Bilderberg i̶s̶ ...̶ ...ce in the world. M... ...othing of its existence. Th... ...who do know little more than that Bilderberg, held each year, is attended by one hundred or so of the richest and most powerful people in the western world, whose decisions determine future world policy. Bilderberg is organised each year by a steering committee based at The Hague, in Holland. Invitations to attend a conference are highly coveted and are extended only to heads of state, leading politicians, top bankers and major industrialists; those who influence the daily lives of millions of people. Yet their debates are unreported in the world's press. Nothing at all of the events at Bilderberg has ever got through the strict security curtain which shields the conference from the outside world.

UNTIL NOW

I, Said the Spy

DEREK LAMBERT

SPHERE BOOKS LIMITED
London and Sydney

A Sphere Book

First published in Great Britain by
Arlington Books (Publishers) Ltd 1980
Published by Sphere Books Ltd 1981
Reprinted 1982, 1983, 1984, 1989

Printed and bound in Great Britain by
Cox & Wyman Ltd, Reading
Set in Intertype Plantin

ISBN 0 7221 5346 5

Sphere Books Ltd
A Division of
Macdonald & Co. (Publishers) Ltd.
66/73 Shoe Lane, London EC4P 4AB
A member of Maxwell Pergamon Publishing Corporation plc

For my not-so-grey eminence – Desmond Elliott

'The world is governed by very different personages from what is imagined by those who are not behind the scenes.'

Benjamin Disraeli

AUTHOR'S NOTE

Bilderberg is fact.

Since 1954 key members of the Western Establishment have met annually at a conference named after the venue of their first meeting, the Bilderberg Hotel at Oosterbeek, Holland.

Bilderberg has been accused of both Right and Left Wing machinations; it has been indicted as a cabal of the elite of both Jewry and Masonry. Its deliberations have always been conducted in an atmosphere of obsessive secrecy and therefore the organisers cannot protest too vehemently at the calumny they occasionally attract. What is indisputable is that, once a year, a nucleus of incalculable wealth and power gathers under one roof. Indisputably, too, the future of the Western world, and therefore indirectly the future of the Communist bloc, must to an extent be affected.

The conference and the château in France in this novel, however, are fictitious, as are the principal characters.

Part One

I

Danzer didn't look like a spy.

He was too sleek, too assured, too obtrusive.

But who does look like a spy? Anderson pondered as he sat shivering in the back of the battered yellow taxi, on loan from the New York Police Department, waiting for the Swiss financier to emerge from La Guardia Airport.

There was no future in looking like a bank robber if your profession was robbing banks!

For three days Anderson had kept Danzer under surveillance at the Bilderberg conference at Woodstock, Vermont, attended by more than eighty of the richest and most powerful men in the Western world.

Earlier that April morning in 1971, Bilderberg had broken up. Heads of state, politicians, bankers, industrialists, were now dispersing, confident that their deliberations had been secret.

Overconfident.

If Anderson's calculations were correct, the conference had been attended by three spies. Certainly two – himself and the Englishman, George Prentice, one-time Professor of Economics at Oxford University.

Anderson was ninety per cent certain about Danzer. Well, eighty-five. . . . The Russians had been trying for seventeen years to penetrate Bilderberg. He had two reasons for believing that with Karl Danzer they had succeeded. Firstly, he was a new recruit to Bilderberg; and secondly, he was the *only* guest whose credentials didn't quite pass intensive scrutiny.

Nothing specific, Anderson admitted, as the wind sweeping across the East River spattered sleet against the windshield of the taxi. Just a gap here, an inconsistency there.

3

Nothing that he could prove to his employers in their headquarters eight miles from downtown Washington D.C., where hunches were regarded with cynicism.

It was to convert a hunch into fact that Anderson had flown on ahead from Boston's Logan airport to follow Danzer when he landed at La Guardia.

It's got to be him, Anderson insisted to himself. *Got to be,* as the eighty-five per cent certainty wavered and fell five points.

'Are you a hundred per cent sure he's flying to La Guardia?' the man sitting beside him asked.

Anderson who was sick of percentages said: 'Sure I'm sure.'

'Then he ought to be here by now.'

Anderson grunted. It always surprised and annoyed him when Miller broke into his thoughts. You forgot that Miller with his thin, greying hair, inconspicuous clothes and gum-chewing jaws was there. That was Miller's strength.

Miller slipped a wafer of gum into his mouth without interrupting the rhythm of his jaws. In front of them, on the other side of a grimy transparent screen, sat the driver, bearded and wild-haired, staring into the sleet.

At regular intervals jets materialised from the cloud, as though suspended from somewhere above the low, grey ceiling; they seemed to hover for a moment, big and vulnerable, before disappearing onto the runway.

Anderson glanced at his wrist-watch. Miller was right: Danzer should have arrived by now. He assumed that the executive jet had been delayed by the weather. Whoever heard of a plane that was not delayed by some unexpected phenomenon?

'Maybe he's meeting someone inside,' Miller said, nodding towards the arrival lounge. 'Maybe he won't be taking a cab,' shifting the wad of gum from one side of his mouth to the other.

Anderson shook his head irritably. 'He told me he was going to take a cab.'

'Maybe he changed his mind. Maybe. . . .' Miller said hesitantly – he was a nervous man and his nerves prodded him into making tactless remarks – 'maybe you blew it.'

'How the hell would you know?'

'Well, you are kind of conspicuous.'

'I'm not the only black at La Guardia. . . .'

'I didn't mean that. But, you know, supposing he recognises you. . . .'

'In this?' Anderson gestured at the sleet; nevertheless he raised the collar of his raincoat so that it touched his tan, snap-brimmed hat, and slid lower in the seat.

'I just hope you're right,' Miller said.

'I am!' Anderson leaned forward, rapped on the partition and pointed at the darkly handsome young man who had just joined the line-up for cabs. The driver, who already knew Danzer's description, nodded his shaggy head.

Although it was 9.35 in the morning, Danzer stood blinking in the daylight as though he had just walked out of the night into a brightly-lit stadium. He was not alone in his reactions: all the other passengers waiting for cabs looked cowered by their meeting with the sleet, which was extinguishing springtime in New York.

'Take a good look,' Anderson said to Miller.

'Don't worry, I already got him.'

Anderson believed him: Miller's eyes were camera lenses. And they had certainly photographed every detail of Danzer's appearance. His wavy black hair, a little too long but not trendily so, the slim athlete's frame, the cleft chin elevating what would otherwise have been ordinary good looks.

He wore a camel-hair coat slung casually over his shoulders, and beneath it the navy-blue mohair suit that he had worn at the conference. (In Anderson's experience Russians who had managed to escape the attentions of Muscovite tailors favoured blue mohair.)

He carried a suitcase made of soft black leather, bearing in gold the initials KWD. The W, Anderson knew, stood for Werner. His black, buckled shoes were custom-made from crocodile skin. The only incongruous item was the shabby brown briefcase he carried in his left hand. Anderson noted that, although he pushed the suitcase along the ground with his foot as he neared the front of the line-up,

5

he kept a tight hold on the briefcase.

Anderson said to Miller: 'Don't let that briefcase out of your sight.'

The driver of the police taxi, capable of speeds approaching 100 mph, started the engine as Danzer climbed into an equally battered cab, with an equally hirsute driver at the wheel.

The sleet continued to pour down as the two cabs, fifty yards between them, joined the expressway. Cabs and cars rode to Manhattan on wings of slush; they reminded Anderson of power-boats racing on a river, except that here on Long Island the race never ended.

The driver of Danzer's cab was in a hurry, weaving in between the other vehicles whose drivers were too disgusted with the weather to brandish their fists or sound their horns. But, whatever Grand Prix ploys he pulled, Anderson's driver kept behind him, theatrically nonchalant with one hand on the wheel, the other adjusting the wave-band on the portable radio stuck together with Scotch tape.

'He's too cool,' Miller said. 'He'll lose him.'

'It'll be the first time,' Anderson said.

Anderson knew that as soon as Miller took up the chase his nerves would stop jangling and he would be as cool as the driver.

Framed in the rear window of the cab Anderson could just make out the outline of Danzer's head. He wondered what was going on in it. He hoped that it was filled with elation at his success in rubbing shoulders with the clique that unofficially moulded the lives of millions of men and women, most of whom had never heard of Bilderberg. He hoped that Danzer was anticipating promotion that had nothing to do with his outward trappings of success; elevation, that was, within the ranks of Soviet Intelligence. He also hoped that he was concentrating on the location where the drop was to be made.

But perhaps, Anderson brooded as the two vehicles crossed Triborough Bridge, he was merely deciding where to have lunch; anticipating, perhaps, a liaison with a beautiful girl. One aspect of Danzer's character had been incontrovertibly established: he liked women; what's more they liked him.

Danzer's cab merged with the traffic pounding along the Franklin D. Roosevelt Drive. To his right Anderson caught glimpses of the dull-eyed buildings of Harlem, marvelling as he always did at the circumstances that had lifted him from a leaning tenement there to a small but luxurious apartment on the East Side.

Danzer's cab took an exit to the right and burrowed into mid-town Manhattan. Here the sleet fell erratically, blown by the winds exploring the canyons between the high-rise blocks, and the streets were wet and clean while the slush piled up in the gutters.

'What if he makes a meet?' Miller asked, jaws quickening. 'Who do I follow?'

'Follow the briefcase,' Anderson said.

'You're the boss.'

On East 42nd Street Danzer's cab slowed down. Anderson could see Danzer's head craned to one side as though he were looking for something – or someone.

'Okay, any minute now,' Anderson said. Unnecessarily, because Miller was hunched against the door, fingers on the handle. Miller's nervousness was infectious; Anderson found that his fists were bunched so tightly that his knuckles gleamed white. 'Don't jump, just pay the driver and get out. Take your time.'

'Okay, okay.'

Danzer's cab stopped at an intersection while pedestrians, heads bowed into the unseasonal and treacherous cold, flooded across the avenue.

Then it took off again, hugging the kerb. They passed the New York *Daily News* building with the huge globe of the world in the window. Danzer's driver was looking behind him, gesticulating with one hand. Anderson imagined what he was saying – 'Why don't you get out and walk? Time's money, buddy. . . .' Odd how your mind chanced on any trivia when you were tensed up. He noticed a gaunt man wearing only check shirt and jeans despite the cold, a poodle trailing a lead and sniffing ankles. . . .

Danzer's taxi stopped.

'You know where to find me?' Anderson asked, and Miller said: 'Sure I know, you told me a dozen times already.'

Danzer was standing on the sidewalk looking around him as his cab departed at speed. He took a notebook from the pocket of his coat, consulted it and peered down the street in the direction of the East River and the United Nations. His suitcase was between his legs but he still held onto the shabby briefcase.

Miller climbed out of the cab onto the sidewalk, timing it well because at that moment Danzer turned and began to walk swiftly in the opposite direction like a man who has suddenly made a decision.

Miller spat out his gum and began to follow.

Anderson rapped on the partition again and the taxi began to edge along the kerb. It was easy enough to keep Danzer in sight: it was Miller the chameleon who kept disappearing.

Once or twice Danzer glanced behind him, saw nothing suspicious and hurried on. Then he disappeared.

Anderson blinked and searched for Miller. There he was, entering a hotel in between First and Second Avenues. Anderson knew it vaguely: it had an English-style pub at the back.

The driver stopped.

Thirty seconds later Danzer emerged without his briefcase. He turned sharply and began to walk towards the taxi. Anderson slid down low in the seat, face averted from the sidewalk.

Danzer hurried past, almost running, like a man escaping from a crime.

The driver turned and looked at Anderson questioningly. Anderson shook his head. There was no point: the briefcase had just emerged from the hotel – in the hands of a balding man wearing a cheap grey topcoat, wide-bottomed trousers and crepe-soled brown shoes.

Anderson kept his eyes on the briefcase as it swung down the street. Miller emerged from the hotel, glanced briefly in

Anderson's direction, nodded almost imperceptibly and began to follow the newcomer.

A Russian? Anderson placed the tips of his fingers together in a prayer-like gesture. Then he lost sight of Miller and his quarry. The next time he saw them they were crossing the bridge spanning 42nd Street.

This time the driver slid open the partition. 'What do you want me to do, Mr Anderson?' His voice was soft and cultured, a contradiction of his appearance.

'Take me home,' Anderson said.

All he could do now was wait.

* * *

The apartment was furnished with impeccable taste.

But was his taste just a little too studied? Anderson wondered in those transient moments of self-doubt that assailed him from time to time.

Olive green, wall-to-wall carpet covered the floor of the living room; the white-leather Chesterfield and easy chairs were low-slung – a little too low for Anderson's long legs; the television peered from fitted bookshelves; abstracts – some bought in Greenwich Village and some painted by a long-ago girl-friend – hung on the walls; in one corner, approached by a zebra-skin lying on the olive-green carpet, stood a small jungle of poinsettias, rubber plants and ferns. The bedroom was all white, the bathroom blue-tiled with a sunken bath, the kitchen shone with stainless steel fittings.

The rent was more than he could reasonably afford and, during those fleeting moments of uncertainty, Anderson wondered whether it was all worth it because, in the eyes of some of his guests, he could discern the patronising appraisal of those who had inherited rather than learned impeccable taste.

To hell with them, Anderson thought, as he took off his raincoat and tossed his hat onto a glass-topped table. But now, as he waited for the telephone to ring, the self-doubt was persistent. It even extended to his clothes – brown

9

Gucci shoes, immaculate fawn suit with vest, across which was looped a gold chain linking a gold watch with a gold cigar-cutter tucked in the pockets. A black dude! The sort of gear affected by a prize-fighter who had punched his way out of Harlem.

Anderson consulted the gold watch. 11 a.m. It would be at least half an hour before Miller called. Anderson decided to take a hot shower to force the cold from his bones – and the questions from his mind.

The water sluiced down over his ebony frame, machine-gunned his powerful shoulders. He turned the handle another degree so that the water ran hotter and steam enveloped him. Ah . . . the doubts dispersed. The man with the briefcase *was* a Russian; any minute now Miller would call and confirm his suspicions; confirm the decision of the hierarchy of the CIA – decision taken after considerable debate – to give Owen Anderson one of the key jobs assigned by the Company. Bilderberg.

The telephone shrilled in the living-room.

Anderson stepped out of the bath and padded swiftly across the carpet, shedding droplets of water as he went.

'Hallo, is that you, Owen?'

'Sure it's me.' The anticipation subsided as he heard the girl's voice; adrenalin stopped flowing in his veins.

'Are you free tonight?'

Standing naked and dripping, Anderson shook his head at the cream receiver in his hand. ''Fraid not, honey.' She was a black model, tall, fine-boned and small-breasted.

A sigh at the other end of the line. 'Are you going cold on me, Owen?'

'I've got work to do, honey.' She knew he was some kind of policeman; probably thought that, with his life style, he was a corrupt one. 'I'm sorry.'

'Yeah, I'll bet. There's a party in the Village. . . .'

'Some other time,' Anderson said. Maybe Miller was trying to reach him now.

'What sort of work, Owen?'

'The usual sort.'

'I won't be going to that party alone.'

'Have a ball,' Anderson said. 'I'll call you.' He replaced the receiver in its cradle.

He put on a white towelling robe and stood at the window watching the sleet pass by on its way to the street, straddling Lexington and Park, fifteen storeys below.

He prowled the apartment. Waiting, waiting. The silent telephone dominated the room. He picked up the *New York Times* and scanned the front page. Spaceshots, political jockeying for the presidential election next year; Nixon on Vietnam, Senator George McGovern on Vietnam.

Anderson threw aside the newspaper, stripped off his robe and went into his daily work-out routine. Fifty press-ups, fifty sit-ups.

The phone rang when he was half way up to the forty-ninth press-up. He collapsed on the carpet and reached for the receiver.

The head porter said: 'Is that you, Mr Anderson?'

Anderson said it was him and, with eyes closed, listened to a complaint that water had been leaking from his bathroom into the apartment below. He told the porter to fix it, that was his job.

He abandoned the sit-ups and considered having a drink. 11.23. Too early. The road to ruin. He sat down on an easy chair, legs stretched uncomfortably in front of him, and stared at the telephone, malevolently cold and impersonal.

Where the hell was Miller? Give him time, for Chrissake. The man carrying the briefcase wouldn't stride straight into the United Nations and hand it to the Soviet Ambassador. Perhaps Miller had lost him; perhaps the briefcase contained girlie magazines. . . .

He switched on the television. An old black and white spy movie, the original *Thirty-Nine Steps*. Anderson had watched every spy film ever made during his training in Virginia; they seemed to think that you could still learn a trick or two from James Bond. Anderson enjoyed the movies, in particular John Buchan's masterpiece with Robert Donat because it had style and he admired style. But not today; leave Richard Hannay to his own devices. . . .

He switched off the television and went into the steel-bright kitchen to make coffee.

Holding a steaming mug in one hand and a chocolate biscuit in the other, he returned to the living-room. It looked unlived-in, which it was because Anderson was rarely there. A show-piece, an extravagance.

He sat down beside the telephone. Ring damn you! And it did, just as he bit into the chocolate biscuit.

He picked up the receiver, swallowed the mouthful of biscuit and said: 'Hallo.'

'Is that you, Anderson?'

'Speaking. Who's that?'

It was Miller.

Two hours later Anderson took a cab to La Guardia and caught the shuttle to Washington.

II

William Danby picked up a white plastic cup of coffee; it was his fourth that morning. Danby who rarely drank liquor – an infrequent beer, the occasional weak whisky at cocktail parties – was fuelled by coffee. This morning he barely tasted it: he was too pre-occupied with the three dossiers and the typewritten report lying on the top of his mahogany desk. They worried him.

Not that Danby ever looked worried. He was a man of medium height, fifty-eight years-old; his greying hair with a suspicion of a quiff, a relic from his youth, was neatly barbered; his pale blue eyes behind horn-rimmed glasses were calm, and his features were barely lined.

Imperturbable, was how his staff described Danby. An automaton with a computer for a brain. A man who, when he removed his spectacles and stared at you with those pale eyes, withered the lies on your tongue.

Nevertheless Danby worried. If you were the head of the largest – or, arguably the second largest – intelligence organisation in the world then you lived with worry. The trick was to discipline the worry, regard it merely as an occupational hazard, and never, never show it.

William Danby, director of the Central Intelligence Agency, subordinated his worry and for the first time savoured his coffee. It tasted like cardboard. He put the plastic cup to rest between the intercom and two telephones, swung round in his swivel chair and gazed over the countryside surrounding his $46 million *castle* close to the highway encircling Washington.

He observed the thin sunlight rekindling spring among the trees. He stared beyond the limits of his vision. From coast to coast, from north to south. The vision awed him as it always did, because he was responsible for the security of the land and the 203 million people inhabiting it.

Which was why the dossiers, two blue and one green, and the report lying on the desk worried him. He was investigating the very people responsible for the prosperity of the United States.

In a way he was guilty of the same suicidal introspection that was racking the CIA (He had just prepared a report on accusations of CIA involvement in the 1970 Chilean elections – despite the fact that the Marxist Salvador Allende had won them.)

But whereas the campaign being waged against the CIA was destructive – instigated by misguided crusaders manipulated by America's enemies – Danby believed that surveillance of the power elite of America was, however unwholesome, necessary and constructive.

Bilderbergers had to be protected against themselves.

He swivelled back to his desk and surveyed the dossiers and the typewritten report stamped PRIVATE AND CONFIDENTIAL. The blue dossiers contained summaries of all that was known about Bilderberg and its participants; the green dossier contained all that was known about Owen Charles Anderson; the report was Anderson's preliminary observations about the 1971 conference brought by courier from Woodstock.

If Anderson was correct, the Russians had infiltrated Bilderberg.

If he was correct. . . . If he wasn't, and his investigations led to his own exposure, then the furore would equal the uproar after the Bay of Pigs fiasco. AMERICAN POWER ELITE PROBED BY CIA. Danby read the headlines of the future. It was difficult even for him to subordinate his worry.

The intercom buzzed. He pressed a button and a woman's voice said: 'Mr Anderson for you, sir.'

'Send him in.'

Danby picked up the green dossier. Anderson had been his personal choice for Bilderberg. Like Danby himself, Anderson represented change.

Danby wasn't an Ivy Leaguer like so many of his predecessors: he was a non-political professional who had learned his trade posing as a diplomat in Guatemala, Moscow and Saigon.

Anderson's claim to represent change was his colour. He had risen meteorically through the ranks since the CIA had been accused of racial prejudice. (In 1967 fewer than twenty blacks had been employed in intelligence work for the Agency.)

A knock at the door.

'Come in.'

Anderson, big, black and handsome, loomed in front of him.

'Sit down.' Anderson sat in the chair opposite Danby: *occupied* it, Danby thought. 'So they all survived, huh?'

'No casualties, sir,' Anderson said.

Ostensibly Anderson worked for the Secret Service. He had been put in charge of Bilderberg security. The perfect cover, thought Danby, who had arranged it.

'Any trouble?'

'Only what I expected. Other agencies tripping over each other's big feet. British, French, German, Feds. . . .'

'Anything personal?'

'How do you mean, sir?'

They both knew that Danby meant his colour.

'Any resentment?' forcing Anderson to concede.

'You'll always find prejudice, sir,' smiling at Danby. There was about Anderson the faintest suspicion of cynical amusement: it had gone against him when he had been put up for the job, but Danby's views had prevailed. They always did.

'Your colour's your greatest ally,' Danby said. 'Coffee?' as he pressed the button on the intercom and, as Anderson nodded, 'Two coffees, please. . . . With milk?' to Anderson. 'Yes, and sugar,' Anderson told him.

Danby released the button. 'Who the hell would suspect that a black security officer worked for the Company?'

'I guess you're right, sir. I'm too conspicuous in all-white company.'

'Precisely.' Danby picked up one of the blue Bilderberg dossiers and extracted the guest list. 'You were in exalted company.' He ran a finger down the list. 'Chairman, Prince Bernhard of the Netherlands. . . .'

'Riding for a fall,' Anderson interrupted him.

'Lockheed?'

'It's got to come out,' Anderson said.

Danby took off his spectacles and stared at Anderson. If Danby had a weakness, it was his admiration for American big business. He had been on intimate terms with corruption for most of his professional life, but he still found it difficult to distingiush between business practice and bribery. It didn't bother him that the smiling extrovert husband of the Queen of Holland might take a fall, as Anderson put it; it bothered him that those who had paid him money might be hurt. And the American image with them.

His finger moved on down the list. 'Rockefellers, Rothschilds . . . British members of Parliament . . . financiers from Belgium, Denmark, France, Italy, Switzerland. . . . You seem to have concentrated your attentions on the Swiss, Mr Anderson.'

They were interrupted by a knock on the door. A grey-haired woman wearing a pink knitted cardigan placed two plastic cups of coffee on the desk and retired. Danby and Anderson sipped their coffee and regarded each other through the steam.

Danby picked up Anderson's preliminary report. 'Have you anything to substantiate your suspicions about Herr Danzer? If you're right, it's a considerable coup considering it was your first Bilderberg.'

Anderson put his cup down on the desk. He opened his jacket and stuck his thumbs in the pocket of his waistcoat, where the gold watch and the cigar-cutter resided. An assertive gesture, Danby decided. Or was it defensive?

Anderson said: 'We put a tail on him in New York.'

'And?'

'He made a drop. A Soviet agent picked up his briefcase.'

'I see. How – '

'The agent was followed to the Soviet Mission at 136, East 67th Street.'

'Then there doesn't seem to be much doubt about it.'

'No, sir.'

'I'm glad for your sake,' Danby remarked. 'The coffee,' he said, 'gets worse,' but he finished it.

Danby stood up and walked round the spacious office. He ran his fingers along the bookshelves of weighty volumes, spun the globe in the corner – the world in which his 12,000-strong army fought daily for American interests. Against enemies outside and inside the States. Danby envied Anderson's lack of appreciation of the canker within.

As the world spun beneath his fingers he said: 'You may smoke if you wish.'

'I don't smoke, sir.'

'Of course, I forgot.'

Danby moved to the desk and picked up the green dossier on Anderson. 'One of your economies to enable you to live in the style to which you are accustomed.'

Danby opened the dossier.

Here we go, Anderson thought.

By *style* he knew that Danby referred to his apartment. It wasn't the first time the apartment had cropped up during interrogation.

And what was about to follow would be a form of interrogation. A tactic to quell over-confidence, to hone the blade of Anderson's perception. A man such as Danby was incapable of conducting an analytical conversation without employing psychological stratagem.

Anderson admired him for it. And it worked! He felt the assurance ebb from him as Danby turned the pages of the dossier. *There in between green cardboard covers is my life.*

The adolescent years in the hovel in Harlem when he was a runner in a numbers racket. (A lot of question marks there, a lot of heavy underlining.)

The street brawls re-directed by an unusually enlightened social worker into the boxing ring. *Showed promise.* . . . But who wants to make money with his fists when he has brains?

Night school resented by his parents, ridiculed by his friends. Long solitary hours with a second-hand speech-training course on a phonograph – 'Now repeat after me. . . .' the invisible tutor's plummy voice scratched by a score of needles.

Danby said: 'I see you play chess.'

'Sir?'

'I see you're a chess-player.'

'Pretty low grade, sir.'

'It's good training,' Danby said, turning a couple of years of Anderson's life.

And then a scholarship to Columbia. (Exclamation marks here probably. *Black, street-fighter, ambitious, educated.* Possibilities.)

Perhaps he had been ear-marked as early as that.

The Army. Military Intelligence. Vietnam with the U.S. Military Assistance Command in 1962. And then the approach (names, assessments, cross references here) by the CIA, followed by another two years in Vietnam, two years in Washington and then New York in a sub-division of the Secret Service.

'Do you know what finally swayed us in your favour for the Bilderberg job?' Danby asked.

'No, sir.'

'French,' Danby said. 'You speak excellent French.'

'I learned it in Vietnam. I believe I have a slight colonial accent.'

'And I see you shoot straight.' (Anderson was Army Reserve pistol champion, having scored 2581 points in the 1970 championships.)

'I'm not popular in amusement parks.' Instinctively Anderson felt for the gun he normally wore in a shoulder-holster; but it wasn't there; you didn't arm yourself to meet the DCI.

'How do you manage to live, Mr Anderson?'

Anderson sighed. 'I believe it's all there, sir,' pointing at the dossier.

'Refresh my memory.'

'You mean the apartment?'

'And that suit you're wearing.'

Blue with a silky sheen to it, lapels beautifully rolled.

'I buy one suit a year,' Anderson told him. 'The apartment is mine. I didn't blow my money in Saigon.'

'But the apartment is not quite paid for, I gather.'

'Not quite,' Anderson said, the anger that was his weakness (all there in the dossier) beginning to rise.

'I admire you.'

The anger evaporated. Danby was a professional.

'So the question is,' Danby remarked, 'what did Danzer get away with?'

'Not a great deal,' Anderson said. 'He was too busy being accepted. Meeting the right people to make damn sure he's invited again. Herr Danzer,' Anderson said, 'would like to be a regular.'

'He must have picked up something.'

'Maybe a line on Lockheed and Bernhard. Maybe the fact that Nixon is going to woo the Chinese. Maybe a few leads on the economic squeeze that's on its way. . . . A few financial killings could be made there if it leaked out,' Anderson observed.

Danby sat down again in the swivel chair facing Anderson. 'It's your job to stem those leaks.' The pale eyes stared across the desk.

'I can't stop the richest men in the Western world trading stories. The critics say Bilderberg rules the world. That whatever is discussed at their conferences just happens to happen. If I were a billionaire then maybe I could do something.'

'There's no law that says the captains of industry shouldn't meet privately.'

Anderson hadn't said there was, but Danby's belief in the American Dream was well-known. He told Danby that, in his view, 'privately' meant *secretly* and then tried to steer the conversation in a different direction – 'My private nightmare is in my Secret Service capacity. All that clout under one roof. One of these days someone is going to get wise to it. . . .'

'An assassination?' Danby smiled thinly. 'Perhaps, Mr

Anderson, that is the reason for the . . . secrecy.' You couldn't deflect a man like Danby.

'Why just one, sir? Supposing a terrorist organisation got wind of the next Bilderberg? They could eliminate the whole goddam bunch of them. Or hold them to an astronomical ransom. Which, of course, they'd pay,' he added.

'It's your job to stop them, Mr Anderson. You had a battalion of police and agents working for you. The Woodstock Inn was more like Fort Knox.'

'As a matter of fact,' Anderson said quietly, 'my private nightmare doesn't concern terrorists: it concerns cranks. Just one. How many assassinations throughout history have been carried out by nuts? And I can tell you this, sir, when it's happened, someone will turn round and say, "He was a guy who kept himself to himself." '

'A sobering thought, Mr Anderson. But the Secret Service has the utmost faith in your abilities. In fact,' Danby said, picking up his now-empty cup, examining it and tossing it into the wastepaper basket, 'they have agreed to upgrade you and increase your expenses.'

'I'm very grateful, sir.'

'So has the CIA. You are now the highest graded black in the Agency. And your expenses will be higher than most whites draw, so keep it to yourself.' Danby closed the dossier on Anderson. 'You'll even be able to pay that last instalment on your apartment. A thousand dollars, wasn't it, Mr Anderson?'

Anderson nodded.

Danby picked up Anderson's preliminary report. 'And now to work,' he said.

'What do we know about Herr Danzer?' Danby asked.

'Not as much as I'd like to. He's Swiss –'

'I know that,' impatiently.

'He's a financier with offices on the Bahnofstrasse in Zurich.'

'What sort of a financier?'

'Currency speculation. If he got wind of a proposal to devalue a currency at Bilderberg. . . .'

'He'd be even richer than he is now.'

'And yet he doesn't live extravagantly.'

'Do the Swiss ever? They live *well*, I believe.'

'And yet he does have a taste for extravagance. It's as if he isn't in control of his money.'

'Funds for the Party?'

Anderson shrugged. 'Maybe.'

'Married?'

Anderson shook his head. 'But he likes women.'

'Any other weaknesses?'

'I haven't had time to find out.'

'Mmmmmmm.' Danby pinched the bridge of his nose where his spectacles rested. 'Then you must find the time. Does he drink?'

'Champagne,' Anderson said. 'The best.'

'I gather you don't regard that as an extravagance, Mr Anderson.'

'It's not an extravagance with his sort of money. But he could have a yacht, a private plane, a penthouse in Monte Carlo. He hasn't got any of those. . . .'

'Does he gamble?' Danby held up his hand. 'I apologise, that's his profession.' He paused. 'Any particular women?'

'The usual. Jet-set. Models, starlets, poor-little-rich-girls. All beautiful,' Anderson said, wondering if a tinge of envy had entered his voice.

'Where does he live?'

'In Zurich. An apartment – more expensive than mine,' forestalling Danby.

'Does Prentice know all this?'

Anderson's head snapped up. 'Prentice?'

Danby said patiently: 'George Prentice, the British agent who has also penetrated Bilderberg.'

Christ, Anderson thought, Danby kept you on your toes. 'I don't know what Prentice knows,' he told Danby.

'We're collaborating,' Danby said tersely.

'As from when?'

'As from now. As you know we have worked closely with Britain's MI 6 since Penkovsky.'

Anderson knew. Oleg Penkovsky had been deputy chief of the Soviet State Committee for the Coordination of Scientific Research. He was also a colonel in Russian military intelligence – and a spy for the West.

But when he had first tried to join the CIA in Turkey he had been turned down. The British had enlisted him and offered to share his secrets with the CIA. The spirit of co-operation that had foundered after the Burgess/Maclean/Philby debacles had been re-established.

At his trial in May 1963 Penkovsky had admitted passing 5,000 frames of film showing Soviet classified information and had been sentenced to death.

'Is it necessary to cooperate in this case?' Anderson asked.

'It's in your own interests. As you probably know Prentice has a good front. Not only is he a professor of economics but he runs an industrial consultancy for an English businessman named Paul Kingdon. He might even know more about the industrialists attending Bilderberg than we do.'

Danby stood up and walked over to the globe in the corner of the office. 'I have a few thoughts about Herr Danzer,' he said, spinning the globe. 'You see, he conforms to a pattern. We've met Karl Danzers before. Soviet agents with a liking for *Western decadence* who don't have the opportunity to enjoy it to the full.'

'You think he can be turned, sir?'

'That's for you to find out. And that's where Prentice will be useful. You see, I figure you might be a little conspicuous here,' as his finger landed unerringly on Zurich on the spinning globe.

III

Zurich is Switzerland's largest city. It is also one of the world's largest storehouses of money and therefore a dull place: bankers do not besport themselves on their own premises.

The streets of the city, divided by the Limmat River, are clinically clean, the night-life as permissive as a whist-drive. It is not, however, without its charm – the historic guild-houses, the twin towers of Grössmunster Church, said to be the finest example of Romanesque Ecclesiastical architecture in Switzerland, the backcloth of snow-crested mountains.

But the language is Swiss francs, and when the leaves of the trees on Bahnofstrasse are ruffled by a breeze from Lake Zurich they rustle like bank-notes.

Dull.

But not when you are twenty years-old and in the arms of the man you love. A wonderful man, a handsome man, an idealist. . . . Idealists are thin on the ground in Zurich.

Helga Keller stirred and looked into the brown eyes of Karl Danzer. 'Tell me again,' she said.

'Tell you what?'

'Tell me about Russia.'

'Ah Mother Russia. The steppes sparkling in the snow beneath blue skies in winter . . . the wind rippling the corn in summer . . . the cottages like fretwork dolls' houses . . . the forests of birch where tigers still prowl. . . .'

'And Moscow,' she said, snuggling up against him on the couch in his apartment. 'Tell me about Moscow.'

He kissed her. 'You will see it one day. Soon perhaps. Hear the music of the skates on the ice in the parks . . . see the domes of the Kremlin gold in the dawn. . . . . Taste the fires of vodka as we drink with our comrades.'

'I like to hear you talk about comrades,' she said. 'I like to hear about people who are . . . alive.'

Neither her father's friends, nor the girls at the finishing school at Basle, had been *alive*.

'They are alive – full of life – because they share. That is the heart of the matter. Sharing. Common endeavour. Even today,' throwing out one arm as though dashing a glass against the wall, ' we still drink to the glorious revolution. The revolution that will one day spread throughout the world.'

Helga Keller glowed with the visions. 'And *we* shall be part of it. If only I could help more. . . .'

'You have helped already,' Danzer told her. 'They are very pleased with what you have done.'

'And to think that until three months ago I didn't spare a thought for this . . . this sharing. I'd read about Communism, but here they talk about it as if it is a crime. . . .'

'To such people,' Danzer said, 'Socialism *is* a crime. Grand larceny. The theft of their privilege. The distribution of their wealth to the underprivileged. . . . Has it been three months?' he asked in surprise.

'Two months, two weeks, three days. . . .' She felt the warmth of the sunshine reach her through the window. Outside, the lake sparkled, the flanks of the mountains were green with young growth. Helga had known from the moment she awoke that the hazy dawn was filled with portent; that June 12th 1971, was one of those days that would change her life; she glimpsed patterns of destiny and was filled with delicious anticipation.

She stretched herself and took in the apartment. It was, she supposed, expensively furnished – she had no yardstick by which to judge expenditure – but certainly not lavishly. (Karl had explained that, to maintain his front, he had to live reasonably well.)

It certainly needed a woman's touch. But there was no chance of a permanent relationship in Zurich. Karl had explained that, too.

Karl put his arm round her. He was wearing grey flannel trousers and a blue silk shirt tapered at the waist; through the silk she could feel the thud of his heart. His hand stroked her waist, then cupped her breast. Wings of fear – or was it excitement? – fluttered inside her. She was so inexperienced, ridiculous in 1971. But if you were the daughter of a Zurich banker. . . . She hoped that he would understand; be grateful, even, that she had kept herself. . . . God, what an antiquated expression. . . .

'Helga.'

She didn't reply. It was ridiculous. They both knew. . . . Did he perhaps think that she didn't want to? How do I show him? Then a thought occurred to her that made her feel suddenly foolish. Supposing he didn't want to? She wasn't a raving beauty. Her long, dark, lustrous hair had been much admired but nothing much else; no one had ever complimented her on her figure, although it wasn't too bad, perhaps a little too full. Swiss! She closed her eyes in mortification and the warmth of the sun no longer reached her.

'I love you,' he said as his hand caressed her breast. Feeling exploded inside her.

He led her to the bedroom which she would remember for the rest of her life. The deep white carpet and the books on the bedside table, and the smell of after-shave and the triangle of blue water jostling with light through the roof-tops. He lay on the single bed and she lay beside him and he kissed her lips, her neck, her breasts which had somehow become exposed.

He went to the bathroom, returning in a dressing gown embroidered with Chinese patterns, by which time she was naked beneath the sheets. Trembling.

Would he know immediately that she was a virgin? In the books that she had read surreptitiously at finishing school – sex was a subject that was never finished, not even started – they always knew and the girl said: 'Please don't hurt me.'

His lips were on her breasts and she was guiding his hands to the warm mound that needed him. His hardness astonished her: it was like warm marble. She slid her fingers along its length, then wanted him inside her. Karl, my love. . . . She lay back and opened her legs and guided him.

And afterwards she couldn't remember whether or not there had been any pain.

* * *

When they began to make love George Prentice removed his earphones and switched off the receiver in an apartment not far from Danzer's.

He removed the tiny cassette that had been recording the conversation between Karl Danzer and Helga Keller, labelled it and stacked it neatly in the wooden cigar box containing the other Danzer recordings. A dozen of them in all.

Danzer, you're not a pro: you should *sweep* your apartment every day. But that, Prentice knew, wasn't true: Danzer was a pro. It was merely that he had become careless, his reactions dulled by the good life – and the mistaken belief that he was above suspicion.

Stupid bitch, he thought, as he considered what Helga Keller was now doing in Danzer's bedroom. Did she imagine she was the only one? She should hear some of the other recordings.

Prentice, lean-framed with scholarly good looks, which he managed to conceal partially by his own indifference to them – that worked, he found, when you were over thirty – lit a cigarette. Acquaintances of Prentice, none of them close, sometimes commented that there was an unfulfilled air about him, that he had sublimated his personality. They were right but they were never able to elaborate: Prentice didn't let them.

He turned his attention to the *Daily Telegraph* crossword. He had been on the point of breaking his record, ten minutes, when he had been interrupted by Danzer and the girl. The clues now seemed more enigmatic than before; he had lost contact with the mind of their author.

In fact the conversation which he had overheard had disturbed him more than he had so far admitted to himself. It was as though he had unlocked a room and found the perfume of a woman he had once loved still lingering there. Stupid bitch, he thought again.

He poured himself a Scotch and soda and wished that Anderson would get back. He should have arrived on the Swissair flight from New York two hours ago, at 11.40 am, to resume his duties. And Anderson's duties – at least when Danzer was in town – were confined to electronic surveillance: you didn't let a 6ft. 2 inch, 220 pounds black loose in Zurich without attracting attention.

Prentice had been surprised to discover that the head of security at Bilderberg also worked for the CIA; Anderson, apparently, had experienced no such astonishment that a former Professor of Economics at Oxford played a dual role. 'It's not Oxford that worries me,' he had said. 'It's those sons-of-bitches from Cambridge.'

The buzzer beside the small grille on the wall sounded. Prentice pressed the button. 'Who is it?' Anderson's voice accompanied by street noises: 'It's me.' ('Owen,' if there was any trouble.)

'Come on up.' ('Okay I'll let you in,' if there were uninvited visitors in the apartment.)

'How did it go?' Prentice asked as Anderson tossed his raincoat and overnight bag onto an easy chair.

'Routine. I had to make a statement for some goddam Senate investigation.'

'Bilderberg?'

Anderson poured himself a beer. 'Christ no. I assume we're clean?' sitting down and drinking thirstily.

'Of course.'

'If it had been Bilderberg I wouldn't have returned. You don't return from the dead.' He grinned. 'How's it been going here?'

'Danzer finally got the girl into bed.'

'You listened?'

'Up to a point,' Prentice said. 'You can take over if you want.'

'You're a cold fish, George,' Anderson said.

Now, yes. But it hadn't always been so.

They appraised each other across the small lounge. A working relationship, nothing more. Prentice guessed that Anderson knew a lot about him; how much he didn't know.

Anderson opened another can of beer and said: 'I wish Danzer would get the hell out of this town. I feel as if I'm in a cell in San Quentin.'

'Thanks,' Prentice said. The cell was his apartment. It *was* small – two bedrooms, lounge, kitchen and bathroom – but, Prentice believed, tastefully furnished if, perhaps, a little bookish; the lounge with its leather chairs was a study, really, and the bedrooms were used only for sleeping.

'Sorry, George. You know something?' Anderson drank some beer. 'You're the least likely looking spy I ever did see. But I thought that about Danzer. People's appearances change when you get to know all about them. Danzer looks like a spy now.'

'You look like a contender for the world heavyweight title,' Prentice observed. 'I always imagine you wearing a red robe waving your fists above your head.'

'Not the champ?'

'No,' Prentice said firmly, 'the contender.'

'Let's see how the champ's getting on,' Anderson said, crossing the room to the desk, switching on the radio receiver and slipping the earphones over his head. He listened for a minute, then removed the earphones and said: 'It's all over. They're back in Siberia listening to balalaikas. Give it ten minutes and they'll be back to politics. Are you political, George?'

Prentice shook his head.

'But you enjoy our game, huh?'

'Of course. Otherwise I wouldn't be doing it.'

Which was true. The game, as Anderson called it, was all he had.

'Motives?'

'I happen to believe in what we're doing. Just the same as I would have believed in fighting the Germans in 1939. We're merely fighting an extension of that enemy. One tyranny succeeds another.'

Anderson tapped his forehead with one finger. 'Do you have a brain or a computer up there, George?' He picked up the *Telegraph* crossword. 'You didn't do so well here. *Ins out a form of art singer.* Sinatra,' Anderson said, filling in the blank squares.

'What are your motives?' Prentice asked curiously.

'Much the same as yours, I guess. Just a little more flamboyantly so. None of that kitchen-sink stuff for me.'

'You enjoy *the game*?'

'It's the only one I know. But I'll be glad when this series is over. How much longer, George?'

'Not long now,' Prentice said. 'Do you want to eat?'

'I assume it's cold roast beef and. . . . What do you call that mess?'

'Bubble-and-squeak,' Prentice told him. 'You guessed right.'

'It wasn't difficult,' Anderson said with resignation. 'We had it the day I left. And the day before. Do you ever eat anything else?'

'I take it you want some?'

'I could eat a horse,' Anderson said. 'Come to think of it, that would make a pleasant change.'

Prentice went into the tiny kitchen and tossed a mixture of mashed potatoes and cooked cabbage into a frying pan.

From the living-room Anderson said: 'Three down. You should have gotten this, George. *Notice without direction an agent.*'

'Spy,' Prentice said over his shoulder.

'How long is *not long*, George?'

The cabbage and potatoes sizzled. Prentice turned them; they were a little burnt on the underside. 'When I get access to his bank account.'

'That shouldn't be too difficult for you. You're the guy with the contacts in Zurich.'

'It's not that easy any more. Article 47 of Swiss Banking Law. It sets out the penalties for divulging bank secrets, i.e. the names behind the number accounts. Jail sentences and fines.'

'So, what's new?'

'The banks are getting very touchy since the British Inland Revenue broke the secrecy.'

'Was that you, George?'

Prentice ignored the question and quoted: '. . . *the banker has no discretion in this matter and, by law, is required to maintain silence about his client's affairs under penalty of heavy fines and even imprisonment.* As laid down by the Swiss Bank Corporation, the Swiss Credit Bank and the Union Bank of Switzerland. The Big Three.' He cut four slices of cold, overdone beef. 'But it's Article 273 of the Swiss Criminal Code that worries me. It states that agents. . . .' He smiled faintly. '. . . . Three down, wasn't it? Agents can be jailed for trying to break numbered accounts.'

Prentice put two plates of beef and bubble-and-squeak on the coffee table in the living-room. When Anderson sat down the table looked ridiculously small.

Anderson began to eat hungrily but unenthusiastically. Between mouthfuls he said: 'You're not trying to tell me that any of this worries you?'

'I merely have to be a little more cautious.'

'If he's stashed away a fortune then we've got him. Maybe we've got him anyway. We know he was born in Leningrad in 1941. We know he was infiltrated into Berlin in 1945 with his parents. We know they turned up in Switzerland in 1947 with forged German-Swiss papers. We also know, thanks to you, George,' liberally smearing mustard on a piece of beef, 'that a lot of the bread that he makes speculating with currency doesn't reach the coffers of the Soviet Foreign Bank.'

'We can't prove that,' Prentice pointed out. 'We need that numbered bank account. When you can wave that under his nose then he's yours.'

'Ours,' Anderson said, pushing aside his half-eaten meal. 'You really enjoy that stuff?'

'I was brought up on it.'

'Jesus,' Anderson said. He washed away the taste with a mouthful of beer. 'But you haven't answered my question. How long is *not long*?'

'Tonight if I'm lucky,' Prentice said. He reached for the sports jacket with the leather-patched elbows. 'See you later.' He nodded towards the radio receiver. 'Happy listening.'

As he crossed the Munster Bridge, heading for Bahnofstrasse, Zurich's Fifth Avenue, George Prentice ruminated on Anglo-American collaboration. It worked beautifully up to a point. That point would be reached when he carried out his instructions to kill Karl Danzer.

*　*　*

The Swiss legalised banking secrecy in 1934. The aim was to conceal the identities of Jewish customers from their German persecutors. Whenever the Swiss are under attack for their fiscal discretion they remind their critics of its humane origins. Then, glowing with self-righteous indignation, they retire to the vaults to tot up the billions entrusted to them by despotic heads of state, Mafia dons, crooked financiers, businessmen avoiding (not evading) the attentions of tax inspectors, oil sheikhs, misers, *bankrupts*, politicians championing the cause of the impoverished; the spectrum, in fact, of humanity embarrassed by riches.

Numbered accounts have their disadvantages: interest is virtually non-existent and, in some instances, a depositor may have to pay a bank a small sum to safeguard his money; he is, of course, buying secrecy and, unless it can be proved that the money was obtained by criminal means, his anonymity is assured.

Such obsessive reticence naturally arouses curiosity, and in the cities of Berne, Zurich, Geneva and Basle there are many agencies dedicated to undermining the system. Among them professionals described euphemistically as industrial consultants, blackmailers and spies.

George Prentice, recruited to British Intelligence when he was precociously teaching at Oxford, represented all three categories. He knew the identities of sixty-nine eminent personages holding numbered accounts – knowledge which had rubber-stamped his entry into the monied Establishment – and was about to make Karl Werner Danzer the seventieth. Although in Danzer's case, he was reversing the process: he knew the name but not the number.

The information concerning numbered accounts is known only to two or three bank executives. It was therefore these worthies that Prentice cultivated. Many proved intransigent – it is difficult to bribe a wealthy banker – a few succumbed readily to Prentice's blandishments.

Danzer banked with a relatively small establishment in a sidestreet near Zurich's railway station. The modest pretensions of the bank had encouraged Prentice: its officials were likely to be paid less than their counterparts in the big banks, and would thus be more resentful of their customers' wealth.

Prentice's contact at Danzer's bank was Hans Weiss. Weiss, plump, middle-aged and embittered, had lost most of the money he earned gambling with currency. He hated Danzer who gambled similarly but successfully.

Prentice met him in a small café frequented by taxi-drivers and printers. It was crowded and noisy and cigarette smoke floated in shafts of sunlight. Weiss was eating a cream cake and drinking chocolate.

Prentice ordered tea. 'Well?' he said as Weiss licked a dab of cream from the corner of his mouth.

'Have you got the money?'

'If you've got what I want.'

'It's here.' Weiss slid his hand inside his jacket. 'Where's the money?' He glanced around the café nervously.

'The information first please.'

Weiss stared at him speculatively. Prentice was used to the expression; it was frequently assumed when people first became aware of the hardness in his voice. And when they suddenly realised that, beneath his indifferent clothes, his body was just as hard.

A waiter brought the tea. The tea-bag had been placed in the milk at the bottom of the cup. Prentice added boiling water but it made little impression on the tea-bag.

Weiss said: 'How do I know you'll give me the money?'

'You don't.'

Weiss sipped his chocolate. His hand holding the cup was trembling. Prentice knew he badly needed the money, two thousand dollars jointly funded by the CIA and MI 6.

'It isn't fair,' Weiss finally said.

The remark sounded ludicrous, the words of a schoolboy negotiating a sale of marbles. 'No one said it was.' Prentice pushed his cup aside in disgust. 'The envelope please.'

Reluctantly Weiss handed it over. Prentice glanced at the contents – a photostat of Account No. YT 43 9/8541. The balance in Swiss francs was the equivalent of five hundred thousand dollars. He asked: 'How can I be sure this is Danzer's account?' and would have forgiven Weiss if he had replied: 'You can't.'

But Weiss' mind was on the money. 'The letter,' he said.

Folded inside the photostat of the account was a copy of a letter signed by Johann Beyer, the manager of the bank. It assured Karl Danzer of the bank's best attention at all times and confirmed the number of the account.

Prentice handed over the envelope containing the money. Weiss snatched it from his hand, ruffled the bills inside with his thumb.

Prentice said: 'Try pa-anga this time.'

'I beg your pardon?'

'The currency of the Tonga Islands. A hundred seniti to one pa'anga. If you're going to speculate you could do worse. But I know what I'd do with that money if I were you.'

'What would you do?'

'Put it in a numbered account,' Prentice said as he stood up and strode out of the café into the sunshine.

*　　*　　*

The cable surprised Karl Danzer. They usually telephoned from the Soviet Embassy in Berne to make appointments. A change of policy, perhaps. The coded message instructed him to report to an address on the Limmat Quai at 10 pm that evening.

Walking to work in the crisp morning sunshine, Danzer considered the immediate implications of the cable. A nuisance, nothing more. He had planned to take Helga Keller to dinner, then to bed. Perhaps not such a nuisance. . . . He would cancel the dinner and still take her to bed, thus avoiding the boredom of answering her ridiculous questions as she gazed at him across the table like a schoolgirl with a crush on a pop star. In bed Danzer found her ardour and inexperience stimulating; soon, he surmised, she would do anything he asked. Except, perhaps, sleep with other men; in that respect, Danzer sensed, she was different to the other girls.

All in all the recruitment of Helga Keller had been a thoroughly worthwhile exercise. Not only was she an assistant in the Investor's Club where financial advice was dispensed free of charge but, being the daughter of an eminent Zurich banker, she moved in influential circles. Already she was learning to hate the people with whom she mixed. When she described a dinner party thrown by her father, Danzer reminded her of the starving millions in the Third World countries; when she mentioned some million-dollar deal of which she had heard, Danzer painted word pictures of peasants reaping the harvest in Russia and sharing their wages.

In fact Zurich, with its secrecy, complacency and affluence, was the ideal location to seize a young girl's confused ideals and give them direction.

Danzer turned into the Bahnofstrasse, glancing appreciatively at the shops filled with gold, jewels, watches and cream cakes. He was really managing his life exceedingly well. He lived well but without excess; he was trusted by his mentors in Moscow; he was accepted at Bilderberg and had been given to understand that he would be invited again; he had salted away enough money to ensure an early retirement, in South America perhaps.

He entered his business premises, discreetly imposing with a brass nameplate and a small, marbled foyer, listened for a moment to the gabble emanating from the room where his staff juggled with telephones and currencies, and entered his own oak-panelled office where his secretary awaited him with the day's business attached to a clip-board under her arm.

The secretary, middle-aged and homely, knew a considerable amount about the affairs of Danzer Associates. What she didn't know was that a sizeable proportion of the profits were creamed off into the hard-currency reserves of the Soviet Union; nor did she know that a percentage was also channelled into the secret coffers of Karl Danzer.

The day progressed predictably. Danzer's sense of well-being swelled as a small fortune was made out of the wobbling dollar and the rock-hard German mark. He took a light lunch and, in mid-afternoon, a sauna.

In the evening he retired to his apartment to change. He had a couple of drinks and set off for the address on the Limmat Quai, blissfully unaware that his euphoria was about to be terminated for ever.

He wondered without any particular concern why the KGB wanted to see him. A development, perhaps, from the information – admittedly sparse – that he had gathered from Bilderberg . . . a lead on the American team of financiers who had just arrived in Zurich . . . a progress report on his latest recruit, Helga Keller. . . .

He stopped outside the guildhouse named in the cable. The moon shone fleetingly from the low clouds that had detached themselves from the mountain peaks to sweep across the lake. From the shadows came a voice: 'Herr Danzer?'

Danzer peered round. The first premonition of danger assailed him, an ice-cold wariness. 'Who is it?'

A figure materialised in front of him. Curiously indistinct, despite a brief parting of the clouds. Then he had it. The man was black. Danzer wished he had brought a gun.

'We've met before,' the man said. He was very tall, broad with it. He emerged into the moonlight. 'The trouble is we all look the same, especially at night.' Danzer could see that he was grinning. 'And yes, I have got a gun, and no, you aren't going any place,' as Danzer tensed himself to run.

'What the hell is this?'

'I'd like to have a little talk with you, Herr Danzer.'

'Who are you?'

'We were both at Woodstock. Does that help?'

The black security chief. 'You sent the cable?'

'Of course, it's time your people changed the code,' and conversationally: 'Shall we take a walk?'

'I don't think so,' Danzer said. 'You wouldn't use a gun here.'

'I have something much more persuasive than a gun, Herr Danzer.'

'I don't know what the hell you're talking about.'

'The number of your bank account, currently in credit to the equivalent of five hundred thousand American dollars.'

They began to walk.

Step by step Anderson detailed everything he knew about Danzer. From his birth in Leningrad to his last deposit in the numbered account. 'You're blown, Herr Danzer,' he remarked as they threaded their way through the cars parked beside the river. 'Blown sky high.'

'What do you intend to do about it?' He couldn't believe it: the comfortable, secure future scythed away, leaving only exposed foundations. Danzer shivered as fear replaced shock.

Anderson said: 'I'm sure you know what will happen to you if I tell your employers about your savings for a rainy day.' Anderson stopped and pointed to a telephone kiosk. 'I could do it right now. One call. . . .'

Danzer had seen the white-tiled cells beneath Lubyanka Prison in Moscow. Had seen a little of what went on inside them. It was enough. 'What do you want for God's sake?'

'You,' Anderson said.

*   *   *

Karl had said he would meet her in the little café they frequented at 11 pm or thereabouts, and she had told her father that she was going to a party with a girl-friend. Not that he objected to Karl. Far from it, but he was a good member of the Swiss Reform Church and he wouldn't have tolerated the moral implications of an 11 pm assignation, especially without dinner beforehand.

She glanced at the slim gold Longines watch on her wrist. 11.23. He had said 'thereabouts' but when did 'thereabouts' finally run out? She would give him until 11.30, she decided, as she ordered another coffee, acutely aware that she looked like a girl who had been stood up.

She hadn't, of course. Karl would come. And he would talk. How beautifully he could talk. And then – and she had no doubt about this – they would go back to his apartment where she would give herself to him. Love was wonderful, just as she had always known it would be.

But how many girls were lucky enough to enjoy love on so many levels? From the physical to the idealistic. Between them they would carry on the fight here in Switzerland, the heartland of the Capitalist Conspiracy. (Such phrases!) They had a cause and it united them.

11.30 pm.

He had obviously been detained by THEM. Helga had only a very vague idea what Karl's employers looked like. Certainly not like the caricatures of Russians she saw in the newspapers.

The waiter was glancing at his watch. What time did they close? Candles were being snuffed out on the small, intimate tables; traffic on the street outside was thinning out.

Unaccountably her lips began to tremble. Her body had sensed what was happening before her brain had admitted it. There were only three customers left in the café. 11.40. . . .

Perhaps he had been in an accident. *Perhaps he's sick of you!* Karl Danzer could have any woman he wanted in Zurich. Why should he bother with someone unsophisticated and, yes, clinging. . . . From college to finishing school to Investors Club with no taste of life in between. . . . What a catch.

A tear rolled unsolicited down Helga Keller's cheek.

Behind her the waiter cleared his throat. She could smell the smoke from the snuffed-out candles. She finished her coffee, paid her bill and tried to smile when the cashier said: 'Don't worry, he's not worth it.'

It was midnight.

She crossed the street to a call-box and dialled his number. Supposing he was with another woman. But it was even worse than that. His voice told her that he didn't care. 'Sorry I couldn't make it. . . . You'll have to excuse me . . . I've got a lot on my mind just now.'

Click.

Desolation.

IV

The message was terse. SUBJECT TURNED.

Anderson transmitted it through one of the three CIA operatives at the United States Embassy in Berne, who would send it to Washington via the TRW installation in Redondo Beach, California.

'So all we do now is feed Danzer,' he said to Prentice who was listening to the news on the BBC World Service.

'Especially at Bilderberg,' said Prentice.

'Provided he's invited again.'

'He will be.' Prentice turned off the radio and lit a cigarette. 'I tracked down some of his financial contacts. He's a dead cert – like you.'

'And you, George?'

'Up to a point. I'm a tame lecturer. They keep one or two up their sleeves. Adds respectability to the set-up. I expect they'll give me a miss next year. It doesn't matter which one of us they invite: we all send them to sleep.'

'So British Intelligence won't be represented at Bilderberg next year?'

Prentice smiled faintly. 'I didn't say that.' He pointed at the receiver picking up transmissions from Danzer's apartment. 'He's taken to his bed. Shit-scared by the sound of him.'

'How do you know?' Anderson asked, sitting down in a leather arm-chair beside the electric fire. The chair sighed beneath his weight.

'The girl called. He sent her packing. We can't have that, of course,' Prentice added.

'Of course not. He's got to keep to his pattern.'

'Exactly. So he's got to continue his recruitment campaign.'

'Has it occurred to you,' Anderson asked, spinning the

bloodstone fob on his watchchain, 'that she could get hurt?'

'It's occurred to me,' Prentice said. 'Does it matter?'

Anderson gave the fob a last twirl and shook his head. 'How did you get like this, George?'

'I worked at it,' Prentice said.

'A girl?'

Prentice said flatly: 'I'm sure you know all there is to know about me.'

'A little,' Anderson replied.

He knew, for instance, that Prentice had belonged to a post-war intellectual elite at Oxford who believed in Capitalism as fervently as other young men at Cambridge had once believed in Communism.

'Any economist,' he was on record as saying, 'must be a Capitalist. Unless, that is, they are tapping around economic realities with a white stick.'

Anderson knew also, from a CIA agent at the American Embassy in Grosvenor Square, London, that at a remarkably early age Prentice had taught economics at Oxford before gravitating to the more exciting fields of industrial consultancy.

The consultancy, as Danby had told him, was owned by the English financial whizz-kid of the late sixties, Paul Kingdon.

The CIA agent, young and keen, had elaborated in a Mayfair pub. 'Kingdon is a smart cookie. As you probably know he's big in mutual funds – or unit trusts as they call them over here. Only, like Cornfeld, he's gone a step further: his funds invest in other funds. To safeguard the investments he started this industrial consultancy and put Prentice in charge with an office in Zurich. It wasn't long before Prentice was recruited by British Intelligence.'

'Does Kingdon know that his prize spook works for MI6?' Anderson asked.

The agent shrugged. 'I doubt it. Why should Prentice tell him? At present he's got the best of two worlds – he's paid by both. Not only that but he believes in the work he's doing.'

'Don't you?' Anderson asked.

'Of course,' hastily.

'Does he believe in the work he's doing for this guy Kingdon?'

'Just so long as Kingdon is making money for the Honest Joe's, he does. At the moment Kingdon is doing just that. His funds have made millions for people whose only hope was the Irish Sweep or the football pools.'

'Mmmmm.' Anderson drank some beer. 'Tell me what makes Prentice tick.'

'Difficult.' Anderson looked up with interest. 'He's deceptively tough. He can read a balance sheet like you or I would read the baseball scores. He's not above breaking into premises to get what he wants. He once killed a Russian who tried to knife him in West Berlin. But about a year ago he changed. . . .'

'His sex?'

'Apparently he became bitter, introverted. Drank a bit for a while. We don't know why,' anticipating Anderson's question.

'Sounds like a security risk,' Anderson remarked.

'The British don't seem to think so.'

'Which means they know why his character changed,' Anderson said thoughfully. 'Prentice sounds an interesting character.'

'If you can get near him.'

'I can try,' Anderson said, finishing his beer.

'A little,' Anderson repeated, his thoughts returning to the present.

Prentice said: 'And that's what you'll have to make do with.' He stretched. 'I'm going to bed. Tomorrow you must introduce me to Danzer.'

'It'll be a pleasure,' Anderson said, shifting his position and making the leather chair sigh again. 'He's got a lot to tell us.'

'How long?' Prentice asked, hand on the door to his bedroom.

'In my experience it can take anything up to six months.

We've got to bleed him dry. And we can't have any professional interrogators out here to alert the Russians.'

'Six months. . . . As long as that?' And when Anderson nodded: 'By that time we'll have to be briefing him what to tell the Kremlin about Bilderberg. It shouldn't take the Russians too long to tumble what we're up to.'

'Don't be such a goddam pessimist,' Anderson said. 'The Kremlin hasn't got a smell of what goes on at Bilderberg. If we play it cool we can use Danzer for misinformation for years. We just have to make sure he doesn't feed them anything which is dramatically wrong.'

'I suppose you're right.' Prentice opened the door of his bedroom. 'Well, good-night. . . .'

'The name's Owen.'

'Good-night,' Prentice repeated and closed the door.

So Anderson knew 'a little'.

He undressed and climbed into bed.

How much was 'a little'?

He switched out the light and lay still, hands behind his head, thinking, as he did every night, about what he hoped Anderson knew nothing about.

*　　*　　*

Annette du Pont had been beautiful.

Flaxen-haired, grey-eyed, full-breasted, just saved from looking like a conventional sort of model advertising tanning cream or toothpaste, by traces of sensitivity on her features that would soon settle into character.

She was, in fact, a student of economics at the old university at Basle, and she came to Prentice for help in her studies.

It was high summer and she was on vacation. While Prentice guided her though the theories of John Maynard Keynes – he had always admired a man who could preach enlightened economics and at the same time make killings on the stock market – he had found that he, too, was learning. How to live.

He bought new suits and Bally shoes, and had his brown

hair fashionably cut. He felt ten years younger than his thirty-three years. Even younger when, as they lay in a field printed with flowers overlooking the lake, she stroked his hair and said: 'You're very handsome, you know. Not a bit like an economist.'

His own awakening astonished him: he had never realised that such emotions lay dormant. There had been other girls, of course, but never rapport such as this.

They crossed the border by car into Germany and, for the first time since they had met two weeks earlier, made love. In a luxurious old hotel in the little town of Hinterzarten. Prentice had experienced sex before, but never anything like this. . . .

They drove through slumbrous green valleys in his silver BMW; they picknicked in forest glades, explored castles, ate and slept and loved in village inns. And shared.

It lasted four days. Then Prentice had to return across the Rheine to attend to the demands of his employers, Paul Kingdon and British Intelligence. As they neared Zurich, Prentice toyed with the idea of proposing marriage.

But how could he? You couldn't ask a girl to share her life with a man whose business was espionage. Or, more specifically, he couldn't conceal his calling from her because a marriage threatened by such subterfuge was no marriage at all.

There were two alternatives, Prentice decided, as he parked the silver BMW 2002 outside the apartment block. He could confide in Annette or he could find another job. He hoped that the latter wouldn't be necessary because, unlike most of the spies he read about in modern fiction, he enjoyed his work.

He decided to fly to England to seek advice. As it happened there was a cable awaiting him, summoning him urgently to London. He told Annette that he would have to leave her for a couple of days; she kissed him and told him that she understood and, in the single bed that had never known anything more orgiastic than the weekly disarray of the Sunday newspapers, they made love with abandonment.

For the last time.

When Prentice arrived at the offices of MI6 in Northumberland Avenue, between Trafalgar Square and the Thames, he was immediately aware that there was something wrong. It showed in the embarrassed greetings from a colleague, in the diffident attitude of Ballard's secretary.

Leonard Ballard was a man in his sixties with the stamp of the Navy about him, but none of an old sea-dog's geniality. Ballard had once been a submarine commander and during World War II he had been deputy chief of the Admiralty's Operational Centre, housed beneath the hideous, bunker-like building in Horse Guard's Parade, known without affection as Lenin's Tomb. Ballard had been in charge of the destruction of U-boats; as an ex-submariner he knew the sort of death to which he was dispatching men; it had seemed to affect him not at all.

To Ballard the pursuit and extermination of the enemy was everything. Now as then. But whereas he was normally urbane, the sophisticated skipper of a clandestine crew, he was today cold and brusque.

'Sit down, Prentice.'

Prentice sat down and nervously assimilated the trappings of the office – seafaring charts, propellers of a ship, a brass compass shining in a shaft of dusty sunlight.

'You look uncommonly dapper,' Ballard remarked.

Prentice didn't reply; there was no reply.

'Dressed to kill?'

'Not as far as I am aware, sir,' regretting the grey lightweight suit and the slightly jazzy tie that Annette had bought him.

'Appropriate for a fond farewell at Kloten Airport?'

A cold finger of apprehension touched Prentice as he said: 'I'm afraid I don't understand, sir.'

'Don't you? Then I shall enlighten you. You were driven to the airport by a Miss Annette du Pont, were you not?'

'As it happens I was. But I don't see –'

'That it's any of my business? I'm sorry to disillusion you. The companions favoured by my employees are always my business.'

Prentice was silent.

Ballard picked up a glossy photograph on his desk and tossed it on Prentice's lap. 'That is Mademoiselle du Pont, I believe.'

Prentice looked at the photograph. Annette looked back at him, smiling. Admiring the tie, he thought foolishly. The apprehension froze into fear. For Annette, for himself, for the future that he had glimpsed in a green field scattered with flowers. He said yes it was Mademoiselle du Pont.

'A student of economics, I am told. I'm sure you were able to teach her a lot. . . .' Ballard picked up other photographs and rifled through them. 'Not that she needed much teaching.'

'I don't think – ' but Ballard interrupted him again: 'You should have *thought* before. You disobeyed instructions. You know perfectly well that you should have checked out anyone who made such a direct approach to you.'

But she approached me for help, stayed with me because she loved me.

Ballard went on: 'I believe you know a man called Karl Danzer?' And when he didn't reply: 'I asked you a question, Mr Prentice.'

Prentice looked up. 'Karl Danzer?' He found it difficult to concentrate. 'Yes, of course I know Karl Danzer. He's a currency speculator. Not very big, but big enough. He also handles the Russians' hard currency for them. I've mentioned him in reports.'

Ballard said crisply: 'He's more than a Soviet bankmaster: he's a spy employed by the First Chief Directorate of the KGB. We've just cracked him through a turned KGB operative in the Soviet Embassy in London.'

Hope surfaced briefly. 'Is that why you brought me to London?'

Ballard sat down behind his desk and faced Prentice. 'We had intended to bring you to London to brief you about Herr Danzer, yes. Now the matter has become more urgent.'

The hope began to die.

Ballard picked up a silver paper-knife bearing a Royal Naval crest and pointed it at Prentice. 'I assume that by

44

now you realise in what direction this conversation is leading.'

'I consider Miss du Pont to be above reproach.'

'Do you now. Very gallant. I'm afraid I shall have to disillusion you.'

Prentice searched for his cigarettes but decided against lighting one, and sat with his hands clasped tightly together.

Ballard sorted through the photographs, selected one and stared at it expressionlessly for a moment. 'Miss du Pont,' he said after a while, 'has been associating with Karl Danzer for at least six months.'

Prentice wanted to protest, but there was no point. He watched the specks of dust spinning in the sunlight as despair settled upon him.

Ballard turned the photograph so that Prentice could see it, saying at the same time: 'You will appreciate that I don't enjoy this. Here, take it,' as though it were soiling his hands.

Prentice took the picture and gazed at Annette's lovely face. At the beautiful, full-breasted body that he now knew so well. And that expression of langorous contentment – as she gazed into the eyes of Karl Danzer lying naked beside her.

Prentice dropped the photograph on the floor.

'The photograph,' Ballard said, 'was taken in her room in Basle a week ago after Danzer had been blown.'

Annette had driven back to Basle a week ago – to fetch some clothes, she had said.

Ballard said: 'The only question that remains – and I am prepared to take your word on it – is, did you communicate anything . . . indiscreet?'

'Of course not. I had intended to seek your advice.'

'And what do you think I would have advised you?'

'Does it matter?'

'It matters now. The liaison must cease.'

'Of course,' Prentice said dully.

'According to our information you were approached merely in your capacity as an industrial consultant. You have made quite a name for yourself in that particular field,

Mr Prentice. Apparently she has no idea – or didn't have a week ago – that you also work for us.'

So they had bugged her room in Basle.

'One more thing,' Ballard said evenly. 'Leave Danzer alone. For the time being, anyway. He's more useful that way,' he added.

'Is that all?'

'For the moment.' Ballard picked up a photograph of another girl on his desk. Her prettiness had been frozen by the lens of the camera; the studio lights and the hairstyle placed her prettiness in the 1940's. 'I'm sorry,' he said. 'I know how you feel. . . .'

The girl was Ballard's wife who had been killed in the Blitz. It was the only time Prentice had heard Ballard apologise.

* * *

No, Prentice assured himself as he turned on his side and prepared to sleep, Anderson knew nothing about Annette du Pont. The story was known only to Ballard, himself and the agent who had reported the *liaison* to London.

He closed his eyes. When a catalyst such as that bitch's voice on the radio talking to Danzer stirred the memories – *'You're very handsome, you know. Not a bit like an economist!'* – it took a long time for sleep to visit him.

During the first few months after the interview with Ballard he had wondered about the identity of the agent who had denounced Annette du Pont. He had never found out, nor had he ever resented the professional's role in the affair.

Instead he had disciplined himself to be just as professional. He had taken a course at an establishment near King's Lynn in Norfolk, run by a cheerful ex-Commando named Saddler, and told Paul Kingdon, his overt employer, that he was taking a vacation.

At the end of the course he was far more than an industrial espionage agent: he was lethal.

Sleep touched George Prentice, but only briefly. He returned to consciousness as he had known he would, as he always did when this train of thought took its inexorable course. Until they reached the point where he was authorised to kill Karl Danzer.

As always it was the photograph that awoke him.

A photograph of a corpse. No ordinary corpse this. Teeth and hair had fallen out, face and body were covered with weals and swellings crusted with dried blood and pus.

The photograph of the man, who looked as though he might have been middle-aged – if, that is, you could imagine him as he was – was in colour.

This time it was Saddler who was displaying photographs – in a Nissen hut in the camp near King's Lynn. His normally cheerful, broken-nosed features were as savage as the wind hurling rain across the bleak Fens.

'His name,' Saddler said, stuffing black tobacco into his pipe, 'was Nemeth. He was a Hungarian. He had worked for us since the revolution in Budapest in 1956. I knew him, he was a good man.' The black tobacco began to glow in his pipe.

Prentice stared at the glossy horror in his hands.

Saddler, blowing out a jet of thick grey smoke explained: 'Thallium. Treated radioactively and introduced into his body. Either forcibly or in his food. The result was the same, his body just fell apart.'

Rain drummed against the corrugated metal walls of the hut and hissed in the chimney of the old stove burning in the corner.

Prentice placed the photograph face downwards on the table Saddler used as a desk. 'The Russians?'

Saddler nodded. 'The Executive Action Department of the First Chief Directorate of the KGB. Once known as Department Thirteen. Renamed as Department V – V for Victor, that is – before the KGB was reshuffled in 1968. For Executive Action read Execution.'

Prentice lit a cigarette. 'Have you got a drink?'

'I thought we'd weaned you off the stuff.'

'I don't *drink* any more. But I like a drink on occasions. This is one of them,' managing a faint smile as Saddler brought out a bottle of Bell's and two glasses from a drawer in the table, saying: 'Not a bad idea at that.'

'The department,' Saddler went on, drinking his whisky neat, 'is run by a gentleman named Nikolai Vlasov. In addition to assassination, its functions are sabotage. It has infiltrated agents into North America and Western Europe to destroy installations in the event of war. But that is not our concern here today. . . .'

Prentice poured a little water from a tap over a sink into his whisky and wondered what their concern was.

Saddler handed him two more photographs. Nothing horrific this time, merely mug shots of two straight-faced young men staring straight into the eye of the camera.

Prentice looked at Saddler inquiringly.

'Both dead,' Saddler told him.

'Murdered?'

'By Department V. Both British agents.' Saddler picked up a pencil in one huge hand and began to doodle; it looked like a gallows to Prentice. 'I trained them both. Both good lads. As far as we know they were both killed cleanly. At least that was something,' as he began to draw a noose.

'Blown I presume.'

'Oh yes,' Saddler told him, 'they were blown all right.'

'Do we know who?'

A pause. A rope joined the noose to the scaffold. 'Karl Danzer. I believe you know him.'

Prentice swallowed the rest of his whisky.

Without waiting for him to reply, Saddler went on: 'Runs quite a harem does our friend Danzer. His girls prey on unwary agents.' Saddler's blue-grey eyes stared expressionlessly at Prentice. 'One of them memorised the names of these poor sods,' pointing at the photographs, 'from a document in a briefcase.'

'In Basle?' Prentice couldn't help himself.

'Vienna.'

Annette? Prentice decided not to pursue it. He wasn't a masochist. He asked: 'Why are you telling me all this?'

'A combination of circumstances.'

The rain-loaded wind sighed in the telephone wires outside.

'It seems,' Saddler said, working on the scaffold, 'that Herr Danzer has managed to penetrate Bilderberg. I presume you know about Bilderberg?' And, as Prentice nodded: 'The annual secret – sorry, private – session of Western clout. Well, Danzer managed to get himself invited this year and will probably make bloody sure that he's invited next year and the year after. Our Company friends in Washington sussed him. They want to turn him, and they want us to work with them. Decent of them, isn't it? What they want, of course, is our intelligence in Zurich. In other words you, George. More whisky?' holding up the bottle.

'No thanks. What do they want from me?'

'Everything you can get on Danzer. I imagine you've got quite a bit already. . . .'

Prentice replied non-committally: 'Quite a bit. I can get a hell of a lot more.'

'Good.' Saddler began to draw a body hanging from the noose. What *we* want is as much information as we can get out of Danzer. Top priority stuff – the names of all the Soviet agents he knows.'

'And then?'

'The CIA,' Saddler said, 'is anxious to use Danzer to feed misinformation about Bilderberg back to the Kremlin. That's fair enough but we have a more conclusive scheme for curbing Danzer's activities at Bilderberg. We want him dead.' He turned over the photograph of the putrified corpse that had once been a man named Nemeth. 'You see, the Americans haven't got this to take into consideration. Nor these. . . .' He tapped the pictures of the other two dead men with his pencil.

'I still don't see – '

'Ballard consulted me.' Saddler put down his pipe, now cold. 'He wanted to know what I thought of your capabilities. He seemed to think that you might like the job. . . .'

Saddler finished drawing the body hanging from the noose. Underneath it he wrote DANZER. 'Now that,' he remarked, 'was very indiscreet of me. The very reverse of what you were taught here, eh, George?' He tore the sketch from the pad on his desk and walked over to the stove; he

49

removed the lid with a broken poker and dropped the sketch into the glowing interior.

Together they watched the sketch burn.

Saddler said: 'But don't forget, George, not before we've bled the bastard dry.'

Raindrops spattered against the corrugated iron. To Prentice the noise sounded like distant gunfire.

* * *

The sequence of events had spent itself. Now Prentice could sleep. He dreamed that he was John Maynard Keynes.

V

In September, 1971, the British, acting with the sort of cavalier authority that had characterised them in the days when they were building an empire, expelled from their country 105 Soviet spies.

This one-way package deal so alarmed the Soviet authorities that Party Secretary Leonid Brezhnev cut short a tour of Eastern Europe, postponed a reception for Indira Gandhi, the Indian Prime Minister, and conferred with members of the Politburo at the airport in Moscow.

One man attending the emergency session was more alarmed than most. His name was Nicolai Vlasov and he was chairman of the *Komitet Gosudarstvennoy Bezopasnosti*, known the world over as the KGB.

The British action had followed the defection in London of a traitor, Oleg Adolfovich Lyalin, aged thirty-four, and Vlasov's alarm was twofold:

Firstly, like everyone else at the Kremlin, he feared that the whole KGB operation abroad was in danger of being blown.

Secondly Lyalin had been a member of Department V (assassination and sabotage) and, before his promotion to chairman, Vlasov had been head of that particular department.

Vlasov had not the slightest doubt that his enemies would store that ammunition in their armoury for future use. So he set out to try and prove that Lyalin wasn't wholly responsible for the debacle; in fact, he didn't believe that he was.

Several weeks later he sat in his huge office at No. 2 Dzerzhinsky Square, Moscow, watching the pellets of snow bounce off the window and reviewing his progress in the Lyalin affair.

It wasn't spectacular.

Vlasov, an elegant man by Soviet standards, with greenish eyes and a skull that looked peculiarly fragile, as though a single blow with a fist would shatter it, pressed a red button on his desk.

Immediately the door opened. A bald-headed man wearing rimless glasses materialised. 'Can I help you, Comrade Vlasov?'

'Has the computer come up with the answers?'

'Not yet, Comrade Vlasov.' The bald-headed man ventured a joke. 'It *is* British made.'

'The British didn't waste any time in September.'

The bald-headed man's expression changed as he realised that the joke had been untimely.

Vlasov said: 'The trouble with the computer is that it's creaking at the joints. Go and give it a kick.'

The door closed. Vlasov shivered despite the fierce central heating that – so they claimed – exhausted his staff. He was never really warm but today he was chilled to the bone. It was that frozen snow, as hard as gravel, sweeping into Moscow from Siberia.

He lit a cigarette with a yellow cardboard filter and poured himself a glass of Narzan mineral water. Theoretically, he shouldn't have to bother about exonerating Department V; as head of the KGB, which penetrated every stratum of life from the Central Committee of the Communist Party down to the smallest commune in Georgia, he should have been the most powerful man in the land.

Theoretically. Not in practice. Acutely aware of the lurking threat of the monster in their midst, successive Kremlin regimes had made it their business to dissipate the power of the KGB. Every move, every appointment and promotion, was supervised by a special department created by the General Committee of the Party.

Vlasov pressed his fingertips to his fragile-looking temples. Another debacle like London and he would be toppled from his throne. But not if I have my way, he thought. It had taken too long to be crowned.

His thoughts descended from the mahogany panelled

office, from the great desk with its batteries of telephones, to the white-tiled cells of Lubyanka Prison somewhere below him in the same building. . . .

A knock on the door. 'Come in.' Vlasov took the lime-green sheet of paper from the bald-headed man and dismissed him.

The computer had printed eight code-names on the paper. The names were the feedback from information compiled by Vlasov during interludes of free time since September.

Each code-name represented a KGB agent abroad. If the aged computer (a replacement was on order) had done its job, each of the agents was above suspicion. With one small qualification: they all demonstrably enjoyed the Western life style.

Not that Vlasov could blame them – he had served in Soviet embassies in Washington, Ottawa and Copenhagen. No, their weakness was their failure to disguise their enjoyment. These eight men, according to the computer, were the most likely agents to succumb to Western blandishments. Just as Lyalin had done.

Not that any of them would be replaced. Just watched. A fatherly eye.

The eighth name was Karl Werner Danzer.

Vlasov sighed and pushed back the heavy drawer of the filing cabinet. The Americans and British had a saying for it: *You can't win 'em all.* Danzer had just been accepted by the powerful elite clique known as Bilderberg: it had been Vlasov's greatest coup since his appointment as KGB chairman.

He picked up one of the telephones, and when the girl on the switchboard answered, told her to arrange for the central heating to be switched up. He wondered if it also heated the cells in Lubyanka Prison.

* * *

Helga Keller was at first so overjoyed by the rekindling of Danzer's love that she didn't notice any difference in his attitude.

53

'But why were you so offhand . . . so cruel that night?' she asked and was completely satisfied when he replied: 'A business deal fell through. It would have netted the Cause hundreds of thousands of Swiss francs. I wouldn't have been good company that night.'

But there had been three more days and nights of misery and she asked him about them, and was again satisfied when he said: 'I was still feeling bad; I didn't want to upset you,' and kissed her.

He was still as eager as ever to hear the titbits of conversation she picked up from her father's dinner table and the Investors' Club. Hints of deals, loans, devaluations, market trends. . . .

He seemed pleased with what she obtained, but she wasn't naive enough to believe that her contributions were devastatingly important and when he suggested that she accept dinner invitations – particularly from American financiers – she reluctantly agreed.

He seemed particularly impressed by one item she innocently extracted from a drunken banker over a champagne cocktail. Astonished even. She had told Danzer that the banker had been celebrating an invitation to Bilderberg.

'Did he know the date?'

'I think it was April 21st.'

'Where?'

'Knokke in Belgium.'

'I didn't even know that,' Danzer said as he stood sipping a gin-and-tonic in his living-room.

'Should you have known, darling?'

Danzer said enigmatically: 'I thought so.'

He seemed distressed, Helga thought. She wished it was because she had been dated by the American banker who was as rich as Croesus. But she was honest enough to acknowledge that it was the mention of Bilderberg that had upset him.

Danzer was depressed for the rest of the day. And it was only then that she realised how much he had changed since that day when he had stood her up. Like it or not, that's what he had done. From time to time she saw him in the company of a big black man and an Englishman – attractive in a shabby sort of way – but it wasn't until much later that she associated them with the change in Karl.

She assumed it was the pressures under which he was working that were affecting him. It was tough enough dealing in currency in Zurich: she could imagine what it must be like when you were double-dealing. And for a goal, an ideal. . . .

The change in Karl Danzer only served to add another dimension to Helga's love: she worried *for* him. Perhaps he was under investigation of some sort; she approached the subject circumspectly once, but he reacted so savagely that she never asked again.

But if he were caught. . . . She stared into a future as bleak as bereavement.

* * *

The snow had settled on the lower flanks of the mountains and still Danzer had not been bled dry. He seemed to ration his intelligence as though he sensed that, when it ran out, so would his usefulness – although Anderson went to considerable pains to assure him that the West needed him for the purposes of misinformation.

One Saturday afternoon just before Christmas, when Anderson was again in Washington, Prentice drove fifty miles from Zurich to the run-down ski-resort where Danzer owned a chalet.

He strapped skis to the roof of the silver BMW and covered everything, except the tips of the blades, with tarpaulin. Under the tarpaulin, between the skis, he slotted a Russian Kalishnikov rifle fitted with a telescopic sight.

The sky was a metallic blue and the white fangs of the mountains were sharp against it. Prentice took the Berne autobahn. The traffic was thin, the Germans in their Mercedes stoically unconcerned as the French drivers overtook them in their big Citroens. Prentice drove at a steady 40 mph; no sense in attracting attention when your baggage included a sniper's rifle; Saddler had taught him never to break small laws when you were about to shatter big ones.

Twenty miles out of Zurich he took an exit to the left. The snow was hard-packed and, occasionally, the heavy-duty tyres spun on the polished surface. He stopped two miles outside the ski-resort. To his left stood a house which he had rented for six months under the name of Gino Salvini. It was a modest establishment by Swiss standards, four rooms built over a garage. Covered with snow and gilded by the sunlight, it looked postively chic. Always sell a car in the rain, they said: in Switzerland always sell a house covered with snow.

Prentice opened the doors of the garage. Inside was an egg-shell blue Alfasud bearing Italian codeplates and registered H52870 MI. He turned on the ignition. The engine fired first time and he drove onto the drive beside the BMW.

The house and the drive were hidden from the road, surrounded by low hills spiked with pine trees. He backed the BMW into the garage, removed the ski-rack complete with the skis and rifle, adjusted it and fitted it onto the roof of the Alfasud. Then he locked the garage, took the wheel of the Alfasud and drove back onto the road.

From the road he could now see the village – a few snow-bonneted houses, a church with a needle-pointed spire, a shop or two and an hotel that had once specialised in package deals before a tour operator had made the astounding discovery that the terrain wasn't a happy choice for ski-ing; the consistency of the snow was never quite right – something to do with a warm wind that nosed through the valley – and the ski-runs were too short.

It wasn't quite accurate to describe the resort as run-down: it had never got up. Nevertheless, a ski-lift served the slope with erratic rhythms, but it was rarely used.

Prentice surveyed the village, the snow-patched valley and the white battlements beyond. Then he glanced across the valley to a cluster of chalets. One of these belonged to Karl Danzer. Doubtless he would have preferred St. Moritz or Klosters but this served his purpose. It was undeniably low-profile.

Prentice drove in second gear down the hill to the village.

Before climbing out he adjusted the neck of his black sweater so that it masked the lower part of his face, and pulled up the fur-lined hood of his jungle-green parka.

He inspected the control cabin of the ski-lift. Like the scarlet cable-cars themselves, it had been constructed with grandiose ideas. But it had a disused air about it and the operator, wearing a plum-coloured uniform shiny with wear, was leaning back in his chair reading a copy of *Der Blick*.

The operator could, if asked, stop the ascending cable-car half way up the valley, at a platform designed to serve the cluster of chalets on the hillside. He looked as if any request would severely disrupt the tempo of his day.

Prentice made a note of the times of the last three ascents, the list on the wall compiled, presumably, in headier days. He tried the handle of the door. It was open. The operator looked up frowning, indicating with his thumb that Prentice should use the staircase to the platform where an empty car waited for passengers, and returned to his newspaper.

Prentice signalled that he understood. Then he set the stop-watch on his wrist and walked rapidly back to the Alfasud. When he reached the car he climbed in and set the stop-watch again. He drove up the hill, beside the thickly-greased cables, to an observation parking lot with room for about a dozen cars.

There were three cars there. One Swiss, one Belgian and one British, a Ford Granada. The boot of the Granada was open and a middle-aged couple were brewing tea on a spirit stove.

Prentice clocked himself from the village to the observation post. It was 4.37: it had taken him exactly three minutes. He glanced around; the bright colours of the day were fading fast and clouds were curdling on the mountain-peaks. The wind that played havoc with the *piste* was iced now, and there was a cruelty about the evening.

Prentice set the stop-watch again, put on climbing boots and set off down the precipitous path beside the car-lot. Almost immediately, he was out of sight from anyone above; not that anyone would be able to see much in the gathering dusk.

He reached a bed of flat rocks a hundred yards beneath the car-lot. It was surrounded by stunted pine trees capped with snow. He checked his stop-watch again and lay down on the rocks and peered through the feeble growth, none of the pines bigger than Christmas trees.

Above him to the right, on the far side of the valley, stood the cluster of chalets. Danzer's was the biggest, made from split pine painted blue with fretted eaves and a balcony on which to drink wine on summer evenings. Prentice had been there several times with Anderson; so, according to the bug in Danzer's apartment, had the girl. And many other girls. . . .

The cables jerked suddenly. He restarted the stop-watch. He couldn't see the descending car but in any case it didn't interest him. He peered down the valley at the ascending car, lit now by a single naked bulb.

As he had expected, there were two men in the car. One was the attendant who had, if anything, an easier job than the operator. The other was Karl Danzer. Stop-watch off.

Danzer passed him about fifty yards away, standing impassively, staring out of the window wearing a black, Cossack-style fur hat and a grey, waisted topcoat. The scarlet car stopped at the landing half way up the slope and Danzer stepped out.

For the rest of the night, Prentice thought, Danzer would worry. Prentice had called him and made an appointment. When appointments were made and not kept, when you were left alone in a chalet high up among the pine trees, you worried. If, that is, you had been reduced to Danzer's mental state.

Prentice began to climb the path. A car engine coughed into life. The English couple must have finished their tea.

Prentice timed himself as though he were replacing the rifle between the skis. Then he drove back through the dusk at speed, skidding round the bends as though he were on the Cresta run. At the rented house he swapped cars, locked the garage and timed himself for the last time.

The dummy run was over. Prentice licked warmth back into his frozen lips as he drove the BMW back to Zurich at a sedate pace, and thought of Danzer framed in the lighted window of the cable-car.

* * *

Unbelievably the Swissair jet arrived twenty minutes early at Kloten Airport. A tail wind, according to the pilot. A girl-friend in Zurich more likely, Anderson thought, as he passed through customs and immigration and told a cab driver to take him to the corner of the street where Prentice's apartment was located.

A lined page from a notebook stood propped up in the bowl of fruit on the table. BACK AT SIX. They were becoming like the Odd Couple, Anderson thought. The note should have added: DINNER IN THE OVEN. Bubble-and-squeak!

Anderson took off his topcoat and glanced at his wristwatch. 5.30 pm. He had half an hour in which to find out what Prentice had been up to during this three-day absence. Searching Prentice's possessions was always an intriguing process because they gave nothing away. Nothing.

Anderson selected a skeleton key on his ring and opened the old-fashioned desk in Prentice's room where he kept his papers. Normally you were assailed by a man's personality when you broke into a desk; an old passport, a key to a forgotten portmanteau, a group photograph – school or Army, perhaps – with the desk's owner staring self-consciously from the ranks; a shabby wallet containing a happy snap of a long-forgotten girl; letters, bank accounts, cheque stubs. . . . A man's imprisoned past clutching at the sleeve of the experienced investigator.

Not in Prentice's desk. It contained relics from the past but none of them had a message. It was as though Prentice had sterilised his possessions. Anderson glanced at the contents expertly: nothing had been moved since he last inspected them: as if they were as foreign to Prentice as they were to him. The collected trivia of a stranger.

Prentice, Anderson thought, had nothing except his professionalism and that was beyond doubt, its strength being its deceptiveness. With another key, Anderson opened the rudimentary safe in the wall of the bedroom – coded reports on Danzer and himself, left there no doubt for Anderson to read.

As he slotted a third key into the built-in wardrobe, Anderson heard the elevator stop outside the door of the apartment. He froze. Then the scrape of a key being inserted into the lock of the apartment across the way. He turned his own key and peered into the wardrobe. A minimum of clothes, a few pairs of shoes. He wondered what Prentice would look like in a tuxedo; attractive to women without a doubt – it was his remoteness that would appeal, that and the hint of ruthlessness.

Running his hands along the line of hanging clothes, Anderson momentarily experienced a flicker of . . . what? Shame? He shook his head. It was, as they said, all in the game. But he wished just for that moment that he was playing the game during a time of war, when the excuses were more flamboyantly obvious. But it's always war, it never ceases.

He stretched out one hand to the rear of the wardrobe where, behind his shabby suitcases, Prentice kept a Russian rifle in a Dunlop golfing bag. The bag was still there. He was about to peer inside when the elevator stopped again. By the time Prentice opened the door Anderson was in the living-room pouring himself a whisky.

Anderson, who was playing black, moved his knight and said: 'I'm beginning to agree with you about the girl.'

'What about the girl?' Prentice also moved a knight.

'She's a stupid bitch. She could be sending guys to their deaths with the information she's passing on.' He brooded over the board for a moment before moving his king's knight's pawn one square.

Prentice made his next move quickly, and then applied himself to the *Daily Telegraph* crossword.

Anderson thought: 'Arrogant bastard,' and, moving a bishop quickly, too quickly, said: 'You know, the stuff she comes up with. Nothing spectacular but all part of a pattern. Those patterns spell out death sentences. . . .'

Prentice shrugged. 'We're at war,' voicing Anderson's earlier thoughts. 'We've got our Helga Kellers. It all balances out in the end. I've moved,' he added, pointing at a pawn.

Anderson castled. Prentice immediately moved a bishop and returned to the crossword puzzle, filling in the squares as quicky as though he were writing a letter.

Anderson pored over the board. 'She heard about Bilderberg before him. That shook the bastard.'

'Did he pass it on to Berne?'

'Of course. All to the good. We want Moscow to go on thinking he's on his toes. By the way,' Anderson said, moving a pawn to queen's knight three, 'I picked up the guest list in Washington. Danzer's on it. You're not,' he added with satisfaction.

'I know. I calculate that I'll be invited every three years. Any new names?'

'A few. . . . Have you nearly finished that goddam crossword?'

'Nearly. One more clue. No way near my record, though.'

'Tough,' Anderson said.

'What are the new names?'

'How can I concentrate on chess when you want names?' Anderson took a photostat of the list from the inside pocket of his jacket and tossed it to Prentice.

Prentice moved a pawn down the rook's file, completed the crossword with a fairly simple anagram and picked up the list.

Anderson moved a pawn, anticipating the sacrifice Prentice intended to make. Prentice took the pawn, offering the sacrifice, a bishop, and said: 'I see Mrs Claire Jerome is on the list for the first time.'

Should he accept or decline the sacrifice? All his instincts said: 'Take it.' You had to be a hot-shot to keep the upperhand if you were a bishop down. Prentice was good, but was he that good? Anderson took the proferred bishop.

Immediately Prentice moved the pawn another square down the rook's file. Anderson took the pawn, and for the first time Prentice deliberated over his next move.

He filled in the time by asking: 'Why Mrs Jerome?'

Anderson leaned back and said: 'It was about time. She is one of the richest women in the world and it is the age of sex equality. Have you got much on Mrs Jerome, George?'

'A fair bit.' Prentice's hand hovered over the board, then returned to his lap. 'We have to keep track of arms manufacturers.'

'We?'

'The British Government. Paul Kingdon hasn't so far shown any interest in her companies.'

'I'm surprised Kingdon hasn't been invited,' Anderson remarked.

'So is Kingdon.'

Anderson wondered how much Prentice knew about Mrs Claire Jerome's interests. Did he, for instance, know that she was of great assistance to the CIA? *And why doesn't he take my bishop with his rook?*

Prentice took the bishop. This time Anderson moved quickly, his castled king.

'You play a good game,' Prentice said reluctantly.

'We play it every day, George.' He leaned over the board and tapped the list. 'As you will see, there is another significant newcomer, Pierre Brossard. A lot of clout there, George. One of the richest men in Europe.'

'And one of the meanest.'

'I guess that's how he got rich.'

'He became rich helping to rebuild Europe after the war.' Prentice made his move and relaxed a little, regarding Anderson watchfully. 'Has Danzer got the list?'

'Nope. Just the invitation.'

'How much longer do you reckon before he's told us everything he knows?'

'About a month maybe.' I think I've got the bastard now, Anderson thought; but you could never be sure with someone like Prentice; you could never be sure of anything with him. He moved his queen imperiously across the board. It looked an obvious move; perhaps it was too obvious. 'But that doesn't mean we've finished with him. We've got to brief him about Bilderberg.'

'Of course. But you think the interrogation will be over some time in January?'

Anderson looked up, frowned. 'I figure that, yes. Why?'

'Check,' said Prentice moving his queen.

'Shit!'

Anderson rested his head on one hand and stared intently at the board. It was seven minutes before he moved his king.

Prentice moved his queen again. But this time she didn't look so regally powerful.

Prentice asked: 'What made you change your opinions about the girl?'

'I didn't change them. I didn't have any strong opinions. It was only when I knew that she had passed on the venue and date of Bilderberg that I realised what damage she could do. Supposing one of the terrorist organisations working with the KGB got wind of it now. They could plan six months ahead' – putting his bishop in front of the white queen with a flourish – 'and hold the whole bunch to ransom.'

'Or just blow the whole bloody lot up,' Prentice remarked, frowning at the board. 'But Danzer would have known within a few days anyway. . . .'

'Sure, in this instance. But supposing one day there isn't any Danzer? She can still pick up that sort of information and pass it on. One thing's for sure – something's going to happen at that convention one of these days. All that power, all that bread. . . .'

'. . . under one roof.'

'It's your move,' Anderson said as Prentice sank back in his chair and lit a cigarette.

'I resign.'

Anderson felt ridiculously elated by the victory.

Prentice said: 'I should stick to cross-word puzzles.'

'I had an advantage,' Anderson said. 'I was playing black.'

* * *

Two days later Paul Kingdon telephoned from London.

Listening to his Cockney voice snapping over the wires, Prentice smiled faintly: unlike most people he had a soft spot for the whizz-kid. He imagined him now, sitting at his desk overlooking the rooftops of the City of London, wolfish features tense with impatience.

Kingdon said: 'We need everything we can get on Marks International and its subsidiaries.'

Prentice raised his eyebrows. Marks International was Mrs Claire Jerome. Coincidence? Possibly. Certainly an easy assignment: he already had plenty on Marks International. He knew, for instance, that Mrs Jerome was a good friend of the CIA.

He asked: 'Who wants to know?'

'I do.'

'You and who else?'

'Does it matter?'

Prentice didn't reply. Only he was allowed to treat Kingdon like this. After all, where would Kingdon be without him? In jail most likely.

Finally Kingdon said: 'Pierre Brossard.'

After Kingdon had rung off, Prentice stayed beside the telephone drumming his fingers on the table. Four months to go and already the Bilderbergers were beginning to stretch out invisible hands towards each other.

VI

It took until the second week in January, 1972, to bleed Danzer dry.

On January 11th Prentice and Anderson celebrated the accomplishment with a bottle of Bell's whisky. At 7 am on January 12th Prentice set out to kill Danzer.

Anderson was still asleep when he left the apartment, having drunk most of the whisky.

Standing on the landing outside the apartment, Prentice heard Anderson laugh in his sleep; laughter from a sleeping man, he reflected, was more eerie than a scream.

He walked down the three flights of stairs and stood shivering in the darkness outside. He wore thick flannels, the roll-neck black sweater and the jungle-green parka; but winter had made a come-back. Ice particles glittered in the glow of the street-lamps, the cold prickled in his nostrils, ice crunched under his feet as he made his way to the BMW.

As he drove towards the autobahn, flakes of snow were peeling from the black sky. He could just make out the outline of the mountains. But he wasn't sure whether he wanted the snow to thicken. Like a fog, a blizzard can be a Godsend and a hazard to an assassin. He prays for a parting in the veil when he takes aim, then pleads for the veil to be drawn again as he flees from vengeance.

After a few minutes it began to heat up inside the car. Prentice longed for a glass of orange juice followed by a mug of hot black coffee. If he felt like that, what would Anderson feel like when he woke up?

He had told Anderson that he would be driving to Berne early in the morning, usual contact number. But his true destination had been decided by Danzer speaking from his bugged apartment.

'Let's go to the chalet tomorrow.'

'That would be lovely, darling.'

'I've got a few things to do in town. Perhaps you could go on ahead and get the place warmed up.'

'Put the champagne on ice?'

Stupid bitch!

'And slip into something exotic. . . .'

'Mmmmmmm.'

'I'll be a little late. The last cable car probably.'

'I'll be waiting.'

Seeing the face of Annette du Pont, Prentice had switched off the radio.

Headlights swooped along the highway. He could see the silhouettes of the mountains clearly now, rimmed with pale green light. He took the exit to the left and parked the BMW in the driveway of the rented house. He drove the Alfasud out, substituting the BMW.

Then he went upstairs, drank a glass of orange juice as though he had just staggered out of the desert, made coffee and sat in front of the picture window to watch the dawn flushing the mountains.

He sipped his coffee. The snow was beginning to fall more thickly. He wondered what it would be like by dusk.

*   *   *

Anderson finally got out of bed at 11.30.

His head ached and he felt sick; it was a long time since he had drunk so much whisky. Prentice, of course, had risen bright and early and gone about his business without an ache in his body. Well, Prentice wasn't human; thank God they could split up now.

Anderson wandered into the bathroom, dropped a couple of Alka Seltzer tablets into a glass of water and watched them fizz. He tossed back the drink and stumbled into the kitchen to make coffee. Unwashed plates were piled in the sink. No more bubble-and-squeak, Anderson thought. Never.

He took his coffee into the living-room, drew the drapes and stared with disgust at the empty, whisky-smelling glasses. Later, he decided, he would call Washington, then in a couple of days drive to Knokke in Belgium to begin the preliminary checks for Bilderberg.

As soon as he learned the subjects for debate – probably as deceptively dreary as they had been at Woodstock – he would be able to brief Danzer about his leaks to the Kremlin.

Anderson wondered how long they could keep that up. Two or three years maybe if the mixture fed to Moscow was finely balanced, i.e. equal parts of harmless truth and misleading fiction. Finally, of course, the KGB would tumble what was happening. . . . Danzer was not a good risk for a life assurance policy.

But the information Danzer had provided, blended with the intelligence supplied by Oleg Lyalin, had been dynamite. Trust the British to expel the Soviet diplomats in London. A gunboat in Kensington! Unpredictable as always. Anderson had never believed that the British had been as naive as it seemed with traitors such as Kim Philby, Guy Burgess and Donald Maclean; he believed that, like Karl Werner Danzer, they had been used for misinformation. One day, he supposed, all the others – men like Anthony Blunt – would come crawling out of the woodwork; and even when they did, the British would keep up the deception.

George Prentice, Anderson thought, was a classic of Anglo-Saxon unpredictability and deviousness.

The philosophising intensified Anderson's headache. He went back to the kitchen and fried some eggs and bacon. He stared at the sizzling food for a few moments, then poured the contents of the frying pan into the garbage bucket.

*　　*　　*

At the same time that Anderson was disposing of his brunch, Helga Keller was driving her grey beetle Volkswagen out of the drive of her father's house. She had called the Investors' Club and told them she was sick.

As she drove through the streets of Zurich, watching the snow peel off the bonnet of the car, she sang to herself. She had with her information that she thought would please Karl

– a photostat of the guest list for the April meeting of Bilderberg *borrowed* from the American banker. Karl's name was on it.

After they had drunk champagne and eaten and made love, she would broach the subject that had been on her mind for weeks. She wanted to go to Russia, to see for herself the picture gallery that he had painted in her mind.

Ah, love and shared ideals. I'm so lucky, she sang to herself, as she turned off the autobahn and drove through the swirling snow towards the ski-resort.

From the picture window Prentice could just see the road. He saw the Volkswagen pass by the end of the drive. He glanced at his watch. 1.30. He would give it another three hours.

Anderson showered, shaved and dressed slowly. He could think of only one course of action that might revive him. He picked up the telephone and called a girl named Rita Geiser, whom he had met filling in the Christmas vacation from university at a toy store on the Bahnhofstrasse. The children had been absorbed with the excellent German and Swiss mechanical toys on her counter, and there had been no shortage of fathers accompanying them because she was very well built and her blouse was cut unseasonably low.

Yes, she said, she would be delighted to have dinner with him and, yes, it would be a good idea to have a few drinks at his apartment first. Anderson began to clean up the apartment, moving like an automaton, keenly anticipating the period between drinks and dinner.

His thoughts wandered as desultorily as his movements. When had Prentice received the summons to Berne? Certainly not last night; well, not as far as he could remember. . . .

Anderson yawned and activated the cassette that had been recording Danzer's conversation in his apartment. The tiny tape whirred smoothly but without sound. Anderson pressed the playback button.

'Let's go to the chalet tomorrow.' (Today)

'That would be lovely, darling.'

Anderson listened to the end. So he wasn't the only one planning recreation for the evening. . . . He frowned: there was something disquieting about the tape. What was it? He played it again. Then he had it. It *wasn't* the end of the conversation. Prentice had abruptly terminated it. As though he had made a decision.

Anderson stood in front of the window watching the snow pouring from the sky. The disquiet persisted. He consulted his address book in which the digits of all telephone numbers were shuffled. He found the contact number Prentice had given him months ago in Berne. He reshuffled the digits, called the number and asked for Kimber, Prentice's code-name.

'Who's calling?' A woman's voice.

'Parsons.' (Apparently a man named Parsons compiled the crossword in the *Sunday Telegraph*. Somewhere, well hidden, Prentice had a sense of humour.)

'I'll see if he's available.'

Then a man's voice, wary: 'Who is it?'

'Parsons.'

A pause. 'I'm afraid Mr Kimber isn't here.'

'But I thought – '

'Thought what, Mr Parsons?'

'Wasn't he summoned?'

A lengthier pause. 'Not so far as we are aware. Would you care to leave a message?'

'No,' Anderson said, staring at the receiver in his hand, 'no message.'

Anderson paced around the living-room. Unease gnawed at him. He tried the handle of Prentice's bedroom; it was locked. He took the skeleton key from his ring and opened the door. The room was tidy except that the bed was unmade.

Anderson crossed the room to the built-in wardrobe. Locked. He opened it with another key. There was the Dunlop golfing bag. Even before he had opened it he knew. . . .

Empty!

Holy shit! The disquiet splintered into panic. He grabbed

a sheepskin jacket, shoved a Magnum pistol in the pocket and ran out of the apartment.

His rented white Mercedes 450 SE was parked in a side-turning. It looked like an igloo. Anderson swept the snow from the windshield and windows with his arm.

The starting motor whined. Come on, you sonofabitch! The engine fired, faltered, then roared the third time. The clock on the dashboard said 4.48 as the Mercedes took off, rear wheels spewing snow.

Rita Geiser would have to buy her own dinner tonight.

Prentice slipped a Walther automatic, two lengths of wire and a roll of masking tape into the pocket of his parka and left the rented house in the blue Alfasud at 4.40 pm. It was still snowing and already the day was assuming the sullen textures of an early winter evening.

He drove slowly, watching the snowflakes charge the windscreen before veering away. He stopped at the brink of the hill leading down to the village. There was a light burning in Danzer's chalet, the girl warming the nest. The other chalets appeared to be unoccupied.

The cables were motionless and Prentice doubted whether the cars had been in use that day. He drove on down the hill and parked the Alfasud across the empty square from the control cabin.

The windows of the car began to steam up. Good. He adjusted the neck of the black sweater and pulled the hood of the parka forward. A little girl ran across the square pulling a puppy behind her. Otherwise the place was deserted. Forgotten. Preserved in snow and ice.

Here and there lights from the windows of the old-fashioned village houses lit the falling snow. He could hear a choir singing in the church. It was possible, Prentice thought, that the cable-car operator might confer with the two attendants – one stuck at the top of the mountain, poor sod – and decide to call it a day. In which case Danzer would have to walk up to the chalet through the pine trees; he would still die, but the execution wouldn't be so neat. . . .

Prentice remembered the colour photograph of the Hungarian whose body had disintegrated. He felt many things as he recalled the weals, the bloody swellings, but compunction was not among them.

He consulted his watch. 5.20. The light was fading. An orange Porsche drove into the square and stopped. A man climbed out, locked the doors and began walking towards the control cabin. It was Danzer.

At least he knew the way. Had driven to the chalet half a dozen times before to interrogate Danzer.

Anderson left the autobahn too fast, skidded, drove into the skid and straightened out onto the side road.

What was it with Prentice? Anderson pressed his foot down on the gas-pedal. Danzer had said something about the last ski-lift. Well, that would be about now give or take a few minutes.

The wheels spun on the hard snow beneath the day's fall, then gripped again.

Anderson assumed that Prentice intended to kill Danzer when he reached the chalet. *Which means that I've got to catch that last lift.*

The Mercedes reached the top of the hill. Below lay blurred lights. The village. Anderson steered the car down towards the lights. The snow poured down from the darkening sky.

Danzer walked briskly across the square. He felt elated, truly elated, for the first time since Anderson had stopped him that nightmarish evening. The interrogation was finally over; if he behaved shrewdly – and he always did – then the rewards of acting as a double-agent should be handsome.

Ahead lay a bottle of champagne on ice, a good meal and a mistress who was attentive if not practised. Tonight I shall teach her a few tricks, Danzer decided.

He vaguely noticed an Alfasud parked beside the cobbled sidewalk. Italian registration. He wondered what an Italian tourist was doing in this dump. Unloading lire probably. He forgot the Alfasud and rapped on the window of the ski-lift control cabin.

The slovenly-looking controller was buttoning a torn parka over his plum-coloured uniform preparatory to leaving. He looked aggrieved, then recognised Danzer who had in the past made a habit of tipping him well. He smiled. Danzer pointed upwards with his thumb and the controller nodded. No great favour, Danzer thought, because they had to bring the attendant at the top down to earth again.

He climbed the slippery steps and told the attendant to go home: he was perfectly capable of negotiating the doors at the platform adjoining his chalet. Rules were made to be broken and tonight he would enjoy breaking any rule in the book. He wondered if Helga Keller loved him enough to. . . .

He rubbed his cold hands together as the scarlet car jerked and, swinging a little from side to side, began its last ascent of the day.

Prentice waited until the homeward-bound attendant had got half way across the square. Then he walked swiftly to the glass-door of the control cabin. It opened as it had opened before. The controller swung round in his seat and stood up.

Prentice prodded the barrel of the Walther in his stomach and said: 'Keep quiet and you won't get hurt. When I tell you to stop the cars stop them. Understand?' He spoke with a thick Italian accent.

'But –'

Prentice jammed the gun deeper into the flabby belly. 'Understood?'

The controller nodded, sweat already glistening on his lumpy face.

'Good. Then I'm going to put this round your mouth just to make sure you don't shout, and this,' tossing the two lengths of wire onto the panel of dials, 'round your wrists and ankles.'

Prentice stared up towards the cable-car, barely visible in the falling snow. He consulted his stop-watch, in thirty-five seconds the car should be opposite the rocks nestling among the little pine trees.

'What controls the lights in the cars?'

The controller pointed at a switch to Prentice's right.

Prentice nodded towards a grey fuse-box with one red and one green button on it. 'Does that affect the lights in the cars?'

The controller shook his head and a few beads of sweat fell on the flickering dials.

'Right. Now!'

The controller pulled a lever. The cables stopped. Shuddered. Prentice pulled the grey fuse-box from the wall. Sparks showered around him.

He told the controller to turn round. He put down the gun and stuck the masking tape round his mouth. 'Now lie face down with your hands behind you.' It took Prentice less than a minute to bind his ankles and wrists.

Then he locked the door from the outside and ran across the square to the Alfasud. As he drove up the hill the outline of the cable-car became clearer. Danzer was standing with his hands and face pressed against the glass. Suspended in space, facing the firing squad.

Anderson saw the lighted cable-car hanging motionless in the gorge and thought: 'Christ, what a target!' But, because his attention was concentrated on negotiating the road down to the village, it was a couple of seconds before he stamped on the brake. The Mercedes slewed first to one side, then the other, before stopping. Anderson jumped out and ran back up the road.

The snow had thinned out and the figure of Danzer was quite clear. A standing target. There was one car in the parking-lot, an Alfasud. Anderson glanced inside. On the front passenger seat lay a newspaper thickly folded so that only a completed crossword puzzle was visible.

Where was he?

Anderson stared wildly around in the fading light. To the right a pathway. Freshly kicked tracks in the snow. Anderson drew his Magnum and charged down the path.

With the night field-glasses, which Karl had used more and more frequently since the change in his personality, Helga Keller stared down the valley.

She saw him enter the cabin. Happiness expanded inside her. She smiled. Her hand went to her throat. She closed her eyes for a moment; when she opened them again the cable-car had begun its ascent bringing him to her.

She could see him quite plainly through the powerful glasses. She stretched out a hand as though to touch him.

Then the cable-car stopped.

Helga saw the frown on his face.

She focussed the field-glasses on the control cabin below to see if she could find the cause of the stoppage. There didn't appear to be anyone there.

An avalanche higher up, perhaps. Her hands shook a little as she traversed the length of the cable with the field-glasses. On the far side of the valley, directly opposite the stationary car, she noticed a movement.

She refocussed the glasses. A man. One of the men she had seen with Karl. . . He was holding . . . a rifle. . . . She opened her mouth to scream but no sound issued from her lips.

Another figure entered the picture. The big black man whom she had seen with Karl. . . .

This time the scream found its voice – at the same time as the crack of the rifle shot. Two of the windows of the cable-car shattered, the figure of Karl Danzer disappeared.

Helga Keller, wearing the low-cut evening gown that she had bought especially for this evening, ran into the snow. Still screaming.

And it wasn't until she saw the blood splashing on the broken shards of glass still attached to the window-frame, that she collapsed in the snow and the screams were stilled.

'Hold it, you stupid fuck!'

Anderson aimed the Magnum at Prentice's head. But he hadn't recovered his balance from his headlong descent down the path. He slipped and Prentice, kneeling, swung at him with the butt of the rifle, catching him on the shin. Anderson fell into the snow, dropped the pistol.

He gazed down – into space. They were on the brink of a

precipice. The last echo of the rifle-shot lost itself in the mountains; the wind whined through the jagged holes in the cable-car windows.

And then Prentice, who had discarded the rifle, was on him. Hard and wiry. Instinctively, Anderson began to employ the unarmed combat that he had learned a long while ago; his movements were brutal and measured but his instincts were out of control: he wanted to kill.

They rolled nearer to the edge of the drop. Anderson got his knee into Prentice's groin and thrust upwards; Prentice catapulted backwards, teetered on the brink, then fell forwards towards Anderson.

As Prentice tried to get up, Anderson went for his throat. And realised, too late, that his instincts had taken over from his training. Prentice twisted to one side and chopped at Anderson's neck with the side of one hand. Pain leaped up Anderson's neck into his skull. . . .

Then Prentice was free, crouching, coming at him with both hands slicing and chopping. Anderson put up a hand to defend himself but he couldn't fend off those hands. Like the blades of a machine, he thought, as one of them caught him just below the ear and he fell back unconscious in the snow.

Prentice picked up the rifle and started up the hill. Before climbing into the Alfasud, he gazed briefly at the cable-car suspended in the darkness below and wondered who had killed Danzer: it certainly hadn't been him.

The Swiss are never over-anxious to publicise violent death within their country: it is very bad for their image. Better to bury the details beneath the snow which so perfectly represents their façade of pristine correctitude. Inevitably the killing of Karl Werner Danzer attracted some publicity but, with the intelligence organisations involved reluctant to become overtly involved, the stories soon drifted down-page, leaving behind the impression that jealousy had been the motive for the shooting of the womanising financier.

The cable-car was repaired; fresh snow settled in the valley.

In certain more esoteric circles no such calm was discernible.

In Washington, William Danby, head of the CIA, considered recalling Anderson and assigning the plum Bilderberg assignment to another agent. But, even if he had screwed up the perfect opportunity to feed Moscow with inspired misinformation, Anderson was still the man for the job. He was established.

Nevertheless, Danby did not refrain from informing Anderson, recovering in hospital from a dislocated vertebra in his neck, of his views on the loss of the turned Russian spy. Even more explosively, he made his views known to Leonard Ballard, head of MI6, effectively shattering Anglo-American co-operation in the field of Intelligence.

Helga Keller disappeared completely from Zurich. George Prentice gratefully accepted the offer of an extended leave, completed his investigations on Mrs Claire Jerome for Paul Kingdon, closed up his Zurich apartment and flew to Rio de Janeiro.

Lying in a hospital bed with his neck in a cast, Anderson reflected that he was lucky to have kept the Bilderberg job – any job, for that matter. And, because he had been told to relax as much as possible, he tried not to think about George Prentice (who ludicrously claimed that it wasn't he who shot Danzer) or Helga Keller who had unwittingly lured Danzer to his death.

To assuage the anger that boiled inside him when he thought about either of them, he comforted himself by reflecting that the Russians certainly hadn't succeeded in infiltrating any other agents into Bilderberg.

In that assumption he was entirely wrong.

Part Two

VII

Bilderberg, according to an article in *The Times* of London, 'is best known for the fact that no one knows anything about it.' Not strictly true, of course. A lot of people know a lot about Bilderberg; but they keep it to themselves.

Among them was Owen Anderson. Sitting up in bed in his apartment (now paid for) in New York, doing his homework for the 1975 Bilderberg at Cesme in Turkey, Anderson gained little satisfaction from his inside knowledge. As always, it seemed to him that they were setting themselves up to be destroyed.

It was only a matter of time. The American way of death. Clandestine manoeuvring followed by suicidal, well-publicised soul-baring. Like the God-awful Watergate mess. . . .

What the American people didn't seem to realise, Anderson brooded as he swung his legs out of the paper-littered bed and made his way to the kitchen to make coffee, was that by over-indulging the democratic processes they were destroying democracy. Playing into the hands of tyrants who sat back and enjoyed the suicidal ceremonies. . . .

Could anyone imagine Leonid Brezhnev being served with subpoenas for refusing to release Kremlin tape-recordings?

Anderson tightened the belt of his white robe and drank some coffee, hoping it would drown the disillusion. He gazed out of the window at the windswept February morning. Far below, office-bound crowds strode the sidewalks, heads ducked into the wind blowing in from the East River. Not one of them, Anderson was willing to bet, was aware that in two months time a hundred or so men – and a couple of women – would meet secretly to discuss policies that would control their lives. . . .

So, in a way, by protecting those who attended the convention, he was protecting the people on the sidewalks beneath him. If the logic was flawed, then Anderson chose not to analyse it. He returned to the bedroom with his coffee, sat on the edge of the bed and began to read what little had been written about Bilderberg.

*　　*　　*

It was born in the early '50s when a Polish philosopher, Joseph Retinger, and an American, George W. Ball, approached the urbane Prince Bernhard of the Netherlands and asked him to preside over a series of conferences.

The aim amounted to an attempt to re-unite European-American relations that had been thrown out of gear by the Cold War. Not everyone agreed that the intent was so innocent. . . .

The first meeting was held at the Bilderberg Hotel, near Arnhem, in Holland, from May 29–31, 1954. And one of the first critics to voice an opinion about the Bilderbergers, as they were subsequently called, was the syndicated American columnist Westbrook Pegler.

Pegler picked on the fifth conference at St. Simon's Island, off the coast of Georgia, after a reader had told him that an almost deserted hotel there was crawling with FBI and Secret Service. Pegler immediately compared the meeting with a conference held on Jekyll Island, Georgia, in 1908 when the currency of the United States and the world was secretly 'manipulated'. Pegler claimed that at the 1908 meeting, convened by Senator Nelson W. Aldrich, of Rhode Island, the Federal Reserve System was secretly hammered out.

Anderson knew about that meeting. It had been chronicled in a book by B. C. Forbes, former editor of Forbes magazine, in a book *Men Who Are Making America* published in 1917. And it was true that a new currency system had been written on the aptly named Jekyll Island. A government outside the government. . . . Just what the critics claimed Bilderberg was.

Of the 1957 Bilderberg, Pegler wrote: 'The public knows substantially nothing about the meeting nor even who selected the company to attend or on what qualifications.'

Well, the guest-list was drawn up by an international steering committee, and Bilderberg had a Secretariat located at Smidswater 1, The Hague, Holland.

The bedside telephone buzzed and Anderson reached for it.

'Mr Anderson?' The nasal voice of the janitor.

'Speaking. What is it, the bathroom?'

' 'Fraid so, Mr Anderson, another complaint from the folk underneath.'

'How many times is that?'

'About ten, I guess.'

'Well fix it, goddam it,' Anderson said with the full authority of a man who owned a property. He cradled the phone, drank some cold coffee and picked up a sheaf of ammunition supplied by the Liberty Lobby.

The Liberty Lobby, with offices at 300, Independence Avenue, S.E., Washington D.C., was the sworn enemy of Bilderberg. Over the years they hadn't achieved much; small wonder when they were pitted against the power-elite of the West. But they *were* a thorn in the sides of Prince Bernhard and the other participants.

Anderson ran one finger down the list of Bilderberg meeting places. . . .

1955 – Barbizon, France, and Garmisch-Partenkirchen, Germany; 1956 – Fredensborg, Denmark; 1957 – St. Simon's Island and Fiuggi, Italy; 1958 – sleepy little Buxton in England; 1959 – Yesilkoy, Turkey; 1960 – Burgenstock, Switzerland; 1961 – Quebec, Canada; 1962 – Saltsjobaden, Sweden; 1963 – Cannes, France; 1964 – Williamsburg, Virginia; 1965 – Lake Como, Italy. . . .

Anderson, who hadn't become the Bilderbergers' guardian angel until 1971, was sorry he had missed that one. They had stayed, of course, at the best hotel, the baronial Villa d'Este, said by some to be the best hotel in Italy. And the guest list had, as always, been impressive. Among those present, the Duke of Edinburgh, George W. Ball, one of the two innovators and Under-secretary of State, David Rockefeller (a regular), Lord Louis Mountbatten, Denis Healey, Britain's Minister of Defence and Manlio Brosio, secretary of NATO.

Writing about the Lake Como get-together, Walter Lucas of *The Christian Science Monitor*, had commented: 'But there is nothing mysterious or sinister about it all.'

A good Christian conclusion, Anderson thought. If a little naive. . . .

1966 – Wiesbaden, Germany; 1967 – Cambridge (surely a dangerous location!), England; 1968 – Mont Tremblant, Canada; 1969 – Copenhagen, Denmark; 1970 – Bad Ragaz, Switzerland.

Then Woodstock, followed by Knokke in Belgium – a golden opportunity to screw the Russians sabotaged by George Prentice, Saltsjobaden once again, Megeve in France and now Cesme.

He thumbed through the documents supplied by the Liberty Lobby, stopping at an extract from the *Congressional Record* dated September 15, 1971. John R. Rarick, of Louisiana, had once again raised Bilderberg in the House of Representatives – his fifth foray that year.

Rarick asserted that he had tried, so far unsuccessfully, to get the U.S. Attorney General to take action against Bilderberg on the grounds that it violated the Logan Act.

He also inserted into the *Record* a revised article by two authors, Eugene Pasymowski and Carl Gilbert, which first appeared in the *Temple University Press*. The article was the most comprehensive Anderson had come across.

It drew attention to the preponderance of members of the Council on Foreign Relations, among the American participants. It also underlined the ties with NATO and the big bands of the West.

But even these two writers, who had obviously exhaustively researched their subject, had failed to discover what was actually said during discussions on such subjects as the 'contribution of business in dealing with the current problems of social instability.'

They should have access to my little bugs, Anderson thought.

The critics, of course, claimed that Bilderbergers schemed outside the conference chamber. Claimed, for instance, that after the Woodstock meeting, American speculators dispatched billions of dollars to West Germany – and made billions when Richard Nixon devalued the dollar a few weeks later.

Well, only the mentally-retarded would believe that fluctuation in currencies, in gold and silver, was outside the interests of Bilderbergers; that they didn't concern themselves with political manipulation, the removal of unfriendly regimes, supplies of armaments and raw materials to the right people. . . .

The few Bilderbergers who had ever discussed the meetings – albeit uncommittally – had agreed that *contact* was everything. Only a simpleton would accept that they didn't profit from that contact.

The Vietnam War that had ended for America on January 23, 1973, had undoubtedly taken up much of their time – Henry Kissinger frequently attended the meetings. . . . Soon the Prince Bernhard scandal would break. Would the fact that their illustrious chairman had accepted bribes be the end of Bilderberg? Anderson doubted it: that sort of clout could ride any storm.

One of the most succinct comments in Anderson's file was made by C. Gordon Tether in the London *Financial Times*. On July 10, 1974, he ended an article with the words: 'It might be added that, if those foregathering at the Bilderberg shrine want to demonstrate that there is nothing questionable about their "humane activities", they could with advantage go to more trouble to avoid fostering the opposite impression.'

Anderson considered the list of participants at the meeting to be held at Cesme. Even if Bilderberg secrecy was undented, changes were being wrought: sex equality had touched its calculating soul.

Among the women invited was Mrs Margaret Thatcher,

leader of the Conservative Opposition in Britain. Which, Anderson thought, was a happy omen for Mrs Thatcher. The Western world's leaders, so it was said, were drawn from the ranks of Bilderberg. Gerald Ford was a relatively unknown member of the House of Representatives when he attended.

Anderson yawned and stretched. Not for him to pass judgement on the deliberations of the Brotherhood. It was his job to stop them being spied upon – or killed.

He turned his attention to two stacks of dossiers piled up beside the bed. One contained the computerised background on newcomers to the conference; the other, material on regulars which had been substantially revised.

He began with the second stack and picked up the top two files. Mrs Claire Jerome and Pierre Brossard. He decided to study Mrs Jerome first: not only was she prettier but she had an appointment later that day with the President of the United States.

* * *

In a penthouse two blocks away from Owen Anderson's apartment, Claire Jerome was luxuriating in a bathtub gazing at a building which may or may not have been the Taj Mahal. In a blue pool in front of the building a muscular young man was swimming energetically in pursuit of a girl who looked not unlike Dorothy Lamour in her prime. It had so far taken him five years to catch her; perhaps, Claire pondered lazily, she should recall the painter and shift the young man a little nearer to his goal on the mural.

She lay back in the black marble bath, toyed with the foam and breathed the perfume rising from the water. The bathroom really was decorated in atrocious style. Which was just how she wanted it. For fifteen minutes every day she escaped from convention. Black back (gold taps), white-tiled floor, a multitude of steam-proof mirrors and the wall-painting, which looked like a still from an early colour movie, was just about as vulgarly unconventional as you could get.

Claire adored the place. She glanced at the Philip Patek watch on her wrist: she still had five more minutes left in which to let her thoughts roam away from board meetings, executive decisions, business luncheons, scheming colleagues. . . .

She stretched out one leg and squeezed a sponge over it. Why did girls advertising baths or bath-salts always do that? Four minutes left. . . . Her thoughts drifted into the future; recently this was the direction they had been taking, accompanied by a vague sense of dissatisfaction. Unfulfilment? Now she was becoming her own psychiatrist. Perhaps she should restrict her therapy to ten minutes.

She stepped out of the bath and surveyed herself from every angle in the mirrors. Pushing thirty-eight, not bad. Full firm breasts, flat belly; the figure of a woman ten years younger. And yet there *was* something unfulfilled about it. You're getting neurotic, she told herself; she towelled and annointed herself, removed her shower cap and let her jet black hair fall over her shoulders.

The unease dispersed.

Mrs Claire Jerome, fifth richest woman in the world, *de facto* head of Marks International, the multi-national corporation founded on armaments, strode into the bedroom and gazed dispassionately at the man propped against the pillows in the big round bed reading a copy of *Time* magazine.

'I see we made it again,' he remarked, tapping the magazine with one finger.

'We?'

'Okay, you.' He yawned. 'Are you always crabby like this in the morning?'

'I enjoy my privacy.'

'Then why didn't you tell me to get out last night?'

'I thought I did,' said Claire, sitting in front of the dressing-table and beginning to apply foundation cream.

'I'm sorry. I guess we both fell asleep.'

Claire observed him in the mirror. Crisply handsome and physically in good shape, age only beginning to show in that tautness of the facial muscles peculiar to men who had knifed their way to the top, and knew that other blades were flashing behind them.

Well, almost to the top. Stephen Harsch was in his early forties, an age when you could still be described as 'an up-and-coming young executive.' Forty-five and you were a middle-aged fixture. Harsch was No. 4 in the Marks hierarchy and was anxious to become No. 3 as quickly as possible.

Which, Claire knew perfectly well, was why he was in her bed. Ostensibly he was at the moment very pro Claire (No. 2) and her father, the titular head of the business. A proxy vote was looming and Harsch was marshalling the stockholders behind father and daughter. When he had won that round, Harsch would be agitating against them.

The knowledge didn't disturb Claire. She understood the Harschs' of the world: she was their female counterpart. And her reasons for wanting Harsch in her bed were equally calculating: sexual satisfaction. *And to have someone beside you,* an unsolicited voice whispered.

Angry with herself, she smudged her lipstick.

Behind her Harsch began to read aloud from the *Time* article in the Business and Economy section headed ARMS AND THE WOMAN. It struck her, as she erased the smudge with a tissue, that the article contained exactly the sort of ammunition that Harsch would direct against her when/if he got the No. 3 job.

When is an enemy of Israel not an enemy? When he's a Persian, according to U.S. arms dealers assuaging their consciences about the destination of their weaponry in the Middle East.

Few armaments manufacturers would overtly clinch deals with states committed to anti-Israel policies. But for a long time Pentagon officials have succeeded in the not-too-daunting task of persuading them that the pro-West Iran falls into a different category. That by strengthening Western clout in the Middle East they are, in fact, helping the cause of the beleagured Israelis. In 1974 a staggering $3.9 billion of the total $8.3 billion arms sales went to Iran.

Currently facing the dilemma of whether or not to help

satisfy the Shah's insatiable appetite for the most sophisticated arms is Mrs Claire Jerome, 38, head, in all but title, of Marks International, the California-based conglomerate. Mrs Jerome is Jewish and she has in the past proved to be intransigent on her Middle East policy to supply only the Jews. But this time the Shah from his Peacock Throne is dangling a $1.5 billion carrot. Can Mrs Jerome, bearing in mind the interests of stockholders and employees, afford to disregard it?

'Well,' Harsch asked, 'can she?'

Claire Jerome began to brush her shiny hair. 'You'll have to wait and see,' she said. 'And Stephen. . . .'

Harsch looked up inquiringly.

'I think I *did* tell you to get the hell out of it last night. Would you oblige now please?'

'Okay, okay.'

'And shower in the other bathroom, would you. This is strictly private.'

Harsch gathered together his crumpled clothes and headed for the door. In the circumstances, Claire thought, he managed to muster a little dignity.

At the door, shielding his nakedness with his clothes, he turned and said: 'You know you'll have to make up your mind about that order from Iran pretty damn soon.'

She said: 'I'm flying to Washington today to discuss it.'

Harsch frowned. 'Who with?'

Claire Jerome enjoyed her moment. 'With the President of the United States,' she told him.

Happier now, she put on a dark-grey, two-piece suit and red cashmere roll-neck sweater, fetched her mink and went down in the elevator to the lobby, where the driver of her Rolls Corniche was waiting for her.

* * *

1.43 pm. The Oval Office of the White House.

Claire Jerome entered nervously. The President rose to greet her. It was odd, she reflected, that a couple of years ago she would have been quite composed in the presence of this man; now because he was President by default she was agitated.

The President, tall and hefty and a little gangling with pale thinning hair, did his best to put her at her ease. He wagged his pipe at her. 'Do you mind this?'

She managed a smile and shook her head. 'But I don't care for cigar smoke.' He probably smoked them in secret.

'I wish,' the President said, 'that every business tycoon I met looked like you.'

Claire began to relax because he was so relaxed.

'I want you to meet Bill Danby,' the President said. He corrected himself. 'Although I think you two know each other already.'

Danby inclined his head and smiled. 'We have met.'

The last time had been in Danby's office on the outskirts of the city, when she had assured him that she intended to continue Marks International's policy of collaborating with the CIA.

A steward in a red jacket served coffee. Claire declined and the President said: 'Bill will have your cup. He lives on the stuff. Would you prefer tea?'

Claire, who would have preferred a beer, shook her head. So did the President; perhaps he would have liked a beer too. Danby sipped his coffee – contained and watchful as always but not as omnipotent as he seemed in his own office. The Oval Office did that to people.

As Claire glanced around the room, history enfolded her. Oil-paintings of Lincoln and Washington resurrected the past; so did the furniture – an antique chest of drawers, a grandfather clock loudly ticking away the present into the past.

The President – or his wife – had taste.

The Presidential desk and its environs, however, were an island on which the man's own personality was stamped. Behind his swivel seat, between desk and the gold-draped windows, was a table on which stood photographs of his family; on the desk was a pennant bearing the name of a College baseball team.

The President relit his pipe and said: 'It's been Cambodia day today. Do you think we should cut aid, Mrs Jerome?' He peered at her through a cloud of smoke.

'It's in my interests to say no, I guess. But to be truthful, I don't think it's going to do much good. The Government will fall however much we send them.'

'I'm afraid you're right. But we can't reduce our commitment. Never let it be said that the United States has been niggardly.' He pointed his pipe at Danby. 'Bill, I think agrees with both of us.'

'That's how I keep my job,' Danby remarked. His spectacles glinted in the light pouring down relentlessly from the ceiling. The only hint of human frailty about him was the suspicion of a quiff in his hair, a relic of innocence. 'In fact, I do agree with both of you. Yes, we should stick to our commitment, no it won't do any good.'

The President traversed the Asian continent and said: 'I hear you've been offered the opportunity to provide aid where it might do more good, Mrs Jerome.'

Claire noticed clips from *Time, Newsweek* and a couple of newspapers on his desk. 'I'm not so sure about the latter part of your remark, Mr President.'

'Indeed? Why not, Mrs Jerome?'

'I believe our commitment' – their phraseology was infectious – 'in Iran is becoming gross. The Shah hoards arms like other people hoard gold. He needs advice, not guns.'

'Well, Bill,' the President said easily, puffing on his pipe, 'what do you say to that?'

'Simple. No prevarication this time. I think Mrs Jerome is wrong. The Shah needs us, we need the Shah. According to our information, he's in a strong position and we need to keep him that way. What's more,' Danby added, 'I don't think Mrs Jerome is being totally honest with herself.'

Claire Jerome understood Danby's resentment: it was the first time since her father had agreed to sell arms to U.S. Intelligence customers that she had questioned the Agency's judgement.

She said: 'I presume you mean the fact that I'm Jewish. Well, of course, you're correct up to a point. In the Middle East I'll only sell to Israel. One day Iran could become actively hostile to the Jews.'

'I rather doubt that,' Danby remarked, reaching for the cup of coffee intended for Claire.

Claire said: 'I think you rather underestimate the power of Islam. Come to that, so does the Shah.'

Danby said: 'The Iranians are not in the same bracket as Libya or Syria.'

'They worship the same God,' Claire said. 'And as you probably know,' wondering if he did, 'Persia was conquered by the Arabs in 671 A.D. and their principal language, Farsi, is written in Arabic script.'

The President grinned. 'I'm learning,' he said. 'Does it amount to this, Mrs Jerome, that irrespective of the pros and cons about Iran, you have no intention of doing business with the Shah?'

'None whatsoever.'

'I wonder,' Danby said, taking off his spectacles and polishing them with a white handkerchief, 'what your stockholders will think about losing one and a half billion dollars worth of sales.'

The President's manner became less easy-going. 'That's a private matter for Mrs Jerome,' he said. 'Doubtless she will be able to handle it and doubtless some other company will be only too pleased to accommodate the Peacock Throne. I hear,' he said to Claire, 'that you will shortly be visiting one of the Shah's neighbours.'

Claire looked at him sharply. She realised suddenly that this was the reason for the summons to the White House, not Iran. 'You mean the Bilderberg convention in Turkey, Mr President?'

'Exactly. Bilderberg worries me, Mrs Jerome.'

'But –'

He held up one large, well-manicured hand. 'I know what you're going to say. I'm an old Bilderberg hand myself. Well, that's true enough. It would have been very stupid of an obscure politician to refuse their invitation, now wouldn't it.'

'I guess so,' warily.

'You are in an extremely advantageous position, Mrs

Jerome. You are not, as yet, a member of the clique. You haven't completely thrown your hand in with them.'

Did he want her to spy on them? If so, why hadn't Danby made the approach? She glanced at the Director of the CIA; he had replaced his spectacles and his face was expressionless.

'I am suggesting, Mrs Jerome, that you are in a unique position to be able to report back to me any . . . any extra-curricular activities. Trends in the sale of the commodities in which you specialise – and anything else which you think would be in the interests of the United States.'

'But surely –'

The President cut in: 'I will, of course, receive many reports. One of my assistants is attending. But your contacts will be rather special, Mrs Jerome.'

'But surely Mr Danby has such matters in hand.'

The President said: 'I don't doubt that Mr Danby is also represented at Bilderberg. I *do* doubt that his representative – or . representatives – will operate in the same circles as yourself, Mrs Jerome.'

For the first time Claire Jerome sensed hostility between the two men. The President wanted an end to intrigue outside his authority. And he wanted Danby to know that he wanted it.

She said 'You know, of course, that there is a gentleman's agreement not to divulge anything that happens at Bilderberg.'

'I know that very well, Mrs Jerome. But you are not a gentleman. You are a woman. And, if I may say so, a very attractive one.'

The President's heavy-handed charm reached her; what saved it, was its apparent sincerity. Flattery will get you everywhere. 'Mata Hari, Mr President?'

He smiled. 'Everything hinges on your priorities. Which is more important: Bilderberg or the United States of America?' He swivelled round in his chair and Claire caught a glimpse of the President's responsibilities – in his family photographs. Wife, children, dogs . . . millions of them.

She asked: 'What worries you about Bilderberg?'

He answered promptly: 'Their power and, paradoxically, their vulnerability. Can you imagine what a temptation they must present to the enemies of the West?'

He stood up, towering over them. 'Lunch-time, all fifteen minutes of it. Bill has got to be on his way too – to decide whether or not his organisation ever contemplated assassinating Fidel Castro.'

Danby stood up unsmiling. 'Not to mention the Kennedys, John or Robert, take your choice.'

The President clumped him on the back, a considerable clump. 'Don't be bitter, Bill. All I seek is a little honesty. God knows we need it.'

Danby said tersely: 'I'm sure the Russians agree with you,' and walked swiftly to the door.

As the President escorted her out of the office, Claire said: 'Do you mind if I ask you just one question?'

'Fire away, Mrs Jerome.'

'Do I gather from our conversation that you believe that Bilderberg constitutes a greater authority than the Presidency?'

'A good question, Mrs Jerome. Perhaps you will help me to answer it.'

The door closed behind her.

*   *   *

The Golden Dolphin Hotel – or *holiday resort* as the management prefers it to be called – is located in the Turkish village of Cesme overlooking the Aegean Sea. It is a modernistic complex of buildings, boasting 900 rooms and private moorings for those guests who own yachts.

On Friday, April 25, it was virtually a fortress. Armed Turkish troops and police stood guard, and the casual visitor – if he were allowed to get that far – might well have assumed that terrorists were holding a bunch of wealthy guests as hostages. (Had this been so, the captors would have been in a position to demand an astronomical ransom; what's more they would probably have got it.)

The *prisoners* were, in fact, there by choice. A wise choice because Cesme is remote, and 'easily accessible' is not a phrase that lightens the hearts of Bilderbergers gathering in force.

Sitting in the sun on one of the balconies, a middle-aged Frenchman with a long lean body and sparse hair combed into grey wings above his ears, was disputing a bill for a bottle of Perrier water with a waiter. The host country picked up the tab, but Pierre Brossard queried all financial transactions on principle.

The waiter who, like the rest of the hotel staff, hoped to make a killing in tips, gazed with astonishment and chagrin at the Frenchman who, he had been told, was one of the richest men in Europe.

Brossard, clad only in a pair of briefs, his disciplined body glistening with sun-tan oil, ignored the waiter and concentrated on his pocket calculator while he converted Turkish lire into French francs. 'Preposterous,' he finally remarked in English.

The waiter looked stunned; even he could just about afford a bottle of mineral water at the Golden Dolphin.

'I shall take it up later with the management,' Brossard told him and dismissed him with a wave of his hand.

Well satisfied with the one-sided exchange, Brossard leaned back in his canvas chair, contemplated the sparkling blue sea, and considered the good fortune that inexorably came his way these days.

His empire was flourishing. New office blocks were shooting up in Paris, Marseilles and Montreal; his oil tankers hadn't yet lost any cargoes through the fuel crisis; the circulation of his financial newspaper published in Paris was climbing steadily, thanks largely to its prestigious columnist, Midas.

Pierre Brossard found this particularly satisfying; Pierre Brossard *was* Midas.

He applied more sun-tan oil, feeling the whippy muscles on his body. He had just completed a course at a health farm and he was trim after ten days of starvation and exercise. Brossard planned to eat well at Cesme, at other people's expense.

He slid a plastic protector over his nose to prevent it peeling and turned his attention to his less publicised enterprises. Brossard acted as middleman in oil and armaments deals. He represented many countries, Israel included, but not, to his regret, the hard-line Arab states who dealt exclusively through the debonair Mohamed Tilmissan and Adnan Kashoggi.

At Bilderberg there was much business to be negotiated.

He sipped his Perrier water. What a target we represent, he thought. On the charter plane from Zurich to Izmir, fifty miles from Cesme. Here at the hotel, despite the security.

Brossard didn't want any harm to come to the Bilderbergers. And not merely out of consideration for his personal safety. If the rumours were to be believed, he was about to be asked to become a member of the steering committee. Brossard calculated that, when he was on the committee, he could expect to be present at the next five conferences. Then he would retire – from Bilderberg and business life. After a coup, already burgeoning in his mind, that would shatter the financial structure of the Western world.

The bell on the door to the hotel room rang and Brossard called out: 'Who is it?'

'Mrs Jerome.'

Brossard removed the nose-protector, slipped on a Navy blue sports shirt and let her in. 'Right on time,' he said leading her onto the balcony. 'But in my experience Americans are usually punctual.' He moved a seat into the shade for her. 'Can I get you anything?'

'Why not? It's on the house. How about some tea?'

Brossard called Room Service and sat down opposite her. She was wearing a white skirt and a pink silk blouse with a rope of pearls round her neck. With her black hair shining in the sun, she looked attractive and ten years younger than her age.

But not my type, Brossard thought. During sex she would be passionate and practised but at the same time watchful, looking for weakness. Like so many successful American women.

Not my type at all. Pierre Brossard thought of the blonde girl in the black corselette in Montmartre, whose apartment he had vacated prior to catching the plane to Izmir. The pain had been truly delicious, the weals beneath his shirt and briefs there to remind him of it.

Claire Jerome would interpret such sexual behaviour as a sign of decadence, weakness. Why? He remained strong and purposeful and his preferences hurt no-one; no-one but himself that is.

The waiter served the tea, glancing nervously at Brossard. Brossard signed the bill without looking at it and the waiter fled.

Claire Jerome added sugar and lemon and said: 'Don't you ever tip them?'

'I presume service is included,' Brossard said.

'You certainly live up to your reputation.'

Brossard smiled thinly. 'You flatter me. Have you just arrived?'

'No, yesterday. I stopped off at the Efes Hotel in Izmir to see how Bernhard handled the Press.'

'And how did he?'

'Effortlessly. He told them that they hadn't got a hope in hell of getting into the Golden Dolphin and that's about all he told them. But it was hilarious really. As you know, the United States imposed an arms embargo on Turkey this year because they invaded Cyprus. The Turkish journalists think that's why we're all here.'

Brossard stretched and winced; the blonde girl had perhaps been a little too zealous. 'I have no doubt the arms embargo will be discussed,' he remarked. He picked up an agenda. 'What have we here? *The Economic, Social and Political Consequences of Inflation.* Well, I think we all know the answer to that – things become more expensive.' He shifted his position in the chair; odd that the residue of pain gave no pleasure, only its infliction. 'And here's another item. The Arab-Israel Conflict. A titillating subject, Mrs Jerome.'

'Stop sending arms to the Arabs,' Claire Jerome said. 'That would resolve it.'

'And stop sending them to the Israelis?'

'The Israelis are under siege.'

Brossard shrugged. 'Anyway, this is a pleasant setting in which to do business.'

'Bilderberg always seems to choose well.'

'Shall we go into the bedroom, Mrs Jerome? Our voices may carry out here. . . .'

In the bedroom he wiped the oil from his face with a towel, and said softly: 'Have you come to a decision about the Iranian deal, Mrs Jerome?' adding: 'I'm assured that the rooms have all been debugged.'

'You know I have. Frankly I don't know why –' But Brossard interrupted her: 'One and a half billion is a lot of money, Mrs Jerome.'

'And a lot of commission.'

'You make it sound immoral. I don't think an arms dealer should ever sound moral, do you,' and, walking across the room, he said: 'Will you excuse me a minute.'

In the bathroom he examined the weals. They were really quite painful. But how could he ask anyone to bathe them? He managed to sprinkle talc on his back, then slipped into a soft, towelling robe.

'Well, Mrs Jerome?' he said when he returned to the room. He glanced at his watch. 'I haven't much time. I have other interested parties. That's what's so convenient about these get-togethers.'

'The only Middle East country I sell to is Israel.'

'Then I can't fully understand why you bothered to come up here.'

'I thought you might have other business to discuss.'

'I might have had. But there are other Dealers in Death. . . .'

'And there are other middlemen dealing in death.'

She picked up her purse and strode out of the room.

In the lobby Claire noticed a big black man immaculately turned out in a pearl-grey lightweight suit. Vaguely familiar . . . something missing . . . the waistcoat and the watchchain . . . the American head of security at the Knokke conference.

He smiled at her and said: 'Howdy, Mrs Jerome.'

She smiled back. 'You looked naked without it,' she said.

'Come again, Mrs Jerome?'

'The vest – and the chain.'

He relaxed. 'You're very observant, Mrs Jerome.'

'And you have a very good memory, Mr –'

'Anderson, ma'am. Take care,' as she walked towards the reception desk to see if there were any messages.

One. *Please call Mr Stephen Harsch.*

To hell with Mr Stephen Harsch, directing the anger aroused by Pierre Brossard at the Marks International executive in New York.

In the corridor leading to her room, she heard a whistle. She swung round. The only other occupant of the corridor was a diminutive pageboy with an angelic face.

The anger subsided. If pageboys whistled at you in your 39th year, things couldn't be all that bad. Suddenly she hadn't the slightest doubt that she could handle the stockholders.

She advanced upon the pageboy who stood staring at her, terrified. 'Here.' She handed him a five-dollar note. 'Go and buy yourself a new whistle.'

* * *

For three days Pierre Brossard listened attentively to what the Bilderbergers had to say in their debates. They sat alphabetically and they were allowed five minutes to air their views – longer if Prince Bernhard, who exercised control with red and green lights, thought they merited it.

At cocktail time Brossard stayed in his room making notes. Then he adjourned to private chambers and suites to meet government ministers, bankers, industrialists, financiers, heads of family dynasties, men even richer than himself. . . .

He suggested deals, clinched deals. He heard many secrets. From Western hawks and doves; from the EEC and

NATO (in particular the intent of Turkey which had closed four of America's bases and listening posts in reprisal for the arms embargo); from men juggling dollars, marks, francs, yen, pounds. . . . He heard about sanction-busting in Rhodesia, diplomatic overtures in China to counter Soviet expansionism . . . about arms and oil – or lack of it – which were his specialities.

At midnight he retired once again to his room, where he collated what he had learned. Then slept fitfully, awoken from time to time by disquiet. Power and wealth paradoxically created weakness. Every guest in the Golden Dolphin was vulnerable – to the assassin's bullet, to blackmail. . . .

The conference wound up without a hitch, and on Sunday evening Brossard boarded the Zurich-bound charter with the other Bilderbergers and their women-folk who had been accommodated at the Efes Hotel at Izmir.

At dawn on Monday, April 28, Brossard drove to the Bois de Boulogne from his house, taking with him a briefcase containing his Bilderberg notes and observations – and a memorandum outlining the embryo of his plan to wreck the Western economy and bring the American dollar to its knees.

He handed the briefcase containing the notes to a thickset man in a raincoat named Shilkov. By lunchtime the notes, transported by diplomatic bag, were in the hands of Nicolai Vlasov, head of Soviet Intelligence.

VIII

Most of those who harboured fears about the eventual outcome of the Bilderberg conferences – and that included the President of the United States – thought big. In terms of international conspiracies or multi-kidnapping by such terrorist organisations as the Black Septembrists, the Red Brigade or the Bader Meinhof – or, worse, a combined assault by guerilla groups.

Only a few realised that the future of Bilderberg could be jeopardised by relatively insignificant individuals. Or that the threat could be posed in events of seemingly little importance.

One of those who *did* appreciate such imponderables was Owen Anderson. He had taken the trouble to study history in the context of his profession . . . an officer of no consequence inadvertently leads his men across a border and the guns of war erupt . . . a nonentity with a deranged mind fires a gun and a head of state drops dead. . . .

Anderson was fully aware that history does repeat itself, and it was therefore the menace of the obscure and insignificant that worried him more than the presence of the obvious and infamous. How could you combat an unspoken threat from obscurity?

As he feared Anderson *was* quite powerless to influence two unrelated happenings involving men of whom the world was largely unaware. Each was destined to endanger two of the Bilderbergers' most precious possessions.

Their privacy. And their lives.

* * *

In London, a little-known journalist named Nicholas Foster,

was ordered by the editor of a Sunday newspaper to write a follow-up to the resignation of Prince Bernhard of the Netherlands from all public positions.

The Bernhard scandal had astonished the world and stunned the Dutch people, who had long believed that he had achieved the impossible: the fusion of the Royal family and big business.

Bernhard was the director of dozens of companies, including the KLM airline. He had been a pilot with the RAF in the war, commander of armed forces outside Holland. With a white carnation in his lapel, he was the symbol of the new post-war spirit of Holland. And he even found time to launch the World Wild Life Fund.

What few people suspected was that, owing to his life style, the prince was short of cash. The revelation came when an executive of the Lockheed Corporation appeared before a U.S. Senate subcommittee on Multinational Corporations.

He was asked if Lockheed had paid any money to Prince Bernhard and replied: 'I wish you hadn't asked that question.' The Dutch were aghast and set up their own committee to investigate the allegations.

The committee confirmed that the swashbuckling prince had taken bribes, and for a while it looked as though the Monarchy might tumble.

When Nicholas Foster was handed the story, he was confronted with the problem that haunts every Sunday newspaperman: he had to find an aspect of the scandal that would not be covered in the daily papers.

He discovered Bilderberg.

Because of the Bernhard furore, the 1976 conference destined for Hot Springs, California had been cancelled. Wasn't it reasonable to suppose that, if the chairman took bribes, then he had been presiding over an organisation where such practices were commonplace?

The crusading spirit consumed Foster.

He was twenty-three years old and with his dark wavy hair and slightly cleft chin was often taken for an Irishman, which he was not. He was determined to succeed without the assistance of his father, who owned a world-wide chain of hotels, and, such was his determination, that he was occasionally inclined to be impetuous.

He studied the thin envelope of cuttings on Bilderberg supplied by the newspaper library; he contacted the Liberty Lobby in Washington; he tried to interview participants.

'No comment, no comment. . . . Not available for comment. . . . Out of the country at the moment . . . I'll call you back' (they never did). . . .' And from one evasive humorist: 'Bilderberg? Never heard of it – sounds like a construction kit for children.'

When Foster put down the telephone for the last time, he found that like other reporters tackling the same subject before him, he was singularly ill-equipped to write a factual exposure.

But he tried. And, as he sat in the newsroom tapping away on an ancient typewriter chained to a green-topped desk – a precaution, he assumed, against scrap-metal thieves – anger began to smoulder among the words. Worse, opinions became a substitute for missing facts; somehow, although he didn't altogether realise it at the time, the resentment he had always felt towards his father, doyen of the Establishment, got mixed up in his writing.

Ordinarily the story wouldn't have got farther than the news-desk. But, unfortunately for Nicholas Foster, the editor demanded to see the copy just as he finished it.

Ten minutes later he was summoned to the editor's office.

The editor, an austere but nimble-brained Scot, held Foster's copy up by one corner and asked: 'Just what is this supposed to be?' as though Foster had dropped a soiled handkerchief.

Fear of failure gripped Foster. He saw his father's patronising expression; heard him saying: 'Now you've had your fling, let's map a decent career for you.'

The editor said: 'As you don't seem to know, I'll tell you what it is. It's crap.'

The fatal quick-temper, which helped to give the impression that he was Irish, began to rise. '*I* don't think so, sir.'

The editor pointed to a chair in front of his desk, now

strewn with paper. Foster sat down. 'You are, of course, entitled to your opinion. The fact remains that I asked for a follow-up to the Bernhard scandal. Which this,' holding up the copy again, 'manifestly is not.'

Foster said: 'With respect, sir, I think I found an angle which the dailies missed. It's been proved that Bernhard has been taking bribes, and all the time he's been presiding over meetings of some of the most influential men in the West –'

'Which hardly indicts them,' the editor interrupted.

'No, sir, but –'

'How long has Bilderberg been meeting?'

'It first sat in 1954.'

'More than 20 years. Is that news?'

'Surely investigative journalism always involves digging up old facts.'

The editor winced. 'Facts? Where are the facts?' He tossed the copy on the desk.

Foster began to enumerate the facts, aware, as he spoke, of their paucity.

The editor held up his hand. '*New* facts, Foster. Everything you've said so far has been written before. What you've produced here is a cuttings job tarted up with opinions.'

Foster said: 'I'll admit that I've drawn inferences. Surely I'm entitled to when everyone involved clams up. . . .'

'Inferences! Since when did a newspaper depend on inferences? So-and-so last night refused to comment on allegations that. . . . That contrivance went out with the ark.'

A part of Foster's consciousness accepted the criticism, but it was over-ruled by frustration so he said: 'The fact is' – facts or lack of them were dominating the exchange – 'that Bilderberg is a secret society and, because of the Bernhard affair, we have a peg on which to hang an exposure.'

The editor leaned forward across his desk; when he was angry his Scots accent thickened. '*If* you had come up with an exposure, Foster, I would accept what you've said. But as you've come up with a hotch-potch of antiquated facts and unsubstantiated accusations, I don't. Has it ever occurred to you that these men are entitled to their privacy?' He picked up the copy and spiked it.

Afterwards Foster wasn't sure whether it was the spiking of his copy or the editor's last remark that plunged him into the brief duel, from which there could emerge only one winner.

With words overtaking thoughts he snapped: 'Privacy – that's their word. Mine is secrecy.'

'So Bilderbergers and I share a common vocabulary. . .'

'No newspaper that I know of has ever had the guts to expose Bilderberg.' Foster had by now dropped the *sir*.

'A conspiracy of silence? I'm surprised you didn't use that immortal phrase in your story. It's very popular, you know, with reporters who fail to dig up any facts.' There was a cutting edge to the editor's voice. 'Am I to assume that you are including me in this category of . . . ah . . . gutless newspaper editors?'

'I'm merely observing that it's odd that no-one wants to publish anything about Bilderberg.'

The editor stood up. 'You are suggesting that I'm suppressing news?'

Despair engulfed Foster, but he heard himself say: 'The facts speak for themselves.'

The editor leaned over, pulled the story off the spike and handed it to Foster. 'I suggest you hawk it somewhere else,' he said, 'because you no longer work here.'

At first Foster nurtured his sense of injustice. He drank too much and swore to other journalists, who displayed little interest, that he would expose Bilderberg for what it was – whatever that was. *A one-man crusade.* A glorious, swashbuckling phrase.

It wasn't until several weeks later, when he discovered that no other editors were interested in employing him, that Foster sat back and took stock. Then he telephoned a reporter named Lucas who worked for the *Financial Times* and arranged to meet him in a pub in the City.

Lucas was a tall, beaky-faced, prematurely-balding man, who had once worked with Foster on a weekly newspaper in the suburbs. Foster admired him and listened to him.

In the pub, a relic of Dickensian London, Lucas ordered two pints of bitter and, while smoke from the coal fire billowed past them, asked to see the story Foster had written.

Later Foster decided that it was the moment that he crossed the border from professional adolescence to maturity.

Lucas said: 'So the editor thought it was crap. Well, you know, I'm inclined to agree with him.'

'Thank you,' Foster said. 'Thank you very much.'

'And I think you agree with me,' handing Foster the copy.

He hadn't read it since he had been fired: it was crap. 'You're right,' he said.

'Which doesn't, of course, preclude you from writing a story, or a series of stories, about Bilderberg. But this time you'd have to mount a campaign. Plan a long time ahead, find ways to infiltrate a conference. . . .'

'First of all,' Foster said, 'I've got to find myself a job.'

'Can't help you there, I'm afraid,' Lucas said. 'You're not really *Financial Times* material.'

'All this flattery is going to my head,' Foster said.

'Why don't you try an agency? Your shorthand's good, you're fast, you're accurate — except when the madness takes you. Then you can plan your attack. But, by Christ, it had better be good if you're going to penetrate Bilderberg. Better men than you have tried. . . . And I'll have another pint,' as he put down his empty tankard on the shining copper bar.

Foster ordered two more pints. 'A good detective,' he said, 'has good informants. Can you help me?'

'I'll see. In fact I wish I could write the story —'

'But it's not exactly *Financial Times* material. . . .'

Lucas patted his head, as though, Foster thought, his hair had been stolen. 'What you've got to be prepared for,' Lucas said thoughtfully, 'is a bloody great disappointment.'

'No story?'

'Not quite.' Lucas swallowed half of his beer. He drank gallons of the stuff and never put on any weight. The bright blue eyes in the hawkish face were thoughtful. 'Not quite,' he repeated.

'What then?'

'You know what they say, *There's no such thing as good news*. Not necessarily true, of course, but it's a fact that most news is bad. Wasn't there a paper once that tried to publish only good news? I don't think it lasted very long.'

'So you think I might find a lot of good guys under one roof?'

'I don't think that either. That's stretching the imagination a bit too far. But I think you might find that a lot of what they discuss is constructive. For the West, that is. If you intend to write a balanced report you'd have to include that.'

'Of course.' A few weeks ago he would have accused Lucas of being part of the conspiracy.

'You see,' Lucas went on, picking up his tankard and eyeing it thirstily, 'I believe in Capitalism. Communism is the equal distribution of poverty. Capitalism is – or should be – the equal distribution of wealth. Have you been to a Communist country?'

Foster shook his head.

'Victorian England all over again. All the money goes towards armaments and expansionism, while the man in the street queues for goodies and lives in an apartment built with a do-it-yourself kit.'

Foster said: 'It's your turn to buy a drink.'

Lucas delved into the trouser pocket of his pin-stripe for some change, ordered two more beers and went on: 'Whereas the sort of man you'll meet at Bilderberg provides employment, pays good money and expands his business – not his country's borders. You've only got to compare West and East Germany,' Lucas added.

'You'd make a good spokesman for Bilderberg.'

'On the contrary, I abhor secrecy. Every self-respecting journalist does. What I'm trying to say is that if you manage to break down their barriers – a bloody great *if*, I might say – then you've got a marvellous opportunity to give a complete, composite story.'

Foster was silent, planning ahead.

Lucas said: 'Of course, you're bound to uncover a few *diabolical plots*. It's up to you how you present them. You'll have to learn how to differentiate between sharp practice and business practice . . . the borderline is very thin.'

Foster said: 'I'll tell you what you can do for me.'

Lucas' blue eyes searched his face.

'Find out where the Bilderbergers are planning to meet and let me know well in advance.'

'I should be able to manage that. When?'

'When I'm good and ready,' Foster said.

'It's reciprocal, of course.'

'What do you mean by that?'

'If you infiltrate Bilderberg I'd like a few crumbs –'

'From the poor man's table.'

'It could make you a rich man,' Lucas said. 'Bilderberg seems to affect people that way.'

Foster went to the toilet; when he returned Lucas was tackling his fourth pint.

Foster said: 'Just one more thing.'

Lucas looked at him inquiringly and Foster pointed at his pint and said: 'Just tell me where you put all that stuff.'

It took Foster longer than he had anticipated to prepare himself for his campaign. He managed to get a desk job at Reuters. There his talents, now disciplined, were noticed and he was given foreign assignments. He was sent to Rhodesia to cover the interminable negotiations and the guerilla war; he flew to Beirut where he was shot in the thigh by a sniper's bullet. Moslem or Christian, he was never quite sure.

He returned with a limp to a desk. But he had entered journalism to avoid sitting behind a desk. He brooded, planned, called Lucas and told him that he was ready to tackle Bilderberg.

When Lucas finally came up with the necessary information, the Nicholas Foster who was poised to take on the power elite of the Western world was a very different person from the impetuous young man who had presented a newspaper editor with a self-opinionated cuttings-job. He was now a professional – competent, calculating.

The venue of the next Bilderberg: the Château Saint-Pierre, forty miles south of Paris.

Foster picked up the telephone and called his father.

* * *

The other event of little consequence – to everyone, that is, except the protagonists – occurred much earlier in the small French alpine resort of Mégève, twenty miles from the Swiss border.

Georges Bertier, aged forty, an anarchist with a history of mental illness, was stopped on the road leading to the luxurious Hotel Mont d'Arbois where a Bilderberg conference was being held.

It had been the intention of Bertier and a handful of muddle-headed followers to storm the convention. The French police guarding the hotel suggested politely that Bertier and his little band should disperse.

The courtesy of the French police when civic disturbance is threatened has never been robust, and when Georges protested they set about him with batons and gloved fists.

Among the supporters, dedicated more to vandalism and irrational violence than the doctrine that all governments should be abolished, was Georges Bertier's twin brother, Jacques. Jacques rushed to defend Georges, but was thrust contemptuously aside by the police, as were the rest of the *anarchists* who, in any case, preferred to give vent to their spleen when opposition was minimal.

As far as Jacques was concerned, it was the story of the life he had shared with Georges. Only momentarily were they ever mistaken for identical twins – the same shortish stature, pale sleek hair, neat but undistinguished faces; then the dynamism of Georges asserted itself and new acquaintances examined them and said: 'No, no, you're not the same at all,' as they compared the hawkish expression on Georges' face with Jacques' air of docility. Now, as always, he had been rejected.

It may have been due to the savagery of the beating, or it may have been the effect of a single blow on Georges' already abnormal brain – the doctors never decided with any certainty – but, after the incident on the road leading to the Hotel Mont d'Arbois, Georges Bertier was never the same again.

He was taken first to a hospital in Grenoble and later transferred to a mental institution at Lyon. Sometimes when

Jacques visited him he was raving and it was impossible to converse with him; at other times he was relatively articulate, and it was during one of these periods of lucidity that Georges told Jacques what he must do.

Since Georges had been hurt at Mégève, Jacques had been aware of a change in his own personality. While he lay on the road, watching the batons ram into his twin, he had felt the blows. Actually felt them. Now, when he sat beside Georges' bed, he felt as if his twin's strength was flowing into his body. As though he were Georges, and it was Jacques lying there between the sheets.

Jacques came one day with books – nothing political, nothing to upset Georges – and red grapes from the village in the great vineyard where they had been born within minutes of each other. And he sat beside Georges and touched his hand, and felt the power ebbing from Georges' body into his own.

'So,' said Georges after he had lain there gazing at the wall for a while, 'it's come to this.'

'You'll be better soon,' Jacques told him, lying, but lying with the sort of purpose that had eluded him in the past.

Georges shook his head, winced. 'Do you ever think about the old days, Jacques?'

Jacques did, all the time.

'We had some good times. You know, the two of us being one. Somehow we could enjoy two things at once, couldn't we, Jacques?'

To Jacques it had always seemed that they each owned separate aspects of one character. In an individual these aspects tempered each other: divided and undisciplined, they became exaggerated; thus Georges' aggression boiled over while he became increasingly more submissive.

In the playground at the village school, Georges had always defended him. Handed out beatings that more than compensated for any injury Jacques might have suffered. It had been Georges who had decided that they, always *they*, would leave home 'because we're not peasants like the rest of them,' meaning the other four children and their parents, the placid, uncomplaining mother and father who drank vast quantities of wine and had become as purple as the grapes he harvested.

It had been Georges who had found them work in an hotel on the outskirts of Paris; Georges who had called a strike and threatened the owner with a knife; Georges who had got the girls – and the girls had made it clear that it was Georges, not Jacques, that they favoured; Georges who, when money and success eluded him, had turned savagely on the wealthy and privileged and, taking Jacques unprotestingly with him, had turned first to Communism and then, because doctrinaire politics cramped his style, to the wild, wide-open spaces of anarchism.

'Yes,' Jacques told his sick brother, 'we did have good times.'

Georges gripped his arm. 'And I want you to carry on.'

Jacques was surprised by the feebleness of his brother's grip. 'Of course I'll carry on. Of course I will, Georges.' And it came to him again that it was Jacques lying there on the bed with fevered eyes and shaking hands.

Georges said: 'Oh those bastards. If only we'd reached them. . . .'

'We will, Georges.'

'Because those Bilderbergers represent everything that we've been fighting. Carry the fight to them, Jacques, carry it. . . .' His hands were clenching and unclenching and his eyelids were flickering; Jacques knew the symptoms – soon he would be mouthing wild nonsense, and a nurse would come and slide a needle into his vein and bring him temporary peace.

Georges continued to hold Jacques' arm, making an effort – Jacques knew this because he could *feel* it – to control himself. He said: 'There's something I must tell you. . . .'

'I'm listening.'

'Bilderberg must be destroyed. It's evil. . . . For the sake of the world you (not *we* any more) must kill. . . .' He bit his lip and blood flowed.

'Easy,' Jacques said softly. 'Take it easy.'

'You must plan, Jacques. Because, you see, there will only be you. You were always the cool one. You can succeed where I failed. Your brains, my fists. A nice combination, eh, Jacques?'

Jacques smiled at him.

'And you'll have both. . . . Now listen to me,' and his voice dropped to a whisper.

Jacques bent his head while his brother talked about their childhood. About the days during the German occupation of France and during the fighting when the Allies had swept across Europe. 'You remember how we used to go out collecting things? Anything we could lay our hands on – pieces of shellcasing, spent bullets, even a gun or two. . . .'

Jacques said he remembered, wondering where it was leading.

'Well, I cheated a little. I made some really sensational discoveries – and I hid them. I didn't know why then; I was just greedy, I suppose. Perhaps I didn't think you were the right half of us' – smiling up at Jacques – 'to have such things. But now I know why I hid them. A part of me knew that one day I would need them.'

'What, Georges?'

The trembling in his hands had spread to the rest of his body. 'You remember the barn?'

Jacques nodded.

'I buried them under the floor beside the old water tank. . . .'

'Buried what? For God's sake, what?'

And then Georges Bertier screamed and the nurse came running into the room, and Jacques Bertier walked out into the green-walled corridor.

Or was it Georges?

Three days later Georges Bertier died.

Jacques grieved, but the intensity of his grief was dissipated by the knowledge that everything that had motivated Georges had been passed on to him.

We are now one, he thought, as he methodically set about implimenting his twin's plans, Georges' compulsions blending perfectly with his own cautious approach to life.

First he drove their grey Citroen van to their birthplace.

His father was in hospital dying from alcoholism; his mother still cooked and cleaned; his sister had married a travelling salesman and gone to live in Limoges, and his three younger brothers worked among the vines, beginning to tipple as enthusiastically as their father.

Jacques, a stranger to his family, went out to the barn and with a garden fork began to dig beside the rusty old water tank. Almost immediately the prongs of the fork hit metal. Fifteen minutes later he gas gazing at a tin chest to which patches of dark green paint still adhered. It was padlocked and Georges had told him nothing about a key; he fetched an axe and smashed the rusting lock with three blows.

Inside were a few collector's items and a rifle, German of course, fitted with a telescopic sight; it had been oiled and greased and, as far as Jacques could make out, was in perfect condition. At the bottom of the chest was a long wooden box covered with greased brown paper. Jacques levered open the top with the blade of the axe – and stared with dawning comprehension at the means with which Georges Bertier had hoped one day to exterminate the very core of the Capitalist Society.

Hoped. Jacques was beginning to realise that his twin had not been as purposeful as he had supposed.

He loaded the chest into the back of the van.

In Paris he bought a trunk, also made of tin but bigger than the chest. He transferred the contents of the chest into it, fitted it with a double padlock and stored it in another hotel, where he had found employment as a porter after the abortive strike called by his brother in their previous workplace.

Then he considered his priorities: he needed a new identity and, with it, a new occupation; he needed to know where the Bilderbergers intended to meet in the future; he needed money. His ally was time: of that he had an abundance.

First money.

The hotel, just off the Place Pigalle, was frequented by businessmen from the provinces who slept there with women other than their wives. Hostesses, mostly, from expensive night-clubs. Overcome by the *joie de vivre* of Paris, the businessmen were frequently careless with their money and Jacques Bertier was able to rob three of them. They complained to the hotel but took it no further because of the circumstances. . . . As the police weren't involved, the hotel manager scarcely bothered: you were lucky, he reasoned, if there was only one thief among an hotel's employees.

Through a member of the kitchen staff, Jacques obtained an introduction to the Parisien underworld which flourished all around the hotel. There, with the substantial sum of money he had stolen, he accomplished the remainder of his priorities.

He bought himself a new identity. The man to whom the documents had belonged, he was assured, was weighted by concrete at the bottom of the Seine; he had only been missing a couple of days and there was no reason why Jacques shouldn't continue his life from where he had abruptly departed it. He left the hotel and the friendly hostesses – some of them appeared willing to be more than friendly (that was the Georges in him!) – went to night-school and found himself a new job.

He had studied the brief reports in the Press about the Bilderberg meeting at Mégève and, when he read that the European honorary secretary, a Dutchman, was staying at the Hotel Meurice on the Rue de Rivoli, he paid a professional hotel thief to break into his room.

The robbery went unnoticed. One document from a briefcase bulging with papers. . . . But enough to provide Jacques Bertier with all the information he needed – the probable venues for the Bilderberg conferences for the next few years.

He ran his finger down the list. Stopped at the last entry. Perfect. It gave him all the time he needed and it was nearby. The Château Saint-Pierre near the small town of Etampes, not all that far from Paris.

The man, who now applied himself assiduously to the task of multiple assassination, was the personification of the character that Owen Anderson had always feared. A psychopath who kept himself to himself.

IX

You're getting too old for this sort of thing, George Prentice thought as pain from his injured ankle shot rhythmically up his leg.

It was his fortieth birthday. He had planned spending the latter part of it in the casino in Campione d'Italia, a pinprick on the map of Europe that had never quite made up its mind whether it was Italian or Swiss. But he had hurt his leg scaling a wall, the safe he was cracking was proving obstinate and there he was still inside the house of a German industrialist at 11.30 at night.

Prentice's assignments on behalf of Paul Kingdon took him to tax havens around the world. Many of them delightful spots in which to sojourn, but each permeated by a sense of shifty unease for anyone but the *bona fide* tourist or genuine inhabitant. The Bahamas, Cayman Islands, Panama, Bermuda, Monaco, Luxembourg, Liechtenstein. . . .

Campione is one of the least known havens; in fact it is not always recognised as one. But it does provide sanctuary for the rich, in particular Germans who are not intimidated by the currency which is Swiss francs.

Officially Campione is Italian. But its minute acreage (pop. 3,000) is embedded in Switzerland on the shore of Lake Lugano. Its money is Swiss – lire is used only for games of Monopoly – its postal and telephone systems are Swiss, as are most of its lawyers, and it relies on Swiss banks to conduct its business.

Foreigners pay no tax and the attitude of the Italian Government to Campione's dual standards is benign, because it collects a considerable percentage of the takings from the Casino, reputed to be the most prosperous in the world.

Prentice's attitude to life had changed since the death of Karl Danzer. He made a point of enjoying to the full the benefits of his profession. He stayed in the best hotels and frugally ate and drank with a gourmet's palate; the change was apparent in his dedication to enjoyment: it had become a substitute for all he had lost with the revelation of Annette du Pont's treachery. He even gambled at the tables, employing a progression system which he had perfected: he had proved to himself that the roulette wheel could be beaten; it was a painstaking process but Prentice enjoyed beating the odds. He had not made love to a woman for six years. . . .

The safe gave itself up as the tumblers finally obeyed him. It had been a mathematical certainty – like his roulette system. But, like the system, a long and arduous business.

Prentice shone a flashlight into the safe which had been amateurishly hidden behind a gilt-framed mirror. The German, he supposed, wasn't too bothered about losing the wads of German marks and Swiss francs stuffed inside the stainless-steel cavity in the wall. What was a few thousand dollars to a millionaire? Nor would he appreciate that anyone might be interested in the documents relating to the palatial house in Campione.

Prentice removed the money and placed it on a desk. Then he reached into the safe for the documents. In doing so, he altered his balance. Pain swept up his leg like a flame. A sprain – he hoped. He limped down into the German's well-stocked cellar in case the electronic flash on his camera could be seen through the drapes covering the windows in the lounge, and photographed the documents.

He then replaced the papers and the money, re-set the combination, locked the safe and replaced the rather cheap-looking mirror. He glanced at his digital wrist-watch: it had taken him two hours. Outside, the German shepherd dogs would be stirring from the sleep induced by drugs inserted into generous portions of raw fillet steak.

Prentice, who had previously defused the burglar alarm system – Prentice acknowledged only one equal in electronic surveillance, the arrogant, knuckle-head American, Owen

Anderson – let himself out of the French windows into the courtyard. It was a cold February night; it was also moon-lit.

Moonlight. An injured ankle. Waking guard dogs. All he needed was an inquisitive patrol of carabinieri!

One of the three dogs lying beside the brick-built kennels growled. Breaking in, Prentice had scaled the 12-foot high wall in the interests of speed. Breaking out, he had intended to manipulate the lock on the lofty iron gates. Not now, not with guard dogs who probably preferred human flesh to fillet steak on the move.

One of the dogs stood up and opened its mouth. A noise which was part yawn, part whine, part growl, issued from between its jaws. The other two dogs stirred.

Dragging one foot, Prentice made for the wall. When he had broken in, it had been pitch-dark and black trousers and roll-neck sweater had merged with the night. Not now. He felt as though he had been picked out by the beam of a searchlight.

One of the dogs was loping after him.

He reached the hinged, rubber-stepped ladder with the grappling hooks, which he had used to climb the wall. It reminded him of a coiled snake lying at the foot of the wall.

The dog following him began to bark. The other two took up the chorus. They were all on their feet now. At least they would have hangovers, Prentice thought.

He picked up the ladder. Took his weight on his injured foot. The pain made him cry out. The first dog advanced as though smelling blood.

He hurled the two hooks at the top of the wall. Missed. Pain, anger, frustration. Too old. . . . The second time the hooks caught. Prentice began to climb as the dog hurled itself at him, lips curled, teeth white in the moonlight.

Prentice kicked back with his good leg, taking his weight again on his injured foot. The sword-thrust of pain nearly made him lose his grip on the ladder. His good foot made contact with the dog; it fell back to be joined by the other two.

As he began to climb, all three dogs hurled themselves at

him. One set of fangs ripped the leg of his trousers. Gashed his flesh? He wasn't sure, his whole leg was on fire with pain. . . .

Then he was above their reach. Their bodies thudded against the wall, their barking filled the night. . . . At the top of the wall he paused. He could hear running footsteps and raised voices. But he couldn't jump, not with that foot.

He hauled up the ladder, turned the hooks and let it down the other side of the wall. He began his descent. The footsteps grew nearer; moonlight pinned him against the wall. . . .

He hit the ground with his good foot and jerked the ladder free. Two carabinieri appeared as, running like a man on invisible crutches, he rounded the corner.

One more corner and there was his dark-blue rented Fiat, parked in the shadow of a tree. He paused for a moment and tossed the ladder over the wall of the house adjoining the one he had burgled.

Then he climbed in the Fiat and coasted down the hill. The carabinieri must have stopped where the dogs were barking; then they would find the ladder next door. . . .

Half way down the hill, Prentice braked and started the engine of the car. It was, thank God, automatic and he could rest his injured foot. He pressed his good foot on the accelerator and headed for the autoroute leading to Milan.

*   *   *

Paul Kingdon sat down beside the bed and said: 'So, did you get it?'

'Aren't you going to ask about my foot?'

'I know about your foot,' Kingdon said. 'Your ankle is broken in two places and the fractures were aggravated by use.'

'If I hadn't used it, I would be in an Italian jail instead of the London Clinic. And, yes, I did get the documents.' Prentice pointed to the locker beside his bed. 'They're in there. Tell me something, Paul, were they worth all this?' gesturing at his foot which was in plaster.

'Of course. As you know the West Germans passed a law called the *Aussensteuergesetz* in 1972. It stated that it didn't matter a monkey's toss whether a German became a resident in a tax haven, because he'd still have to pay tax in Germany if he was also a resident there. So our friend won't get away with it.'

'Do you think he really intended to try? He's as rich as Croesus. . . .'

'The rich, as you know bloody well, don't like giving their money away. Wasn't Paul Getty said to have a pay-telephone in his house?'

'So those papers,' as Kingdon took them out of the white locker, 'are ammunition. . . . Blackmail, Paul?'

Kingdon slipped the papers into the inside pocket of his jacket. He shrugged eloquently. 'A lever. Only a fool conducts business without a lever. . . .'

'A scalpel,' Prentice suggested. He opened the cardboard box with the fancy handle that Kingdon had brought with him. Peaches. He moved them out of Kingdon's reach and said: 'So you're moving into Germany, Paul?'

'Where else? That's where all the work's done, and so that's where all the bread is.'

'Logical,' Prentice said biting into a peach. Juice ran down his chin. The private ward in the Clinic, he thought, was more like a room in the Savoy. 'What's the deal?'

As Kingdon explained, Prentice stared at him curiously. As though he were appraising a stranger, which Kingdon most certainly was not. He saw a man in his mid-thirties, sharply but not elegantly dressed in a fawn suit with a chocolate shirt and yellowish silk tie; sleek brown hair; features wolfish – that was the only way to describe them – as yet bearing no evidence of the immense strain of being head of Kingdon Investments.

In the past Prentice had regarded Kingdon with affection. With his mutual fund enterprises he had actually helped small investors get rich in a world dominated by the privileged. But the affection was waning; Kingdon was getting greedy.

A pretty nurse came into the room, fussed around to no

obvious avail, asked: 'Have you got everything you want, Mr Prentice?' and departed smiling when he held up a peach and said he had.

Kingdon crossed his legs and asked: 'Were you listening to me, George?'

Prentice said he had been listening.

'I don't think you absorbed a single bloody word I said.'

'You know me, Paul. It's the field-work that I enjoy. I don't give a damn what you do with it afterwards.' Which was no longer strictly true; he cared if the small investor was getting hurt.

'You're an enigmatic sod, George. You know as much as I do about our . . . our business associates. And yet you're content to let me make all the bread.'

'Once a spy always a spy. I wasn't cut out to be a tycoon.'

'And you carry all those dossiers around up here. . . .' Kingdon tapped his temple with one finger. 'Which is your biggest dossier, George?'

Prentice smiled. He was, after all, being discharged tomorrow; he would take his system and his plaster-weighted foot to Monte Carlo for a week or so. He said: 'The biggest dossier? That's easy. Paul Kingdon.'

* * *

The foundation for Paul Kingdon's fortune, invested these days largely in diamonds, had been a rust-coloured ten shilling note, No. 79C 867324, now obsolete.

Aged sixteen, Kingdon had wagered the ten shillings on the second favourite in the Derby and lost. From that moment he had become convinced that all gamblers were fools. Lesson: take their money, there's one born every minute.

He had borrowed ten shillings in coins and recovered the ten shilling note from a startled bookmaker, who engaged him the following day as a runner in the East End where he was born.

Street fights . . . knuckles hardening, razor in his sock –

he was stockily built but when you were on the shortish side (5 feet 7 inches) you needed that razor. Promotion to a betting shop from which, behind the grille, he observed cupidity and gullibility; his resolve to capitalise on these weaknesses hardened.

But the real money wasn't in an Aldgate betting shop. It was up the street, in the City of London. On Sundays he roamed the slumbering streets of the City, keeping company with cats and caretakers and patrolling policemen. He brooded about the fortunes lying dormant inside the great sooty buildings. Money should never be dormant.

On the eve of his 18th birthday he borrowed a pin-stripe suit and, armed with forged certificates asserting his academic accomplishments, presented himself for an interview for a job with a small stock-brokers and got it.

The company was later hammered but by that time, Kingdon, having learned the basics of Stock Exchange practice, had formed his own company with negligible capital.

His premise was simple. Instead of buying shares, laymen were now buying unit trusts, or mutual funds – hedging their bets by investing in companies that spread the money in well-balanced portfolios.

Why not go one better? Create a fund, or trust, that invested in other such funds? Create a force of silver-tongued salesmen who, inspired by generous commissions, could persuade the public – and charge them for the privilege – to hand over their money.

Paul Kingdon was not quite the pioneer that he professed to be: but he learned from the mistakes of the crusading spirits and elaborated on their techniques.

The first priority was to go offshore to a tax haven to avoid tiresome laws designed to part the entrepreneur from as much of his profits as possible. Kingdon chose B.V.I. – the British Virgin Islands, eighty kilometres east of Puerto Rica. Not only was B.V.I. favourably disposed to the formation of private companies but one of the sixty islands was reputed to be Robert Louis Stevenson's *Treasure Island*!

Kingdon then broadened his interests by borrowing 30,000 dollars and starting the first of his own mutual funds, which was hawked all over the United States and any country in the world that did not protest too hysterically about the outflow of capital. His own salesmen were committed to invest in Kingdon Investments; but their investments were not realisable until the day Kingdon decided to make them available on the open market.

Kingdon also expanded into real estate. Investors in his real estate funds were persuaded that property represented a slower but sounder investment than company shares; the fees charged to clients represented a far-from-slow growth rate for the fund.

Kingdon anticipated British legislation to clamp down on the use of tax havens and took appropriate avoidance measures. But his inspiration was his industrial consultancy, his private spy ring. Through the investigations conducted by Prentice, his fund managers were able to assess glamour stocks – get in quickly and get out twice as fast – and equity with long-term prospects.

By the age of twenty-seven, Paul Kingdon was a millionaire. By the age of thirty-five, his plans for his money were getting out of control.

* * *

'Are you sure you didn't fall on your head?'

'I beg your pardon?' Prentice closed the dossier and returned to the present.

'Are you sure you didn't suffer brain injuries? You seem to be in a trance.' Kingdon leaned forward. 'You cocked up that job a bit, didn't you, George?'

''Fraid so. I'm getting old. Like all of us – from the moment we're born. But still,' Prentice added, 'you got what you wanted.'

Kingdon's voice hardened. He was no longer visiting a patient: he was conducting business. 'I want a lot more,' he said, 'before you're finally over the top of the hill.' He clenched his hands together and the knuckles shone. 'Did you get an invitation to Bilderberg this year?'

'Not this year. I get invited in cycles of three year intervals.'

'At least you get invited. . . .'

'Your day will come.'

'That's a racing certainty,' Kingdon said. 'But not because the fucking Bilderbergers want me. I'm not Establishment, I didn't go to Eton, or Oxford,' staring at Prentice. 'I'm not a member of a cosy family bank, I don't have Royal connections, I don't contribute to party political funds, I'm just –'

'An *entrepreneur*?'

'And vulgar with it.' Kingdon stood up and paced the private ward. 'But I'll get an invitation because I'll force their hand. And do you know why?'

Prentice shook his head. He tried to shift his foot which was beginning to ache but failed. 'Why?'

'Because I want to get in there and beat them at their own game. If I could get in there among them, George, I could make the sort of killings that would make Slater and Cornfeld look like feather-weights. Do you realise what Bilderberg is? It's a world summit conference, that's what. Held in secret. If I knew what was discussed there I could bring off deals that would. . . .'

For once words failed Paul Kingdon.

'Which is it,' Prentice asked, 'the money or revenge?' His foot was beginning to itch as well as ache.

Kingdon stopped pacing and considered the question. His hungry face was framed in a shaft of wintry sunlight. Finally he said: 'Both.' Paused. 'Yes, both. The bastards have patronised me for too long.'

'So where do I come in? I'm only an economist as far as they're concerned. A professional front man.'

Kingdon sat down again, shifted his chair nearer the bed and said: 'I'm not bothered about your down-the-bill appearances at the meetings. What I want, before you're in your dotage, is dossiers on every regular participant. Then,' tapping the plaster lightly with his finger. 'I'll be in a position to negotiate with the bastards.'

'If you get invited.'

'I'll get invited, don't you worry about that.'

'You don't have to torture me. . . .'

'What the hell are you talking about?'

'Stop tapping my plaster,' Prentice said and then, discarding the peach-stone in an ash-tray: 'So you intend to keep me fully employed.'

'It shouldn't be too difficult. Not with your contacts in Zurich. The names behind the numbered accounts for a start.'

Prentice said thoughtfully: 'Of course, we've got a good deal of material on a lot of them.' He recited a string of names. 'Plus Mrs Claire Jerome – at the request of Pierre Brossard.'

'And, as it happens,' Kingdon said, withdrawing from the bed, 'Mrs Claire Jerome again wants anything new on Pierre Brossard.'

Prentice laughed. 'That shouldn't be too difficult, either.'

Kingdon stood up. 'So, will you do it, George?'

'I'll think about it.'

'Think hard, George. I'll pay you well.' He turned and walked to the door, where he paused again and said: 'I'll call you tomorrow from Paris.'

'Paris?' Prentice was mildly surprised.

'I'm flying there in two hours time.'

Prentice's mind vaulted ahead. 'To see Pierre Brossard?'

'Of course. My entrée into Bilderberg. He's on the steering committee these days.'

'By the way,' Prentice said, 'my leg's much better, thanks.'

But he was addressing a closed door. He selected another peach, picked up the *Daily Telegraph* and started the crossword. Perhaps today he would beat his record.

*   *   *

Two days later, Prentice, on crutches, went to the MI6 offices in Northumberland Avenue and reported what he had discovered, on behalf of Kingdon Investments, about the German industrialist. A middle-aged, desk-bound intelligence officer who had been permanently crippled 'in the course of duty' read the two typewritten sheets of foolscap paper with minimal interest, expressing his opinion with an apparently uncontrollable series of yawns.

In five years time I'll be like that, Prentice thought. Maybe sooner if he continued falling off ladders in the dark.

'Thanks anyway,' yawned the intelligence officer. 'Every little helps. Perhaps one day. . . .' Whatever might happen one day was swallowed by another cavernous yawn. 'Care for a cup of tea?'

'No thanks.'

Prentice picked up his crutches and made for the door. The yawns were infectious; they were still with him when he stepped out into the fast-fading daylight. Around Trafalgar Square the starlings were beginning to chatter.

He collected his baggage from the Clinic, then caught a cab to West London Air Terminal and a coach to London Airport. From Heathrow he caught a plane to the Côte d'Azur airport at Nice. Three hours later he was sitting, with his crutches beside him, playing roulette at the casino in Monte Carlo. He made a steady but modest profit with his system. What, he wondered, would happen if everyone played the same system?

*　　*　　*

At about the same time that George Prentice was collecting chips at Monte Carlo, a girl of about twenty-five years of age with a voluptuous body and a chalk-white skin was taking off her clothes in a night-club in Paris.

'To your taste?' Pierre Brossard nodded at the girl as she peeled off long black gloves in the time honoured manner.

'A little amateurish, isn't it?'

Brossard gave a professional French shrug. 'It's what's underneath that counts, I suppose.'

The girl certainly wasn't his preference. She was too passive, he suspected; she moved on the small circular floor like a robot! He had recently made the acquaintance of a red-headed girl with a vicious temper; more accomplished, even, than the blonde who had got married.

In slow-motion the girl began to remove one of her fish-net stockings. 'In Manchester they'd be throwing beer-cans at her by now,' Kingdon remarked.

He poured them both whisky from the bottle of Johnny Walker Red Label that had cost him £50. (Black Label was much, much more.) Brossard was aware that Kingdon was picking up the tab because it gave him a tactical advantage. So he believed.

'Really?' Brossard pushed at the greying wings of hair above his ears with his fingers. 'I doubt very much if I shall ever have the pleasure – if that's what it is – of watching striptease in Manchester.'

'It's what's underneath that counts,' Kingdon told him as the girl came close to their table and tossed him a stocking. She smiled at him but her eyes were somewhere else.

The club was full. Businessmen mostly – some in tuxedos – and a few wives and girl-friends. Brossard and Kingdon wore lounge suits, Brossard's a little threadbare around the cuffs. A revolving ball of mirror-fragments suspended from the ceiling spun flecks of light around the walls.

The second stocking came off. The brassiere, Brossard thought, would take an eternity.

Kingdon sipped his whisky and water and said: 'Well, everyone to his own taste. But not quite yours, eh, Pierre?'

Brossard stared speculatively at the brash Englishman who would have looked more at home in Marseilles. What did he know about his sexual tastes? Another shrug. 'I must admit that I, too, prefer something a little more sophisticated.'

'And a little more painful?'

Fear fluttered briefly inside Pierre Brossard. A fear that owed its origins to an incident a long time ago. He squeezed his fingertips, a habit of his. Still, if you employed private detectives, which was what, on a grand scale, industrial consultants were, there was always an element of risk. . . . But you certainly couldn't threaten a Frenchman with his sex life. Confidence returned to Brossard. He smiled at Kingdon almost conspiratorially. 'If you say so.'

The girl tossed her brassiere into the audience, where it was retrieved and kissed theatrically by a fat man smoking a cigar. Her breasts, Brossard perceived, were smaller than he had imagined; the brassiere must have been padded. Unless. . . .

He said to Kingdon: 'Is *she* your preference?' as the girl began to wriggle out of her panties.

'She's all right.' Brossard suspected that Kingdon didn't have a great sexual drive; all his libido was concentrated in his work. 'Not bad,' Kingdon said pouring more whisky.

'That's interesting.'

Kingdon gazed at him over the rim of his glass. 'What's so interesting about it?'

Brossard nodded at the *girl* who was now naked, shrivelled penis in full view.

'Jesus Christ!' Kingdon swallowed his whisky. 'I didn't realise –'

'Nothing to be ashamed of even if you had,' Brossard said, retaking the initiative. 'What does sexual taste matter if it hurts no-one?' *Or what does it matter if it does hurt?* The *girl* skipped coyly from the floor while the audience applauded half-heartedly. 'What was that you were saying . . . ?'

'Your point.' Kingdon licked his finger and scored a one on an imaginary blackboard. 'Of course, we get to know a hell of a lot about both the people we're asked to investigate and the clients who employ us.'

'Of course. You must have a veritable library of information about the captains of industry. All stored away for a rainy day?'

'It's always useful,' Kingdon said non-committally.

A girl who was indisputably female came onto the floor, followed by a muscular young man who was indisputably masculine. They lay on a black satin mattress and began to make love.

Kingdon said: 'Do you mind if we talk business?'

So, the initiative had certainly been snatched from Kingdon. 'Why not? That's what we came here for, wasn't it?'

'You don't find that a distraction?' Kingdon pointed at the two writhing bodies.

'Not if you don't.'

'I want to get an invitation to Bilderberg. I understand that you're now on the steering committee.'

'Your information is good. As always. As for the request. . . . It's very difficult.'

'Come off it, Pierre, you can swing it.'

'I would have to be very persuasive.'

Momentarily Kingdon lost his temper. 'Why, because I make a lot of money outside the Establishment? Because I came up from the gutter?'

'That's the best place to come *from*,' Brossard soothed him. 'It's only unpleasant when the process is reversed.'

Kingdon splashed more whisky into their glasses. 'All right, all right. . . . But don't give me any bullshit, Pierre. I know perfectly well what I am and I know perfectly well what the sort of people you mix with think of me. As you've pointed out I do have a lot of information –'

Brossard prodded one finger at Kingdon. 'Let me stop you before you utter a threat. I don't react to threats.' Which, Brossard reflected, was the most outrageous lie of the evening.

Kingdon held up his hand. 'Okay, I'm sorry. But can you do it?'

'It's just possible. But it will take time.'

Kingdon sank back in his chair. 'Thanks, Pierre,' he said softly. 'See what you can do. Maybe then we can do a lot of things together.'

'We'll see. Meanwhile go on collecting your diamonds.'

'So you've been investigating me?'

Brossard shook his head. 'Everyone knows about the Kingdon collection of diamonds. The only commodity, apart from the Swiss franc, that can be relied upon to keep up with inflation.'

Kingdon held up his glass. 'Here's to Bilderberg. Long may it flourish.'

'I'll drink to that,' Brossard said.

On the floor the couple finished their act. Whether or not

they had satisfactorily accomplished what they had set out to do was not apparent.

Pierre Brossard, however, was completely satisfied with the outcome of the evening. He had been planning to ask Kingdon if he would like to attend Bilderberg: instead of that the Englishman had come begging.

Furthermore he had paid for the bottle of Scotch.

Part Three

X

Claire Jerome read her invitation to the Bilderberg convention at the Château Saint-Pierre in France, while she was lying topless beside a scimitar-shaped swimming pool in the Bahamas on an autumn day in 1979.

In theory, the invitation should have been addressed to her father, the president of Marks International. But the world knew that it was Nathan Marks' daughter who controlled the empire – with executive vice-president Stephen Harsch, now No. 3, fretting in the wings.

Beside her on a blue and white sun-lounger lay a man with the body of a football quarterback and a heavy moustache. He dozed in the sun, an old straw-hat tipped over his eyes.

Claire tossed the invitation onto the white table beside the pile of mail and said: 'How does a trip to France grab you?'

'Uh-huh.'

'What's that supposed to mean?'

'It's supposed to mean uh-huh.' He yawned.

'Some bodyguard. Supposing someone came busting in and pulled a gun on me.'

'Wham.' Pete Anello kicked out in slow-motion. 'I'd break his arm.' Sighing deeply, he sat up, rested his weight on one elbow and flicked the straw-hat to the back of his head. 'Why did you wake me?'

'Because awake is what you're supposed to be. Sleeping on duty is a court martial offence.'

'After last night I've got every right to be exhausted.'

Claire smiled at the recollection. She was, she acknowledged, lucky to be able to. She was in her early forties (no longer specific) and he was thirty-five. But at least she still didn't look her age; genuinely didn't. Her hair was as glossy as the tresses of a girl who brushes them 100 times a day, her breasts were firm, her complexion that of a Jewess in her prime. Except, perhaps, late at night when the years slyly presented themselves at the corners of her mouth, and around the eyes.

She said: 'So now you're awake, what about it?'

'What about what?'

'France. I've got an invitation to meet the rulers of the world. Heads of state, prime ministers. . . .'

'Any emperors?'

'No emperors.'

'Forget it,' Anello said.

'I'm going. It's a male chauvinist affair but I've always been accepted.'

'The second – or is it the third? – richest woman in the world usually is.'

'Fifth,' Claire said. 'And if I go, you go. It's in your contract.'

'Okay by me. I guess I can't guard you by remote control.'

'As if anyone would notice any difference.'

'No kidnaps so far.' Anello slumped back on the lounger and the straw hat slipped back over his eyes.

Claire dipped one hand in the water, more blue than the ocean in its bed of cobalt mosaic, and thought: 'He doesn't give a damn. The first one. Or was he merely more subtle than the others?'

Anello's breathing had returned to its shallow rhythms as he dozed again. She examined his body. Chest matted with black hair, power in the muscles sloping from neck to shoulder, belly taut – disfigured by a knotted scar. And wearing frayed Navy shorts. He bore no resemblance to a gigolo.

And yet. . . .

She stood up, stretched and strolled across the lawn, skirting the sprinklers tossing diamonds into the hibiscus blossom.

When her father had first bought the white, colonial-style mansion at Lyford Cay, on the island of New Providence, she had once picked a hibiscus bloom and thrust it into her hair before visiting the bars and clubs of Nassau and Paradise Island; no-one had told her that the hibiscus flower closes at nightfall.

She paused beside a stone wall and, shielding her eyes against the sun, gazed back at the man lying beside the pool. He was an enigma. Self-sufficient, apparently lazily content.

But what were his motives? She was rich, middle-aged, alone despite the riches. A gift from the gods for anyone on the make, especially anyone astute enough to realise that time-honoured ploys would be recognised for what they were.

She had met him five weeks ago in the casino on Paradise Island, the sliver of land on the other side of the toll bridge spanning the harbour from Nassau, once known less romantically as Hog Island before Huntington Hartford had developed it.

She had been playing roulette, losing steadily. When she had lost around 1,000 dollars she said to her companion, a svelte young man in a white suit: 'Take my seat for a few minutes,' and had headed for the rest room.

A big man, wearing a blue, light-weight suit as though he resented it, detached himself from one of the slot machines and beckoned to her.

'No offence, ma'am. But would you care to look in your purse and see if your wallet's still there?'

She opened the jewelled evening purse. No wallet.

Before she could speak, he said: 'The young guy who was standing behind you in the white suit. Why don't you ask him to give it back? Maybe he was just minding it for you,' a smile creasing his face.

'Carlos? Don't be ridiculous. He's – '

'With you?' The big man shrugged. 'Nice looking guy. The last person you'd suspect. But I'm telling you, lady, he's a thief. Why don't you ask him? I can tell you this, he isn't a pro. If he was he'd have passed it on by now and he hasn't – I've been watching him.'

'Are you the house detective?'

'No ma'am. Not even a shamus.'

She hesitated. 'I can't accuse him of robbing me.'

'You could ask him nicely. Maybe I should hang around.'

Claire returned to the table as the croupier was raking in the chips. Carlos, twenty-five years old, Argentinian, swung himself from the chair and smiled apologetically. 'I continued your losing streak.'

Claire said: 'I lost more than I reckoned on. Someone's stolen my wallet.'

The green eyes widened. 'That's terrible. Are you sure you haven't dropped it?' kneeling and searching the carpet at their feet.

'No, Carlos, I haven't dropped it. And don't think I'm going to enjoy what I'm about to say. If I'm wrong please forgive me. If I *am* wrong then whatever was in that wallet is yours.'

'I don't understand.'

'Did you take the wallet?'

He took a step backwards. 'That is a disgusting thing to say,' and sadly she knew it was true.

What did she do now, frisk him?

The stranger intervened. 'You know something, Carlos, you should have been an actor. Why don't you get your ass over to Hollywood?'

Wariness settled on the Argentinian's features. 'Who is this man?'

'Don't bother your pretty little head about who I am,' Anello said. 'Give the lady back her wallet.'

'I happen to be this lady's escort.'

'Do you want the big scene here or outside?'

'I don't give a shit.'

'Language, Carlos.' Anello gripped the lapels of the white suit; heads turned. 'Here or outside?'

'Okay, okay. Get your hands off me.' Anello let go of his lapels; the Argentinian slipped his hand inside his jacket and withdrew the black leather wallet. 'I was looking after it.'

'Beat it,' Anello told him.

'But –'

'Do what the man says,' Claire said, 'or I'll call the police.'

The Argentinian smoothed his crumpled lapels and, re-assembling his dignity, strode away.

Claire opened the wallet. 'Would you be insulted if I offered you a reward?'

'It takes more than that to insult me. But I wouldn't take it.'

Claire tried to assess him. Carlos in a different guise? 'Well thank you anyway, Mr –'

'Anello. Pete Anello.'

'Thank you, Mr Anello.'

'You look tired,' he said. 'Maybe you should go home.'

She took a compact from her purse and examined her face. He was right.

'Don't worry, you look great,' he said. 'Just tired.' He took her arm and they walked towards the exit.

'I don't need an escort.'

He ignored her.

Outside the sky was scattered with stars. She could smell the sea and the message of the waves was loneliness.

She stopped beside her red Maserati.

'Classy,' Pete Anello remarked.

She wished she'd come in the beach buggy.

'Well,' she said, 'thanks again.' And hesitantly: 'Maybe you'd like to drop by for a drink tomorrow evening. We're having a few people round.'

'We?'

'Me and my father.' She handed him a visiting card embossed with a pair of duelling pistols.

'Lyford Cay.' He whistled as he read the address. 'So you're really loaded.'

'Is that a crime?'

'Depends how you got the load.'

'Well, come along if you've nothing better to do.'

'I'll be there,' he said, slamming the car door.

But he wasn't.

Nor the next day.

On the third day he called her. 'I forgot the address at Lyford Cay.'

'It was on the card.'

'I know. I only found it today in the pocket of that suit.' A pause. Then he said: 'I thought maybe we could go for a drink someplace. One of the joints. Blackbeards, Charley Charley's, Dirty Dick's. You name it.'

They went to Charley Charley's, where they drank beer and ate half-pound hamburgers and listened to Latin beat.

As they left she said: 'Tell me truthfully, why did you call me?'

'I always wanted to drive a Maserati,' he said.

Then he'd gone missing for a week. 'Skippered a yacht,' he said when he returned.

Later that day, back at the house at Lyford Cay – where the rich and the very rich lived – she asked him: 'Do you want a job?'

'Depends.'

They were sitting at the safari bar leading into the pool room. Tiger skins lay on the floor; an ancient fan idled from the ceiling. She was sipping a champagne cocktail, he drank from a can of Budweiser. He wore Levis and a patched blue shirt, looking more at ease in the imitation hunting lodge than he had at the casino.

'You look as if you can take care of yourself,' she said.

Anello shrugged.

'And other people,' she said.

'You?'

'Everyone has a bodyguard these days. Three hundred bucks a week and your keep.'

'More than I get now,' Anello said.

'Are you accepting?'

'Best offer I've had so far.' He grinned at her and poured beer down his throat from the can.

'Then you can start now.'

'It's a deal.' He suddenly leaned across the bar and kissed her and, tremulously, hope expanded.

'Where's the old man?' he asked.

'He flew back to New York this morning.'

'To do an arms deal?'

'I do the deals,' she said.

'How about that,' unimpressed.

'I wasn't boasting. It just happens to be a fact.'

Later that night they made love on the big round bed hung with blue silk drapes, and it was as it had never been before. She thought: 'At my age, crazy.'

But it was true. Possessed and possessing. And yet afterwards he was so casual.

I have to find out, she thought, as she stood bare-breasted in the sun gazing at the sleeping figure beside the swimming pool.

She went up to him and whispered in his ear: 'How about earning your living?' She removed the straw hat and he opened his eyes.

'Huh?'

'Like we did last night.'

He blinked sleepily. 'Did you say *earning* my living?'

She nodded and thought: 'You stupid bitch,' but she had to know. If he was like all the others he would spring smartly to attention and follow her to the bedroom, and if he wasn't he would get angry and she would laugh and tell him that she had been joking and it would be beautiful.

He stood up, yawned, stretched. Then he dived into the pool and ploughed powerfully through the water. She became frightened.

He hauled himself out of the pool and dried himself with a towel bearing the duelling pistols motif.

She put her arms round him and said: 'Pete, I was only joking,' but he pushed her away and said: 'Better put that bathing top on, you might catch cold.'

He started to walk towards the house.

'Where are you going?'

He didn't reply.

She retrieved the top of her bikini, cupped it round her breasts and ran after him down the avenue of poinsettias leading to the house.

But he was loping along now, and by the time she reached the steps he had disappeared inside the house.

When she reached the bedroom he was putting on his Levis and patched blue shirt.

'Where are you going?'

'Haven't decided yet,' he said, taking a scuffed leather bag from the closet. 'I hear there's a millionaire loose in Nassau looking for hands for his yacht.'

She touched his arm. 'Stay here. I didn't mean it. You must know that. I . . . I was trying to test you.' Everything she said made it worse.

'And did I pass?'

'With flying colours,' trying to smile.

'Wow!'

'Please stay.'

He reached into the bag, searched around and pulled out a cigar box. He opened it and took out a thick roll of dollar bills. He handed them to her. 'Payment for services rendered. You'll find it all there.'

He picked up the bag and walked down the marble staircase.

When he opened the heavy oak door a shaft of sunlight lit the entrance hall.

He saluted and said: 'Take good care of your wallet, Mrs Jerome.'

'How are you going to get into Nassau?'

'Hitch I guess.'

'I can drive you.'

'What, in that old Maserati? I'm not used to travelling in anything less than a Rolls.'

And he was gone. And she was left weeping, watched curiously by a black servant hovering in the shaft of sunlight.

She found him two days later feeding coins into a slot machine in the casino.

He looked up. 'Hi.'

'I want to talk to you.'

'Shoot.'

'Can we go somewhere?'

'Here's fine.'

'I want to say I'm sorry.'

'Accepted.'

'You see,' she said, as he pulled the handle and the bright coloured symbols whirled in front of them, 'I just had to know. All my life . . . ever since my husband died, that is . . . I've been surrounded by phonies. You know, Carlos, that kind of guy. . . .'

'Poor old Carlos,' Anello said, feeding another quarter into the machine. 'He was an amateur.'

'Let me finish. You were the first . . . you know, I just couldn't believe it, and because I couldn't believe I would ever fall that lucky I just had to find out. A sort of death wish, I guess. . . .' She ran out of words. 'Will you come back, Pete?'

Anello stared at the last quarter in his hand. 'Let's ask the machine.'

He pushed the quarter into the slot, pulled the handle. The symbols spun, blurred into streaks of colour, began to slow down.

Please God.

The symbols stopped with a jerk.

Coins showered onto the carpet.

'Okay,' he said, shovelling them into his pockets, 'let's go. Where's the Maserati?'

'I brought the beach buggy,' she said.

They didn't make love that night. For a long time they held each other very close in the big round bed, and for the first time Claire Jerome sensed that perhaps the man in her arms wasn't as self-sufficient as he made out.

Once he dozed and woke up screaming. About guns and fire and a man who wanted to plant trees. . . . And when she woke him to break the dream she was aware that her feelings towards him had changed. Found a new dimension. It was strange: hearing him cry out, *she* wanted to protect *him*.

Why, she wondered, did so many men want to appear invulnerable? It was a weakness in a way. She was glad Anello had a weakness; she was glad she no longer looked only for strength.

She switched on the bedside-lamp. Her eyes re-focussed

in the light and he said: 'Did I call out?'

She nodded.

'That dream,' he said. 'Always that dream.'

And somehow she knew that it wasn't just a dream and knew that she shouldn't ask him about it.

He put his hands behind his head and stared at the ceiling. 'We don't know a damn thing about each other,' he said. 'It's about time. . . .' He turned his head to look at her. 'You first.'

*   *   *

Claire Marks was born in New York in the early '30s when the United States was still shuddering from the '29 crash.

Her father, Nathan, reacted to the recession with delight. It had always been his philosophy that adversity was the breeding ground of success – perhaps because, being a hunch-back, he had always viewed the world from a disadvantageous angle.

When he lived in Germany not even the mounting anti-Semitism there had failed to curb his incorrigible optimism. 'Time to get out,' he had announced cheerfully. 'Harness failure. Use your enemies, *use* the bastards.'

He had closed down his small-arms factory in Berlin and booked a passage for himself and his pregnant wife on a cargo boat bound for New York. His wife didn't protest – he never listened – merely lay on a bunk on the heaving ship, hands clasped across her taut belly, gazing with adoration at her diminutive husband as he bustled in and out of the cabin planning deals on the other side of the Atlantic. 'A bear market,' he would gloat. 'What could be better?'

But Nathan Marks' small-arms were very small indeed. A few hundred finely-tooled pistols a year. The duelling pistol motif made no impact on the American market.

Claire was born in conditions of adroitly concealed poverty in an apartment belonging to another Berlin Jew in the Garment Centre between Broadway and Ninth Avenue.

Nathan, who had openly coveted a son, was unperturbed as he gazed at the baby born with a shock of black hair and her mother's lustrous eyes. 'A girl. Wonderful! An heiress to a fortune,' a statement which confused his most devoted admirers.

By the time his daughter was four, Nathan Marks was still optimistic about his decline in fortune. (He was by now helping to manufacture print frocks and investing his meagre profits in a warehouse in Jersey City.) 'Soon there will be war and then we shall be made. You see. The Germans are playing into our hands. We'll use them yet.'

But Claire's mother hadn't the will to wait for this phenomenon. She died in 1938, placidly content at the short journey on which Nathan had taken her, confident that he would care for their daughter.

Two months after her death Nathan was visited by two middle-aged men wearing grey suits, white shirts and striped ties.

They said vaguely that they represented the United States Government and Nathan nodded impatiently as if to say: 'What kept you so long?'

'We've got a proposition to put to you, Mr Marks.'

'Yes, yes,' the hunch on his back a symbol of his impatience.

'But we'd like to ask a few questions first.'

Tweedle-dum and Tweedle-dee, thought Nathan Marks, offering lemon-tea and sugar-crusted cakes in the fusty little apartment as though he were president of Krupps. 'Sure, sure, go ahead.'

'Who are the firms leading German re-armament at the present time?'

'At the present time Grossfuss at Döbeln; Walther at Zella-Mehlis; Erma-Werke at Efurt –'

Tweedle-dum held up a hand. 'Fine, Mr Marks. That's just fine.'

'And your political affiliations?' Tweedle-dee asked.

'I'm a Jew, isn't that enough?'

They asked more questions which Nathan answered without hesitation. Yes, he thought the persecution of the Jews was the most terrible crime Mankind had ever perpetrated: the Germans were vomit. War was inevitable, but he understood the isolationist movement in the States even though it was doomed to disillusion.

'What are *your* priorities, Mr Marks?'

Promptly: 'Myself and 'my daughter in reverse order.'

The older of the two men, grey-eyed and sharp-featured, said: 'We are interested in your views on isolation. The extreme isolationists tend to be pro-German and anti-British. How would you like to join their ranks?'

Nathan bit into a sugared cake. 'Explain yourselves, gentlemen.'

The younger of the two, who had a soft voice and a scarred face, told Nathan that Roosevelt believed that the only way to stem German expansionism was to buttress Europe. And at the same time undermine the Nazi war effort. 'That's where you come in,' the younger man said.

The older one carried on: 'We want you to prepare a complete treatise on German arms manufacture. In particular its most vulnerable aspects. In return you will find your business account – such as it is,' smiling, 'credited with 500,000 dollars. We wish you to expand your warehouse in Jersey City – and go back into your old business.'

By the end of 1940, when Great Britain was the only country in Europe left to be 'buttressed', three German arms factories in Essen, Dortmund and Berlin had mysteriously been sabotaged and Marks International was in full, lethal production. Nathan Marks was *using* the enemy.

He took his daughter, maid and nanny, to a penthouse on the East Side, where he joined the anti-British faction of Manhattan society and attended a dinner thrown at the Waldorf Astoria to celebrate the German victories in Europe. Future trade between America and the New German Empire – after Britain had been vanquished – was among the topics discussed.

Dutifully the little hunchback reported back to Anglo-American Intelligence headquarters at the Rockefeller Centre where, in Room 3553 at 630 Fifth Avenue, he talked with the British director, William Stephenson, and J. Edgar Hoover, head of the FBI.

Nathan agreed to supply arms to Nazi sympathisers in

Mexico and South America – Brazil in particular – through a front company with a Gentile board of directors to avoid upsetting the Aryan sensibilities of the purchasers.

Thus the Nazis, assembling beneath the belly of the United States, became the proud possessors of great arsenals of weapons and ammunition – most of it dud and much of it booby-trapped. The good stuff was distributed among the American armed forces or dispatched across the U-boat infested Atlantic to Britain.

After that Nathan Marks never escaped from his mentors, the FBI, the OSS and its successor, the CIA. Nor did he wish to: the fortunes of war and its aftermath had made him a multi-millionaire.

But, while his products equipped the armies of the world, Marks International remained a family business. The major stock-holder and senior vice-president was his daughter, Claire.

When she was sixteen, ripening into extravagant beauty, he sent her to Paris and London. Then back to New York for instruction in the subtleties and brutalities of big business. By the time she was twenty-three he believed he had developed a protégé capable of holding her own against any male.

She was beautiful, sophisticated, tough as the boss of the Teamsters' Union. Not bad for the daughter of a penniless, deformed German-Jewish immigrant.

But one outstanding problem faced Claire: the problem that faces any woman who possesses a strong character, a good brain and the trappings of wealth: the choice of a man.

Claire believed that she had found a man as arrogantly accomplished as herself in Michael Jerome, heir to a family oil fortune, reputed to be on paper in the region of 15 billion dollars. Nathan, now in his late fifties, approved of the choice: arms and oil. And if Jerome didn't meet the requirements he sought, then he could be jettisoned.

Michael Jerome had one other asset in addition to wealth and apparent business acumen: he was extraordinarily handsome. Dark curly hair, Byronic profile, athlete's body adorned by Savile Row tailors.

After the wedding in New York the couple flew to London to a suite in the Savoy overlooking the Thames. There Claire, still a virgin but aching not to be, discovered that Michael Jerome's dynamism ended at the bedroom door.

The honeymoon wasn't a fiasco. They made love many times. But it seemed to Claire that she was always the instigator; that, although he responded, he regarded her passion as somewhat distasteful.

She became pregnant on the honeymoon, and nine months later a baby boy was still-born. She never saw him and, because this had been Nathan's wish, she forever wondered if there had been a hunch on the tiny body.

When she finally surfaced from the grief, there might still have been a chance for the marriage. Until she discovered that Michael's vaunted business capabilities were a charade. And she knew then that the partnership was over because somewhere there had to be respect.

She was divorced four years to the day after the marriage.

There were many other men in Claire's life, many of them sophisticated, affluent and physically attractive, but they always failed her. She didn't seek domination from a partner: merely equality. But as she thrust herself into the forefront of the business world, the equality became more elusive.

By the time Nathan was sixty-five, Claire was in virtual command of an empire that now included copper mines in Zambia, oil in Alaska, a chemical plant in Britain, thousands of acres of prime real estate in South America.

Claire, in her mid-thirties, was still devastating. Beautiful, powerful, rich. Newspapers and magazines speculated endlessly about her wealth and her lovers. But none of the writers ever suspected her clandestine activities.

American Intelligence had founded Marks International; throughout the fifties and sixties the company, which had moved its heaquarters to Los Angeles, continued to repay the debt, arming and financing CIA operations all over the world. Claire revelled in the atmosphere of intrigue and was able on one occasion to tell an ecstatic CIA director in

Washington that she had concluded a deal to sell anti-freeze to the Russians who were accustomed to using vodka. Marks International installed a staff of two in an office in Moscow, one of whom was a CIA agent.

It wasn't until she was peering into middle-age – and Nathan was an old man to whom the past had become more real than the present – that Claire paused for a stock-taking. Realisable assets of around a billion dollars, houses in the Bahamas, Switzerland and Mexico, penthouses in Manhattan and Los Angeles, apartments in Paris and London, private jet, yacht moored at Antibes. . . .

But to her astonishment Claire Jerome discovered that she was discontented. She peered ahead and saw that there was nowhere else to go. Worse, there was no one with whom to share what she had achieved.

Until she met Pete Anello.

Now Anello knew most of what there was to know about her. (Nothing about the CIA connection, of course.) But he didn't reciprocate; she hadn't really expected him to. Whatever it was that he dreamed about was private property. No trespassers. One day perhaps.

Claire wondered if she had told him too much about herself. Then she thought: 'It's a pity we have to think that way; it shouldn't matter.'

For a while she was content and it wasn't until the evening of the last day of her vacation in the Bahamas that, as a cool breeze came in from the sea, her fear returned.

They had taken a picnic lunch to a deserted stretch of beach fringed by tamarind trees and, after they had swum and eaten, they had made love on a towel, tasting the salt on each other's bodies. And the hiss of the waves and the cries of sea-birds had been part of the love-making.

'You know something,' he said at the wheel of the buggy, driving back to the house, 'you once told me that all the men you'd known had been weak. Well, I'm just about the weakest goddam article you're ever likely to meet.'

'I was wrong about them. Well, a lot of them. I just nosed out their weaknesses like a dog searching for truffles. I didn't stop to observe their strengths, I judged them by one set of rules. They were lucky to escape.'

'Since the Army I've never done an honest day's work in my life. Except, perhaps, on boats.'

He drove the buggy fast and expertly, and the airstream whipped at his dark hair, the sunlight finding a few strands of grey.

When she didn't reply he said: 'So what are you going to do about me?'

'Nothing,' she said.

'Come on. The Bahamas' fine. Wall Street, Washington, dinner with the Krupps . . . no way. Can you see me in the boardroom with my ass hanging out of a pair of jeans?'

She laughed. 'Stay here for a while. We'll work something out.' Of course he was right; there were shark-fins in the waters ahead.

But it was her last day. She exerted her will and the shark-fins submerged. She concentrated on how it had been on the beach that afternoon.

'That scar,' she said. 'I always meant to ask you. How did you get it?'

'Vietnam.'

'And you don't want to talk about it. . . .'

'That's right, I don't want to talk about it.'

But later, during dinner, he did indirectly. Pete Anello, it transpired, was anti-armaments.

And he chooses our last meal together for at least a month to tell me, she thought, and said: 'You know, I've heard all these arguments a hundred times before. Couldn't we forget it? Just for tonight?'

'If you wish,' shrugging and helping himself to the lobster, prawns and scallops glistening in their bed of ice. 'If you figure it's not important.'

She sighed. 'Okay, let's get it over. You know which was the most powerful anti-arms lobby in the thirties? The Communists. And why? Because while they moralised about profiteering from guns and bullets Russia was re-arming. If the American arms manufacturers had heeded the lobby, the United States would have been crushed. By the Japs . . . by the Germans . . . and then by the Russians if the others had

146

missed out. Arms dealers are accused of fermenting war to line our pockets. Bullshit. That's just the tired old rationalising of the jealous. It has nothing to do with armaments – just envy of riches. The riches which are distributed to provide jobs for the people who gripe.'

'Not for me,' Anello said mildly. 'Nobody's ever provided work for me in a long time.'

'So the guy whose yacht you skippered wasn't wealthy?' He smiled. 'And you, of course.'

'When I hear these stupid arguments I always quote a certain Englishman named Maurice Hankey. He was giving evidence at an inquiry into the arms trade back in the thirties. And this is what he said:

' "Doctors, pharmaceutical chemists and nurses depend for their profit on ill-health and disease. It would be outrageous to suggest that for that reason they try to encourage epidemic disease or are lukewarm in their promotion of public health." '

'Maybe,' Anello said, lifting up his shirt and pointing at the scar, 'you made the bullet with my name on it.' He removed the shell from a prawn and chewed the white flesh. 'Are you into percussion bombs or napalm?'

'Neither. And no, we didn't make your bullet because we don't manufacture arms for the enemy,' reflecting that this wasn't entirely true.

'How can you be sure? Let's face it, the British manufactured the rifles with which the Turks shot them in World War One.' There was a new note to his voice; it was a stranger's voice and it scared her. 'Have you ever seen the end product of one of your production lines? Have you ever seen a man cut in half by a burst of machine-gun bullets?'

She had to fight back. She said: 'Have you ever seen the atrocities perpetrated on innocent people because they didn't have arms with which to defend themselves?'

Anello shook his head slowly. 'No, nor have you. But I have seen a soldier tearing at his guts with his bare hands trying to get a bullet out.' He cracked a lobster claw. 'Have you ever considered pulling out of armaments?'

'Are you serious?'

'Stick with oil and copper and anti-freeze and you'll still be a billionaire.'

'Are you a Communist, Pete?'

'No way. Just a simple soul. No arms, no wars. It's got to start somewhere. Why not with you?'

'Forget it,' she said.

'Maybe I'll do just that.'

'And what's that supposed to mean?'

He shrugged.

The shark-fins re-appeared. She shivered. 'Why? Why tonight?'

'At this moment someone somewhere is getting killed by a bullet.'

'Let's have a real ball,' she said, 'and talk about hydrogen bombs.' She pushed her plate away. 'I'm going to take a bath and go to bed. Are you coming?'

He seemed to soften. 'Sure I'm coming.'

As they passed the front door she noticed an envelope lying on the floor. She picked it up. 'Odd. Someone must have pushed it under the door.'

She opened it.

On a sheet of cheap blue notepaper was a date cut from the page of an old newspaper. October 10th, 1943.

'What's that supposed to mean?' she asked frowning. She handed it to Anello. 'Does it mean anything to you?'

'Damn right it does.'

Another nudge of fear.

'It was the day I was born,' Pete Anello said.

XI

Pierre Brossard received the details of the 1980 meeting at the Château Saint-Pierre while he was sipping lemon juice with distaste and eating dry toast on the terrace of a health farm in the Swiss Alps.

He scanned them with satisfaction. It was to be his last Bilderberg. A sumptuous setting for his last coup which now had the enthusiastic support of Nicolai Vlasov, the head of the KGB in Moscow.

The sound of cow bells reached him from the green valley below. The sky was blue but the mountain peaks above him were already sprinkled with snow and there was a hint of ice in the air; like the trace of crushed ice lingering in a Martini cocktail, Brossard thought. For Martini he substituted champagne ('61) from a friend's vineyard near Epernay. And then, by Gallic logic, his thoughts progressed to food – *truite au bleu, beurre blanc crême*.

His mouth watered. A Frenchman on a diet: it was a contradiction in terms. But necessary if you were nudging sixty, still working an eleven-hour day with a tendency to put on weight around the belly. And a pot belly in a six-foot-tall, lean-fleshed man was more ridiculous than an immense corporation in a man who was uniformly fat.

His hands strayed beneath his bath robe. Most of the excess fat had been shed. By God he was trim compared with most of his contemporaries. And virile in his own particular way. He wondered if his secretary, Hildegard Metz, realised this. But the question would always be unanswered: not on your own doorstep: one of life's rules.

Hildegard Metz came through the French windows onto the terrace. Neat and dark and efficient and, he supposed, attractive if she ever broke loose and tossed away her spectacles. She looked older than twenty-eight, he thought.

149

She smiled at him politely and said: 'A beautiful morning, Monsieur Brossard.'

'Like champagne. I only wish I was drinking some.'

'Only two more days.'

'And then I shall eat like a pig.'

She sat down at the table. 'Not you, m'sieur.'

The remark pleased him: she recognised his self-control, his discerning palate.

She crossed her legs – good legs – and placed a pad on one knee. 'Any letters this morning, Monsieur Brossard?' glancing at the gold watch as thin as a coin on her wrist – an extravagance, Brossard thought. 'In ten minutes you have to be in the gymnasium. And then the sauna.'

Brossard sighed. A few other guests were wandering around the lawns, printed with autumn crocuses, trying to forget their hunger by admiring the scenery.

He said: 'A few calls Fraulein Metz. Could you telephone Madame Brossard and confirm that I shall be flying back on Thursday.' He could have called her himself but why compound the tedium of the day? 'Also call Mayard and see what he proposes to put on the front page on Friday.'

Of all Brossard's possessions it was the financial newspaper, published once a week in Paris, that brought him most satisfaction. It was prestigious and informed and its columns exercised great influence on the stock markets.

Brossard had always been scrupulously honest in his handling of the paper. One contributor who had suggested that a stock was weak, bought heavily when the shares fell and sold immediately they re-attained their rightful price, had been fired.

The spearhead of the paper was Brossard's own column, Midas. Followed, feared and respected. Midas could elevate a struggling company to stardom, destroy a giant trying to conceal its crumbling foundations.

'Anything else, m'sieur?'

'See if you can contact Paul Kingdon in London. Tell him I'll call him at four this afternoon.'

Brossard's stomach rumbled. He sighed. 'Have you eaten breakfast this morning, Fraulein Metz?'

'I won't tantalise you.'

'An English breakfast perhaps? Eggs and bacon?'

'You're a masochist, m'sieur. In fact I had croissants with rich Swiss butter and peach confiture and hot chocolate. It was delicious,' Hildegard Metz said smiling.

'And you're a little sadist,' wondering if it could be true. 'There's just one more thing,' as his stomach groaned again, 'could you acknowledge these details about Bilderberg. There's the address – The Secretariat, Smidswater 1, The Hague.'

'Bilderberg again. They obviously think very highly of you.'

'I am on the committee,' he reminded her.

In the gymnasium he pedalled two miles on a bicycle and sculled half a mile on a rowing machine. A male attendant in a white uniform took his pulse and remarked: 'You are in very good shape – for your age.' Brossard wished he hadn't added the qualification; still, the flattery pleased him.

He adjourned to the sauna where four other men sat stoically enduring the dry heat, towels wrapped round their waists. Two of them were plump – one a banker from West Berlin with almost feminine breasts; the third was scrawny; the fourth, brown and muscular, a film star from Rome fleeing from the temptations of pasta.

They sat in silence.

As the heat enveloped him, Brossard lay down on one of the wooden benches and let his thoughts drift back to the last Bilderberg he had attended in Torquay in Devon, England. How did Bilderberg describe itself?

'. . . a high-ranking and flexible international forum in which opposing viewpoints can be brought closer together and mutual understanding furthered.'

Fine as far as it went.

But, of course, intrigues weren't discussed in a forum. They were concocted in ante-rooms, private chambers, penthouses and executive suites.

You would have to be very gullible, Brossard thought turning onto his stomach, to believe that the elite of the Capitalist world gathered between four walls and did not come to a few *arrangements*. . . .

The film star got up and left. Brossard seemed to remember him having a screen love affair with Sofia Loren. Or was it Gina Lollobrigida?

This time the venue was only sixty kilometres or so from his house in Paris. He knew the château fairly well, not far from the autoroute to the south but cloistered among woods and fields. The food there was excellent, the wine irreproachable . . . his stomach made a noise like a drain emptying. But it was too expensive.

Brossard cooled down in the splash pool, put on his robe and returned to his room, decorated in autumnal colours, to compose his column. This week it would be innocuous – anecdotes and gossip and appetisers for the column the following week – because he had been away from his office for too long to have any hard facts to hand.

And facts, cold, hard and often sensational, were what the public expected from Midas. Over the years he had built up a reputation for total credibility.

Which was just as well. You needed such a reputation when in six months time, at the end of the Bilderberg conference, you intended to publish a sensational story that was totally false.

Half an hour later Brossard broke off for his mid-morning snack – half an apple and a glass of warm water on which a slice of lemon floated.

He ate the apple, chewing the skin carefully, and nibbled the flesh of the lemon up to the rind. Then he read what he had written on the portable electric typewriter. Bland, very bland. But readable. He switched on the typewriter again and his thin fingers glided over the keys. Half an hour later it was finished; Hildegard could send it to Paris on the health farm's Telex.

Standing at the window, gazing at the mountains, their peaks now wreathed with cloud, he wondered, as he had wondered over the past three decades, how his readers would react if they knew the identity of his real masters.

He telephoned Hildegard Metz. When she came in she

placed his correspondence on the table where he had been typing; on top was a carbon copy of his acknowledgment to Bilderberg together with the details.

'Will there be anything else, Monsieur Brossard?'

A steak as thick as a fist!

'Nothing more, Fraulein Metz. You can go and besport yourself in the fleshpots of the village.'

Would she? Could she? Dark hair contained so severely by tortoiseshell combs, waisted grey costume, spectacles. . . .

'I think I'll take a walk, Monsieur Brossard. There's a beautiful little church in the valley that I want to see.'

'Very well. Send this to Paris,' handing her the typewritten pages, 'and take the rest of the day off.'

She thanked him and went out of the room, closing the door softly behind her.

He picked up the typewritten statement from the Bilderberg Secretariat and absent-mindedly turned it over in his hand.

He froze.

On the back, printed in purple letters – the sort of lettering contained in a children's printing set – was a date.

March 21st, 1942.

Coldness swept up through his body to his brain.

His legs began to give way and he sat down abruptly on the edge of the bed and lowered his head between his knees.

The faintness passed.

He lay back on the bed trembling.

At 9.30 on that March morning the French Resistance had blown up a German ammunition dump fifty miles northwest of Paris. Fortuitously a posse of German officers, including two generals, had been inspecting the dump at the time and had been blown a hundred feet or more into the air during a series of explosions which were likened by the local population, both ecstatic and fearful, unto a volcano erupting.

Immediately the area was sealed off by SS and regular Wehrmacht troops, while plain-clothes Gestapo interrogated suspects in the town and the surrounding villages.

Pierre Brossard, aged twenty-two, son of a property developer, already known before the German invasion for his keen business instincts and his appreciation of life's luxuries – complicated by his reluctance to spend money on them – relaxed while the Germans went about their business. He was a member of the Maquis but he assumed he was above suspicion; his father was a collaborator – like father like son.

Pierre, slim with aloof good looks, assumed too much. Seeking a little additional charisma with the daughter of a Parisien businessman, he had hinted that he was engaged in clandestine activities against the Germans; unbeknown to him the girl was also sleeping with an SS major.

The Gestapo called for him while he was drinking a glass of Chablis in the lounge of his father's house, watching the rain streaming down the windows and re-living the almost orgiastic pleasure he had experienced when the explosion had occurred.

They dragged him out of the house, bundled him into a Mercedes truck and drove him to an improvised interrogation centre in the village school.

When the truck stopped outside the school, he could hear the screams of men being *interrogated*.

His own interrogation, conducted in a class-room adorned with children's paintings of soldiers in field-grey, didn't last long.

There were two Gestapo officers in the room. They both wore leather coats. One was tall and smooth-cheeked with pale, almost colourless hair; the other, his subordinate, was squat with powerful shoulders and pock marks on the back of his neck.

The officer in charge said: 'It would save us a lot of trouble if you collaborated with us – like your father.' He spoke perfect Parisien French.

'I don't know what you're talking about.'

'Come now, an ammunition dump is blown sky high and two generals with it, and you don't know what we're talking about?'

'I heard the explosion of course,' Pierre said. Fear knotted inside him.

'You not only heard it, you helped to arrange it.' The officer rested his elbows on the teacher's desk and stared at Brossard. 'You see you've been under surveillance for a long time. We hoped you would lead us to the ring-leaders. Unfortunately they struck first.'

'I had nothing to do with it, I promise you.' Belonging to the resistance movement had brought a new swagger to Pierre's life; but he had never anticipated anything like this. *Please God, don't let them hurt me.*

'Let's not waste any more time,' the officer said. 'What we want from you, my young hero, are the names of all the Resistance agents in this area.'

'I don't know them, I swear it.'

The officer picked up a piece of chalk and snapped it between his fingers. He said to his assistant: 'Show him, Schapper.'

Schapper opened the door leading to another room. Pierre saw a young man with whom he had been to school lying naked on a trestle table. Blood dripped from the wounds where his fingernails had been; electrodes were attached to his genitals. He was unconscious.

Schapper said: 'A temporary respite. When he comes to they'll start again.' He shut the door.

Pierre swayed, steadied himself against a desk.

The officer said: 'You want to go through all that?'

'But I don't know the names.'

'Schapper, the box.'

Schapper opened a black metal box and took out a pair of pincers. 'Your hand please.' His voice was thick with pleasurable anticipation.

'No! Oh Christ no!'

'The names!'

'I don't know them.'

Schapper said: 'I asked for your hand.' He reached out and grasped Pierre's wrist with his left hand. In his right hand the pincers, their jaws open.

From the room next door a scream. From hell.

Pierre felt the cold of the steel of the pincers on one finger.

'I'll tell you. I'll tell you anything you want to know. For God's sake put those things away.'

Reluctantly Schapper let go of his wrist.

'That's better,' the officer leaning on the desk said. 'Much better.' He picked up a document and read from it. 'Low resistance to pain. How accurate. Really, our intelligence is getting better and better. Now the names please,' as the man on the trestle table began to scream again.

One hour later the twenty-two men named by Pierre Brossard were herded into a barn. Two gunners opened up with 7.92 mm MG 34's, lazily swinging the barrels of the machine-guns as the bullets tore through the wattle and plaster. Then they set fire to the barn.

Pierre was forced to watch.

And I didn't even lose a fingernail, he thought later, as he sat in the classroom listening to the senior Gestapo officer.

Would he care to act as an *agent provocateur* in the future? If not he could fill in the next hour or so helping to dig a mass grave for the charred bones of the executed traitors; he would then, of course, be consigned to the grave himself. Alive.

Pierre closed his eyes and whispered: 'You already know the answer.'

'I must congratulate you on your foresight. The Third Reich does not forget those who serve it well.'

Between March 21st, 1942, and the German surrender Pierre Brossard betrayed 113 members of the Resistance, most of whom were tortured and executed. And so expertly was his dual role concealed that he believed that, apart from one or two Nazis who had no desire to reveal their own role in such deceptions to the Allied inquisitors, no-one knew his secret.

And continued to believe it until 1950 when Soviet Intelligence enrolled him as their banker and spymaster in West Europe. The Gestapo officer who had enrolled Brossard had been uncovered in East Berlin masquerading as a taxi-driver.

During interrogation, when he exhibited a low resistance to pain, the former Nazi had revealed the names of all the agents and double-agents under his control during the war. Among them Pierre Brossard! The Russians were astonished and delighted: fat cats were not often delivered to them in their baskets.

Brossard, emerging as one of the principal re-builders of war-shattered Europe, was visited in his offices in Paris by two members of a Russian trade delegation, ostensibly to import Brossard technology into the Soviet Union.

They told him that if he didn't co-operate with the KGB then his role as traitor would be revealed 'to the appropriate authorities' – bureaucratic phraseology slipping precisely off their lips – and he would then be tried and executed unless, of course, the families of the men he had sent to their deaths got to him first.

There was no alternative. He had been a traitor once, why not again? But this time he would at least have style. Wealth, position and power. Brossard made it quite clear to the KGB that they would have to contribute to his coffers.

The Russians agreed, and for the next thirty years Pierre Brossard acted as banker and spy in an espionage network at levels of power and prestige within the Western Establishment to which not even Kim Philby had aspired.

But who had printed the date on the back of the sheet of paper? And why?

Pierre Brossard, travelling tourist class on Swissair Flight 704 from Zurich to Paris, stared down at the green and gold French countryside and once again tried to work it out.

All the Frenchmen who knew that he worked for the Resistance had been shot and burned on that terrible day that had changed his life. As far as he knew, any Nazis who knew about his dual role were by now dead. (The Gestapo officer who had interrogated him had long since died, broken by the Russians.)

Which left the Russians themselves. But what could the KGB's purpose be in resurrecting the date? A reminder, perhaps, that he was embarking on his last operation? All espionage organisations enjoyed a flourish of melodrama.

Brossard who had regained some self-composure since the first shocked reaction in the bedroom of the health farm, decided that the Russians must be the culprits.

He turned to Hildegard Metz. 'Would you care for a drink?'

'A beer would be nice.'

Brossard pressed the button above him and the stewardess took the order for a beer and a coffee.

'Tell me,' Brossard said as she sipped her beer, 'did you take a close look at the details about the Château Saint-Pierre when they arrived?'

'Bilderberg? I glanced at them. Why?'

'Did you notice anything on the back?'

'There was a date printed there, I think.'

'Do you remember what it was?'

Hildegard Metz looked surprised. 'No, but if you wish. . . .'

'No, it doesn't matter,' said Brossard who had the sheet of paper in his briefcase.

Mayard was waiting for them at Orly in his '79 sage-green Rolls-Royce Silver Shadow, an unwarranted expenditure in Brossard's opinion; but, with Mayard at the wheel, it enabled him to be chauffeured in the manner expected of him.

Mayard had been editor of the paper for nine years and he was all things that a financial journalist should be: astute, correct and uninterested in speculative ventures. He was paid a handsome salary and this Brossard did not resent paying; he never questioned the need for expenditure in business. Mayard owned a magnificent town house in Neuilly, a château on the Loire, a yacht moored in Cannes – and the Rolls.

Ostentatious. But forgivable, Brossard conceded, if you were short, stout and somewhat lacking in presence.

'Thank you for forwarding the mail,' Brossard said as they glided through the suburbs of Paris.

Mayard stroked his neat moustache. 'It was nothing,'

sounding surprised at the compliment. 'My secretary took care of it.'

'Fraulein Metz replied to the Bilderberg correspondence.'

'Bilderberg?' Mayard allowed the driver of a small Citroen the pleasure of overtaking a Rolls. 'When is the next meeting?'

'You don't know?'

'Should I?'

'I suppose not,' and when Mayard said: 'I hope you don't think I've been reading your personal mail,' Brossard said hurriedly: 'I have been thinking about referring to Bilderberg in my column.'

Both Mayard and Hildegard Metz, who was sitting beside Brossard in the back of the Rolls, exclaimed in astonishment.

Mayard said: 'I don't think that would be a good idea. You would upset a lot of good contacts.'

'I suppose you're right,' Brossard said in a conciliatory tone.

'Anyway,' Mayard remarked, 'I liked your column this week. Not red meat this time. Not steak tartare. But a soufflé is acceptable from time to time, eh?' He braked gently at an intersection. 'Where to first, Pierre – home, office or newspaper?'

Brossard didn't particularly want to go to any of them. He had more exhilarating activities in mind. But for the sake of convention, he said: 'Newspaper first, then the office.'

They dropped Hildegard Metz who made her way to the offices, the hub of the Brossard empire, near the headquarters of Radio France. Brossard and Mayard entered the undistinguished post-war block off the Place d'Italie that housed the newspaper.

Mayard's office was for him austere, although touches of self-indulgence were visible – the hinged bookshelves ajar to reveal bottles of Chivas Regal whisky and the Beefeater gin, a silver box containing Havana cigars on the desk.

Brossard, wearing an off-the-peg blue suit, and Mayard dressed in a grey three-piece which must have cost 4,000 francs, faced each other across the desk.

Brossard picked up a proof of the front page. 'So,' he

said, 'how's the dollar holding up?'

Mayard jabbed downwards with his thumb. 'The President will have to get even tougher because, believe me, the Arabs are going to. And God knows what's going to happen in Iran. . . . American intelligence was very badly informed there. It was almost as if they were deliberately misinformed.' Mayard pulled at his small moustache. 'Has it ever occurred to you,' he said, 'what an opportunity Bilderberg presents for spreading misinformation? It is so strong and yet so vulnerable. . . .'

Brossard said nothing.

Mayard went on: 'Gold is poised once again to hit the ceiling – if such a ceiling exists.' Mayard unbuttoned the jacket of his suit; the tailoring of the waistcoat was consummate but, Brossard observed, it still failed to hide the bulge of Mayard's little pot belly. 'The trouble with the once-almighty dollar,' Mayard said, 'is that they printed too many of them. Multiply any commodity and you dissipate its value. What would happen if the Russians released all their diamonds?' He smiled. 'Tiffanys would go bust and so would de Beers. And, of course, Monsieur Kingdon.'

'Which reminds me,' Brossard said, 'I forgot to telephone Kingdon in Switzerland.' He had forgotten most of his business calls the day he had seen the date on the back of the Bilderberg details.

'I think Monsieur Kingdon got rich a little too quick,' Mayard remarked.

'You think he's suspect?' Brossard, who relied on Mayard to provide much of the background to the Affluent Society, looked interested.

'He's always been suspect,' Mayard said. 'You know that. Now I hear rumours of a revolution within his court. Crazy speculations – with the investors' money of course. And reports that he's been sanction busting in Rhodesia.'

'Who hasn't,' Brossard remarked. 'In any case that will shortly become academic.'

'Just the same he's displaying classic symptoms of desperation in financial straits.'

'But Kingdon will never starve,' Brossard said. 'He's put his own money into diamonds.'

'As I just said –'

'The Russians will never flood the market,' Brossard interrupted impatiently. 'They would be cutting their own throats.'

Mayard shrugged, took a cigar from the box. 'Do you mind?'

Brossard grimaced. 'Go ahead, it's your office.'

Mayard made a performance of lighting the cigar, blew out a jet of smoke and said: 'Maybe he has got diamonds. They won't do him much good in prison.'

'As bad as that?'

Mayard shrugged. 'Possibly.'

Brossard said carefully: 'I don't think we want to publish anything just yet.'

'As you wish. In any case I haven't got enough facts.'

'But I do want you to up-date our file on Kingdon.'

'It shall be done.' Mayard examined the smouldering tip of his cigar. 'I've been thinking about what you were saying in the car.'

Brossard looked puzzled.

'About referring to Bilderberg in your column.'

'I think you were right,' Brossard said. 'It would upset too many of our contacts. In any case we have touched on it in the past.'

'Only a few innocuous paragraphs – like every other paper. I mean the real story. What a scoop!' Mayard drew strongly on his cigar and a segment of ash fell onto his desk.

Brossard leaned across the desk, flicked aside the ash and said: 'I would never break any confidences.'

'Why not? They're like rules, meant to be broken.'

'Not at Bilderberg.' The lack of deference displayed by the tubby little editor with the postage-stamp moustache always irritated Brossard; but he couldn't afford to lose him so he remained silent.

'Perhaps,' Mayard said carefully, 'if you leaked a story to your editor. . . .'

'That's ridiculous.' Brossard had never considered Mayard to be naive. 'Everyone at Bilderberg – everyone in the world, for that matter – would know the source of the information.'

Mayard said: 'I was thinking ahead.'

'How far ahead?'

'To when you retire. You're not getting any younger, Pierre. What a way to sign off – with the exclusive to end all exclusives.'

Brossard, who intended to retire in six months time, said: 'I've got a few years to go yet.'

Mayard stared at him impassively.

Brossard said defensively: 'I've never felt fitter.'

Mayard waved his cigar, managed to reach the ashtray before more ash fell. 'I don't deny that you look fit. But you know what they say, "Quit while you're still in front."'

A disturbing thought occurred to Brossard. Did Mayard know? All this talk about retirement. . . . No, impossible. How could he?

He said firmly: 'I can assure you I have no intention of retiring for a long time to come.'

Mayard shrugged.

Brossard had promised to sell him the newspaper at a knock-down price when finally he did retire. Perhaps that was what he was hinting at. 'But when I do,' Brossard said, 'I shall hand over the reins to you, as I promised.'

'Just the reins?'

'Everything. At the price we agreed.'

Mayard seemed to relax. His cigar glowed brightly. 'Do you want me to pay you in gold?' He smiled; it was a joke.

'Anything except roubles – or lire.'

'Did they discuss gold at the last Bilderberg?'

'I forget.' Really, Mayard was getting impossible. But not for much longer. 'And now, is there anything that won't keep until tomorrow? I've got a heavy day ahead.'

'Not a thing,' Mayard said. 'Please don't let me detain you,' as though he knew where Brossard was going. Or am I becoming too sensitive? Brossard wondered.

He told the editor that he wanted to call Paul Kingdon in private, nodding perfunctorily as Mayard left the office. He picked up the telephone. Kingdon's Cockney accent was very pronounced over the phone; Brossard was never quite sure whether it was deliberately exaggerated.

'Good afternoon, Paul.'

'*Bon jour*, Pierre. What can I do for you?'

A lot, Brossard thought and said: 'Nothing in particular. I shall be passing through London next week. I thought perhaps we could have lunch together.'

'Of course. Do you have any news?'

'About Bilderberg?'

'It's been a long time. . . .'

Brossard, who believed in the psychology of keeping people waiting, said: 'I told you to be patient.'

'How patient, Pierre?'

Brossard made soothing noises. He wondered if Kingdon intended to threaten him. Probably not: Kingdon's star was in the descent. He could imagine how desperately he wanted an invitation. As far as he knew one was in the post. . . .

Kingdon said: 'I'm assuming that you will have some news by the time we meet.'

You can assume what you wish, Brossard thought, saying: 'Make it Wednesday.'

A pause. 'Rules – at twelve-thirty?'

'That would suit me perfectly.'

'All right, see you.' The line went dead.

When Brossard emerged from the Metro in Montmartre half an hour later, it was beginning to rain. The air smelled of wet dust and dead leaves. He stopped outside a grey, three-storey house squeezed in between a bookshop and a patisserie and rang the bell.

A woman's voice issued through the grille beside a window-box filled with geraniums. 'Who is it?'

'Pierre.'

'Pierre who?'

'Pierre Darrieux,' Brossard said humbly.

'Ah, that Pierre. Come up, you bastard.'

The red-haired girl in the black peignoir regarded him sternly when he shut the door behind him in the room curtained with red velvet drapes and furnished with quilted chairs and a big double-bed. 'Where have you been?'

'On business, *ma chere*.'

'You could have called me.'

'I'm very sorry. I tried but you were out.'

'You're lying,' said the girl. 'You will have to be punished.'

'Don't be too hard,' Brossard pleaded. He put three 500 franc notes on the table beside the bed.

'The price has gone up,' the girl said.

'How much?'

'Two thousand.'

It was ironic, Brossard thought, taking another note from his wallet, that in these circumstances he actually enjoyed being robbed. It was a kind of sexual foreplay; he wondered what his limit would be.

'Now get undressed.'

The girl went out of the room while Brossard stripped off his clothes. When she returned she was wearing black stockings, garter belt and stiletto-heeled shoes.

'Now you will pay for your lack of consideration,' she said. 'Lie on the bed,' reaching into the closet beside the bed.

As the first stroke of the leather thong seared Pierre Brossard with delicious pain, he heard again the soft voice of Schapper the Gestapo officer: 'Your hand please.'

*   *   *

At the same time that Pierre Brossard was enjoying his punishment, Hildegard Metz was sitting in her studio-apartment in St Germain des Prés typing a report.

She had left the office almost immediately because she, like Mayard, knew that Brossard would not be conducting any more business that day.

She was happy to be home. Away from Brossard. Away from Switzerland.

The apartment on the top-floor of a dilapidated terrace

house was small but personal, as though she assembled here the personality which she so conspicuously lacked outside it. One wall was lined with books and a coal fire burned in an old-fashioned grate. The few pieces of furniture clustered around the fire were old, not antique, a *chaise-longue* with a loose leg rested against a chest of drawers, and on the walls were a few paintings of Parisien scenes, rain-slicked streets mostly – the French, unlike the English, seemed to revel in their rainfall.

Hildegard Metz liked rain, too. It isolated her in her room, exaggerated its cosiness. As she typed, rain began to tap on the skylight. She liked to think that an impoverished artist had once painted beneath the skylight; and found fame, or at least recognition.

She finished her typing and slipped the report into a manilla envelope. On the mantelpiece an ornate gold clock chimed. Two-thirty. In fifteen minutes the shop-assistant from the bookshop, close to the Sorbonne, would call by to pick up the envelope.

She went into the kitchen to make coffee. From the tiny window she could just see the spire of St Germain des Prés Church, the oldest in Paris.

While she waited for the kettle to boil, she stared through the rain trickling down the window. She had one reservation about rain: it made you introspective. And your thoughts became dominated by one word. IF.

If she hadn't met a man named Karl Danzer she might still be Helga Keller, successful career woman in the male-dominated financial circles of Zurich. Or she might be married to some worthy banker with a rosy-cheeked nanny to look after her two children.

If Karl Danzer hadn't been shot dead she might never have spent two years in Moscow. (Karl, she knew, would only have wanted her to make fleeting visits.) Almost certainly, she would never have changed her name, her personality.

If. . . . The kettle whistled her back from the past. She made the coffee and went back into the little living-room.

She took a record from its sleeve – Borodin's *Nocturne* – placed it on the record-player and sat beside the fire staring into the glowing coals.

Sharp at 2.45 the door-bell rang. She moved to the window and peered down into the street. She went downstairs and let the shop assistant into the building. She led him upstairs, re-boiled the kettle of water and made him coffee.

The shop assistant was young, bearded, intense. She quite liked him but there was no spark between them. They talked in a desultory sort of way for a while. He left at 3 pm for an appointment at 3.45. With the same man, Shilkov, to whom Pierre Brossard had handed his report on the Cesme conference.

Helga Keller stayed for ten minutes or so gazing into the fire; then Hildegard Metz fetched her umbrella and walked out into the rainswept streets.

XII

Sixty-five . . . 70 . . . 75 mph. . . .

Paul Kingdon pressed his foot on the accelerator as he swung his powder-blue Ferrari out of the last of the round-abouts clustered to the south of London's Heathrow Airport and drove down the A 30.

Speed always relieved his tensions. Bled them. And today there had been a surfeit of tensions. Disastrous annual profit figures, a harrowing discussion with George Prentice, the phone call from Brossard. . . .

Why did Brossard want to meet him? Dossiers on the newcomers to Bilderberg? Well that could be arranged – Prentice had been working on all the possibilities. They had even installed an optical wiretrap in the house of a Swedish banker and televised him opening his own wall-safe!

But am *I* among the newcomers?

If not, Brossard could forget the confidential dossiers he wanted. The research wouldn't be wasted: other Bilder-bergers had sought background about their fellows. But he *was* the only member of the steering committee who had asked for information.

And if I am to make a sensational come-back I need that invitation to the Château Saint-Pierre.

80 mph. . . .

Kingdon had considered bringing pressure to bear on Brossard. But ammunition was in short supply. Brossard was a mean man and therefore a careful man; he covered his tracks.

The only weak spot in his defences appeared to be his sexual activities. Weak but not weak enough. If I could reach the source of Brossard's masochism, Kingdon thought, then it might be different. It had to be guilt, of course. Discover the reason for Brossard's guilt and you had him wriggling on a hook.

A chilling thought occurred to Kingdon as he fractionally increased his speed. How much did Brossard know about the decline in the fortunes of the Kingdon Investment Corporation and its subsidiaries? No-one had so far seriously doubted their solvency: They were too big and brawling. But Brossard was a journalist, the owner of one of the most influential financial newspapers in the world – and he had that fat ferret Mayard working for him.

Ostensibly, Kingdon Investments radiated good health. Just as many a tubercular patient looks like an advertisement for tonic wine. But a balance sheet reflects the past and not the future; much had changed since the Kingdon balance sheet had been struck.

The disastrous investment (of investors' money) into an area of the North Sea that contained no oil or gas. . . . The floating of tax avoidance schemes to save his lieutenants from crippling capital gains taxation. . . . The investigation by the London *Sunday Times* into his sanction busting activities in Rhodesia which, Kingdon feared, might extend into other operations. Happily, publication of that august and inquisitive journal had been stopped by an industrial dispute; but doubtless it would return.

Meanwhile it only needed one hatchet-wielding journalist such as Midas, i.e. Pierre Brossard, or one aggressive creditor to expose the wasting disease behind Kingdon Investment's buoyant figures. Kingdon had no feeling of guilt about the figures; everyone manipulated balance sheets. Good-will – that inspired euphemism for loss; fixed assets which were wonderfully reassuring except that they earned nothing. . . .

Kingdon relaxed a little: the speed was fulfilling its therapy. The *Sunday Times* was out of action and he would have known if Midas had been on the warpath. As for the annual profit figures. . . . Well, for the time being he would stick to his original estimate – just over twice what the figures revealed – and go public.

He was still the whizz-kid of the '70s. Why not the '80s

as well? Big Business certainly wouldn't knock him. He might not be Establishment but he was still a torchbearer for Capitalism; in an age when it was considered criminal by some to make a personal fortune, he actually made money for the masses. Or claimed to.

Behind him in the gathering dusk came the sudden glare of headlights on full beam. Kingdon glanced into the driving mirror and the sudden spurt of confidence spent itself.

He drew into the side of the road and waited while the white police car pulled in ahead of him.

'. . . travelling at a speed of eighty-miles-an-hour. . . . Is there anything you wish to say?' One peak-capped policeman knelt beside the door while his colleague examined the road fund licence on the windscreen.

'I didn't know I was speeding.'

The policeman wrote down this gem and said: 'You should keep your eye on the speedometer, sir. Could I see your driving licence?'

Kingdon slid the green licence in its plastic cover from his wallet and handed it to the policeman. In the other hand he held two £10 notes.

The policeman eyed the notes. 'I should put those away if I were you, sir, they might blow away in the wind.'

Another of the incorruptibles: they were always the danger. Kingdon didn't subscribe to the theory that everyone had his price; just the same he wondered how the policeman, young and ginger-haired, would have reacted to a bribe of £1,000.

The policeman wrote down Kingdon's name and address and told him that he would be reported for consideration for prosecution. 'And watch the speedometer, sir, this isn't Silverstone.'

Kingdon continued his journey at 30 mph and turned into the Wentworth Estate, hidden behind barriers of laurel and rhododendron amid the salad-green fairways of the golf-course.

He parked the Ferrari in the drive of his mock-Tudor mansion and walked round the gardens where, in the evenings, he liked to cool off after the day's in-fighting. Another kind of therapy. The air was cool and the first frost of the year had rusted the blooms of the late roses and the chrysanthemums; a few brown oak leaves floated in the swimming pool.

From beside the pool Kingdon surveyed the house in the dusk. Of all his homes this gave him most pleasure. It was tranquil and dignified and it had breeding – the quality Kingdon's enemies found lacking in his character. It was, he told himself, the sort of property they would have bought if he hadn't broken them first.

He shivered. Therapy was doomed this evening.

Did George Prentice have a therapy? Kingdon doubted whether he bothered. Prentice was imperturbable, inviolate. It seemed as though he had always been present, cynical, assured and wise. My anchor, Paul Kingdon thought.

Only once, eight or nine years ago, had Prentice seemed unsettled. Kingdon never knew why; he only knew that, whatever it was – he couldn't imagine Prentice having a personal crisis – he had come out of it more dispassionate than before.

Kingdon knew little about his private life. A bachelor, like himself, with no desire for domestic permanency. Leave it at that. Kingdon harboured only one resentment against Prentice: he was always right.

Like this morning when he had summoned Prentice to his office in the City to discuss the lamentably low annual profits, $16 million instead of the estimated $34 million.

As he began to retrace his footsteps towards the house, heels crunching faintly on the soggy grass that was just beginning to freeze, Paul Kingdon brooded with admiration and anger on the man who had sat opposite him, dispensed advice – and revealed that *he* had been invited to the Château Saint-Pierre.

* * *

The offices of the Kingdon Investment Corporation occupied half a high-rise building. It was known as Kingdon House and it was uninspiring rather than ugly. Another slab of concrete.

Only Kingdon's office had style, and that was painstaking. Wilton carpet, mahogany cupboards, two double-barrelled Parker pistols (circa 1810) on one wall across the room from an oil-painting of some unidentified patriarch.

The view, however, was spectacular. Especially this morning, with fragile autumn sunshine lighting the rooftops, spires, domes – and skyscrapers – of the Square Mile.

'Well' – Kingdon impatiently tapped the leather-topped desk with a silver paper-knife – 'what do you think?'

Prentice was gazing at the view. He was, Kingdon admitted, a handsome bastard. Looks that had once been donnish were now hawkish. If only he would take an interest in his clothes. How long, for God's sake, had he been wearing that herring-bone sports jacket with the leather elbows?

Prentice said: 'A pity we can't adjourn to a coffee shop. It's that sort of day. The sunshine's a hundred years old.'

'No poetry for Christ's sake,' Kingdon snapped. He filled a plastic cup with iced water from the dispenser, the only concession to the 20th century in the office. 'I need your advice, George, your help.'

Prentice stared at Kingdon. 'First of all,' he said, no poetry in his voice now, 'you tell me what went wrong.'

'You know bloody well what went wrong. Everything. We were among the pioneers in the offshore game. Others followed and improved. Anyone that leads gets left behind. Britain launched the Industrial Revolution. Look at Britain now.'

'I think,' Prentice said, 'that you are over-simplifying the situation.'

'The only way to keep ahead is to keep pioneering. New ventures. As you know we're doing just that. We're lending securities to brokers who're short – charging fees of course – and we're underwriting big financing operations through our banks.'

'Could I put that last one a bit more bluntly?'

'If you must.'

'You're using your clients' cash to float bonds which you yourself are pushing.'

Kingdon shrugged. 'So what? The name of the game in this country is Unit Trusts. The customer's got to have trust.'

'And in the States it's Mutual Funds. The customer should be mutually involved.' Prentice lit a cigarette. 'And now you're into real estate in a big way, eh, Paul?'

'In the States, yes. Why bring that up?'

'Your customers will have to be *very* trusting in those ventures.'

Kingdon undid the top button of his shirt, loosened his tie and put his feet on the desk. 'I have their trust.'

'Swampland in the Bahamas? The name of this particular game is brokerage, isn't it, Paul? You're buying with mortgages but taking your brokerage fees on the total cost, i.e. if you buy the Eiffel Tower for ten million dollars and borrow the remaining thirty million you take five per cent of 40 million. Which is two million dollars for Paul Kingdon and associates.'

'Not bad business, eh, George?'

'It could be called exploitation,' Prentice remarked. 'But I'm sure you haven't brought me here just to give you advice. No one does that. They merely seek approval of what they intend to do anyway. What do you intend doing, Paul?'

Kingdon said abruptly: 'I intend sticking to my estimate of profits.'

'I thought you would.'

'And I intend going public.'

'I thought you would.'

'Doesn't anything surprise you?'

'You've always surprised me, Paul. It's merely that I've come to expect your surprises. How much do you hope to raise?'

'Thirty million pounds,' and when Prentice looked sceptical: 'Anything wrong with that?'

'Nothing wrong with it. Provided the shit doesn't hit the fan before the offering.'

'Your command of the English language continues to

ámaze me,' Kingdon said, reaching for the plastic cup of water.

'Like sanction busting hitting the fan.'

'Do you really think the City, Wall Street, gave a monkey's toss about sanction busting? They might have expressed distaste but they knew it was big business and secretly they were thinking, "Kingdon has done it again." Anyway the sanctions will be lifted soon.'

Prentice went on: 'I think the real danger will come from within your empire. Your lieutenants who have been promised a slice of the pie when you go public. Know what they'll do? They'll sell pretty damn quickly and then turn on you. The money's been re-cycled into the pockets of the few for too long and the recent investments have been bloody awful. When word gets round everyone will dump and your shares will be worthless.'

'Thank you, Mr Jeremiah Bloody Prentice. But –'

Prentice held up his hand. 'Don't tell me. You'll find ways of buying your own shares to prop up the price. I don't have to tell you that in this country that's against the law.'

'Sod the law,' Kingdon said. 'All I need is breathing space. Thirty million pounds worth of it. You should see what I've got lined up for the punters when I've raised the bread.'

Kingdon tossed the prospectus for the public offering across the desk. It was as thick as a short novel.

Prentice flipped the typewritten pages. Ten banks . . . eleven trust funds . . . real estate . . . investment banks . . . 'Limitless opportunities for the future.'

Prentice dropped the manuscript on the desk. 'So, what's your problem?'

'Underwriting,' Kingdom told him. 'Just one bastard underwriter.'

Prentice looked surprised. 'Just one?'

'Just one. I've got dozens from Tokyo to New York City. But one's holding out.'

'Who?'

'Gerards.'

'British or French connection?'

'The British end of the family,' Kingdon told him, crackling the plastic cup in his hand. 'The British bastards.'

'So what's so disastrous about that? I presume you've got half a dozen lead underwriters?'

'You know bloody well what's disastrous. Whatever one Gerard house does the other follows. Until now. It's unprecedented for the British side of the family not to follow the French. Supposing the Press start asking questions about the break in tradition? Supposing some bloody City page reporter contacts Gerards?'

'They'll say, "No comment." They always do.'

'Supposing this same reporter speculates about Gerards' reasons for not underwriting us? If the shares bomb then we're finished.'

'No reporter could speculate adversely after he's read this,' Prentice said innocently, tapping the draft manuscript on the desk. 'Your prospectus seems very comprehensive.'

'Don't be funny,' Kingdon said angrily. 'No prospectus stands up to examination under a microscope.'

'Some better than others.' Prentice stood up and walked to the window. In the silence they could both hear the muted sounds of the biggest money market in the world. Prentice turned and said: 'I may be able to help you.'

Kingdon looked up expectantly.

'I've been invited to Bilderberg again.'

'Again?' For a moment Kingdon almost hated him. 'Christ, that's the third time, isn't it?'

'Fourth,' Prentice said. 'But don't sound so appalled. You know as well as I do that they always invite a few people like me. Just to make it all seem democratic and decent.'

'But why you?'

'What you mean,' Prentice corrected him, 'is why not you.' He sat down again. 'In any case you should be pleased. The London end of Gerards will be there. Robert Gerard.'

'That doesn't surprise me.'

'Maybe I'll be able to influence him a little. . . .'

'Lean on him?'

Prentice shrugged. 'We've got time on our side. I *am* an

industrial consultant. I haven't got round to Gerards yet but I'm sure they're not completely untainted, not with all those billions at their disposal.'

'Very well, George.' Kingdon had his anger under control now. 'I'm very grateful. If there's anything I can do. . . .'

'None of your lousy shares, please.'

'Why the hell do you want to help then?'

'I'll tell you if you like, but you won't enjoy it. Originally I helped out because you were providing a means for the impoverished millions to make a few bob. Invest fifty quid and in no time they'd have five hundred: colour telly or a holiday in Majorca. You enticed them away from the doldrums of saving to the high-flying excitement of investment. You performed a public service, Paul. You gave the masses a little hope.'

Kingdon watched him impassively, accepting the plaudits, awaiting the indictment.

'And it worked well. You had your espionage net spread over Europe. With your knowledge – *our* knowledge,' he corrected himself, 'it wasn't difficult to invest in the right properties. The millions rolled in –'

'For God's sake, get it over with,' Kingdon snapped. 'You're a good spy, a lousy preacher.'

'You know what went wrong. You got greedy. Instead of using the client's money for their benefit you used it for your own.'

'My trouble was that the sales managers got greedy. They lived like millionaires. Some of them *are* bloody millionaires,' Kingdon added.

'You were the boss,' Prentice said.

'You haven't answered the question: Why do you want to help now?'

'I want to save some of the money all those poor sods invested. As simple as that. One headline in the *Financial Times* – GERARD AGREES TO BACK KINGDON INVESTMENTS – and you might, just might, be back in business.'

'You could say you're compounding a crime.'

Prentice stood up and walked towards the door. 'I admit it. For a good cause. So what you've got to do is persevere with your astonishing estimate of profits and make your prospectus at least half plausible.'

* * *

Paul Kingdon swore softly as he reached the house. Pools of mist had gathered in the hollows in the garden. The silhouettes of the trees against the darkening sky were forbidding.

In the oak-beamed lounge Kingdon tried to shake off the sense of apprehension. He warmed his hands in front of the blazing log fire and rang the bell for Willett, his manservant.

Anticipating his request, Willett brought a bottle of Chivas Regal, ice and water, and poured Kingdon a drink. Kingdon gulped it down and poured himself another.

Willett said: 'There are a couple of messages on the machine, sir.'

'Anything important?'

Willett shook his head. 'One woman sounded a little crazy, sir.'

Kingdon accepted his judgement. Willett was astute enough. He performed many functions – valet, butler, cook in a basic sort of way, and bodyguard. He was fifty years-old, perhaps a little too muscular for black jacket and striped trousers. His features were seamed, his hair thick and grey and neat. Kingdon had known him in the East End; he had given him the job when he was released from prison after serving a sentence for assault. Kingdon trusted him more than he trusted most people.

Apart from the woman who came in to clean the house every day, Willett was the only domestic servant.

'It's your night off, isn't it?'

Willett nodded; he spoke sparingly.

'Where are you going?' Kingdon felt the need for conversation.

'I thought I might go up east, sir.'

'Well, don't get into any trouble.' Not that he ever had in the ten years that Kingdon had employed him.

'No, sir.'

'I envy you.'

And in a way he did. After Willett had gone the house echoed with emptiness.

Kingdon poured himself another drink, paced the spacious lounge. The floor-boards creaked beneath his feet. He threw a log on the fire, settled himself once more in a leather armchair and switched on the television with the remote control button.

The news. The police had been awarded a pay increase! Kingdon switched the television off.

Somewhere in the house a window banged.

In the garden a guard dog barked.

Kingdon turned off the lights and went to the window. It was dark and the first stars were cold in the sky. A shooting star traversed the heavens, disappeared. A death? Again Kingdon shivered. Christ, what was the matter with him? One bad day and he was anticipating the arrival of the Fraud Squad.

He chinked the cubes of ice in his empty glass. Stared at them and smiled, and fetched the keys to the cellar where solace, immutable, arrogant and flawless, awaited him. A therapy that never failed.

But first he had to deal with his own security. Industrial espionage had helped to create an industry: electronic surveillance. That in its turn had created a side product: surveillance detection. Kingdon's house bristled with anti-surveillance equipment – bug alerts, wiretrap warnings, telephone analysers. No-one was going to trap Paul Kingdon at his own game.

The cellar was a strong-room. Steel doors a foot wide, the combination of the lock known only to Kingdon; a wireless/television monitor; ultrasonic warning beams and an electronic system that alerted the local police station. Kingdon closed the steel doors behind him and disconnected the surveillance apparatus.

The vault which Kingdon now entered was dimly-lit. He switched off the conventional lighting and flicked a switch that activated a single beam of light from a halogen bulb.

His fear receded as the fears of other men recede in the arms of a woman. As far as Kingdon was concerned power was more important than sex, and his power was crystallised in diamonds.

In the beam of light, on a bed of satin, stood a beautiful stone, its 58 facets flashing fire at him.

Kingdon's contingency plans were centred around the one diamond for which he had paid the highest known price since Harry Winston sold the 75.52-carat Star of Independence for $4 million in New York in 1956. The Kingdon Diamond was 87.38 carats; when the ratings of the world's most illustrious diamonds were re-assessed it would find a slot in between the Star of Persia, now 45th, and the Spoonmakers which was 46th – ten notches above the pear-shaped diamond that Richard Burton had given to his then wife, Elizabeth Taylor.

The Kingdon Diamond was now worth about $10 million; the Kingdon Collection in the region of $30 million. One day, perhaps, if the unthinkable occurred and Kingdon Investments collapsed, he would elope with them. His riches, his passion.

Kingdon stared at the single stone glittering on its cushion. Reluctantly he saw it for what it was: a fake.

The real Kingdon Diamond lay in a vault in the City of London. If any thief managed to penetrate the fortifications outside the cellar in the house, he would have access to a simulant made from strongium titanate.

But Kingdon felt calmer now. Thank God he could still fall for the wiles of a beautiful imposter.

Back in the lounge he stood in front of the fireplace and examined the exhibit in the glass case above the mantelpiece. The old ten-shilling bank-note on which he had founded his fortune. . . . His thoughts were interrupted by the sound of tyres crunching on gravel. He walked across the lounge and activated the closed-circuit television. In the small black-and-white screen he saw a girl photographed outside the door with infra-red beams. The doorbell chimed.

He opened the door and the girl walked in, noticed the

surprise on his face and said: 'You mean you forgot?' She tossed her red fox jacket onto a chair.

'I forgot.' He kissed her. 'Sorry.'

'Well, it's a new experience I suppose.'

The girl was long-legged and small-breasted; her black hair shone with bluish lights and her features were flat and beautiful. She was Eurasian, born Betty Winkler in Cardiff's Tiger Bay, but renamed Suzy Okana by the escort agency which had first employed her.

She had graduated from the agency to be the chosen companion of famous men such as Paul Kingdon. Her name had been linked with Royalty and she featured regularly in the columns of William Hickey in the *Daily Express* and Nigel Dempster in the *Daily Mail*.

She wore slit skirts because it was expected of her, and on occasions swore like a dockland whore. Many men eulogised over her beauty – oriental, enigmatic – but none ever noticed the expression that shadowed her face in unguarded moments. Lost innocence settling into disillusion: the expression of a girl in her teens searching for what the woman of twenty-five suspected was no longer attainable.

Her relationship with Kingdon suited her. All he needed was a fashionable woman to display publicly.

Kingdon, who had invited her to dinner, grinned. 'Can you cook?'

'Again a first. No-one's ever asked me before. And the answer's no.' She poured herself a whisky and lit a cigarette. 'In any case I understood we were going out. I thought you liked us to be *seen* together.'

'Not tonight,' Kingdon said. 'It's been a shitty day.'

She shrugged. 'Okay, open a few tins.'

'You'll find an electric tin-opener on the kitchen wall. It shouldn't be too difficult to operate.'

'Oh boy,' she said and disappeared into the kitchen.

While she was away Kingdon played back the recorder attached to his telephone tap alert. Willett's voice ordering liquor supplies: then Willett talking to a woman.

Willett: 'Mr Kingdon's residence.'

A woman's voice: 'Is Mr Kingdon there?'

'No, madam, he's at his office.'

'Can you give him a message?'

'Of course.'

'Tell him November 12th 1978.'

Kingdon frowned.

Willett's voice: 'I'm afraid I don't understand.'

'It's simple enough. A date. Make a note of it.'

The woman repeated the date.

Willett: 'Is that all?'

Click.

Kingdon switched off the recorder and wrote down the date on a memo pad. He tore off the page and went into the kitchen where Suzy had opened cans of chicken breasts, salmon and paté de fois gras.

'Not exactly a scene from Jennifer's Diary,' she remarked.

'Did you telephone me today?'

She looked at him in surprise. 'No, why should I have done?'

He read out the date. 'Mean anything to you?'

She shook her head.

The feeling of unease returned. He sat down and began to eat without appetite.

'Would you rather I went home?' She was dressed in a maroon and gold thread lamé trouser suit with a ruby pendant necklace at her throat. 'I don't feel quite adequate for the occasion. I'm not dressed for understanding wife consoling worried hubby.'

'The date,' he said. 'What the hell is that date? I'm ex-directory, I had the number changed last week. A woman calls. Leaves a date and hangs up. What the hell do you make of that?'

'Not a lot,' she said. 'A practical joke?'

Kingdon pushed aside his plate. 'Champagne?'

'Shouldn't it be a mug of cocoa?'

Kingdon took a bottle of Bollinger from the fridge and eased off the cork. He poured the champagne into two tumblers, gulped half of his.

'That's all I needed,' he said. 'A bloody mystery.'

'This is all I needed,' she said. 'A night out in an ancestral kitchen. Do you mind if I watch television?'

'Go ahead.'

'And spend the night?'

'Do as you please.'

'You really know how to make a woman feel wanted.'

She went into the lounge, leaving Kingdon sitting in the kitchen watching the bubbles spiralling in the bottle.

Half an hour later he went up to bed. As midnight struck on the grandfather clock in the hallway he heard her go to her room.

He slept fitfully for a while. A breeze had risen and the branches of a tree clawed at the mullioned window panes.

He awoke abruptly as the clock struck two. His mind clear, the date surfacing from his dreams.

The date on an elegant receipt. . . . 'A day to remember, Mr Kingdon,' as he signed the cheque and handed it to the dealer.

November 12th, 1978, was the day he bought the Kingdon Diamond.

But next day was better.

On top of the pile of mail on his desk in his office was an invitation. To Bilderberg.

XIII

The original Château Saint-Pierre was built by François the First, the additions by various successors to the French throne, and the red-brick annexe by a builder from Orléans who later admitted that he had little sense of history.

Annexe apart, the château was a mellow and dignified place. Two wings reached out protectively from the main building, but they were the only concessions to geometric design; successive architects had discovered ancient foundations and built on them, with the result that the extensions tended to wander and guests sometimes took a couple of turns round the corridors before finding their rooms. The outside walls were terracotta, the turrets and clock-tower verdigris green.

Orderliness to the general picture was restored by its frame – the gardens. Lawns as green and fine as moss, an open-air theatre fashioned from holm-oak, carp-filled pools surrounded by stone balustrades, patterned gardens set in clasps of silver Helichrysum, several foundations and a maze which, despite its internal convolutions, looked neat and compact from the outside. The gardens were enclosed by fifteen-foot high railings spiked with gold-painted barbs.

It was these railings that were occupying the attention of Owen Anderson one showery day in March six weeks before the Bilderberg conference was due to assemble. They gave him little encouragement, a professional would be up and over them like greased lightning.

He took a micro-recorder from the pocket of his belted raincoat and spoke into it. 'Install electronic burglar alarm system plus closed circuit television surveillance.'

The Château Saint-Pierre, Anderson concluded as he continued his reconnaissance, posed two forbidding security problems. One was its rambling design; the other was its situation. On one side lush fields and clumps of trees; on the other meadows and orchards separating the château from the village half a mile away; during the conference it would be patrolled by armed guards, but it wasn't impenetrable; the actual gardens, he hoped, would be.

The most likely threat from a sniper's bullet lay on the village side of the château, where there were several vantage points. Again Anderson spoke into the black and silver recorder: 'Make sure guests with the most clout occupy rooms on the opposite side to the village.' Snipers wouldn't want relative nonentities in their sights.

At the heavy, gold-barbed gates, Anderson paused to survey the château. This year's manifestation of his annual nightmare. One bomb, one clutch of bullets and World War III could be ignited. Especially this year after the seizure of the American hostages in Iran and the Soviet invasion of Afghanistan. If only the United States had in the past presented a stronger face to its enemies instead of internally savaging its own security.

Well, for the last time he would do his damndest to safeguard the unofficial Summit as it debated the tenuous future. He had already told Danby that he wanted to be relieved of the Bilderberg responsibility. It had been a long time. Danby had been remarkably sympathetic.

Anderson began to walk along the lane, which was flanked by hedgerows leading to the village. The sun shone warmly after a recent shower and steam rose from puddles. As he walked, he planned six weeks ahead. To Anderson, the château wouldn't be a sequestered retreat: it would be Fort Knox. And the 'pleasant pastoral setting' (the brochure's description) would be a theatre of war. . . .

In the dripping woods and thickets would be day-and-night patrols equipped with guns and two-way radios – primarily from the host country, France, but augmented by security guards from other countries – and electronic beams *tripping* intruders.

In the interior of the château there would be surveillance and detection equipment, ranging from simple bug alerts and analysers to a central alarm system relaying ultrasonic waves to the security HQ on the ground floor and the nearest police station.

In fact, the usual array of equipment, except that each year it became more sophisticated.

One of the main obstacles to be overcome was friction between the security organisations. In three weeks time they were meeting in Paris to thrash it out. Anderson, who had been through it all before, guessed that the meeting would end in complete agreement, which meant that the discord would ferment below the surface.

You couldn't blame any of them: they *were* clandestine organisations.

The most difficult to appease would be the French. Understandably – the convention *was* being held in their country. What they would resent most was his overall authority which, although tacit, was blazingly obvious.

Anderson had a great regard for French Intelligence. He deeply regretted that they seemed to be following the example of Britain and the United States and rounding on their own security service instead of the enemy's. Only two months ago they had appointed a conventional gendarmerie officer to head the security section of the SDECE, the French intelligence service, in place of a veteran espionage expert. The security service had been accused of conducting a witch-hunt! The Russians, Anderson thought, must have been transported with joy.

He saw a children's home-made house perched in an oak tree. It could be used. . . . He noted it in the tiny recorder.

He entered the village. It was quite small, with a cobbled main street glistening after the rain, a church with a green dome, a few snug shops nestling between thin grey houses, plane trees with flaking barks sparsely lining the side-streets. Old men in black berets were emerging like cats after the rain; the smell of new bread issued from the *patisserie;* the breath from the inn was overpowering. About 800 inhabitants, Anderson guessed, warily independent and suspicious of strangers.

Children pointed at him and stared as he recorded some notes. He was, he supposed, something of a phenomenon –

184

a black dude talking into his closed fist.

Half way down the main street he sensed that he was being watched with more than usual intensity. Or perhaps imagined it; you developed an exaggerated wariness over the years; a bug in every cocktail olive.

Or perhaps he *was* under surveillance – by the French.

He paused outside the church. Ah, the belfry. The hunchback of Notre Dame! The point was, could you see the château from the belfry?

He walked past the wet gravestones. Daffodils bloomed in the grass, spring teasing the long-dead.

A priest greeted him at the open doors. He was a cadaverous man – more like an undertaker, Anderson thought – any animation that he might once have possessed, paralysed by the village iniquities confided in the Confessional. Or so it seemed. Then the priest smiled and was transformed. 'Good morning, my son.' No surprise at beholding the black Mafia seeking sanctuary. 'What can I do for you?' And in perfect English.

'I'd like to see your church, father.'

The priest smiled again. Sunshine lighting a craggy cliff. 'And so you shall. Are you interested in any particular aspect?'

Anderson paused. He was described in his own file as 'well-read'. But his erudition didn't extend to ecclesiastical architecture.

'The belfry perhaps?' the priest said.

Anderson stared at him.

'You are no ordinary tourist, are you?' Then taking Anderson's arm and leading him into the scented gloom: 'I n an that you are not here merely to soak up the atmosphere of rustic Gallic life.'

'Not exactly,' Anderson said, about to make his prepared statement – seeing the country before taking up a position at the United States Embassy in Paris.

The priest said: 'I'm very fond of Shaft.'

The prepared statement took flight. 'Good God! – sorry, father.'

'And James Bond, of course.'

'You really read that stuff?'

'Why not? It isn't one of the deadly sins as far as I am aware.'

'It encompasses a few.'

'So does the Bible, my son.' The priest pointed to a wooden spiral staircase. 'Those lead to the belfry, I believe that is what you are interested in.'

'How did you know?'

'You remind me of Shaft. And, after all, Bilderberg is only six weeks away.'

Anderson spread his hands. 'I give up. Are you Father Brown?'

'My favourite,' the priest said as he climbed the worn stairs in front of Anderson.

The bells hung huge and impotent from the domed ceiling. To the right of them, Anderson noticed a small aperture that had once contained glass. He peered through it – and saw the château.

The priest said: 'An ideal spot, eh?'

'I'm afraid so.'

'Then we shall have to keep our belfry under lock and key.'

Downstairs Anderson slipped a fifty-franc note in the offertory box and thanked the priest.

'Can I be of any further help?' the priest asked.

They walked into the sunshine; Anderson thought he noticed a movement to the side of a big, arched gravestone. Imagination? Or the French police. . . .

'I wondered –'

'I'm afraid my help cannot extend to revealing the secrets of the Confessional.'

Anderson grinned. 'You must be psychic.'

'Divine guidance, my son.'

'But you might be able to give me some . . . some indications. You see, father, terrorists aren't really the greatest danger in a situation like this. We can contain them. You wouldn't believe the precautions we take. You pluck a blade of grass and wham! we've got you.' He shook his head. 'No, the greatest dangers are nuts . . . lunatics. They are totally unpredictable, imponderable. Especially the ones who act normally.'

'Like you and me?'

'I sometimes wonder about myself, father.'

The priest smiled his wondrous smile again. 'And you want me to list any likely candidates.'

'If you would, father.'

'I'm afraid you're going to be disappointed. Do you know, I can't even think of one. We've had our fair share of unfortunates who have been deranged. But they've been taken to hospitals.'

Anderson shrugged. 'Well, if you come up with anything give me a call. I'm living at the château.'

'A wonderful setting,' the priest said.

'For what, father?'

'A murder mystery. Simenon, perhaps?' He took his smile back with him into the church.

After checking out the village Anderson returned to the château to vet the staff – 123 of them – concentrating on anyone who had been employed within the past six months. Chefs, pastry-cooks, waiters, cashiers, chambermaids, telephonists. . . . Some of them lived in the village, some in the annexe of the château.

He was half way through the list, checking references and credentials, when he came upon the name Nicholas Foster. Very English. What was a Mr Foster doing in a French château working as a trainee manager? Anderson added his name to a short list of staff to be double-checked.

The following day he began the preliminary sweep inside the château. He had been joined by a colleague from the Secret Service in Washington, an FBI agent, a member of Britain's Special Branch and a French detective inspector named Moitry. There was a Moitry at every conference, the local police officer who was blamed if anything went wrong.

Together they swept every room and corridor with detectors. No bombs, of course. But they were able to eliminate, or pin-point on a plan of the hotel, every metal item that might confuse a later search.

Then they turned their attention to the hotel's antiquated

telephone system. Only eleven lines but more would be provided.

Watched resentfully by the French inspector, he checked the switchboard, using an analyser that monitored the lines for a distance of ten miles and located the position of any eavesdroppers. Nothing. Not yet.

That evening more electronic equipment arrived in two packing cases, shipped via the American Embassy in Paris. The United States was more conscious of security than the other nations involved: they had to be: they couldn't afford to lose Americans as influential as those on the guest list.

On his fourth day at the château, Anderson interviewed members of the staff on his short list, recording their replies on a voice stress analyser. The degree of stress provoked by a lie was conveyed to the interviewer on a numerical readout.

To intimidate his subjects, Anderson conducted the interviews in an imposing ante-room, lined with Italian marble and hung with 18th century Beauvais tapestries, overlooking the fountains and the maze.

'Have you ever been a member of any political organisation?'

The room-service waiter, slightly-built with the dated good looks of a French film star in the '40s, said firmly: '*Non, monsieur.*'

The stress analyser thought otherwise; the number on the readout was high.

'Are you sure?'

'Of course.'

Anderson consulted all the available information on the waiter compiled by a computer in Paris. 'You will excuse me asking this, but do you have any particular sexual preferences?'

The waiter smiled. 'Handsome black police officers. Does the fact that I am gay, as you Americans put it, have any effect on security?'

Privately Anderson didn't think it mattered a damn. In this day and age homosexuality didn't make you any more vulnerable to blackmail than heterosexuality.

'You were truthful about that. Why did you lie about your political activities?'

'If you know about them, why ask?'

Anderson, who hadn't the faintest idea what the waiter's political affiliations were, asked 'How long were you a Communist?'

'A couple of years, maybe less. That is no crime, not in France.' He combed his sleek hair with the tips of his fingers. 'All that matters, Monsieur Anderson, is that you are enjoying yourself. A Communist pervert. What a catch!'

'You're wrong, comrade, I'm not enjoying it one little bit.'

Once he had enjoyed the game. Not any more. Not since the advent of the Holy Brigade, the self-appointed censors of intelligence procedure; the same genre that decried the ill-treatment of terrorists and ignored the horrors they perpetrated. What was the point in defending America against its enemies when Americans were doing the enemies' job? Even if things had got a little better since Iran.

'Well?' The waiter had become more nervous during the pause.

Anderson said: 'When did you leave the Party?'

The waiter mustered his failing resources. 'I quit when I felt like it. As I quit my job now.' He stood up, lips trembling. 'If this interrogation is part of democracy, I shit on it.'

He turned and walked quickly out of the ante-room, built up heels of his shoes clattering on the marble floor.

You've got a point, comrade, Anderson thought, you've got a point. He struck the waiter's name off the list, one who wouldn't have to be temporarily relieved of his duties during the conference.

Nicholas Foster walked in and sat down as Anderson waved him to the carved oak chair on the opposite side of the table.

'I'm sorry about this,' he said to Foster, scrutinising him. Somehow the black jacket and striped trousers didn't quite go with the man. Hotel managers had to be disciplinarians, but there was a controlled aggression about Foster that was out of place.

'No need to be sorry.'

Observing the cleft chin, dark wavy hair and grey eyes, Anderson asked: 'Are you Irish by any chance?'

Foster grinned at him. 'Not a drop of Liffy water has touched my lips.' He'd been asked that one before, Anderson thought.

'Do you mind telling me how you got that limp?'

'Not at all. A drunken idiot with a spear-gun mistook my leg for a fish. In the Greek Islands,' he added.

Anderson made a note on a pad, then asked:

'Mr Foster, why did you decide to take up hotel management at the ripe old age of twenty-eight?'

'I'm sure you know, Mr Anderson. My father owns a chain of hotels and I'm training for the family business. I left it a little late. It was my privilege.'

'But this hotel isn't one of your father's.'

'My father is a friend of the owner, Monsieur Gaudin.'

Anderson glanced at the analyser which, from Foster's side of the table, looked like an open brief-case. The figures revealed nothing suspicious about Foster's answers. Anderson wondered if stress would be revealed in the voice of an accomplished liar; or perhaps someone accustomed to the thrust and parry of an interview – a journalist perhaps. 'What exactly did you do after you left college, Mr Foster? There seems to be a blank in the hotel records.'

'Not a lot,' Foster said. 'I travelled. Bummed my way around.'

'Financed by your father?'

'No, Mr Anderson, not financed by my father.'

'Any political affiliations?'

'I voted for Mrs Thatcher.'

'Good on you, Mr Foster. Any youthful indiscretions?'

'I was caught in bed with the matron at school.'

'I meant political, Mr Foster.'

'I've never been into politics, I don't intend to kidnap the former American Secretary of State, and I haven't the slightest intention of robbing any of the millionaires.'

No excessive reaction from the analyser. 'I'm glad to hear it. You wouldn't get very far.' Anderson stared through the window at the trimmed hedges of the maze. 'How are you enjoying your training here?'

'It's fine. You can't beat the French at this business.'

'And your French?'

'It's adequate,' Foster told him.

'You know why I'm here, of course?'

'Of course,' Foster said. 'Bilderberg.'

'Did you know about Bilderberg when you applied for this job?'

Foster shook his head; nothing the analyser could do about that.

'When did you find out?'

'A week or so ago.'

'An impressive guest list for a trainee manager.'

'A challenge,' Foster replied.

'For me too,' Anderson said grinning. 'Okay, Mr Foster, thanks for your time. Take care.'

Anderson advised Gaudin, the proprietor, to suspend two members of the staff with criminal records, and one who had been seen in the company of members of an urban guerrilla movement in Paris.

Gaudin had once been an Olympic fencing champion, individual foil. He was now middle-aged, commanding quiet authority and distant charm, a former head waiter at Maxims, who was now acknowledged to be one of the best hoteliers in France. Gaudin was honoured by Bilderberg's choice, but not overwhelmed like his co-directors.

He pointed at a pile of correspondence from his fellow directors on his desk. 'The excitable French, the foreigners' conception of us.' He spoke in English.

'What's worrying them?' Anderson asked, easing his bulk into a Louis Quatorze chair.

'Security mostly.'

'You can't blame 'em. It worries me.'

'You don't look as though anything ever worries you.'

'Thirst does,' Anderson said.

Gaudin, dressed in a neat charcoal-grey suit, opened a refrigerator cased in walnut. 'A glass of wine? An aperitif?'

'A beer would be fine.'

'As you please.' Gaudin poured a beer and a glass of white wine for himself.

Anderson drank some beer and spread a plan of the château on the desk. 'One of our biggest headaches is where we're going to house the delegates.'

'I'm sure you have some ideas,' Gaudin remarked.

'Only from experience.' Anderson consulted a notebook. 'I assume there will be no other guests?'

'Correct. We had sufficient warning to refuse all bookings for this period.'

'Okay, heads of state in the best suites. Adjoining spare room for those who bring their own security guards. At Torquay, Helmut Schmidt brought his own German shepherd guard dogs. Do you have kennels, Monsieur Gaudin?'

Gaudin nodded. 'And stables if anyone brings their own horses.'

Anderson grinned: he and Gaudin understood each other; one of the main hurdles already vaulted.

'And the former United States Secretary of State travels with his own security. At least he did in Torquay. They fitted the locks with gadgets to stop the hotel keys working and blocked the fire exit. The guards were hopping mad because the British police wouldn't let them tout their guns around the town.' Anderson drank some beer. 'What's your total staff?'

'At the moment a hundred-and-twenty-three.'

'Do you expect it to change?'

'The figure? No. But hotel employees change all the time.'

'We can cope with that,' Anderson said. 'How many live out?'

'About fifty.'

'They live in the village?'

'About forty of them I should say. The rest in Etampes.'

'I'd like to know who lives where.'

Gaudin nodded. 'Very well, it shall be done.'

Anderson made some notes. 'Now what about entertainment? Anything special laid on for the Bilderbergers?'

'Nothing much,' Gaudin told him. 'They like to keep

themselves to themselves. But we do throw a cocktail party. Whenever we have a conference, Jules the barman comes up with a special cocktail. This time it will be the Bilderberg Special. Frankly,' Gaudin said, 'I think it's the same mixture every time.'

'Like Bilderberg,' Anderson remarked. He prodded the plan with one finger. 'Another thing – we've got to be diplomatic. Representatives of various countries in blocks if possible. Friends close by and enemies apart. I happen to know some of their likes and dislikes. In a few cases it might be tactful to make their rooms . . . accessible.'

'I understand,' Gaudin said. 'We French have an advantage in these matters. Or so the world believes. They also believe we are a nation of thinkers. How does that explain some of the drivel that our politicians talk?' He reached across the desk and poured the rest of Anderson's beer for him. 'You seem to have an extraordinary knowledge of our guests' habits, Monsieur Anderson.'

'My job.' Anderson consulted the plan again. 'Another thing,' he said. 'The most important guests on the west side.'

'The most expensive side,' Gaudin commented.

'Sure – and the safest. Open fields in front of them. Any vantage points for a sniper lie to the east.'

'Do you think it's possible that anyone might try?'

'What amazes me is that no-one's tried before.'

'We share the same nightmare.'

'As for a certain Mr George Prentice,' Anderson said, 'you can house him in the east wing. In the most vulnerable position.'

Gaudin looked surprised. 'Any particular reason?'

'A private one,' Anderson said. 'I just don't happen to like the guy.'

'I shouldn't have thought you were the sort of person to allow personal feelings to interfere with your job.'

'They don't. It's just that if someone's got to get shot it might as well be Prentice.'

* * *

That afternoon, the man who had once been known as Jacques Bertier, gazed across the meadows from his cosy bachelor apartment above the *tabac* in the village in the direction of the château and thought: 'Only six more weeks.'

He could scarcely believe that the time had almost come. For revenge. For the chance to rid the world of the elite of Capitalism. Heads of State, bankers, financiers, heads of family dynasties.

Filth!

Excitement and hatred expanded inside him. He began to shiver and went to the sideboard where there was an array of bottles. He poured himself a rum and tossed it down his throat. Then another; the shivering subsided.

He lit a cigarette and returned to the window. In the sunlight he could just see a corner of the château. A haven for the rich and the privileged. But never again, not after the conference. No-one would ever stay at a hotel where a hundred guests had been killed. And there was no way those guests could escape. No way at all: he had planned their destruction for too long.

From the other window of the apartment he had observed the black American security officer inspecting the village, wandering through the gravestones to the church. He looked dangerous, but there was nothing he could do. No way he could combat the unknown.

Jacques Bertier, snugly established in his new identity, accepted now that his twin brother, Georges, would not have implemented the plan. Poor Georges had been limited to words and violent tantrums. That scene on the road near the hotel in Mégève . . . Georges and his little band had never stood a chance of reaching the hotel and Georges had known it all along.

Not that Jacques' new awareness diminished his feeling for his lost twin. Georges had meant well; but he had only possessed one side of their character. His death had been preordained – to rectify the accident of conception that had led to twin births. Now they were one, calculating and controlled.

He crossed the room, furnished with shabby but homely furniture, and went into the bedroom. From beneath the brass-bedstead he pulled the tin trunk. He unlocked the padlock, lifted the heavy lid and surveyed the contents that his brother had looted from the battlefields of World War II.

A German helmet. Luger pistol. Swastika armband. Ammunition belt from an MG 34 light machine-gun. A German flag. The field-grey arm of a jacket perforated by a hole, rimmed with a brown stain.

And the rifle – a Karabiner 98K rifle fitted with a telescopic sight. He stroked the long barrel of the rifle lovingly, thrust the butt into his shoulder and, standing well back from the window, peered through the sight.

In a bedroom in the visible corner of the Château Saint-Pierre, a middle-aged man in a blue dressing-gown opened a window and began to breath deeply.

He pulled the trigger of an unloaded gun. Click! The man in the dressing-gown closed the window and disappeared from sight, unaware that he had just been shot.

That was the only window of the château he could see from the apartment. Not that it mattered. He had found a really beautiful vantage point to be utilised when the time came. He replaced the rifle and caressed the prize trophy that lay at the bottom of the trunk, the long green box. His hand lingered on the box and he smiled.

But before he used its contents he would use the rifle. Just one bullet. A diversionary tactic with a bonus: he would be able to stand back and watch their futile attempts to escape the inevitable. Count the hours, the minutes. . . .

Tonight he would move the trunk to the cellar of a deserted farmhouse eight miles from the village, in case the police searched premises in the village.

A knock at the door.

He called out: 'Just a minute,' locked the padlock and pushed the trunk back under the bed.

He opened the door and a plump woman with impossibly-black hair came in and kissed him – as she might once have kissed Georges.

'Did anyone see you?' he asked.

'Only the old crone in the *tabac* and she is well paid to keep quiet,' said the woman, who was the wife of the innkeeper down the street. 'But it's a nerve-wracking business. A little drink perhaps?' sitting on the sofa.

He gestured at the bottles on the sideboard. 'You know I always have a good stock. What would you like?'

'Cognac?'

'*D'accord.*'

As he poured the brandy, and another rum for himself, she said: 'And what have you been doing with yourself?'

'Not much.'

'You never do.' She swallowed the cognac. 'Do you fancy –'

He smiled. 'What do you think?'

In the bedroom she freed her heavy breasts from her brassiere, sighing like a woman removing too-tight shoes. 'I've been thinking,' she said as she attended to her slip and stockings. 'On your days off, before I come up that is, you should find something to occupy yourself. You know, something really exciting.'

'Funny you should mention that,' he said, reaching for her. 'I was just thinking that myself.'

* * *

In his room in the annexe Nicholas Foster wrote out his notes for the day. Starting with the sweep with metal detectors and concluding with his own interrogation by Anderson.

It was his intention to present one newspaper with a complete dossier on Bilderberg and to whet their appetites with a sensational hard news story. He had decided to give his old editor on the Sunday paper first refusal; in a few weeks time he would write to him advising him, without being explicit, that an exclusive story would be on its way. He would also give Lucas a few snippets that might find their way into the columns of the *Financial Times*.

Lucas had been very helpful. After Lucas had found out

the venue of the 1980 Bilderberg they had met in the same old pub near St Paul's Cathedral. The chimney hadn't been fixed and a high wind gusting through the streets of the City pumped smoke from the coal fire back into the saloon.

The barman placed two pints of bitter in front of them on the bar.

'Well,' Lucas said, 'did your father fall for it?' He poured beer down his throat; Foster watched his prominent Adam's apple bob up and down.

'He welcomed me back into the fold with open arms. "So you've seen the light at last," he said. "We'll make a hotelier out of you yet." '

'Don't like him much, do you?'

'I like him more than I used to. I feel sorry for him; he's a captive of his own hidebound values. I think he probably got like that after my mother died.'

'I'm sure he doesn't feel sorry for himself.'

A particularly acrid cloud of smoke billowed out of the chimney enveloping the customers – bank clerks, messengers, detectives from Snow Hill – eating bar snacks washed down with beer or Spanish wine.

Foster said: 'Anyway, he was delighted that I wanted to learn the hotel trade. And quite happy that I should start in the Château Saint-Pierre. I suppose it wouldn't have been good for his image to have a greenhorn twenty-eight year-old son in one of his own hotels.'

'Mmmmm.' Lucas ordered two more pints. 'It's your image you've got to work on now. You'll stick out like a sore thumb and the security police will check you out. You'll have to shed your journalistic past.'

'I've thought of that,' Foster said. 'Do you fancy a snack by the way?' When Lucas shook his head he ordered a plate of macaroni cheese and said: 'They'll approach my father, of course. I'll warn him in time. He'll be quite willing to forget that I was ever a journalist.'

'What about the bylines you had when you were abroad?'

'I'll have to risk them. I worked for an agency and not many papers used my name.'

'American papers?'

'I doubt it. They mostly take AP or UPI anyway.'

Foster began to eat his macaroni cheese. A lot of macaroni, very little cheese.

Lucas ordered two more halves, handing the barman their tankards, both of which were much more than half empty. The barman raised his eyes to the heavens and filled them up.

'They'll put you through the police computer, of course,' Lucas remarked. 'Anything there?'

'Only a couple of fines for speeding. All part of the playboy image.'

'Credit cards?'

'American Express and Visa. All paid up.'

'What about your income tax returns and National Insurance contributions in this country?'

Foster pushed aside his plate of macaroni, half-eaten. 'I've thought about that too,' he said dabbing his lips with a napkin. 'There's not a hell of a lot I can do about them. But we're talking as two people who *knew* that I was a journalist. There's no reason why anyone at the Château Saint-Pierre should ever suspect that I was. If I play my cards right – and my father plays his – they'll accept that I was a layabout. Anyway,' he said, 'it wouldn't be much fun if there weren't any risks.'

'Like a bullet in the head from a trigger-happy security guard.'

Foster patted his good leg. 'Or another one there to even things up.'

Lucas pounced on the remark like a terrier and said: 'You'll have to have a convincing reason for that, too,' and Foster thought what a bloody good journalist he must be and hoped the *Financial Times* appreciated him.

He said: 'A motor-cycle accident – when I was speeding.'

Lucas finished his beer, beaky face alive and alert *despite all that beer!* 'A scar from a bullet wound doesn't look much like a scar from a motor-cycle accident.'

Foster drummed his fingers on the bar. 'Right, as always. How about an accident with a spear-gun while under-water fishing? Part of my dissolute past . . . somewhere on the Greek islands, perhaps.'

'Better,' Lucas said, picking up his briefcase. 'Much better. You'll make a spy yet. By the way, as soon as you can get your hands onto a guest list you might let me have a copy. There'll be the usual crowd, I suppose. Rockefellers, Rothschilds, a smattering of blue-blooded English financiers. . . . It's the newcomers that interest me,' Lucas said as he made for the door. 'Keep in touch.'

Foster had mailed Lucas a copy of the guest list he had *borrowed* from Gaudin's office shortly before he had been interrogated by Anderson. He inserted his own copy into the file containing his notes. The notes were also in duplicate – one copy to be kept in his room, one copy to be posted daily to an accommodation address in London.

He lay down on his bed in the small, barely-furnished room and read through his latest observations.

Suspect members of staff, including myself, vetted by black American Secret Service agent named Anderson – a redoubtable opponent who might have given Muhammad Ali a run for his money. Used some type of lie detector. (Check this out.) Assume I escaped detection because, being a journalist, I was able to anticipate the questions. . . .

. . . . Other security police arriving for preliminary check. Suspect friction between Anderson and French. Gallic temperament etc. . . .

As background material, it was adequate. But what I have to do when the time comes, Foster thought, is find out what happens *outside* the conference chamber.

And to present that credibly he would also have to obtain verbatim reports on the deliberations *inside* the chamber. There was only one way to achieve that – bugs.

He picked up his ballpoint pen and appended a footnote to his day's observations. *What a story if there was an assassination attempt!*

*   *   *

The following day was a long and tedious one for **Owen Anderson**. It rained, and the few guests at the hotel stayed in and got in his way and asked awkward questions. Then an FBI agent who had come direct from a course on electronic surveillance arrived and trailed around after him making suggestions, while Anderson, who reckoned that he was, if nothing else, unbeatable in that particular field, found difficulty in controlling his temper.

At 10.30 in the evening he escaped from the guests and the FBI man – he had contemplated planting a bug in his bedroom – and retired to the bar which was empty.

The barman, Jules Fromont, was mixing a cocktail.

Jules was famous for his cocktails. He was a quick, neat man in his late forties and was popular with guests because he adapted to their personalities. He could share the maudlin grief of a man with an unfaithful wife; he could swap stories with the breezy extroverts; he could discuss politics or religion or sport. Or he could keep quiet. His only concession to his own personality was a theatrical manner with the cocktail shaker.

Anderson sat down on a stool.

'What can I get you, m'sieur?'

'God knows. What's that?' pointing at the cocktail shaker in Jules' hands.

'A Saint-Pierre Special.'

'A bit late, isn't it?'

'One of the guests asked me last night to mix him one as a night-cap. But you're very welcome. . . .'

'Okay,' Anderson said, 'I'll try it. Add a slug of bourbon while you're at it.'

Jules looked affronted. 'There's already bourbon in it, m'sieur.'

While the barman concluded his act with the cocktail-shaker, Anderson looked around him. It was the first time he had been in the bar. He examined the engraved mirrors behind the bottles and ran his finger along the deep-shining mahogany counter.

'From a café in the gardens of the Palais Royal,' Jules said, nodding towards the counter.

'It's got style.' Anderson picked up his drink. 'Here's mud in your eye.' He smacked his lips appreciatively. 'Is this the Special you're going to serve to the Bilderbergers?'

'Something similar,' Jules said reprovingly. 'I have been known to vary the recipe. . . .'

'Sorry,' Anderson said. 'Can I buy you a drink?'

'I'll take a glass of Vichy water, m'sieur. I don't touch alcohol when I'm working.'

'I guess this conference is going to test your ingenuity,' Anderson said, taking another sip of his Special.

'I think I shall be able to cope,' Jules said.

'Around twenty nationalities. That's a lot of different brews.'

Jules Fromont shrugged. 'Most of them drink Scotch anyway. It's just a question of knowing the brands. Malt whisky for the English aristocrats, J and B or Cutty Sark for the Americans, a drop of Jamiesons or poteen for the Irish. . . .'

'Do the staff drink here?'

'No, m'sieur, they have their own bar in the annexe.'

'I'll take another of those,' Anderson said, pushing his glass across the bar and, as Jules mixed the cocktail: 'Many drinkers among them?'

Jules smiled. 'Show me the Frenchman who doesn't drink wine and you show me an imposter.'

'But they're not all French,' Anderson remarked. 'The trainee manager for instance, he's a limey.'

'I beg your pardon, m'sieur?'

'Foster, he's an Englishman.'

'Then, of course, he drinks warm beer.'

'He seems a pleasant enough guy. Any idea what he did before he came here?'

'No, m'sieur. I think he is that breed of Englishman who doesn't do very much until it is almost too late.'

They eyed each other across the bar. Then Anderson said: 'This doesn't fool you one little bit, does it, Jules?'

'M'sieur?'

'All this small talk.'

Jules gestured eloquently with his hands.

'I'll be honest with you,' Anderson said. 'I need your help.

Always consult the barman, one of life's unwritten rules.'

'And in your profession the chambermaid?'

'Right,' grinning. 'I know all about you and I reckon I can trust you.' He consulted a black notebook. 'Born 1932, went to school at Saint Christophe en Brionnais in Burgundy. Good wine there, huh, Jules?'

'And poultry and meat,' Jules said.

'And you've worked here for three years. Do you want to hear any more?'

Jules shook his head.

'I want you to keep your ears open. More indiscretions are committed in bars than beds, contrary to popular opinion.'

'And –'

'You will be suitably rewarded. How does five hundred dollars grab you?'

'With pleasure, m'sieur!'

'Half now, half when the conference is over.' Anderson slid 250 dollars across the bar and left.

Jules Fromont stared at the money for a moment. Shrugged and slipped it into the inside pocket of his blue jacket.

He was just finishing his mineral water when the guest who had ordered the Special came in. He was a Frenchman, and he worked for the security section of SDECE.

'I was just mixing your drink, m'sieur,' Jules said, reaching for the shaker.

The Frenchman sat on the stool vacated by Anderson and said: 'This bar, it's beautiful. I meant to remark upon it last night.'

'From a café in the gardens of the Palais Royal,' Jules said, giving the shaker a final dramatic flourish.

XIV

The muscular young man was still in hot pursuit of the girl in the swimming pool.

Lying in the black marble bath, Claire Jerome gazed at him – and thought of Pete Anello, now waiting for her in London while she tied up some business deals prior to the meeting at the Château Saint-Pierre.

Her thoughts warmed her with the sort of pleasure that she would not have thought possible a year ago. Since the night in the Bahamas, when they quarrelled about armaments – the night when the envelope containing his birthdate had been delivered (still a mystery) – their relationship had developed wonderfully. He didn't intrude into her business life but he was nearly always around. He even wore suits without looking as though he wanted to tear them off.

There were, of course, still those shark-fins of danger just below the surface. Their age difference for one. But dieting, exercise and her mental approach to life kept her young. Not to mention Anello himself.

The far greater peril was Anello's principles which, since the Bahamas, he had kept sublimated. What, she wondered stepping out of the bath, would he have made of the extraordinary deal that had been negotiated the previous day?

Claire Jerome had never been troubled by a conscience in her business dealings. She always invoked the arguments of arms manufacturers throughout the ages: weapons maintained a balance of power. And: 'If I don't provide them someone else will.'

'If Britain had been adequately armed in 1939, World War II might never have happened,' she was fond of pointing out.

Nor did she have misgivings about the business practices involved in her calling. The purchase of arms was usually controlled by a few influential people; for security reasons the deals were often secret; it was therefore inevitable that commissions, inducements – 'Bribes if you like' – had to be offered.

'Why not? If we don't oil a few palms, then the French, Swedes or British, not to mention the Russians, will walk right in there.'

And: 'Right, I agree, I'm also out-bidding American firms. So, what's so goddam wrong about that? Competition's healthy. I provide employment for thousands of men and women. Do you want me to let them starve?'

She had been involved in many such arguments since the Lockheed and Northrop scandals in the mid-seventies and the subsequent revelations that, in five years, fifty of America's largest corporations had paid out a hundred million dollars.

The results of the scandals – and the size of America's arms commitment to Iran – had been the Humphrey Bill of 1976–77, designed to control the outflow of arms.

Like other arms dealers, Claire Jerome negotiated the Bill smoothly. Congress could now halt sales of weapons worth more than 25 million dollars – except under extraordinary circumstances.

Extraordinary circumstances proliferated. And as the bill specified that nothing should 'impair the U.S. competitive position in foreign arms sales' business was much as usual.

Although one of the 'extraordinary circumstances' was abruptly terminated when the Shah of Iran was overthrown. Then the arms manufacturers had to find other outlets. Among them Saudi Arabia which, in 1976, had already bought 2½ billion dollars worth of arms from the U.S.

Now, according to two men who visited Claire Jerome in her New York office on Madison Avenue, Arabs were hoping to buy wire-guided missiles and conventional weapons manufactured by Marks International.

There Claire's conscience baulked.

She was Jewish and she had never sold arms to Arabs. Not even to Saudi Arabia, even though its attitude to Israel was less belligerent than its neighbours. Once the arms had been delivered, she argued, they could be handed over to Israel's immediate enemies.

The two visitors were diplomats from the Israeli Embassy in Washington. One named Eyal was a first secretary in the Chancery division, the other named Bein was an assistant armed forces attaché.

Although Claire at first didn't realise it, the two men were re-enacting a scene similar to that played nearly forty years ago when two American intelligence agents had visited her father, now a frail eighty-year-old.

Except that these two visitors had no desire to conduct their sort of business in her office: these days the only safe place to talk was the open-air.

Eyal was stocky and intense; Bein was taller with a face that looked as though it had been stamped indelibly by the sun over the Sinai desert.

'Very well,' she said when they told her they wanted to leave the office. 'But where?'

'Nowhere in particular,' Eyal told her. 'We'd just like to take a walk.'

With Claire in between the two men, they strolled in the spring sunshine down Park Avenue like tourists bewildered by the bustling lunch-time crowds.

Claire guessed that the two men represented Israeli intelligence, probably its third arm, Mossad, the external agency, more explicitly known as the Central Institute for Information and Espionage.

As they waited for the lights to change to WALK on one of the fifties, Bein said: 'You have been a good friend to Israel, Mrs Jerome.'

'Of course. Could it be any other way?'

Bein waited until they had crossed the street before he told her that she would soon be approached to see if she would be willing to supply arms to Arabs – the Saudis.

'Whoever's going to make the approach must be crazy,' she snapped.

'Not necessarily. Throughout history, arms dealers have sold their wares to friend and foe.'

'This is different for God's sake. I *am* Jewish.'

'Someone will provide those arms, Mrs Jerome,' Eyal said.

'But not me.'

Bein continued as though she hadn't spoken. 'The request will be for your new machine-guns that fire eight hundred .380 bullets in a minute, weigh only four pounds and have a revolutionary silencer. The perfect weapon for a terrorist.'

'And your latest wire-guided missiles,' Eyal added.

'So? Why are you telling me all this? You surely don't want me to supply them.'

'As a matter of fact,' Bein said softly, 'we do.'

Claire Jerome stopped walking. 'Is this some sort of a hoax?' Passers-by glanced at them with mild interest; a row was always stimulating, especially when it involved a beautiful woman who looked as if she had walked out of the pages of *Vogue*.

Bein took her arm. 'Let me explain,' he said. 'According to our information the man who will approach you is Mohamed Tilmissan.'

'That bastard!'

Tilmissan was a Lebanese who, when the Arabs began to flex their muscles, had made a fortune negotiating deals with the West. With the millions he had made, he had become a multi-national salesman owning banks, real estate, hotels. For his personal convenience he had acquired a jet airliner, a yacht, homes in the business capitals of the world, and the companionship of the world's reigning beauties.

He saw himself as the leader of the Arab crusade founded on oil. He had helped them re-discover their pride: now he had to help them destroy the enemy. Israel.

'Yes,' Eyal said, 'that bastard.' His voice had taken on a new bitterness.

Bein, who was clearly the senior of the two, told Claire: 'Tilmissan will approach you very soon. He will tell you that the arms are destined for Saudi Arabia –'

'And I –'

'Please let me finish, Mrs Jerome. We believe he will also suggest a way by which you can achieve this without invoking the fury of every decent-thinking Jew in the world. In short, the overt destination of the arms will be Pakistan.'

Eyal took over the story as they turned into Paley Park, the tiny oasis on 53rd, where cascading water muted the roar of traffic. 'Mr Tilmissan,' he said in his still-bitter voice, 'is an enterprising man. As soon as the Soviets invaded Afghanistan, he saw the possibilities of its neighbour, Pakistan. In fact, Pakistan has become the Eldorado of arms dealers. As I'm sure you are aware. . . .'

'I don't understand,' Claire said flatly, sensing Eyal's hostility – the familiar attitude to Merchants of Death.

Bein said quietly: 'Of course you don't, Mrs Jerome.' He was the soldier, Claire thought, with his harsh, dark features – ironically just like the history-book picture of a Bedouin – and yet officially he was the diplomat. 'Of course you don't. No-one expects that you should.'

They stood for a moment absorbing the peace that splashing water conveys. A businessman carrying an umbrella in one hand and a dripping hamburger in the other sauntered past; a girl with fashion-model looks smiled at them. What a beautiful day, her smile said.

Bein said: 'The point my colleague is trying to make is that Tilmissan now uses Pakistan for his own purposes. Of course he supplies a few arms to the Pakistanis, but basically there's no call there for a middleman.'

'I still don't see –'

'You will. So we now have a situation where, to save your face, arms intended for Saudi Arabia are apparently being dispatched to Pakistan. You understand that?'

'Of course.'

'How would you transport your merchandise to Pakistan, Mrs Jerome?'

Claire shrugged. 'By sea. There are several possible routes. . . .'

'Only one in this case,' Bein told her. 'Tilmissan will ask you to freight them across the States and ship them from the East Coast, across the Atlantic, through the Mediterranean and down the Suez Canal.'

'Except,' Eyal interrupted, 'that they won't get farther than Port Said. Tilmissan has a set-up there. They will be off-loaded and transferred to another ship.'

'And shipped to Saudi Arabia?'

For a moment neither of them answered. When Bein spoke his voice was taut. 'No, Mrs Jerome, to the Palestinians.'

As she began to protest he took her arm again and led her out of the park, back into the bustle of Madison Avenue.

'You see,' Bein said as they began to walk back in the direction of her office, 'Mr Tilmissan is a very devious gentleman indeed.'

'But no match for you two gentlemen. Can you please explain why I should sell arms to Pakistan which I believe are going to Saudi Arabia but are, in fact, going to the Palestinians?'

'Yes, Mrs Jerome, I believe I can,' Bein said. 'Tilmissan will ship the arms from the East Coast – we're not sure where yet – on his own boat. We,' dropping any pretence that they were conventional diplomats, 'have three men on board that ship. Your arms, Mrs Jerome, will be doctored en route to Port Said. So in a way you will be emulating your father. Years ago he undertook valuable work for the Allies in World War Two. I don't know if you are aware of the details, but what he did was to manufacture sub-standard weapons for the Germans. What we are asking you to do is not so very different.'

'The men on board the ship are weapons experts,' Eyal said. 'They also hold Lebanese passports. And they are aware of certain deficiencies in the first batch of machine-guns off your assembly lines which were written off.'

'You're nothing if not thorough,' said Claire, who had exhausted her reserves of surprise.

Eyal said: 'We have to be. We are a small nation.'

Bein said: 'On board the ship, the process by which the faults in those first guns was corrected will be reversed. It is a fairly simple procedure, I believe.'

'What about the missiles?'

Eyal said: 'That, too, is comparatively simple.' He smiled thinly. 'The guns will blow up in the Palestinian's faces. The missiles may well back-track on them as well.'

They stopped outside Claire's offices in a modest high-rise near the IBM Exhibit Center. 'I think,' said Claire, 'that we should walk a little more.'

'As you please,' Bein said. They crossed 57th. 'You must have a lot of questions.'

'An understatement.' They threaded their way through a party of thick-bearded orthodox Jews sightseeing. Rubbing shoulders, in all probability, with fanatical Arabs. Pick a conflict and you could find its participants in Manhattan. 'One question in particular comes to mind. Why me? Why did Tilmissan pick on a Jewish arms dealer?'

'Because we paved the way,' Bein told her. 'He has been persuaded that you are cast in the mould of the great Sir Basil Zaharoff, who at the turn of the century was quite happy to sell arms to friend and foe. As you know, Mrs Jerome, unlike that other celebrated middleman, Adnan Khashoggi, Tilmissan is a militant.'

'Now he can afford to be,' Eyal said.

'And it will give him great pleasure,' Bein continued, 'to believe that he has persuaded a Jew to help the Arabs fight the Jews.'

Claire glanced at her watch. 'We'd better be getting back. I'll make a list of the other questions. There will be plenty of them, believe me.'

'One other matter,' Bein said as they re-crossed 57th. 'We would also like to buy some of your products. The Knesset has authorised the purchase of a considerable quantity of arms. In particular your new submachine-gun and wire-guided missiles.' A trace of humour in his voice.

'If I go along with your other plans?'

'No strings attached, Mrs Jerome. But I would remind you that, if you collaborate with us, you will be a heroine of the Israeli people. But, I'm afraid, an unsung one. If it became known that you were selling arms to the Arabs then my guess is that one dark night your factories would join the satellites circling the earth.'

They stopped outside her offices, three lunch-hour strollers parting company.

Claire had already decided to collaborate with the two

Israelis. One thing bothered her. 'Tell me,' she said, 'will one consignment of flawed arms really make so much difference to the final outcome of the struggle?'

It was Eyal who answered her. 'Oh yes, Mrs Jerome. You see the Arabs don't forgive or forget. And they won't forgive Mohamed Tilmissan for double-crossing them. You will be ridding Israel of a powerful enemy. You, Mrs Jerome, will be writing his death certificate.'

After she had bathed and dressed Claire called Anello in London to tell him that she was again going to see the President. No reply. No reason why there should be – it was mid-afternoon in England.

At 10 am she flew from La Guardia to Washington. At 2.15 she was in the Oval Office facing the President, successor to the big, even-tempered man she had met before.

He was smaller than she had imagined but, beneath the bright lights, radiating.

He looked physically fit but his features seemed to have been aged by awesome decision-making. The toothy smile, however, remained. He was dressed in a plain dark blue suit and a maroon tie.

An aide with pepper-and-salt hair and wary features, sat unobtrusively to one side.

The President smiled that smile and said: 'I'm afraid I can only spare you a few minutes, Mrs Jerome. I have rather a lot on my plate. . . .'

Claire said: 'I understand perfectly, Mr President.'

Which she did. She used up a day; this slenderly-built man consumed it. How, she wondered, could anyone have the stamina to cope with domestic matters dominated by the fuel crisis, the Confrontation over Afghanistan, the shift in relations with China, the hostages in Iran – and the campaign for Democratic nomination.

He gestured with one hand at the aide. A pre-arranged signal. The aide left the room, smiling faintly at Claire.

'You are, I believe, attending a conference in a few days' time. . . .' the President said.

'I've been invited to Bilderberg, yes.'

'Did my predecessor consult you about this?'

'He did.'

'I thought as much. Well, Mrs Jerome, I have a request to make and I imagine it is very similar to his. Unfortunately, Mr Danby cannot be here today. . . .'

The telephone buzzed. The President picked up the receiver. Claire glanced around. The Office didn't look all that different – except for the family photographs.

The President said: 'Tell him I'm busy right now, I'll call him back in fifteen minutes.' He replaced the receiver and continued as though there hadn't been an interruption: 'As you know better than I do, vital policies are discussed at Bilderberg meetings. This year, perhaps, more vital than ever before.' He leaned forward. 'After the conference, Mrs Jerome, I'd like to hear your views on them.'

'Of course, Mr President. But. . . .'

'Yes, Mrs Jerome?'

'Surely there are more important people there than myself.'

'Importance is in the eye of the beholder, Mrs Jerome. I won't insult your intelligence to suggest that you will be the only guest who will be considerate enough – and patriotic enough – to confide in me. The point is that you are a specialist. You will be in a unique position to judge the trend in supply and demand of weaponry. Those trends will tell us a lot, Mrs Jerome, and when you return I have no doubt that Mr Danby will be here to assimilate them.'

He stood up; the smile returned. The meeting was over.

Mohamed Tilmissan called her half an hour after she had got back to her apartment in New York. He had, he said, a proposition to make to her. Would she care to join him on his yacht anchored off Corfu?

Claire accepted the invitation; but when she replaced the receiver she wondered if anyone had eavesdropped. The two Israeli agents had heightened her awareness.

Supposing, for instance, Stephen Harsch knew that she planned to deal with an Arab middleman.

* * *

Tilmissan said: 'You have me at a disadvantage, Mrs Jerome, I am more used to catering for the tastes of male arms dealers,' gesturing towards two tanned hostesses with long legs and plump breasts.

'You'll have to adapt, Mr Tilmissan. It's a woman's world as well as a man's today.'

Tilmissan smiled. 'Not in the Arab world.' He snapped his fingers and one of the hostesses walked across the lounge of the 85-foot yacht Tiffany, pushing a trolley bearing a bottle of champagne in a silver ice-bucket and two slender glasses.

Tilmissan said: 'I pretend it's not alcohol. Do you care for champagne, Mrs Jerome?'

'Champagne will be fine.' She studied the small, dapper man sitting opposite her. He radiated suppressed energy and his manicured hands were never still. He wore a navy-blue brass-buttoned blazer and grey slacks.

Fifteen years ago Mohamed Tilmissan, the son of a dealer in precious stones, had been poised to enter the family business in Beirut after an education in England and the US, where he had studied at the Graduate Business School of New York University. But the now cosmopolitan young man had realised the far greater potential of another of the earth's riches. Oil.

He made his millions first through oil. Then from the arms and technology that the Arabs had suddenly found they were able to buy as they hiked the price of that oil.

Now he held sway in the feudal court of Saudi Arabia, all the other Arab states with money to spend and in the emporiums of the world's arms manufacturers, demanding payment from both vendor and purchaser. By the mid-seventies, if you wanted to deal with the Arabs you had to negotiate through Adnan Khashoggi or Mohamed Tilmissan.

For an hour Tilmissan and Claire Jerome had sparred verbally about the deal. As the scarlet-uniformed hostess poured the champagne, Tilmissan asked: 'Don't you feel any qualms about arming Arabs, Mrs Jerome? You are, after all, a Jew.'

'Why should I? According to you the Saudis want the

weapons to protect themselves. Against a possible uprising amongst their own people, against a possible threat from Iraq. . . .'

She sipped her champagne. She wondered if Pete Anello had ever crewed a yacht like the Tiffany, as elegant as the Royal Yacht Britannia, with its sculptured blue hull and cream funnels. The floor of the lounge was covered with white, wall-to-wall carpeting and furnished with antique furniture, a grand piano topped with silver candelabra and a TV equipped for video. Her own cabin had a mirror on the ceiling and she wondered how many salesmen had been persuaded to increase commissions beneath its heaving reflections.

Tilmissan watched her reflectively for a moment. Then he said: 'The Israelis don't have quite the same tolerant attitude towards the Saudis as yourself, Mrs Jerome.'

'I am a businesswoman. If I don't sell those arms someone else will.'

'I seem to have heard that argument somewhere before.'

'I am not here, Mr Tilmissan, to argue about the principles of dealing in arms. Do you want these guns and missiles or don't you?'

Tilmissan waved one hand eloquently. 'You're right, of course. Let's not waste any more time on moral issues. Who wants them?' He stood up. 'Perhaps a stroll on deck? None of my, ah, entertainments here will take the edge off your business instincts. Maybe I will be luckier with the aesthetic approach. Corfu is looking particularly beautiful today.'

And it was. A wall of green olive and cypress trees with a white house lodged half way up it; a few small yachts at anchor, the sky blue and the green water ruffled by a spring breeze.

From behind the trees came the sound of breaking crockery.

Claire looked at Tilmissan enquiringly.

'It's Easter Sunday tomorrow. Today the Corfiots hurl crockery from their upstairs windows. Don't ask me why,' hands spread wide. 'I can only tell you about Moslem celebrations. At midnight on Sunday an illuminated cross is switched on with the words *Christos Anesti* underneath it. Then fireworks.'

'Talking of fireworks. . . .'

Tilmissan thrust his hands into the pockets of his blazer. 'Talk away, Mrs Jerome.'

'How many guns do the Saudis want?'

'Of your very special guns? Something in the region of 30,000. And ammunition of course.'

'And wire-controlled missiles?'

'Five thousand,' Tilmissan said. He leaned over the rail and stared down at the sea. 'Not the biggest deal in the world but we have to consider the future.'

'Meaning?'

'I believe your plant at Los Angeles is geared to produce a revolutionary ground-to-air missile system.'

'You have good information, Mr. Tilmissan.'

'Of course, the best. I understand that the missiles reach unprecedented heights and that an enemy plane stands no chance whatsoever.'

'At the moment it doesn't. But, as you know, countermeasures are always discovered. It's the history of our business.'

'The French are also working on a similar system. But it looks as though Marks International is going to be first. The Saudis would also like to be the first nation in the Arab world to possess your system.'

'It's possible,' Claire said, listening to the smashing of crockery across the water.

'But of course we can wait for the French.'

'How much, Mr Tilmissan?' Claire asked abruptly.

'For myself a million dollars. A mere bagatelle.'

'More like poker,' Claire said.

'A million for me. Billions for Marks International. And I assure you I am not particularly interested in the million. I am interested in Arab pride. We are in the driving seat these days; we intend to stay there.'

'Then if it's the Arab cause that motivates you, why a million dollars? Why not five hundred thousand?'

Tilmissan clasped his hands together and smiled. 'I am an

Arab. Arab pride you see. And I can assure you, Mrs Jerome, you are not in a position to bargain.' His brown eyes searched her face. 'Tell me, what would your reactions be if one of your missiles shot down an Israeli plane?'

Claire turned away, stared at a shoal of silver fish approaching the yacht. Like marauding aircraft, she thought. 'I would grieve, of course. Just as I would grieve if it was shot down by a French missile.' She turned and faced the middle-man. 'A million dollars, Mr Tilmissan. Do we have a deal?'

He shook her hand. 'Very well. But I can assure you that it has been a unique experience for me doing business with a woman – and a Jew,' he added. 'And now some lunch?'

They went below deck to the dining-room where, on a rosewood table, a waiter served *dzadziki* and *dolmades*, *feta* and red mullet, and one of the hostesses, a Californian blonde, dispensed wine.

After lunch Claire Jerome retired to her cabin and for a long while stared at the face regarding her from the mirror on the ceiling. Then she slept.

While she was sleeping, the Californian girl rowed herself to the shore in a dinghy.

From a waterside hotel she made a long-distance telephone call, high heel of one white sandel tapping impatiently as the plump girl on the switchboard phlegmatically made the connection.

Then she closed the door of the booth tightly and spoke urgently into the receiver. 'The bitch has made the deal.'

* * *

Nathan Marks was watching television. An old black-and-white movie about the Second World War.

Nathan preferred the past to the present and frequently retired there. 'In the old days we had to beat the odds. These days it's all laid on a platter. . . .' Although he *was* optimistic about the new crises facing the United States.

He lived with two servants in a neat grey house, squeezed between two high-rise blocks in the eighty's close to Central

Park. He should, Claire knew, have retired years ago. But when the occasion demanded it he could still put in an appearance, snappy and bird-like, as President of Marks International, so long as Claire was there behind him like a belligerent attorney.

Sitting in a leather chair too big for him, the hump in his back thin and sharp beneath a worn, red-silk dressing-gown, he looked frail and brittle; like an autumn leaf, Claire thought, as she tidied the room, while on the television some long-forgotten star with boyish good looks garotted German sentries who were forever looking the wrong way.

Eventually wave after wave of American bombers flew in to finish the job and Claire switched off the set. Nathan leaned painfully back in the chair. 'Those were the days,' he said. His rheumy eyes focussed on Claire. 'But I tell you, things are beginning to look up again.'

'If recession is good news they are, papa.'

'Recession, recession. . . . The best thing that could happen. No-one ever built a fortune on prosperity. Look, the Germans played into our hands, now it's the Russians, so what's different? I tell you, Claire, this country needs a challenge. Already they're rising to it. And as for Marks International, a good time ahead, Claire. . . .' He noticed that Claire wasn't dressed for watching television; she wore a dark-green waisted suit and her hair had just been styled. 'You going someplace?'

'Dinner with Stephen Harsch,' she said. 'Business.'

'Harsch, huh? He's a smart boy.' Stephen Harsch was over forty-five. 'Something going between you two?'

'Sure there is. He wants my job,' said Claire, who hadn't slept with Harsch since the day she ordered him out of her apartment.

'Maybe the two of you could get something together. You should get married, Claire.'

She said affectionately: 'I married Marks International, papa,' and thought about Pete Anello.

She smoothed her father's wispy grey hair, folded the collar of his striped pyjamas over the dressing-gown. 'Anything I can get you, papa?'

'Feed something into that video gadget. I'll watch another movie and then go to bed.'

'Anything special?' As if she didn't know.

He told her *Citizen Kane*, but she was already fixing it. It was his favourite movie.

* * *

They dined in a small Italian restaurant fitted incongruously with lots of glass and stainless steel. She chose lasagne verde with meat sauce while Harsch, weight-watching, ate a fillet steak with spinach, and ordered a bottle of Barolo.

The conversation was strained; not only did he resent her power with Marks International but he still smarted from his peremptory dismissal as her lover. He was clever and zealously youthful but, as far as sex equality was concerned, old-fashioned.

'You know something, Stephen,' she said as he re-filled her glass with wine, 'you try too hard.'

'Is that bad?'

'When it shows.'

'What's that supposed to mean?'

'You aren't thirty-five any more. Why try to act it?'

He straightened the knot of his fashionably thin grey tie; there was still a crisp determination about his features, but it looked strained. A mask that was slipping.

He sliced a morsel of steak and said: 'When I'm fifty maybe I'll admit to forty. A good age for promotion,' coming to the point of the dinner.

Claire drank some wine. 'Promotion to where?'

'Look,' he said, putting down his knife and fork, 'I know how you feel about your father. But it is time he retired. In fact, let's face it, he *is* retired.'

'In that case,' Claire said calmly, 'it doesn't matter, does it?'

'Okay, so you're the power behind the throne. But it's time you occupied that throne for everyone to see.'

'I haven't heard any complaints.'

'Perhaps you don't listen too much. There's a lot of ill-feeling in the boardroom. And elsewhere.'

'I remember the last time you said something like that. Father and daughter, as I recall it, won hands down on a proxy vote.'

'That was a hell of a long time ago. Things have changed.'

'No they haven't,' Claire said abruptly. 'And you haven't changed either, Stephen.'

'Oh yes I have. I'm more honest these days. Like I told you, I want to hustle along.'

'What would be the difference, Stephen? I'd be president and you'd be number two.'

'Better than number three,' Harsch said and, as a waiter hovered: 'What would you like to follow?'

'Cheese,' Claire said. 'And some more wine.'

Harsch said to the waiter: 'I'll take the fruit.'

When the waiter had gone Claire said: 'You don't really expect me to put my father out to grass, do you?'

'You've put it crudely, but he is eighty.'

'With an alert mind.'

'Let's stop kidding,' Harsch said. 'It's *your* mind.'

'You can forget it anyway,' Claire told him.

There was a pause while the waiter placed the cheese-board and a bowl of fruit on the table. Another waiter uncorked the new bottle of wine.

Harsch pared an apple carefully and began to speak. It sounded, Claire decided, like a rehearsed speech.

'Look, Claire,' he said quietly as the length of peel uncoiled from the apple, 'we've worked together for a long time now. Okay, so something went wrong a few years back. I don't know what the hell it was; maybe you can tell me. . . .'

Shaking her head, Claire said: 'Come to the point, Stephen.'

'Marks International needs strength at the top.'

Claire pointed to herself. 'It's got it.'

'You're in your forties, right? I guess that's not a smart remark to make to a woman. But we understand each other.'

'Oh yes,' Claire said, 'we understand each other all right.'

'As you get older it's going to get tougher.'

'So am I,' Claire said. She cut a slice of gorgonzola cheese and placed it on her plate.

'It'll be lonely up there.'

Claire nibbled a piece of cheese, washed it down with wine, then said: 'Stephen, are you proposing marriage for Christ's sake?'

'As a matter of fact I am.' The peel finally fell in a neat pattern on his plate and he began to slice the apple into quarters. 'Okay, so let's be honest, it might seem like a business arrangement. But I think we'd make out, Claire. I once thought we did. . . .'

Harsch's marriage had broken up years ago because for him it had been a convenience – according to the rules young executives were supposed to be married. After the break-up he had still been accepted because, it was said, his wife hadn't understood his ambition. And that was all Harsch had been left with, his ambition. Momentarily Claire felt sorry for him because she guessed that, occasionally, he glimpsed the lonely future. Yes, she thought, I understand that.

She pushed her plate aside and said softly: 'I'm sorry, Stephen, it wouldn't work. How could we leave the office, occupying the positions we do, and then go home and carry on as though we'd just returned from different jobs? It's my fault, I guess; I'm a tough old bird.'

'Just as you please.' His face was bleak. 'Now I'll put the alternative. You've got a fight on your hands, Claire. At the next Board-meeting there's going to be a motion to force your father to retire.'

'No way will it succeed.'

'You're wrong. You're out of touch. Perhaps you've been too occupied with your personal life.'

Claire's anger flared. 'Personal life means just that. KEEP OUT.'

'I respect that. I've no wish to compete with Mr Anello. . . . He's a nice guy, I'm told.'

'You were told right.'

'Coffee?'

She nodded. 'And cognac.'

'While you've been . . . otherwise occupied' – Harsch

smiled without humour – 'I've been looking into your figures.'

'Booming, huh, Stephen?'

'Sure they're booming. I see we've even exceeded our own expectations.' He reached into the inside pocket of his jacket and brought out a sheet of paper. 'I see we've doubled our quota of arms for Pakistan. A decision taken arbitrarily by yourself two days ago.'

The anger was replaced by fear, but she managed to say: 'Then the Board should be very pleased with me.'

'I wonder. . . .'

'What do you wonder, Stephen?'

Harsch waited until the waiter had brought the coffee and cognac. Then he said: 'I called Karachi this morning. They don't seem to know a goddam thing about it.'

The businesswoman accustomed to dealing with emergencies took over. She smiled at him. 'The President of the United States does, Stephen.'

But, she thought as she let herself into her apartment later that night, Harsch could check on that too.

XV

A sunny spring Sunday in London and Pete Anello was bored. All morning he had walked the quiet streets, listening to the church bells, feeding the pigeons in Trafalgar Square, riding a red double-decker bus, drinking his first pint of English beer and observing with awe other customers sinking pint after pint of the stuff, smiling at the nannies out with the children in the parks.

Central London was fine as it awoke slowly on a Sunday morning. But fully awake in the afternoon, it lost its dignity, even Park Lane where Claire Jerome owned an apartment. Street vendors selling Union Jacks and soft porn, garbage outside elegant portals, whores assembling for the evening trade.

He walked to Hyde Park Corner to listen to the orators shouting, pleading, gesticulating, lecturing on anything: Rhodesia, Women's Lib, the death penalty, the hazards of smoking.

'. . . . without the Merchants of Death the world would be a safe and decent place for your children to grow up in. . . .'

The speaker was small and shabby and fanatic, standing on a soapbox addressing an audience of five. Anello joined them.

'. . . but we can still win battles, ladies and gentlemen. We can fight their guns and bombs with our own weapon — the might and wrath of God.'

A small girl asked her mother: 'What's he talking about?'

Her mother shook her head. 'I don't know, dear. Some film called the Merchants of Death.'

'I think he's barmy,' said the girl.

The speaker thrust out his arms, a line of froth on his lips. 'What about the concussion bomb?'

'What about it?' asked a thin youth eating potato crisps.

'You, sir,' pointing at Anello, 'you look an intelligent human being. Do you know about the concussion bomb?'

Anello nodded. 'Sure.'

'Ah!' The speaker was ecstatic. 'An American. Am I right, sir?'

'Sure, I'm American.'

'And proud of it. So you should be.'

'Why?' asked the youth.

'Because they banned the concussion bomb, that's why. Am I right, sir?'

'We banned its sale to foreign countries.'

The orator shook his head in wonderment, overcome by such shared knowledge. 'I knew you were an intelligent man, sir. You're absolutely right. And do you know what that bomb could do? It could crush bodies. Crush them!' pounding one fist into the palm of his other hand.

The youth tossed away his empty crisp packet and said: 'They might have banned it. They also made the sodding thing.'

'But had the strength to cast it aside. There has to be a beginning. Now we have to unite our forces. President Carter gave the lead; it's up to us to follow.'

Anello strolled away. He walked across Hyde Park and lay down beneath an oak tree, using his denim jacket as a pillow.

The sun reached him through the budding leaves of the tree; children played on the new grass; lovers lay entwined in each other's arms.

Anello closed his eyes.

And the Viet Cong were stumbling out of the jungle, clothes blazing after the Napalm attack, and you could smell burning flesh and the young soldier beside him was screaming and running towards the burning men and the sergeant was shouting: 'Get your head down you, stupid fuck' but the soldier kept on running, throwing aside his Armelite rifle, and Anello knew he was going to die.

The previous night, lying in their sleeping bags in a tent ten miles behind the line, they had talked about what they would do when they got back to the States after the opera-

tion tomorrow, which would be the last for both of them. The young soldier, whose name was Dave Armstrong, had shown him pictures of his girl and told him he was going to study forestry at night school and get into Conservation, and Anello had said: 'You know, I might go along with you because I sure as hell haven't done anything with my life so far.'

And Dave Armstrong was shouting: 'For Christ's sake forgive us' as the machine-gun opened up from behind the flames and practically cut him in half, and Anello was cradling his head and the last thing the young soldier said was 'All those green trees' and died as the machine-gun spent itself, the last bullet hitting Anello in the belly.

Another gun fired. Beside him in the park. A cap-pistol brandished by a small boy wearing a green school cap. Anello leapt up and knocked the pistol from his hand.

The boy stared at him, then his lips began to tremble.

'Hey.' A middle-aged man wearing braces over a white shirt was running across the grass. 'Hey you, leave my kid alone.'

Anello put his hand to his forehead. 'I'm sorry.' He took a £5 note from his pocket and handed it to the boy; then he picked up the pistol and handed it back to him. 'I'm sorry, I guess I was dreaming.'

The man took the note from the boy and examined it as though he suspected a fake. He thrust it into his trouser pocket and said: 'You're drunk, mate, that's what's wrong with you,' taking the boy's hand and walking away.

Awake he could forget. Drift with the tides. Coast along to your destiny. Nothing mattered, not when a dream of green trees could be extinguished in a moment. But asleep you were defenceless and the smell of burning flesh was strong in your nostrils.

By the time he reached the apartment he was calming down. He stripped off his clothes and took a shower. Just a dream triggered by a crazy preacher on a soapbox.

He wandered naked into the living-room, oriental in style with an unbleached Berber carpet, walls covered with raw silk from Bombay, gold statuettes from Thailand on the glass-topped table, Chinese porcelain on the wall shelves. He poured himself a large measure of Scotch.

Without the Merchants of Death the world would be a safe and decent place for your children to grow up in.

So he was an ageing gigolo and his mistress was a Merchant of Death. He gulped the whisky to drown the self-disgust and stood at the window overlooking the park watching the children walking home in the gathering dusk.

When he went out later he was a little drunk. He winked at a black whore tottering along on six-inch high heels and went into a pub in Shepherd Market. It was more elegant than the pub he had visited in the morning, furnished in pastel colours. A Mayfair pub.

He ordered a pint of bitter to dilute the Scotch in his stomach, and surveyed the throng drinking hastily during the brief time it was permitted on a Sunday evening.

A woman came up to the bar and ordered a gin-and-tonic. In her late twenties with long dark hair, attractive.

A hooker? Anello, you're getting old. Girls go into bars by themselves these days.

She had a cigarette in one hand and was fumbling in her handbag. He lit a match and held it out for her. She looked surprised. But was she?

'Thank you,' she said with a trace of unidentifiable accent. There were more foreigners than British in London these days. She accepted the light and nodded; the incident seemed to be closed as far as she was concerned.

Anello said: 'On vacation?'

'No, business. And you?'

'Business. I'm here to sell concussion bombs.'

'An enterprising assignment.'

'You know what concussion bombs can do? Crush people like that.' Fist into palm. 'Like that. Pow!'

'You surprise me,' the woman said. 'I was under the impression that President Carter banned sales of the concussion bomb in seventy-seven.'

'So you know about the goddam bomb.'

'I read the papers.'

'Speaking of bombs,' he said, 'I guess I'm a little bombed

Can I buy you another drink? I'll stay with my beer.'

She looked at him speculatively for a moment. Then accepted.

Later, when they were sitting at a table in a corner of the bar, he said: 'I hope you don't think it was a pick-up. It was, I guess, but that's a hell of a way to describe a meeting. . . .' He wished he hadn't drunk so much whisky in the apartment.

'It was I who was fumbling for my matches.'

'My name's Anello,' he told her. 'Pete Anello.'

'Gretchen,' she said.

'German?'

'Austrian. From Innsbruck.'

'Do you like London?'

She shrugged.

'I guess you have to have someone to share it with,' he said.

She considered this. 'Are you staying at the Hilton round the corner?' as though that classified him.

'No, a friend of mine has an apartment in Park Lane.'

'A rich friend,' she remarked. 'Can't you share London with him?'

'Her. She's in New York. She flies in on Tuesday.' He wanted to add: 'So we have two days,' but he checked himself. Instead he said: 'What's your business in London?'

'Clothes. I'm sales manager for a firm in Innsbruck. We're trying to market Tyrolean styles over here. To be honest,' she said smiling, 'I don't think we stand a chance. Can you imagine an Englishman in leather shorts?'

'You've been to London before?'

'Many times. I went to school here.'

'I was wondering,' said Anello, pulling at his thick moustache, 'if you had any time to spare,' wishing again that he hadn't drunk so much Scotch, 'whether you might be able to show me around.'

'If you promise to wear leather shorts.'

'Sure, and play the piano accordian.'

She finished her drink. 'I have some work to do in the morning. Could I meet you at midday?'

'Where?'

'The Hilton – that's where I'm staying.'

The following afternoon he picked her up in the Jaguar he had rented and she directed him along the tourist routes – Buckingham Palace, Houses of Parliament, Law Courts, the Tower.

On the second evening Anello took her to dinner at Simpsons where they ate roast beef washed down with claret, and Anello confessed that he was consorting with the daughter of Nathan Marks, mistress of death. At the same time he confided his views on armaments `and their manufacturers.

'I don't know why the hell I'm telling you all this,' he added, sipping his wine.

'Because you've been waiting for a long time to tell someone.'

Then he told her about Vietnam. He had never told anyone else about Vietnam.

'One thing puzzles me,' Gretchen said. 'How can you stay with Claire Jerome if you feel as strongly as that about armaments?'

'Most of the time I try not to feel too strongly about anything.'

'But how long can you go on like that?'

'I don't know,' Anello said bitterly. 'I don't know. . . .'

They parted at midnight. A small kiss and a smile in the foyer of the Hilton and that was all. They had shared.

Back in the apartment, Anello slipped between silk sheets and fell asleep instantly, unaware that, Vietnam apart, the past two days had been the most momentous of his life.

*   *   *

She arrived at Heathrow at 2.50 pm. Tall, tanned, imperious, attracting immediate attention in a setting where tans, looks and assurance were commonplace.

She kissed him and he took her bags and led her to the Jaguar. 'Well,' Claire said as he drove through the tunnel leading to the Bath Road, 'how is London?'

'I've done the rounds. How was New York?'

'No change. I got through a lot of business.'

'Dirty business?'

She put her hand on his thigh. 'Not today, Pete.'

He put his foot down on the accelerator and the Jaguar surged past a British Airways bus.

In the apartment they went straight to bed and made love with abandonment. Brutally and tenderly, endearments and obscenities mingling hoarsely. The love-making of a man and woman sharing physical attraction tuned by practice. When he withdrew from her she lay back, eyes closed and said: 'Not bad for an old broad, huh?'

Beside them the cream telephone shrilled.

She picked up the receiver, listened for a moment, then said: 'Okay, I'll take the call in the other room,' and said to Anello: 'Sorry, business, not dirty business,' trying to smile.

She slipped into a robe and went into the lounge, closing the door behind her. She picked up the extension and said: 'Good evening, Pierre, what can I do for you?'

'Just a social call,' Pierre Brossard told her.

'That'll be the day.'

Pierre Brossard was Marks International's middleman in deals with Israel. Since Marcel Dassault, son of a Jewish doctor, survivor of Buchenwald, had sold his first Ouragon and Mystère fighter planes to Israel, there had always been a French connection; overt in the early days, latterly more circumspect.

'What's the weather like in London?' Brossard asked.

'It's great, Pierre, but you haven't called me to discuss the weather. Where are you calling from?'

'Paris.' A pause. 'And how was the weather in Corfu?'

Claire's hand tightened on the receiver. 'Why do you ask?'

His voice hardened. 'Was your deal with Tilmissan successful?'

'I was a guest on his yacht, nothing more.'

'Come now, Mrs Jerome, Tilmissan's yacht is a floating office. Everyone knows that. Was his commission as low as mine?'

So that was it. She said: 'There was no deal, Pierre.'

'That's not my information.' Brossard sounded as though he was enjoying himself. 'It will seem very odd to my Israeli clients to hear that you, a Jew, are supplying the enemy.' He paused. 'In fact,' Brossard said, spacing out the words, 'it will seem very odd to every Jew and Zionist in the United States of America. And, of course, very odd to the Arabs to hear that you are supplying their enemies with exactly the same weapons.'

'Blackmail, Pierre?'

'Not at all. Business. The sort of business that is concluded every day by the great powers. If you don't do this, if you don't sign this, if you don't withdraw your troops . . . we will cut off supplies of arms, oil, technology. *If* – the global unit of negotiation. Only the currency changes. Now America is playing the If Game – with grain.'

'And your *if*?'

'I have the draft of an article that you might like to see. I should like your comments. And possibly your suggestions for revisions.' His voice was silky. 'You might even decide to veto the article altogether.'

'What's the article?' *Bastard!*

'A treatise on the moral implications of a Jewish company supplying machine-guns and wire-guided missiles to both Jew and Arab. Plus a little speculation about a future deal involving the sale of a sophisticated ground-to-air missile system to the Palestinians.'

She stared at the telephone in her hand. Who had betrayed her? Tilmissan himself? A deal between the two middlemen? She waited until the first spurt of anger subsided.

She said quietly: 'I should like to see that article.'

'And so you shall. I believe we have both been invited to a château in France in a few days time. You can read it then.'

'Very well.' She waited for the inevitable.

'There will of course be a charge for reading the article.'

'How much?'

'Two million dollars,' Brossard said.

The line went dead.

Slowly Claire cradled the receiver. Then she went back to the bedroom. Pete Anello was lying on his side, hands clasped as though he were praying. He was asleep.

In the study of his house on the Avenue Foch, Pierre Brossard leaned back in his swivel chair smiling faintly. Then he wrote out a cheque for 2,000 dollars payable to the blonde hostess on Tilmissan's yacht.

He had one regret about the day's business. He should have called Claire Jerome collect.

XVI

Midas, fabled king of Phrygia, whose touch turned everything to gold, sat at the kitchen table wearing a frayed jacket and crumpled trousers.

It was Saturday. Nine days until Bilderberg. Nine days in which to complete preparations for the greatest espionage coup of all time: the destruction of the United States dollar.

Today, Brossard decided, he would compose the Midas column which would help to seal its doom.

'More coffee, Pierre?' his wife asked.

Brossard shook his head.

'Pierre?'

Brossard grunted, barely aware that she had spoken. These days their conversation was minimal; they faced each other across the breakfast table in the mornings, went their respective ways during the day, slept in separate rooms at night. She had never been pretty, but she had been *chic* in the Parisien way; now she was dumpy and her hair was thin and her complexion sallow.

'I need more housekeeping this week,' Simone Brossard said.

'Why?'

'Just this once couldn't you give me a few extra francs without asking why?'

'I'm a businessman. I have to know how my money is being spent. If I handed out money hand-over-fist without knowing why, we wouldn't be living the way we do.'

'Living? You call this living? A huge house – with only five rooms furnished. No staff –'

'You have Marie.' He looked at her curiously; it was unlike Simone to complain.

'Ah yes, Marie. I am grateful for Marie. A fat idle slut

who comes in twice a week and sweeps the dirt under the carpet. Thank you for Marie.'

'Why do you want extra housekeeping?'

'Because I have made some friends. Believe it or not, Pierre, I have some friends of my own. And I want to entertain them.'

Brossard crumbled a croissant between his fingers. 'Who are these friends?'

'Not men friends, I assure you. No man would look at me now; unless, of course, he thought he could find the key to the Brossard treasure chests. What a hope!'

'But who are they?'

'Just ordinary women. Five or six of us who like to get together every week and talk and maybe drink a little wine and eat a few cakes.'

Lesbians? Brossard wondered. No, not Simone. 'How long has this been going on?'

'Not long. A few weeks. Now it is my turn to entertain. I need some money. . . .'

'What do you talk about?' Brossard asked curiously, wary of the unknown.

'Everyday things. Our neighbours, our children – their children,' she corrected herself, closing her eyes for a moment. 'Our husbands.'

'I wonder what you have to say about me,' Brossard said.

She didn't reply, regarding him steadily.

He shrugged. 'How much do you want?'

'A thousand francs would help. I could buy some decent wine. Some pastries. . . .'

Brossard stood up and opened his briefcase on the chest of drawers behind him. He took out a wad of notes, selected a 500 and tossed it onto the table. 'I don't have to feed the five thousand,' he told her.

She stared at the bill, said quietly, 'Thank you. Pierre,' picked it up and put it with her shopping list. 'Strange,' she said, 'that you should have picked a Biblical reference to qualify your generosity.'

Brossard snapped the catch on the briefcase and moved

briskly towards the door. 'Why's that?' he asked, hand on the door-handle.

'Because we are a Bible group. We pray, Pierre.'

'God in heaven,' exclaimed Brossard. He shut the door firmly behind him, relieved that it was nothing more serious than Religion that had upset his wife's normal docility, and walked across the hall, footsteps echoing on the marble floor so loudly that he couldn't hear her sobbing in the kitchen.

But still, he thought as he took the cover off his old Remington typewriter in his bleakly furnished study, it was an opportune time to be gone, with a wife undergoing the irritating disturbances of the menopause.

He slid a sheet of paper into the typewriter, typed the date and slugged the sheet *dollar – 1*. Then he sat back, deliberating on how to incorporate in the column the results of his meeting the previous day with Paul Kingdon.

They had lunched at Rules, the elegant London eating house which had survived from a more dignified era: two aperitifs and you imagined you could hear the sound of horses' hoofs on cobblestones. They ate lemon sole and drank Chablis and, as always, Brossard was surprised at the excellence of English food, so long derided, and the comparative cheapness of good French wine. Although he suspected that the nuances of the palate were lost on Kingdon. Too rich too soon. Undertones of vulgarity in the aggressive cut of his suit, the rings – diamonds, of course – on two of his fingers, his sleek, sharp looks.

'And now down to business, eh, Paul?' as the waiter served black coffees and brandy.

Kingdon shook his head. 'You will have to excuse me. I am pathological about eavesdroppers. Electronic ones. We'll talk in the car.'

A company car was delivered to the door by a chauffeur who tipped his peaked cap and disappeared. Kingdon took the wheel; Brossard sat beside him. 'At least I know the car's clean,' Kingdon said as he steered the grey Bentley through the traffic. 'And I know you're clean.' He grinned and opened one hand, revealing a tiny bug alert. 'So we can talk. I've already thanked you for the invitation to Bilderberg. Now I can be more specific. Thank you for fixing it.'

Brossard shrugged eloquently.

'The microfilms on the newcomers to the conference are in my briefcase.'

'You're very efficient.' Brossard only needed information on two financiers in case they needed further persuasion; he didn't think it would be necessary. 'Do the microfilms include Kingdon Investments?'

'I suspect you have your own dossier, Pierre.'

'I do. Mayard can also be very efficient when he puts his mind to it.'

Kingdon seemed unperturbed. Crude but cool.

The Bentley accelerated down Whitehall, past Big Ben and the Houses of Parliament and over Westminster Bridge. The Bentley, Brossard reflected, was an example of calculated snobbery; there had always been a school that deemed the Bentley to be less ostentatious than the Rolls and Kingdon had joined it. A wasted effort – with Kingdon at the wheel even the Bentley seemed vulgar.

Brossard opened his own briefcase and took out Mayard's report on Kingdon Investments. 'I thought you might like to hear what Mayard has to say about your companies.'

'Is that the reason for your visit?'

'Partly,' Brossard said. He ran a finger down the figures on the first page of Mayard's report. 'Do you mind if I talk in dollars?'

'As you please. The way things are going we'll be papering the walls with them soon.'

The way things are going. . . . Odd, the subject broached already. But there was no way Kingdon could know; the details of Brossard's plan were known only to key members of the Politburo and the KGB, the Soviet Foreign Trade Bank and the Narodny Bank.

'The dollar is more resilient than people seem to imagine,' Brossard said carefully. 'It will need a powerful explosive to topple it. A financial nuclear device.'

Kingdon swung the wheel easily. They passed through

Kennington, then Brixton – 'London's Harlem,' Kingdon remarked.

Brossard said: 'You don't seem very curious, my friend.'

'What's the point? You'll tell me anyway.'

Brossard returned to Mayard's report. 'Kingdon Investments are not quite as buoyant as they might appear.'

'Aren't they? I'm always the last to know.'

'I think you know, Paul.'

'You tell me.'

Mitcham, Rose Hill, Banstead. Rain began to bounce on the Bentley's bonnet and spatter against the windscreen. They were in the countryside now and the houses were big and comfortable.

'Very well, Paul, I will.'

Brossard told him that in the ten years since Kingdon Investments had been in business they had bought shares totalling three billion dollars. And the total income – 'The *total* income, Paul,' – over that period has been nine *million* dollars. If you deducted the capital loss, the profit on the three billion was virtually nothing. Not good business, eh, Paul?' Brossard said.

'How do you explain that the value of each share has increased by sixty-three per cent?' Kingdon replied.

'I can explain it very easily, as I'm sure you can. Your sales managers are instructed to sell, sell, sell, whatever the market. If the market is buoyant, bullish, then now is the time to buy. "Get in while you can. See United Chemicals rose two cents yesterday, buy today, go with the market." But if the market is depressed the sales pitch is a little different.' Brossard smiled faintly and tapped the report on his knees with his finger. 'If the market is in a decline then the investor is told, "Now is the time. You are buying cheaply. The market has never been so good. Get in while you can. Buy, buy, buy."'

'So?'

'The market has been depressed lately but, on the advice of your salesmen, investors have been buying. That money was never invested. You have been able to spread that money that was never invested over the entire fund – and managed to keep its net asset value relatively high.'

'I'm a wizard,' Paul Kingdon said as they drove through the rain along the brow of Box Hill. Beneath them, towns and villages were veiled by the rain; in such small places lived the people who trustingly handed over their savings to Kingdon Investments in the guileless belief that they could still get something for nothing. 'As greedy as the rest of us,' Kingdon murmured.

'Pardon?'

'Nothing, I was thinking aloud.' The Bentley began to descend the green cushions of the North Downs. 'So, what do you want from me? Do you intend to publish all this shit?'

'I don't want anything from you, Paul. I want to give you some advice. Sell, sell, sell.'

'Get out, in other words.'

'Not quite,' Brossard returned the report to the briefcase. 'I have a proposition to put to you. But I am a little tired of talking to you out of the side of my mouth. Is there anywhere else we can go that is . . . ah . . . clean?'

'Of course, my house.'

'I hope so,' Brossard said. 'I sincerely hope so.'

Kingdon pressed the accelerator and the big car accelerated smoothly. Then slowed down as Kingdon remembered the zealous and uncompromising attitude of the British police to speeding.

A girl was sitting on the sofa in the big, oak-timbered lounge watching the Saturday sport on television. A slim, supple girl with Asiatic features and eyes that immediately tried to assess you, as though every man could be typecast.

'Suzy, this is Pierre Brossard. Pierre, Suzy Okana.'

Pierre bowed slightly.

'Afternoon, Pierre.' An accent he couldn't place; a trace of Cockney perhaps? He had once been introduced to a club owner speaking some Scandinavian language; it was explained later that he was a Geordie from Newcastle. The girl's green eyes lingered on him, then returned to the television and rugby football. Brossard felt that he had been assessed and dismissed.

Kingdon said: 'How about running an errand for me, Suzy. Take the Ferrari and drive down to the village and buy me some books.' He wrote out a list and handed it to the girl.

'You want to get rid of me?'

'Business, Suzy, business.'

She shrugged, left the room dangling the car keys on one finger as Kingdon called out after her: 'About an hour, okay love?'

'An attractive girl,' Brossard said as the door closed behind her.

'Not your type, Pierre. Too gentle. A drink?'

'A cup of tea perhaps. I am a confirmed Anglophile. Is there anyone else in the house? Your valet perhaps?'

'No-one. Just you and me.'

'Do you mind if I have a look round?'

'Suit yourself. Do the grand tour while I make the tea and check whether anyone's been trying to bug the place.'

'A beautiful house,' Brossard remarked when he returned. They sat down in easy chairs opposite the unlit fire. He glanced round the room. Reproduction furniture, invitations on the mantelpiece, too many mirrors on the walls. A mess.

'So,' Kingdon said, sipping his tea, 'what's the proposition?'

'According to my information, the American dollar is going to crash.'

'Just like that?'

They regarded each other steadily over fragile pink tea-cups.

Brossard said: 'I can tell you the exact date if you wish.'

'And in return?'

'Your funds have considerable investments in the United States. Hotels, an entertainment centre, an apartment block in Chicago. All built, if you will forgive me, on sand. Within the next eight days I want your managers to sell them. I want you to get rid of everything American.'

Kingdon put down his tea-cup; it chinked melodiously on

the saucer. 'You're joking of course.'

Brossard ignored him. 'How much can you personally raise in dollars?'

'A few million maybe.'

'Then make arrangements for them to be unloaded when the markets open on the morning of April the twenty-fourth.'

Kingdon said: 'You know something? I think you've flipped. But just to humour you I'll hear you out.'

'It doesn't matter if you get a bad price. I can assure you that by the following day they won't be worth the paper they're printed on. I'm doing you a favour, Paul, I earnestly advise you to take my advice.'

'Why are you being so bloody solicitous?'

Brossard leaned forward, tips of his fingers together: 'Can you keep a secret?'

Kingdon shook his head. 'Never could.'

'I think you should – if it means your personal escape from a debacle. If it means money in the bank – German marks, Swiss francs, Japanese yen – when everyone else is jumping off the skyscrapers in Wall Street,' he paused. 'Do I have your word?'

'Okay, Pierre. You have it for what it's worth.'

'I understand on good authority that the Arabs intend to stop all oil exports to the United States. The dollar's never been so weak. If that happens, then the Soviet Union is going to unload its dollar reserves. And I can promise you that the rest of the world will follow.'

Kingdon considered this, then asked: 'Why do you suddenly love me, Pierre?'

'For purely selfish reasons, of course. I am, after all, a journalist. I intend to reveal what I've just told you in my column. That is the vital factor. That is what will start the dollar landslide.'

Kingdon glanced at the old ten-shilling note on the wall. 'Carry on, Pierre.'

'I need your name. You see the world doesn't realise that the Kingdon empire is about to topple. You are still the King, the whizz-kid, the greatest phenomenon since Jacob

Astor; you're the financial genius who took on the Establishment and beat them. I intend to lend weight to my column, which in this instance will be all over the front page, with the news that Paul Kingdon has got out of dollars and everything American.'

Brossard leaned back and observed Kingdon. His name in the column would infuse colour into the story. He hadn't thought it necessary to tell him that the heads of three multi-national business concerns were also being tipped off.

Not even the Basle Club, formed by Europe's leading central banks to preserve the international monetary system, would be able to protect the dollar against the combined pressure of the corporations, the speculators and the Foreign Trade Bank of the Soviet Union.

The dollar would be debased. The United States, pilloried, impotent. Never to rise again from the ashes of the greenback! Another dominant currency would arise, a European Common Market monetary unit, perhaps; a just solution because the U.S. had sabotaged every attempt to create such a currency.

The United States of America brought to its knees because forty years ago a frightened young man had declined to have his fingernails pulled out with a pair of pliers!

And there was a bonus. A savage, beautiful bonus that Brossard had suggested to his mentors in the Kremlin. In 1973 American conglomerates in the know had cleaned up billions of dollars prior to devaluation. And how had they come to be in the know? According to the critics, the devaluation had been blown at Bilderberg.

Brossard had timed his forthcoming coup to synchronise with Bilderberg. Again the accusation of conspiracy would be made. A body blow not only to the dollar but also to the Capitalist elite.

Kingdon said: 'Give me time to think.'

Brossard's voice was brisker now. 'You don't have any time.'

'Today's Saturday. I have tomorrow.'

'You don't have any time and you don't have any choice,' Brossard said. 'I suggest that you continue with this charade of going public to divert attention from other dealings.' He smiled faintly. 'Who knows, the British end of Gerards may even come across?'

Kingdon looked startled. 'How did you know about that?'

'Mayard learned how to find out these things from you, Paul. Industrial consultancy! And I do happen to know the Parisien branch of the family.'

Kingdon stood up. 'All right, it's a deal. As you say, I don't have any choice. Or to put it more colourfully you've got me by the balls.' He stretched out his hand which Brossard grasped without relish.

*　*　*

After he had finished composing Midas' valedictory column Brossard re-read it in his study with quiet pride. A masterpiece of distortion built on a few rocks of fact. With the beautiful dateline: *Bilderberg, Thursday.*

The American dollar is tonight poised on the brink of destruction.

News was leaked to me here today that the OPEC countries have agreed to stop ALL oil shipments to the United States until a Middle East settlement favourable to the Arabs is reached.

The American President immediately conferred secretly with the Treasury Secretary, top aides and financial advisers to thrash out emergency measures to:–

(1) Save the economy.

(2) Save the dollar without which, of course, the first priority cannot be achieved.

According to my information the measures proposed cannot possibly achieve their aims and the Czars of European financial empires are already withdrawing the 277 billion dollars of foreign investment in the U.S.

The Russians have naturally not been slow to react. They are dumping their hoard of dollars on the world markets and by the time you read this column they will be competing desperately with the big European and Japanese speculators to SELL, SELL, SELL.

239

Midas produced figures revealed by *impeccable sources* that showed that the inflation rate in the U.S. was rocketing and that its trade deficits had worsened dramatically.

Far from being *impeccable* the sources were non-existent and the figures grossly exaggerated. Denials would be issued but these days the public paid little heed to them: they weren't far removed from confirmations.

In any case they would be too late. By the time they were issued the Russians – and the financiers with whom he would confer at Bilderberg – would be shedding dollars as though they were infected with bubonic plague. However massively the U.S. intervened on the exchange markets, she would be unable to save her currency.

To put it more succinctly she would be bankrupt.

Among the first to get out of dollars was whizz-kid Paul Kingdon. Astute as always he took precautionary measures last week. . . .

Brossard finished reading the column and leaned back exultantly in his chair. In a couple of thousand words he had exercised more power than any of history's despots.

'Beneath the rule of men entirely great,
The Pen is mightier than the sword.'

He had often speculated to what effect erroneous information could be employed when it was deliberately inserted in a responsible journal. One allegation of criminal practice published on the eve of a political election could destroy a candidate's chances; one snippet of information in the City pages could destroy a company.

I will have destroyed one of the two super-powers. And probably the whole monetary system of the Western world, because once the panic gained momentum all the hard currencies would soar against the plummeting dollar; exchange barriers would be introduced; trade would come to a halt.

A fitting climax to a distinguished journalistic career. And when it happened, he would be taking the sun in a palatial mansion on the Adriatic near the Yugoslav resort of Dubrovnik. Not for Pierre Brossard the meagre luxuries and estrangement of an alien's life in Moscow: he had demanded, and been granted, asylum in Yugoslavia where

Communism was benign and the style of living was comparable to Western standards.

Already vast assets had been banked in Belgrade. He had also invested heavily in gold, silver and diamonds and property bought under assumed identities supplied by the KGB. All he had to do was disappear off the face of the earth on the last day of Bilderberg. And at a leisurely pace. He would drive his Citroen CX 2400 to Marseilles, where he would pick up a similar car with a different registration and continue on his way as Monsieur Marcel Rabier, architect. Then he would cut across the French Riviera and the north of Italy to the Yugoslav border, which he would cross like any other French tourist intent on criticising the wines of another country.

There would be regrets, of course. Paris. How he would miss Paris! As it was now, with the displays of cut flowers in the Place de la Madeleine market; as it was in the autumn, with gold and brown leaves floating on the Seine. But since the day the Resistance had blown up the ammunition dump – and two generals with it – Brossard had always been fatalistic: it had been written and there was nothing he could do to reverse irrevocable processes.

He wondered if his more esoteric tastes would be catered for in Yugoslavia. To be denied masochism was surely the ultimate in masochism! But in his experience his Soviet masters were usually indulgent towards those who had served them well.

Just the same he would take full advantage of his last days in Paris. He let himself out of the house and, with an uncharacteristic gesture, hailed a taxi.

In the apartment at Montmartre, the girl with the red hair said: 'You know perfectly well that I don't work on Saturdays.'

'I'm sorry,' Brossard said meekly.

'Well clear out, I have a real man coming to see me soon.'

'Just this once. I will pay you well.'

'How much?'

'Another 1,000 francs on top of the usual fee?'

The girl stood in front of him, hands on her hips. 'Two thousand.'

'Very well.' He placed the notes on the table.

And when she placed one stiletto heel on his bare chest she said: 'You must have been a really bad boy, Pierre.'

'Very bad,' said Brossard as she reached for the whip. 'Very bad indeed.' What punishment, he wondered, would she have inflicted if she had known just how bad.

* * *

The following day Brossard lunched with Hildegard Metz in an open-air café overlooking the Seine. The waiters wore black trousers and white aprons, the tablecloths were chequered in red and white and the sunlight was dappled by the young leaves of the plane trees overhead. Paris wasn't making his departure easy; perhaps, when the reverberations from the economic earthquake ahead subsided, he might be able to return for a little while. . . .

He sipped a glass of Medoc, reputed to stave off the allergies that beset him in spring and stimulate the appetite, and spoke to the efficient, enigmatic woman facing him.

'So, everything is prepared for Bilderberg?'

'Of course, Monsieur Brossard.' A breath of reproach.

'We have rooms close to each other?'

'As you requested. I have also taken the precaution of ensuring that we are as far away as possible from Mr George Prentice. As you know I suspect that he was trying illegally to get information about your business activities.'

'A very wise precaution, Fraulein Metz.'

A waiter served them omelettes and salad and a beer for Hildegard Metz. Brossard checked out all the details with her one by one – Telex, telephone, transport; she had forgotten nothing; she never did.

Where would we be without the Swiss? Brossard wondered as he speared some chicory with his fork. They survived wars; they survived epidemics; they survived depressions. And they always emerged triumphantly.

They said the Swiss were dull. Cautious, perhaps, feeding on the weaknesses and fears of their more flamboyant neighbours. But who could say they were dull if they had never penetrated that professional reserve? Perhaps they danced naked on moonlit lawns to celebrate the influx of another billion black marks or guilders invested in a numbered account with virtually no interest and extortionate charges?

Had Hildegard Metz ever danced naked on a moonlit lawn? Or anywhere else for that matter? It saddened Brossard to realise that he would probably never know.

She finished her omelette, placed her knife and fork neatly together and looked at him inquiringly through her spectacles. Plain glass, he had discovered. Why plain glass? I shall never know. Perhaps merely to accentuate that impersonal facade.

'You seem troubled, Monsieur Brossard,' she said. 'As if you were going away and didn't know how to say good-bye.'

Brossard smiled. 'Very perceptive. But it is not I who am saying good-bye. It is Midas: I have decided to stop writing the column. The next one will be the last. It will have to be good and that's what I was thinking about. Forgive me if I was preoccupied.'

'But why abandon Midas? It's the most respected financial column in the world.'

'The conflict between inside knowledge and journalistic enterprise is too great. The temptations too enticing.'

'I don't believe you would ever even contemplate anything dishonest, Monsieur Brossard.'

Jamais de la vie! 'It's very touching of you to say that.'

'What will you write about in your last column?'

'Something sensational, have no fear.'

'I'm pleased. But it will be a sad day.' She stood up. 'And now I must get back to the office, there is always a lot to do before Bilderberg.'

A good figure, Brossard mused. But concealed. Unused. . . .

'Tell me one thing, Hildegard.' He was surprising himself. She stopped in mid-stride. Unable to stop himself, he plunged on: 'Why do you wear spectacles? I mean, they are plain glass, aren't they?'

She looked confused. 'I didn't know you knew. . . . Why? To make myself look ordinary I suppose. I don't mean that I am not ordinary. . . . To look like the perfect secretary, m'sieur.'

She walked away self-consciously, one hand touching her spectacles, and Brossard wondered if perhaps she was a little in love with him. For his part he would miss her.

In the afternoon he called on Mayard, who was smoking a cigar far too big for him. He had just been to the barber and the smell of pommade mingled with the cigar smoke drifting across his desk.

Brossard told him he was writing his last column.

Mayard looked surprised. 'But why, Pierre?'

'Time to get out. I've been using your brains for too long. How would you like to become Midas?'

Mayard stroked his small moustache. 'You know I can't write. I'm a make-up man, an ideas man –'

'You know more about finance than anyone in France.'

'That doesn't make me a writer.'

'I'd like you to try,' Brossard said.

Mayard shrugged. 'Okay, you're the boss.'

'Literary flourishes aren't necessary. Just tell the facts – the ones they don't know. Which reminds me. My last column, I want you to put it all over the front page.'

'You mean it's a news story?'

'Oh yes,' Brossard said, 'it's a news story all right. I can't tell you any more at the moment. But I want every word used, nothing cut on the stone.'

'Naturally,' Mayard said, knocking a thick roll of ash into the ashtray. 'Have we ever cut the thoughts of our proprietor?'

Brossard fanned the smoke with one hand and coughed. 'I think the story will surprise you. At the moment I have only an inkling of what it's all about. But don't forget that the source will be impeccable.'

'Bilderberg?'

Brossard didn't reply.

After he had left the editor's office, Brossard walked along some of the famous avenues of Paris. Down the Rue de la Paix to the Opera House. Along the Champs-Elysées to the Place de l'Etoile, where he gazed for a few moments at the French flag rippling in the breeze.

Then he walked home, stooping a little, briefly overcome by the parting that lay ahead. Between himself and Paris.

From the living-room of his house there came the sound of chanting. Surprised, Brossard looked through the half-open door. Six women including his wife were kneeling on the carpet praying.

Brossard's spirits lifted. There was much he would be happy to leave behind.

XVII

The message that Helga Keller dispatched after she had left Brossard said SUBJECT PROCEEDING AS EXPECTED. She coded, dated and timed it.

The subject was Brossard. The Kremlin had never wholly trusted a man capable of sending twenty-two compatriots to their graves to save his fingernails and, since 1976 when she had become his secretary, Helga Keller had monitored his movements.

She telephoned the bearded assistant in the bookshop and met him outside the Hotel de Ville. She passed on the message inside a creased copy of *Elle* magazine which she discarded in a litter bin.

Afterwards she crossed the Louis-Philippe bridge onto the Ile Saint-Louis.

It was spring and it was Paris, and it was like nowhere else in the world. It wasn't just the buds opening on the trees leaning over the Seine; nor the pleasure boats forging arrows in the water; nor the spire of Notre-Dame touching the misty blue sky. It was more, much more. It was re-awakened innocence, it was . . . ah well, it was Paris.

On the cobbled embankment of the river below her, old men camped beside their fishing rods and lovers strolled entwined and intent. As Helga had once strolled. Because today was what it was, Helga let her thoughts drift with the river. And the towers and spire of Notre-Dame became the domes of the Kremlin.

One week after Karl Danzer's murder, Helga Keller had made contact with the Soviet Embassy in Berne. Two months later she had flown to Moscow, telling her father that she had got a job in London.

It had then taken the KGB a month to decide whether

she was a suitable candidate to become a professional spy as opposed to the obedient mistress of one. In the labyrinths of the KGB's directorates her case was argued. Her youth, gullibility and emotional immaturity versus her potential.

It was her hatred that finally won the day. It was like an icicle that never thawed, its icy blade pointing towards the West, towards the two men, one black and one white, who had killed Karl Danzer.

At first, while they debated her case, she stayed in the Ukraine, the great mausoleum of a hotel on Kutuzovsky Prospect. From there, always in company, she was allowed to make the tourist rounds of Moscow, and it was just as Karl had described it to her: the gold cupolas of the Kremlin riding over the snow-white city, skates singing on the ice-covered paths in the parks, the Bolshoi, Metro stations like chapels. . . . Within the vice of winter she could *feel* the united energy of the people.

Finally she was given a tiny apartment off Gorky Street and taken under the wing of Directorate S of the First Chief Directorate, responsible for training agents living abroad under false identities. Because, as it was explained to her, Helga Keller had been blown in Zurich: it would be another girl, a stranger, who would eventually return to Europe. Meanwhile they took her letters for her father and posted them in London.

The indoctrination took months. In vain did she point out that Karl had taught her about Marxism and Leninism; that was not enough; you had to live a cause, not learn it. Her life was then put in the hands of a French-speaking agent named Litvak.

Litvak had been a boy soldier in the last stages of World War II and, like most veterans of a nation that had lost 20 million, he hated the Germans with an intensity that would never weaken. When he had drunk a little too much vodka, the hatred became confused with The Cause. This Helga Keller understood.

He was tall and lean with cropped hair – not unlike an archetypal pre-war Prussian officer – and grey eyes that sometimes looked sad as though he were searching for something that had been taken from him when he was a boy. He was very correct and, Helga suspected, a little in love with her.

Together, as the snow melted and water gurgled in the streets, they walked in Gorky Park and the Lenin Hills. And, when spring arrived to prepare hastily the way for the brief summer, they picnicked on the river beaches where, in their thousands, Muscovites bared themselves to the stranger, the sun.

Although Helga didn't realise it, men who fed souls into computers had decided that in her case, indoctrination should be orchestrated with beauty. That was the way, according to his reports, that Karl Danzer had begun the process and that was the way it should continue. For the time being.

They needn't have bothered. Helga would have embraced Communism working on a factory assembly line.

Only once did Litvak stray from his brief – when they were sitting on a spur of grassland beside a fat curve in the river after lunching on black bread, caviar, cheese, fruit and Georgian wine.

'Perhaps,' he said, lying down with his hands behind his head and staring at the blue sky, 'you shouldn't hate so much. It will consume you, as it did me.'

She looked at him in surprise. 'But you are consumed with ideals. They have replaced the hatred. Except when you have drunk too much vodka,' smiling at him.

'My life was founded on hatred. The Germans killed my parents and my brother. . . . It was sown in me when I was too young. My hatred and my ideals over-lapped. But I never let anyone know. Only you. And I shouldn't. . . .'

She touched his arm, bare beneath the rolled-up sleeves of his white shirt. 'All that matters is the work we're doing. Equality, that's all we should worry about. Then, perhaps, there won't be any room for hatred.'

He took her hand and kissed it. 'There is something that I should tell you.'

She withdrew her hand. She wasn't sure whether she

should be angry. Surely he understood that her life was now a dedication.

He saw the expression on her face. 'I'm sorry,' he said. 'One day perhaps. . . .'

And that was all.

When they thought she was ready for it, they taught her the arts of surveillance – how to implement it and how to avoid it – and the subtleties of choosing between useful and useless information. They taught her self-defence, micro-photography, cryptology, radio-transmission . . . and Russian because it was only right and proper.

They also created Hildegard Metz.

Born 1952 in Vienna in a small street off the Praterstrasse near the railway station. A student of languages and business management, competent in shorthand and audio-typing. (She found the secretarial training more tedious than anything else.)

An only child. Parents killed in an automobile accident when she was eighteen. Determined, when she was qualified, to leave Austria.

The KGB also physically moulded Hildegard Metz. Plastic surgeons filled out her face a little and the Russian diet thickened her waist, but not too much. She wore spectacles and pinned up her long hair. Before the transformation she had planned to visit her father, but she learned that he had died of a heart attack.

Within a year she *was* Hildegard Metz. Except alone sometimes in the tiny apartment.

If she hadn't blindly handed her life over to The Cause, as a nun bequeaths her life to the Church, she might have questioned some of the manifestations of the dream of equality. The cramped quarters with whole families sharing one bathroom; the ubiquitous *upravdom* – the KGB supervisor present in every apartment block; the turgid propaganda in *Pravda* and *Izvestia*; the harassment of dissidents and Jews; the disappearance of critics of the regime into the Serbsky mental institution.

But her tutors explained it all. One day there would be fine homes for everyone and one day, when the American and British spies stopped preying on innocent citizens, there would be no call for the *upravdom*. The Jews. . . . Were they not first and foremost Russians? The dissidents. . . . 'Are they not traitors sabotaging our beautiful ideals?'

She remembered Karl Danzer and saw the blood spurting on the windows of the cable-car and, yes, she believed.

They didn't send her directly to Paris. Instead she joined the ranks of secretaries eager to obtain lucrative jobs with various branches of the EEC in Brussels. She worked for an Englishman and regularly reported to the Kremlin the mounting evidence of Britain's disenchantment with the European Community. She discovered that she revelled in intrigue: it replaced other desires which had been quenched.

In the early spring of 1975 she was recalled to Moscow. She was met at Sheremetievo Airport by Litvak who looked ill. His face was gaunt and his eyes hollowed. He kissed her on both cheeks and led her to his small grey Moskavitch car.

Driving into Moscow, past the monument marking the point where the German advance had been halted, he told her that she was to be uniquely honoured: she was to meet the head of the entire KGB operation, Nicolai Vlasov.

'They must have something very important lined up for you,' he told her. 'Not many people get to meet Vlasov.'

Snow was sliding off the rooftops, the silver birches were dripping. It was the same Moscow that she had once explored with Litvak by her side.

He dropped her outside the Ukraine Hotel, gripped her arm and said: 'Be careful,' and was gone.

The hotel hadn't changed. The vast lobby was filled with tottering piles of luggage and dispirited visitors lining up for keys, passports, currency. . . . She was escorted to a suite of rooms on the floor where the surveillance equipment was located.

Nicolai Vlasov was waiting for her with a bottle of Russian champagne, two pale-green glasses and a plate of canapes.

So this was the dreaded commander of an army which penetrated every walk of Soviet life and infiltrated every capital in the world. He looked positively benign, she thought. An elder statesman rather than the head of the secret police. Except for the eyes, set wide in the fragile-looking skull, that took you apart with one glance. They were green, she noted.

'Champagne?'

She nodded; you didn't refuse.

He poured the champagne into the two glasses and said: 'Please sit down.' He lifted his glass to his lips. 'Here's to your next assignment.'

She sipped her champagne and glanced round the room. A considerable improvement on her earlier accommodation in the hotel. Green carpet, plastic chandelier, furniture made from walnut veneer. Lenin peered down at them from one wall.

Vlasov said: 'You must be wondering why you've suddenly become so important, Comrade Metz.'

'Not many people get to meet Comrade Vlasov,' quoting Litvak.

Vlasov placed the tips of his fingers together and appraised her. 'I have been studying your dossier. Your devotion to our doctrines has been quite remarkable. For a foreigner, that is. And you don't appear to have been spoiled by your daily contact with decadent and bourgeois values.'

'You forget, Comrade Vlasov, that I was born into them.'

'True, true.' He picked up a grey, spring-backed folder; inside were two typewritten sheets of paper. He took them out and scanned them. 'I see you do not entirely deprive yourself of the benefits the West has to offer. Good food and good wine. . . .'

Helga, determined not to be intimidated by this cool, grey-haired, all-powerful policeman, said: 'Naturally, Comrade Vlasov. In the first place I have to act as a single girl in my position would act. I am well paid, I have no attachments. . . . It is only natural that I should live relatively well. Furthermore, I see nothing wrong with taking advantage of some of these good things of life. It is surely our aim that *everyone* should be able to enjoy them.'

Vlasov raised his glass of champagne and picked up a finger of toast smeared with caviar. 'I am hardly in a position to criticise.' He smiled.

Helga smiled back and waited. The central-heating was over-powering and the windows had steamed up. Through the condensation she could see a pigeon perched on the window-sill.

Vlasov put his glass down; he looked, she thought, as though he ate and drank frugally. 'I am giving you the opportunity,' he said quietly, 'to live in even better style.'

She waited.

He frowned, as though deliberating the wisdom of the course of action he was going to take. Then he nodded, to himself it seemed. 'What I am about to tell you is extremely confidential and is known only to a few high-ranking officers.'

She wasn't sure what to say. She said: 'I am honoured, Comrade Vlasov.'

'But as your record is impeccable. . . .' He returned the two sheets of paper to the folder. 'Have you heard of a man named Pierre Brossard?'

'The French millionaire? Of course.'

'He has worked for us for many years.'

Helga expressed surprise.

'He is not the most efficient agent in the world. But he has the contacts, he has the money and he moves in illustrious circles. He has until now been under surveillance by his secretary, a woman named Bouvet. But she is sixty and about to retire. Monsieur Brossard needs a new secretary, Comrade Metz, and we have decided that the secretary should be you.'

'But how can I be sure that he will want to employ me?'

'You will be recommended by Madame Bouvet. Meanwhile you will study the dossier on Brossard and make yourself acquainted with every facet of his character so that when he interviews you, you will be the ideal candidate for the job and he won't bother seeing anyone else. And don't be alarmed by his sexual inclinations; he doesn't mix business with pleasure. He is also very mean but you will find that he doesn't economise falsely where work is concerned, so you will be well paid.' Vlasov paused. 'You realise just how important your new post will be?'

Helga nodded. There had to be some fatal flaw in Brossard's character to merit such a back-up. She wondered what it was.

Vlasov said: 'In case you are wondering why this is necessary, it is because Brossard is a coward. He could be frightened into betraying the cause. He has, according to his dossier, *a tendency to unreliability*. Nevertheless, he is both spy and paymaster. You, comrade, will be his monitor. A far more important job than the one you're engaged upon now.'

'I shall look forward to the challenge,' Helga said.

'You will, of course, discuss it with no one. Not even your friend Litvak. Pierre Brossard has come up with an idea which, if properly handled, could change the whole balance of world power. At the moment it is only an idea, an embryo; we have to wait until the time is opportune. But, from what I am saying, you will realise that you are in an extremely privileged position.'

Helga Keller looked into Vlasov's green eyes and said firmly: 'I shan't let you down, Comrade Vlasov.'

He relaxed suddenly. Poured more champagne – half a glass for himself. 'I don't believe you will. Tomorrow other officers will brief you. Now let us drink once again to the success of your new role.' He raised his glass, drank the champagne, bowed slightly and left the room.

Helga was briefed for two days. Before returning she had one free day with Litvak. He didn't question her about her meeting with Vlasov; he understood.

They walked as they had walked before among the melting gardens of Gorky Park and watched the old men playing chess. 'They would brave a blizzard to capture a bishop,' Litvak remarked.

She told him that he didn't look well and he said it was nothing. She knew that he was lying.

On the following day she flew back to Brussels. Six months later she became Pierre Brossard's private secretary.

She returned once more to Moscow in the winter of 1976. When she saw Litvak he was dying.

XVIII

Paul Kingdon had planned a feast at the Savoy.

Mountains of caviar, oceans of champagne.

Former Government ministers had been invited. (He had always believed in parading pillars of respectability to support his schemes, and was the first to admit that some of the pillars had subsequently turned to salt.) Leading financiers, bankers, actresses and members of the set who were regularly photographed in the fashionable discotheques of London and New York.

The party was originally for all the fund salesmen who had exceeded their quota for the year. As few of them had succeeded in doing this, the invitations had been amended to include 'all those who have made outstanding contributions to an outstanding year.'

Kingdon had planned to take the opportunity to deliver an ebullient speech about future prospects. On the day before the party he announced that he was suffering from an unspecified virus infection, told his deputy to make the speech – and caught the 11.15 Concorde flight to New York.

He watched the dial in front of his seat indicate that the Concorde had reached Mach 1, accepted a glass of champagne from an aristocratic stewardess in pink, and settled back to consider a future that had nothing in common with the sentiments he had intended to express at the Savoy.

He was by no means convinced that Brossard was telling the truth about the imminent fate of the dollar; nevertheless, the Frenchman had provided an incentive; it could do no harm to get the funds' cash out of the bad investments in the U.S. Since he had grown careless, since he had delegated too much authority, the performance of most of the investments was pathetic.

If he sold out judiciously there would be a few million to be recycled through normal channels into his personal accounts in Zurich, Liechtenstein and Andorra. Which he would immediately recycle into diamonds.

If the crash came, then he would have a foundation of compressed carbon on which to build a new empire. At the fount, the glittering Kingdon Diamond which, coldly and aloofly, would appreciate as money became as worthless as fools' gold.

Paul Kingdon licked his lips. The stewardess, imagining he was displaying symptoms of thirst, refilled his glass with Dom Perignon 1970. 'Nothing like a champagne breakfast, sir.' A beautiful, actresses' voice. 'But don't forget that we land at Kennedy at ten o'clock – an hour and a quarter before we took off.'

Before leaving he had visited the vault in the City. Held the diamond in his hand. Gazed into its fires. Forged more than 120 million years ago, 200 kilometres beneath the earth's surface in a reservoir of molten magma and driven up to the surface by explosive forces; transported from South Africa and thence to Antwerp, where its mundane disguise was removed by cutting and polishing and its flawless beauty uncovered.

He glanced at the machmeter. Mach 2. Twice the speed of sound or about 1,320 mph. Outside the sky was dark blue: they were twice the height of Mount Everest and, because of the loss of density, the blue elements of the sun's light were less scattered.

The infinity of the heavens and the eternity of the diamond presented themselves for comparison in Kingdon's mind; the lancing beauty of the Concorde's flight and the perfect facets of the stone. Too much champagne too early! He waved the hovering bottle away.

He spent six hours in New York supervising the sales by startled managers and staff of several million dollars of stock; he then flew to Houston where he authorised the sale of three drilling companies that had discovered a phenomenal number of dry wells; he rounded off the trip in Miami where he unloaded real estate in Florida and the Bahamas.

Two days later he was in a shabby street named Pelikaanstraat in Antwerp where, on credit, he bought 4 million dollars worth of rough and fine cut diamonds, which he brought back to England that evening in diamond parcel papers in the pockets of his trousers.

He showed them to Suzy Okana.

'Supposing you'd got caught?' she asked, impressed for once.

'Speeding is the only crime I get pinched for.'

He lay down on the sofa, hands behind his head. He felt both exhilarated and exhausted. 'Get me a drink, Suzy, there's a good girl.'

She poured him a Chivas Regal.

He drank some and said: 'So, where's it all going to end?'

'Where's all what going to end?'

'Us?'

'I don't know,' she said, 'because it never started.'

'There's a lot going to happen in the next few days.'

'Such as what?'

'Well, we're going to France for a start.'

'Are we? No-one told me.'

'I've got to attend a conference. I've booked you into an inn in the village. I want to show you off to some of the stuffed shirts. They'll have apoplexy.'

'Where are you staying then?'

'In a bloody château, that's where. Delegates only, can't be helped.'

She shrugged. 'Okay, so I stay in the village.'

Then Kingdon said: 'Have you ever thought of making our relationship permanent?'

The slanting green eyes appraised him. 'You think I might be an investment for the future?'

Kingdon felt confused; businessmen were warned not to negotiate deals immediately after a long flight. He tried to

make a joke of it. 'I've always believed in short-term investment. But the market's changing; perhaps I should switch
to long-term.'

'And perhaps I should stick to short-term.'

'I want you to stay with me,' he told her.

'Really? I'm not one of your sales managers. I can take
off tonight without breaking any contract.'

Dusk was gathering. She switched on a table light and
sat in an easy chair opposite Kingdon, legs tucked underneath her; her hair gleamed blue-black in the light and her
face was shadowed.

Kingdon said: 'As I said, there are going to be a lot of
changes. I can't elaborate. But think about it. It will be to
your advantage, I promise you.'

'To my advantage! Christ,' she said, 'You make everything sound like a business deal.'

'You've been happy enough, haven't you?'

'With the business arrangement? Oh yes, Mr Kingdon,
it's been very satisfactory. From both our points of view. I
have my retreat and you have your adornment. If I walked
out of the door right now you'd find yourself another adornment in time for tomorrow's social gathering.'

Kingdon stood up and switched on the main light. 'I
don't want another adornment,' he said.

'What *do* you want?'

Kingdon swayed slightly. Christ he was tired. 'Let's
compromise,' he said. 'Come with me to France and
after the conference we'll decide about the future. Is that
a deal?'

'It's a deal, Mr Chairman.'

'Okay, Suzy,' he said, 'after Bilderberg we'll work something out. And now I'm going to bed.'

As he undressed he thought about Suzy Okana. He had
the diamonds; unlike other unsuspecting capitalists he had a
future. He wanted Suzy with him in that future – in his
villa in Switzerland.

Perhaps they would marry. No-one would believe that
they had never slept together. His appetites had always been
expended elsewhere in obtaining and securing power and

wealth. He had not been celibate but sex had always seemed to him to be a wasting process.

Soon there would be a time for consolidation. Time to enjoy the strange, remote girl who had entered his life. A time for awakening for both of them.

But when he slept he dreamt about diamonds.

XIX

On the morning of Friday, April 18, packages were delivered to Claire Jerome at her London apartment, Paul Kingdon at his mansion at Wentworth and Pierre Brossard at his house on the Avenue Foch.

Packages were also delivered to their respective offices, with accompanying notes that they should be disregarded if the recipients had heeded the original deliveries.

In each case they had.

Each package contained a cassette accompanied by a three-word note: PLAY IT NOW.

Each played the cassette in privacy.

Each heard a date.

Each reacted with shock.

* * *

CLAIRE JEROME.

A woman's voice: 'The date, Mrs Jerome, is October 10, 1943.'

A pause.

'You are aware of its significance?'

Claire Jerome nodded.

The woman's voice: 'The day he was born, Mrs Jerome.'

Another pause, longer this time.

'If you want Mr Anello to celebrate another birthday, make five million dollars available at Bilderberg.'

Click.

The spool still running.

Claire Jerome's head thrust down towards her knees to force the blood back to the icy regions of her brain.

One hand reached out to switch off the cassette player.

Silence.

* * *

PIERRE BROSSARD.

A man's voice: 'The date, Monsieur Brossard, is March 21, 1942.'

A pause.

'You remember it?'

'*D'accord!*' trembling.

The man's voice: 'On that day you sent twenty-two French patriots to their graves.'

A prolonged pause.

'If you do not want the world to know that Pierre Brossard is a coward and a traitor, you will make five million dollars available at Bilderberg.'

The trembling eased a little: dollars would be worthless and he would soon disappear.

The man's voice: 'Do not relax, Monsieur Brossard. Marshal Tito was a very brave man during the war. Yugoslavia is not a safe haven for men who betrayed the cause of freedom.

Click.

Spool still running.

Thin, cold fingers reaching shakily for the switch-off button.

* * *

PAUL KINGDON.

A man's voice: 'The date, Mr Kingdon, is November 12, 1978.'

A pause.

'Do you remember it?'

A shrug. The date he bought the Kingdon Diamond.

'The Jager Formula has been perfected and has come into our possession. This, as you know, could make your investment worthless.'

Kingdon: 'What the fuck –'

The Jager Formula was an experimental process for producing synthetic gem diamonds indistinguishable from natural stones.

The man's voice: 'We can eliminate the formula if you

make five million dollars available at Bilderberg.'

Click.

Spool running.

Stopping as the cassette was hurled across the room.

XX

The first guest to arrive at the Château Saint-Pierre was the West German Foreign Minister. He was so impressed by the view of the hotel from the gates that he ordered his chauffeur to stop his metallic-blue Mercedes.

To the consternation of the security guards deployed discreetly around the hotel, he spent a long time admiring the scene.

With good reason. The sky was grey, thinning here and there into patches of lemon-yellow, through which the sun occasionally broke, misty drizzle was falling and the château had about it an air of impregnability and dignified seclusion.

To the relief of the guards, the Foreign Minister finally had his fill and ordered his chauffeur to drive on.

He was met in the domed hallway by Gaudin, the owner, and a phalanx of receptionists and managers.

The Minister smiled, displayed the black and white identity disc on his lapel and pointed at the nymphs and cherubs adorning the frescoes, the massive chandelier, the bronzes and statues and said: 'It reminds me of Fontainebleau.'

Gaudin nodded: 'You are very perceptive, Herr Otten. There are distinct similarities. You will find many works here by the painters and sculptors who adorned Fontainbleau. Van Loo for instance. And the stairways are said to be the models for the two Louis XIII stairways at the palace.'

Gaudin snapped his fingers. 'Monsieur Foster, please take the Minister to his room.'

Anderson watched from the shadows at the entrance to the ballroom. Foster still worried him. Did anyone really take up hotel management at the age of twenty-eight? He shrugged: there were at the moment greater worries than

Foster, not the least of them the proliferation of security agencies tripping over each other's big feet. The French doing it their own way as usual; the Germans with their shepherd dogs; the British Special Branch as obvious in their tweeds and suede shoes as the two FBI agents with their clipped hair-cuts, chunky black shoes and pistol-bulging suits.

The West German Foreign Minister was followed by two Italians. A newspaper editor and the Minister of Social Affairs together in an Alfa Romeo. Then the head of a Danish Bank, the president of a German Finance Company, the Prime Minister of Iceland, a Norwegion ship-owner, a Swiss banker, two British industrialists, the Dutch Minister of Finance. . . .

Rolls-Royces – Camargues, Corniches and Shadows – Jaguars, Volvos, Ferraris, Mercedes, a few taxis from Paris. . . . You could almost identify nationality and owner by their style of transport.

A Citroen CX 2400 drew up. Out stepped Pierre Brossard. One of the wealthiest men in Europe. The Citroen was a good car but not in the Rolls-Mercedes bracket. You would have thought . . . but no, not Pierre Brossard!

The Secretary General of NATO, the West German Chancellor, a Greek diplomat, a former governor of the Bank of Sweden, a Spanish nobleman and financier. . . .

Still no Americans. Perhaps they had all been eliminated *en route!*

The British whizz-kid himself, Paul Kingdon, sharing his powder-blue Ferrari with a stunning oriental girl. Anderson consulted his notes. *Possibly travelling with girl named Suzy Okana.* She would be the booking made by Kingdon at the hostel in the village. But, of course, he had to parade her first in front of the Establishment.

The President of the Federation of Austrian Industrialists; a Canadian executive from the Bank of Nova Scotia; the Irish Minister of Foreign Affairs. . . .

And then, thank Christ, the first of the Americans, the president of one of the largest oil companies in the world and a celebrated New York banker.

But there were still a lot of Americans to follow. In particular the former Secretary of State, who was due to arrive by helicopter the following day with the French President.

Two English bankers . . . a Tory peer . . . Belgians, Austrians, Scandinavians. Then two more Americans – Mrs Claire Jerome, mistress of arms, accompanied by her personal bodyguard, Mr Peter Anello.

Mrs Jerome smiled briefly at Gaudin and went straight up to her room, accompanied by Anello and a receptionist.

An hour later Anderson had ticked off all the names except the French President and former Secretary of State. He went into the bar where a few delegates had already assembled for a drink before the preliminary session.

He ordered a glass of Chablis from Jules. 'That's from Burgundy where you were born, isn't it?'

'You're very knowledgable, m'sieur.'

'And I hope you will be, Jules.'

'I shall do my best.'

Anderson nodded, drank the cold white wine thirstily and walked out through the French windows leading into the gardens to check on outside security.

Unknown to him there had been one incident after he had left the lobby. Pierre Brossard had returned to reception and demanded to know the price of his room. With service and tax it came to 1,000 francs a night. Outraged, Brossard demanded cheaper rooms for himself and his secretary, Hildegard Metz, who had arrived at the hotel ahead of him.

The young man behind the desk was flustered. 'But, Monsieur Brossard, the accommodation was arranged weeks ago.'

'I don't care when it was arranged. The price is extortionate.'

The receptionist called Gaudin.

Gaudin spread his hands. 'I don't understand, m'sieur. All expenses are paid by the host country.'

'I don't have to remind you that I am French.'

'But the west wing is by far the best, Monsieur Brossard. All your fellow countrymen are in the west wing.'

'You can spare me our calculating national charm,' Brossard snapped. 'If the west is the most expensive then I assume the east is the cheapest?'

'But it gets little sun –'

'I am not here to acquire a tan. Please have my baggage moved to the east wing.'

Gaudin shrugged. 'If you wish, m'sieur.'

'And my secretary's to an adjoining room.'

Gaudin gave the orders and the receptionist began to make the alterations on the plan on the desk.

* * *

In his room in the annexe Nicholas Foster completed his notes for the morning. He put one copy beneath a loose floor-tile under the mat beside his bed, the other into an envelope addressed to the accommodation address in London.

It was 3 pm. The guests were assembling in the conference chamber. Time to head for the village to post the envelope. He took off his black jacket and striped trousers and put on a brown sports jacket, white roll-neck sweater and flannels.

He was stopped at the gate, guarded by two *gendarmes*, by Anderson.

'Taking the air, Mr Foster?'

'I always take a stroll at this time. Doctor's orders – for my leg.'

'Even with such important guests to look after?'

'One hour, that's all. Union rules – you forget I'm English.' He smiled at the big black man.

Anderson consulted a notebook. 'That's right, 15.03 hours on the dot. You seem to have established a routine.'

'It's the only way,' Foster said, 'in a hotel.'

'It's the only way anywhere. Take care, Mr Foster.'

Foster limped down the lane leading to the village. The

banks of grass supporting the hedgerows on either side of the lane were printed with primroses; the air was heavy and verdant as the sun drew the morning's rain from the fields. The setting reminded Foster of days walking in gum-boots with his parents in the East Anglian countryside – before he had reached the traditional age for summary dispatch to boarding school.

A thrush settled on a branch of a tree and began to sing; a cow regarded him through a gap in the hedgerow. Behind the trees and bushes and flintstone walls, there lurked men with field-glasses, radios and guns.

All beautiful background for the eventual story. . . . Already he had recorded in detail the events of the day. The dawn sweep with metal detectors, the check for letter or parcel bombs; the breakfast meeting between the various security agencies, the French uniformed police and the Sureté. He believed he knew the position of every closed-circuit television camera, every electronic beam.

He had made a note of the guests' rooms – all checked for bugs – their clothes, their dietary preferences – Kosher, fat-free, vegetarian – their newspapers, their telephone and Telex arrangements.

The female presence interested him, because these days women competing in what had once been a man's world was always good copy. Hildegard Metz, well she was only a sec-retary. . . . But Claire Jerome would provide excellent colour. Still strikingly attractive for her age, one of the richest women in the world. Foster wondered how Anello, rugged and lazily assured, featured in her life.

Of the men it was Pierre Brossard who intrigued him most. According to Lucas, he was the most influential finan-cial journalist in Europe, although not everyone knew that he was Midas. Supposing he had decided to break the Bilder-berg story. . . . Surely fate couldn't be quite as shitty as that. But if Brossard had wanted to write the story he could have done it years ago. He was, presumably, sworn to secrecy like the rest.

In the village he bought a packet of Galloise at the *tabac* and made his way to the post office, passing the church where a cadaverous-looking priest stood on guard as though protecting God's House against the intrusion of the owners of so many worldly goods. What did the villagers make of the Bilderbergers esconced in the château across the meadows? It was enough to make the underprivileged Communists for life. Except, perhaps, that they didn't regard themselves as underprivileged; preferred bicycles to Rolls-Royces and regarded the security precautions that wealth involved as absurd.

He posted the envelope. Then he called Lucas to make sure that arrangements, in the event of a fast-breaking story, were in hand.

'Everything okay?'

Lucas, speaking from a friend's house in London, said everything was okay. By which he meant that a daily paper had been alerted that it might receive an exclusive tip during the conference; once the tip had been received, the paper's Paris staff would be able to check out details with police, hospitals, ambulances . . . if, that was, it was that sort of story. The editor of Foster's old Sunday newspaper had already been given first refusal on an in-depth exclusive.

Suddenly feeling thirsty, Foster went into the village inn and ordered a beer. The saloon was dark. At first the only person he could see plainly was the woman serving at the bar, plump with dyed black hair. She regarded him suspiciously and served him without speaking.

He threaded his way through the tables and sat down in a corner. As his eyes became accustomed to the gloom he saw that the room was sparsely and cheaply furnished. The flagstones chilled his feet, the air smelled of sour wine.

'It's not the Ritz, is it?'

He turned and made out the figure of a girl sitting two tables away from him. He tried to place the accent, it had a bit of a lilt to it.

'At least the beer's cold,' he said.

'Don't I know you?'

'I shouldn't think so,' Foster said uneasily.

The girl stood up and moved to the next table and stared at him. 'I'm sure I do.'

He studied her profile. Oriental. Unexpected features to find in the recess of a village inn in France. But familiar. . . .

'My name's Suzy Okana,' she told him. 'What's yours?'

Of course he knew. Every week or so she surfaced in the newspaper diaries with some flamboyant pace-setter or fledgling member of the aristocracy. Worse he had once interviewed her!

He said: 'I know you, of course, but we've never met.'

'Come off it,' she said. 'I never forget a face.'

'Well, you've made a mistake this time.' He finished his beer. 'My double probably. My doppelganger. We're all supposed to have one.'

'And if you meet your doppelganger then you die. But you're no doppelganger.' She bit her lip. 'It's coming. . . .'

'Well,' he said standing up, 'I'll see you around. I suppose you're here for the conference?'

'Sort of,' still frowning at him.

'Who are you with this time?' He couldn't resist it; it was his undoing.

'I know – a reporter. I recognise your voice when you ask a question.' She wagged her finger. 'Got it. At the opening of some damn concert hall in South London. I was with Paul. Everyone was asking questions about his taste in music. Music! He doesn't know the difference between Gilbert and Sullivan and Gilbert O'Sullivan. And you asked me if I ever had any difficulty in remembering who I was with at such occasions. Something like that.'

Foster sat down resignedly. 'You're right, we have met.' He grinned. 'Sorry about that question.'

'Forget it. It was the only bright one anyway. And the answer is Yes, sometimes I do forget who I'm out with. At the cinema I have to go to the loo so I can get a good look at his profile on the way back.' She laughed. 'I'm with Paul Kingdon this time – as far as I remember. Can you make anything out of that?'

'I'm not in journalism any more,' Foster told her. He decided to have another beer. 'Can I get you a drink?'

'A glass of red plonk would do nicely. I like plonk. A

good old glass of vino with no one examining the bottle and sniffing it and passing judgement. And a hunk of bread and cheese for lunch.'

Foster, suspecting that she might already have consumed several glasses of plonk, ordered the drinks from the sullen woman behind the bar.

'And do you know what else I like?' Suzy called out from behind him.

He shook his head as he handed her a glass.

'Tizer. It's got a beautiful smell. Reminds me of the little shop at the end of the street.'

'In Tiger Bay,' he said sitting down beside her.

'You've got a good memory.'

'Not really. Almost everyone in Britain who reads a newspaper knows you come from Tiger Bay.'

'That's where Shirley Bassey came from.'

'I know. She's in the newspapers quite a bit too.'

'The difference,' Suzy said sipping her wine, 'is that she's got talent.'

Relieved that the discussion had wandered from the reason for his presence in the village, Foster said: 'I'm sure you've got talents.'

'Oh yes. And we all know what those are.' She put down her glass and rested her chin on one hand. 'Now tell me why you're here.'

'I'm working at the château. I'm going into the hotel business.'

'Pull the other leg,' Suzy said. 'It's got bells on it.'

'I'm a trainee manager. Check it out if you like. I was no bloody good as a reporter.'

'Got the old heave-ho did you?'

Foster nodded.

'Marvellous.'

'I beg your pardon?'

'I'm out with a failure. The first in years. Bloody marvellous.'

Foster burst out laughing.

'You haven't told me your name,' she said.

'Nicholas Foster.'

'Not a bad by-line. Nicholas Foster. Very authoritative. Mmmmmmm, I like it.'

'I'm glad you like it,' Foster said. 'Perhaps I should write it down for you because you'll never see it in print.'

'I can see it now. THE TRUTH BEHIND BILDERBERG. An exclusive report by Nicholas Foster.' She lit a cigarette and quickly blew out a little puff of smoke as though she didn't like it. 'Come off it. It's pretty obvious why you're here, isn't it. All right, so you're a trainee manager. But once a journalist always a journalist.'

'*Are* you with Paul Kingdon?'

She nodded. 'In a manner of speaking.'

Foster considered the possibilities. If he kept up the deception she might tell Kingdon that a journalist was working at the hotel. Kingdon, who liked journalists as much as he liked tax inspectors, would immediately inform Anderson and he would be thrown out. The alternative was to enlist her help. An inside contact; she might stumble on an exclusive; she was bright enough, although a little drunk at the moment.

She solved it for him. 'You know,' she said, 'I could help you. I could be an informant, a grass.'

He sighed. 'All right, I confess.'

And he told her how it had come about.

She said: 'I'll help you if you promise me one thing.'

'Which is?'

'Don't become a rip-roaring great success.'

'Journalists never make any money.'

'Okay,' she said with finality, 'you've got yourself an accomplice. What do you want to know?'

'Everything.'

'That's quite a challenge for a first assignment.'

'And I want you to promise that you won't blow it.'

She licked one finger, dried it on her sleeve. 'See this wet, see this dry, cut my throat if I tell a lie.' She put one hand on his wrist; her hand was small and dry and the nails were shell-pink; like a child's hand, he thought. 'And I know what you're thinking. "She's smashed and she'll forget."

Well, if you find me with my throat cut you'll know I did forget.' She stood up. 'And now let's go for a walk.'

'I'm going back to the hotel.'

'Marvellous,' she said, 'I'll walk with you.'

Outside the air was scented with spring blossom. Daffodils bloomed in window-boxes and the church bells were pealing.

'Why did you get the sack?' she asked, taking his arm as though they had been walking out for weeks.

He told her about the poorly documented article he had written about Bilderberg.

'At least you're honest about it. And the limp?'

'A bullet in Beirut.'

She absorbed this information without comment. Instead of commiserating with him she said: 'I suppose everyone asks you if you're Irish.'

'A lot of them do.'

'I don't think you're Irish,' Suzy said. 'But I can understand people thinking you are. Cleft chin the devil's within. . . . Do you think you'll be able to make anything out of the conference?'

'It depends on my contacts.'

He glanced at her. A breeze ruffled her black hair and there was sunshine in her dark eyes.

In the lane she plucked a blade of grass and nibbled it. 'So,' she said, 'what do you want me to find out? You know, I've got to have something to work on.'

'Well, for a start, I read in the English papers that your Paul Kingdon – '

'Not mine.'

'Well, Paul Kingdon. According to the papers he was indisposed – a virus infection or something – and couldn't attend his booze-up at the Savoy. And yet here he is right as rain.'

'There never was anything wrong with him,' Suzy said. 'In fact he flew to America.'

'Did he now.' Foster frowned. 'And just before Bilderberg. Perhaps you could sound him out.'

'He said something about changes.'

'What sort of changes?'

'I don't know. He was very vague – out of character. But I got the impression that the changes were connected with the conference.'

Foster, instincts aroused, said: 'Anything else? Think carefully.'

'He was very different on the ferry. Broody and snappy. As though something had happened after his return from America. . . . Wait a minute,' she said, hand to her mouth. 'He bought some diamonds.'

'Where?'

'In Antwerp.'

'I thought you said he went to the States.'

'He came back via Antwerp. He showed me the diamonds.'

'Did he seem pleased with them?'

'And himself. So it must have been something that happened after that.'

As they neared the château he said: 'We'd better split up now. Trainee managers aren't supposed to chat up rich clients' girl friends.'

'Companion,' she said. 'I'm his companion.'

'It makes you sound about ninety.'

She disengaged her arm from his. 'How am I going to tell you if I find out anything?'

'We'd better meet again tomorrow at the pub. Same time.'

They stood framed in the sunlight looking at each other, both sensing that something was beginning.

Framed in the sights of a Karabiner 98K rifle.

Jacques Bertier caressed the trigger with one finger. He had brought it back to the apartment over the *tabac* after the search of selected houses in the village.

The man or the girl?

Both.

Temptation flowed from his brain to the finger on the trigger.

He closed his eyes, shook his head.

Madness.

Sweat oiled his trigger finger.

If he killed them he would be sacrificing the task for which he had prepared himself for so long.

In any case, what were they? A lackey of the wealthy and a rich man's whore.

He opened his eyes and lowered the rifle.

XXI

The palatial lobby of the château was crowded with reporters. Instead of trying to keep them at bay outside the gates, Anderson had advised the management to let them into an area where they could be contained and observed.

Stories had already appeared about secrecy and security and the reporters had been issued with a statement that revealed nothing. The statement sketched the origins of the conference:

'In the early 1950's a number of people on both sides of the Atlantic sought a means of bringing together leading citizens, both in and out of government, for informal discussions of problems facing the Western world. Such meetings, they felt, would create a better understanding of the forces and trends affecting Western nations.'

A couple of reporters wearing fake ID cards had penetrated as far as the ballroom, but a French police officer monitoring closed circuit television had checked them against the photographs of the guests and they had been ejected.

Others tried to infiltrate as new members of the staff; several attempted to bribe hotel employees living outside the hotel – the employees took the money and told the police.

When approached by Pressmen, guests replied noncommittally or not at all. The most outspoken was a former British prime minister who said he was looking forward to some good French cuisine 'and wine, of course.'

Photographers were not permitted beyond the gates and their long-focus lenses were examined in case the pistol-grips were designed to fire bullets.

When Claire Jerome wandered through the lobby, a reporter from U.P.I. called out: 'Give us a break, Mrs Jerome. Don't let the male chauvinistic pigs call the tune.'

But she seemed not to hear him, which was unusual for

her, because she was usually good with the Press. She seemed distracted and the reporters turned their attention to the German Chancellor – until the shepherd dogs following him growled.

Claire Jerome had, in fact, just left the conference room in the middle of the opening session on 'Trade Relations between the USA and the Common Market since the European Elections.'

The speeches were relayed in French and English through earphones so that the chamber had the appearance of a United Nations in miniature – except for the murals and immense chandeliers and the vistas through the windows, which seemed to lead back to an era of more dignified affluence.

Claire Jerome couldn't concentrate on the speeches. Instead her thoughts kept returning to the tape. The date. The threat.

In her blue-and-gold bedroom with its high, moulded ceiling and four-poster bed, she called Room Service, ordered tea and sat at the escritoire beside the window overlooking the lawns.

She wondered whether Pete Anello was in his room next door and whether she should consult him. She hadn't so far told him about the threat because it implied possessiveness, an assumption that she would even consider paying a fortune to keep him.

Unsolicited, another consideration surfaced. Could he be implicated? Was he so sure of himself that he knew she would pay five million dollars to save his skin? It wouldn't be the first time that an apparent kidnap victim had been part of the conspiracy.

She remembered the scene in the Bahamas when he had given her back the money and walked out. Had that been part of an elaborate long-term scheme? Perhaps it had begun in the casino. . . . *Pick up the old broad and make her fall for you, but play it cool.* After he had walked out it hadn't been too difficult to find him. . . .

'Please God,' she said aloud, 'don't let it be so.'

Pete Anello was the first one. The only one. Did he find

it pathetic to see a middle-aged woman behaving like a young girl in love?

A knock at the door. A waitress brought in the tea and a plate of wafer-thin tomato and cucumber sandwiches.

When she had gone Claire poured herself tea with lemon and picked up the article that Pierre Brossard was threatening to publish.

It was a clever piece of journalism. The old moral issues about weapon dealers – without any judgement from Brossard; then the revelation of an extension of those issues. *How can anyone with even vestigial principles condone the sale of weapons by a Jew to both the Jews and their enemies, the Arabs?*

Ironic, she thought, that she would have to pay Brossard two million dollars to keep him silent when she was for once in her life acting for idealistic motives. Helping the Israelis to survive.

There was a knock on the door and Pete Anello called out: 'Anyone at home?'

He came in, sat down and began to eat the sandwiches.

'Didn't you have any lunch?' Claire asked.

'Nope. Too busy carrying out my duties. You're still alive, aren't you?'

She watched him devouring the sandwiches. An unlikely blackmailer. She smiled at him. 'You're looking neat.' He was wearing a blazer and flannels bought in London, blue shirt and striped tie. 'You'll be playing cricket next,' she said.

'Sure, and carrying an umbrella.' He poured himself tea.

She was going to tell him about the threat on his life when the telephone beside the bed rang.

The phone was linked to a control system contained in a black box the size of a small suitcase. The system defeated wire-taps and incorporated a scrambler. It had been installed in the rooms of all guests requiring telephonic secrecy.

'*Bon jour, Madame Jerome,*' Brossard said. 'Welcome to my country.'

She said tersely: 'Okay, I've read it.'

'You liked it?'

'What do you think? But the answer is, yes, I'll pay. At the price arranged. How do you want the money?'

Brossard gave her the name of a bank in Monaco and she hung up before he had finished speaking.

When she turned, Anello was staring at her. He said: 'You tell me, how *can* anyone?'

She frowned: 'What are you talking about?'

He pointed at Brossard's article lying on the chair. 'How can anyone with even vestigial principles condone the sale of weapons –'

'You shouldn't have read it,' she cut him off.

'But I did. It was lying there to be read.' He stood up and walked to the window. 'Is it true?'

'Yes,' she said quietly, 'it's true. But there is a reason –'

'Selling arms to the Israelis AND the Arabs! Jesus, it's unbelievable.'

'You don't understand.'

He turned on her savagely. 'And if you don't, someone else will. And all the rest of the crap.'

'Pete, let me explain. Please.'

Hand on the door-handle, he turned. 'Who was that on the phone? Midas, or whatever the hell his name is? How much did you sell out for?' opening the door.

'Pete, there's been a threat . . . on your life,' as the door slammed behind him.

She ran to the door and opened it. He was striding down the corridor and she called out: 'Pete,' but he didn't turn round and then he was gone.

She closed the door and stood still for a few moments. Then she threw herself on the bed and wept.

*　　*　　*

Brossard put down the receiver, attached to the control system in his room in the east wing after speaking to Claire Jerome, and thought: Two million, that leaves three million to find.

That wouldn't be difficult. But should he pay? Blackmailers were rarely satisfied with a first demand. Supposing he handed over the five million and was then betrayed in Yugoslavia?

The last-war guerillas, elderly though they might be, wouldn't tolerate a man who had sent scores of Frenchmen fighting the same battle to their deaths. Nor would they eliminate him commando style because they had agreed to give him sanctuary.

No, they would wait a few weeks. Stage a robbery in his mansion, perhaps. Kill him swiftly and silently. Brossard imagined two grotesque, white-haired killers slipping into his bedroom, felt their knives sliding between his ribs.

But there wasn't really any alternative to paying the ransom. Whoever was making the threats obviously had all the evidence against him.

Escape? Brossard realised that he must have been under surveillance ever since the first enigmatic message had been delivered. If he made a run for it he wouldn't get farther than the gates.

There was nothing to be done except await the next move. But who was behind the blackmail? Lying on his bed, hands behind his head, Brossard stared at the ceiling and tried once again to work it out.

He had initially decided that the Russians were responsible for the first message. A theatrical warning. But he had been forced to dismiss the theory: the Soviet Union would certainly not be attempting to extract a miserly five million dollars from an agent who was about to establish for all time their supremacy over the United States. In any case the Russians knew that, by the end of the week, those five million dollars would be worthless. Today was Monday; his column would be published on Thursday morning, leaving two full week-days for the biggest bear raid in financial history.

Perhaps, somewhere within the KGB, there was an agent with capitalist inclinations. Perhaps a member of another intelligence organisation had penetrated Soviet Intelligence and gained access to the files on him.

Whoever it was, he was almost certainly stalking the

corridors of the Château Saint-Pierre at this moment.

The telephone rang beside him. Hildegard Metz. She said: 'Do you wish me to dictate your column to Paris, Monsieur Brossard? Monsieur Mayard has just been on the Telex.'

'No, I'll take care of that. As a matter of fact I'm just writing it.'

'When shall I tell Monsieur Mayard to expect it?'

'Tomorrow,' he said. 'Some time tomorrow. There's no urgency, the front page is the last to go to press.'

'Very well, m'sieur.' She hesitated.

'Is there anything else?'

'Monsieur Mayard asked if you could give him any idea what the column would be about.'

'Tell Mayard that he will know the contents of the column when I dictate it and not before.'

'Very well, m'sieur.'

Brossard replaced the receiver.

Mayard!

But he was forty miles away in Paris.

A knock on the door.

'Who is it?'

'Room service, m'sieur.'

But he hadn't ordered anything.

He opened the door so that it was still held by the chain. A waiter stood outside holding a silver tray; on the tray was a bottle standing on a white napkin.

Brossard slid the bolt on the chain. 'Who sent this?'

'I don't know, m'sieur. We found it standing on the table in our service room. There is an envelope addressed to you.'

Brossard took the tray. 'Service is included in the bill,' he said as the waiter hesitated. He closed the door.

Inside the envelope was a plain card. WITH OUR COMPLIMENTS. Nothing more.

He picked up the bottle. Slivovitch. The national drink of Yugoslavia.

*   *   *

Paul Kingdon had lunched with George Prentice. A cold buffet – Scotch salmon, York ham, Russian salad, Scandinavian roll-mops. . . .

'The French don't seem to have contributed much,' Prentice remarked.

Kingdon lifted a bottle of Muscadet from a silver ice-bucket. 'They contributed this,' as he poured the wine.

He watched Prentice tackle his plateful of food. 'You eat well, George,' he said. 'Where does it all go?'

'Brain matter,' Prentice replied.

Kingdon had considered telling Prentice about the blackmail threat but had rejected the idea: you didn't share knowledge that provided grounds for extortion. All he could do was wait and see if the blackmailers were genuinely in a position to carry out their threat. Kingdon knew that, despite what the trade claimed, any formula that could produce synthetic gem stones cheaply would debase the value of diamonds.

It was common knowledge that the supply of diamonds was controlled to maintain their value. If the Russians, for instance, released their stocks into the world markets, then their value would slump dramatically. The Russians did no such thing for the basic reason that it was in their interests to maintain their value. No-one in the Western world wanted roubles: everyone wanted diamonds.

'So,' said Kingdon, eating without appetite, 'you're going to deliver an address to Bilderberg.' He glanced round but the adjoining tables were unoccupied. 'What's the subject? Industrial espionage?'

'Capitalism,' Prentice said briefly.

'A wide-ranging subject.'

'And the contribution of Capitalism to the survival of democracy.'

'I think you're preaching to the converted, George.'

'I can always publish the speech afterwards.'

'And forfeit any future invitations to Bilderberg.'

'That wouldn't worry me unduly,' Prentice said.

Kingdon raised a hand to acknowledge the greeting of

Pierre Brossard as he walked past the table. 'What's going to happen to the dollar, George?'

'Nothing especially that I know of. It will have its ups and downs until the fuel crisis is sorted out. Unless, of course some sort of gigantic bear raid is mounted. But I can't see that happening.' Prentice put down his knife and fork. 'And now, I think, some desert.' He returned with a plateful of trifle dripping with cream.

'Don't you feel out of place here?' Kingdon asked as he tackled the sweet.

'Why should I?'

'Well, you've been wearing that jacket for at least ten years to my knowledge.'

'Harris tweed,' Prentice said. 'Never wears out.'

Hildegard Metz walked past and Kingdon remarked: 'Brossard certainly doesn't pick his secretaries for their looks.'

Prentice said: 'She's a stupid little bitch.'

Kingdon looked at him in surprise. 'You sound unusually vehement. You almost sound as if you hate her. Do you, George?'

Prentice watched Hildegard Metz sit down beside Brossard. He had known for three years that she was Helga Keller.

Kingdon said again: 'Do you, George?'

Prentice's voice was cold. 'I just happen to know that she's a stupid bitch.'

'And you're not saying why. . . .'

'That's right,' Prentice told him, pushing his plate aside, 'I'm not saying why.' He changed the subject. 'Do you still want me to tackle Gerard? We didn't dig up much on him. Nothing that can be used as leverage.'

'No,' Kingdon said, 'leave him to me.'

Kingdon sought out Alex Gerard, London-based partner of one of the most illustrious merchant banks in the world, in the bar that evening.

It was 6.30 pm. Most of the guests were sitting at tables. But the British preferred to stand at bars and Alex Gerard, despite his Gallic ancestry, was one of them.

Whatever Brossard predicted about the dollar Kingdon was determined to go ahead with his public offering: he had to maintain ascendancy over the Establishment who, despite the invitation engineered by Brossard, were poised to destroy him. To accomplish that he needed Gerard's support as an underwriter.

He said: 'Good evening, Alex. Can I get you a drink?' He had met Gerard once before at a cocktail party in the Barbican in the City of London.

Gerard, plump and bland, was holding an empty whisky glass. He turned and frowned and thrust out his bottom lip as if trying to identify Kingdon. Two years ago, Kingdon thought, you'd have been grovelling for my custom.

'I don't think –'

'Kingdon. Paul Kingdon. What is it, Scotch?'

'That's very civil of you.'

'Two Scotches,' Kingdon said to Jules. 'Water?'

'Just a little.'

The barman added Malvern water to both whiskies.

They sipped their drinks, appraising each other. Gerard said: 'Your first Bilderberg?'

'Correct. I had dinner with some members of the steering committee. We were discussing the future of my companies and they seemed to think their omission should be rectified.'

'Ah.'

'You know, of course, that I'm going public.'

'Yes,' Gerard said staring at his drink, 'I did know that.'

Kingdon named three members of the steering committee and told Gerard: 'They're going to invest heavily.'

'I'm delighted for your sake.'

'Good business for the underwriters,' Kingdon remarked.

'I believe you have an impressive list.'

'Including the Parisien branch of your family business.'

Gerard inclined his head and pointed at Kingdon's glass. 'May I get you the other half?'

Jules refilled the glasses.

'I wondered,' Kingdon said, 'why you hadn't followed the example of your French cousins.'

282

'As you know we are quite independent of each other.'

'But it's the first time you haven't taken part in an offering when the French side of the family has.'

'As I have said, Mr Kingdon, we reach our decisions independently.'

Kingdon fought to curb his anger. Smug, self-satisfied and patronising, Gerard personified the type of businessman that he had out-smarted. When the money was rolling in from all over the world, Kingdon had been fêted in the City. Now men like Alex Gerard were circling like vultures for the kill. He hoped Brossard was right in his predictions: he hoped that Gerard was up to his fat neck in dollars. He opened his briefcase and produced a ten-page précis of his proposed prospectus.

'If you could spare the time,' Kingdon said, 'I should be grateful if you would have a look at this.'

Gerard held the folder in one hand as though it was infectious. 'What precisely is this, Mr Kingdon?'

Kingdon told him.

'But we have already looked into your prospects, Mr Kingdon.'

'This crystallises them. There are some new ventures which might interest you.'

Gerard handed the folder back to Kingdon. 'I think not, Mr Kingdon. We have made our decision. If you must know, we came to the conclusion that some of your claims did not quite measure up to the facts.' He glanced at his wrist-watch. 'And now if you'll excuse me, I must go and change for dinner.'

Kingdon returned the folder to his brief-case. A salesman with a door slammed in his face! In his early days he had produced a booklet setting out the pitch which a salesman should use to close a deal. Number one: Never give up. But Gerard was already walking swiftly away.

A voice intoned over the Tannoy: 'Would Mr Paul Kingdon please call at reception.'

Suzy Okana was waiting there. 'They won't let me in,' she said. She was shielded from reporters by a black security guard.

'Okay,' he said to the guard, 'I'll vouch for her.' He and Suzy walked across the lobby to the elevator.

In his room he paced up and down the carpet while Suzy sat in an easy chair watching him.

'Do you want a drink?' he asked.

'A Perrier water, please. I had too much local plonk at lunch-time.'

'Call Room Service then.'

She stretched her long legs, the slits in her yellow dress reached to the top of her thighs. When the mineral water had been delivered she said: 'What's the matter? You look as though you've lost a tenner and found a fiver.'

'I've just been talking to a member of the aristocracy. An aristocratic pig.'

'You mean he wouldn't do what you wanted him to?'

'If what I think is going to happen does happen, he'll come to me on his knees.'

Suzy sipped her Perrier water. 'And what's that?'

'It doesn't matter.'

She shrugged. 'When is this *thing* going to happen?'

'At the end of the conference.' He stopped pacing and sat down on the bed opposite Suzy. 'You remember what I said?'

'About staying together?'

'Stay with me and you'll live like a queen.'

'I'm not very regal,' she said.

'I'm very fond of you, Suzy.'

'At film premieres,' she said.

'More than that.'

'I wish,' she said frowning, 'that I knew what you were talking about.'

'You will.' He leaned forward. 'How about it, Suzy?'

She shook her head. 'Let's just stick to our bargain. We agreed that either of us could pull out when they felt like it.'

'And you feel like it?'

'I didn't say that.'

'I'm going to live in Switzerland,' Kingdon said abruptly.

She looked at him in surprise. 'Why?'

'If I told you that the financial structure of the world is going to change, would you believe me?'

'I wouldn't believe you and I wouldn't disbelieve you.'

'And Switzerland will be about the only place to be for a year or so. Or somewhere behind the Iron Curtain, but I can't see myself sharing my roubles. I never did believe in equality.'

'Is this what you've been hinting at?'

Kingdon nodded.

'And how is the financial structure going to change?'

'Just take it from me that it is.'

'And I assume you're going to make a fortune out of it.'

'Of course.'

'And other people will lose millions?'

'Including Alex Gerard.'

'Who's Alex Gerard?'

'The pig I've just been talking to.'

'And ordinary small people. . . . They'll lose fortunes – or what seem to them to be fortunes?'

'It's never been any other way.'

She digested this. 'I suppose you're right. They don't even have any say in wars, do they?'

'I'm not responsible for what's going to happen,' Kingdon said.

'But you could prevent it?'

'I doubt it.'

'You could try. Paul Kingdon's name still means something.'

'Then I would be finished.' He tried to take her hand but she snatched it away. 'If I tell you something in confidence, will you promise not to tell anyone?'

'I suppose so,' draining the glass of mineral water.

'I'm being blackmailed.'

Her hand jerked as she was replacing the glass on the bedside table and she knocked over the bottle. It shattered on the tiles between the carpet and the wall. She knelt and began to pick up the shards of glass. 'Blackmailed? By whom?'

285

'I don't know.'

'What sort of blackmail?' She swore as she cut her finger on a piece of broken glass.

'No details,' he told her. 'I just thought I'd tell you. They want five million dollars,' he added, handing her a silk handkerchief to staunch the bleeding.

'Is that a lot of money? You know, I realise it's a fortune. But businessmen make and lose sums like that in a day. In a way that sort of money becomes pointless, doesn't it. I've known men who deal in millions and resent taking their wives for a week's holiday in Brighton. Pierre Brossard for instance.'

'What do you know about Brossard?'

She sucked her finger, wrapped the handkerchief round it. 'Only what I've read. He'd pick his own pockets. His appearance confirmed it when I met him at your house. A lecherous old sod, too.'

'Five million dollars is a lot of money to anyone,' Kingdon said. 'I can raise it all right, but hell, why should I?'

'That's right,' Suzy said, 'why should you? You haven't told me yet.'

'I have your promise?'

'You have my promise.'

'They claim they can make my diamonds worthless.'

'Make them worthless? Diamonds? They must be out of their tiny minds.'

'Oh no they're not,' Kingdon said.

And he explained why.

* * *

That evening reports of a violent quarrel between three unlikely protagonists spread among the staff of the hotel and reached one or two of the guests.

The quarrel was first heard by a chambermaid who was making her way from room to room along a corridor in the east wing removing the bedspreads, turning back the sheets and punching the pillows into shape. She stopped outside the door and, pressing one finger to her lips, beckoned to another chambermaid to come and share the entertainment. Together they lurked in a doorway across the corridor.

They were joined by a whistling pageboy who, after he had been forcibly quietened, also listened. It was he who spread the word but, because neither he nor the two maids had been able to understand much of what was said, it was an embroidered and garbled account that reached the chefs, kitchen-maids, waiters, porters, assistant managers and finally Monsieur Gaudin himself.

The room in which the quarrel took place was occupied by the English professor, Monsieur George Prentice. According to the pageboy, a woman's voice had been heard screaming abuse. Suddenly the door had been flung open and the security officer, Owen Anderson, had stormed out.

At this point the trio listening in the doorway dispersed, but not before they had glimpsed Prentice and the girl – identified by one of the maids as Hildegard Metz – facing each other, shouting. Fraulein Metz's hand was raised, said the pageboy, as though she was about to strike the Englishman.

Waiters later noted that both Anderson and Prentice arrived late for dinner in the banqueting hall when the brandy and liqueurs were being served. Prentice sat with Paul Kingdon, Anderson by himself; both appeared tense and distracted.

When Gaudin heard about the affair, he called Anderson into his office and said: 'Monsieur Anderson, no one would dispute that normally quarrels are private affairs.' His voice hardened. 'But not when they are aired so noisily that they become public. I do not like such scenes in my hotel. You of all people should not get yourself involved in such situations.'

Anderson apologised.

'I seem to remember,' Gaudin said, 'that you once indicated that you didn't care for Monsieur Prentice.'

'I guess he doesn't care too much for me either,' Anderson said.

'And Fraulein Metz. . . . How did she become involved in the quarrel?'

Anderson said quietly: 'It was something that happened a long time ago. Fraulein Metz has good reason to dislike both Prentice and myself. I'd rather not go into details. . . .'

'Very well, but I should be grateful if you would restrain your enmity until you have left my hotel. You do have rather more important matters to deal with, Monsieur Anderson. Tomorrow morning the President of my country and the former American Secretary of State are due to arrive here.'

'I'm truly sorry,' Anderson said.

'Very well. We'll say no more about it.'

They shook hands and thereafter acted as though the matter had been forgotten.

* * *

By 11.30 p.m. the château was quiet.

Because the delegates had to be fresh for the morning session, most of them had retired early. They lay in their beds stripped of the outward trappings of wealth, as vulnerable in sleep as the poor. From time to time one or the other would cry out as, in their dreams, a market crashed or a government toppled.

In one or two rooms, deals were clinched that had little to do with the avowed purpose of the conference. In Pierre Brossard's room, for instance, where three financiers attending the conference discussed dollars. Billions of them.

But, by and large, the guests were in the cradle of the great equaliser, sleep.

In the stone-flagged kitchens below, where herbs hung in bunches from the oak beams, grills and pans and saucepans, freshly scoured, stood in readiness to provide a hundred or so breakfasts of astonishing variety.

Room service was still alert; the night porter was checking his list of early calls and requests for newspapers; occasionally a dozing telephonist would awake with a jerk and place a call to a distant city where, in daylight, business was still being transacted.

The journalists had called it a day. In the grounds, guards patrolled in the moonlight as the clock in the village church tolled the hours across the fields.

In the bar, the last drinker finally gave up and went to bed.

As Jules was drying the last of the glasses Anderson walked in; Jules had expected him. 'A nightcap, Monsieur Anderson?'

Anderson shook his head wearily. 'Anything for me, Jules?'

'Nothing much. In fact, I don't really know if you'll be interested in what I've heard. It's only gossip. . . .'

'Shoot,' Anderson said.

'A couple of investment bankers were talking about dollars?'

'So?'

'I got the impression that they were planning some sort of coup.'

'Aren't they always?'

Jules shrugged. 'I only heard snatches of the conversation. You know how it is. In any case they would hardly go into details at the bar. . . .'

'Who were they?'

Jules gave him two names and Anderson jotted them down on the back of an envelope.

'Okay, it isn't really anything to do with security but I'll bear it in mind. Anything else?'

'Not really. And I wouldn't bring this up except that you mentioned the trainee manager, Nicholas Foster. He went to the village this afternoon. Did you know that?'

'I knew it.'

'Did you see him come back?'

Anderson shook his head.

'Well I did. You can see the lane from the French windows. He came back with that Chinese girl, the friend of the Englishman, Paul Kingdon.'

'Did he now.' Anderson made another note on the envelope. 'Lucky bastard. Anything else?'

'Not really, m'sieur. . . .'

'Come on,' Anderson said, 'out with it.'

Jules picked up a glass and began to polish it. 'There really is nothing,' he said.

'What you mean is that the best gossip you've heard concerns me.'

Jules shrugged. 'I heard there had been some sort of difference of opinion.'

'The understatement of the year. But it proves that you've got your ear to the ground. Keep it there, Jules.'

As Anderson walked out of the bar, he gave a mock salute to the French intelligence officer who was coming in for a nightcap. A Saint-Pierre Special.

XXII

The newspapers were deposited outside bedroom doors at 6.30 am, by which time many guests were showered and shaved and drinking their first cup of tea or coffee.

Outside Rooms 203 and 207 in the west wing and 82 in the east wing, the newspapers were accompanied by manilla envelopes of varying size on which were printed the occupants' names and one word: URGENT.

In Room 82 Pierre Brossard was awakened by an early call a quarter of an hour later than usual; but the benefit was cancelled out by the fact that he had hardly slept. He shuffled into the bathroom and stared at himself in the mirror; his age was showing; these days he needed his sleep.

He cleaned his teeth, doused his face with cold water and returned to the bedroom as a maid knocked and entered bringing him his tea; he barely noticed the pout of her lips or the expanse of leg as she bent to pick up the newspapers and envelope outside the door.

'Will there be anything else, m'sieur?'

Any other time, perhaps. Not this morning.

He glanced at the *Wall Street Journal* and the pink pages of the *Financial Times,* rushed from Paris to the château by courier service. Then he noticed the bulky envelope.

He opened it with trembling fingers.

Inside was a sheaf of papers, copies of old documents. All German. Some were signed by low-ranking Gestapo officers serving in France during the Occupation; one was signed by Reinhardt Heydrich, head of the RSHA which incorporated the Gestapo, and one by Ernst Kaltenbrunner, who took over when Heydrich was assassinated in Czechoslovakia. All incriminated Brossard as a traitor.

The trembling spread from Brossard's hand to his entire body.

He sat on the edge of the bed for a moment staring at the photostats. Then he picked up the typewritten letter stapled to the first copy. It was in French.

You will see from the attached documents that the evidence against you is comprehensive. Arrangements are in hand to distribute further copies of these documents to the Préfecture de Police in Paris, the offices of Le Monde, and the appropriate authorities in Belgrade.

These arrangements will be instantly cancelled when we receive confirmation that five million dollars has been deposited in Account No. CR 58432/91812 in the United Bank of Switzerland, Zurich, before the close of Swiss banking hours the day after tomorrow, April 24th.

We realise that you may harbour doubts as to whether all the evidence will be destroyed. You have only our word, but we would point out that five million dollars is sufficient for our needs and we would hardly repeat the risks involved in this operation.

We would also point out that you have no choice.

The letter was unsigned.

Brossard went into the bathroom and vomited.

He returned to the bedroom and copied the number of the Swiss account into an address book. Then he burned the photostats and the letter in the bath and washed away the charred paper with the hand-shower.

Five minutes later he made a phone call to Paris.

* * *

Claire Jerome awoke groggily in Room 203. She had taken two sleeping tablets before going to bed and the drugs were still in her bloodstream. Daylight entered the room gently through the blue curtains.

The telephone rang beside her.

'Madame Jerome? It's seven-thirty.'

She put down the receiver and pulled herself up onto the pillows as her memory returned. 'Pete,' she whispered, 'where are you?'

She pulled back the sheets and went to the bathroom

where she put on a shower-cap and let cold water sluice over her. Then she stared at herself in the mirror and thought: 'Look at you, you poor bitch.'

Ten minutes later a maid brought coffee and fresh orange juice. She put the tray on the table by the window and drew the curtains; light flooded into the room. She placed the newspapers on a chair beside the table, envelope beneath them.

Claire decided to drink her juice and coffee, put a face on and go into Anello's room to explain about the arms deal. He would probably still be asleep; some bodyguard, she smiled.

She glanced at the papers. Fuel. The dollar. Iran, Afghanistan. . . . She picked up an English tabloid. On an inside page was a story about whizz-kid Paul Kingdon whisking Oriental model Suzy Okana from the clutches of Bilderberg security and transporting her to his bedroom.

She put on bra and panties and returned to the bathroom.

The sleep and the drugs had lulled the fear. The blackmail threat was the work of a nut; when she explained the arms deal to Pete he would understand. And he would understand that she had to pay off Brossard because any publicity would wreck it.

She applied a foundation, attended to her eyes and mouth and slipped into a black cashmere sweater and a cream gaberdine two-piece. Round her neck she hung a rope of pearls.

She tidied the newspapers – and saw the envelope.

Her hand went to her throat.

With one scarlet fingernail she slit the envelope.

In case you are thinking otherwise, Mrs Jerome, our threat was quite serious. If you wish to see Mr Peter Anello alive again please deposit five million dollars in Account No. CR 58432/91812 in the United Bank of Switzerland, Zurich, not later than the conclusion of Swiss banking hours the day after tomorrow, April 24th.

She dropped the letter and ran to the door and into the corridor. She banged on Anello's door. 'Pete, Pete, open up, it's me, Claire.'

No movement, no sound.

A housekeeper in a white coat paused and stared at her. Claire turned and said to her: 'Have you got the pass key?'

I have, Madame, but I don't – '

'I think there may have been an accident. . . .'

The housekeeper took a bunch of keys from the pocket of her coat, selected one and inserted it into the lock.

The door swung open.

The room was empty.

At that moment Pete Anello was in a motel room ten miles away, staring down the barrel of an Uzi sub-machine gun.

*   *   *

Paul Kingdon opened the door of Room 207 to pick up the newspapers before the maid arrived with his tea, and spotted the envelope immediately. He wasn't surprised.

He slammed the door, ripped open the envelope. Inside were three photostats each bearing the heading THE JAGER FORMULA.

Kingdon sat down and perused them.

For at least a century, chemists had claimed to have manufactured diamonds – synthetics as opposed to simulants. The first to receive serious recognition was James Hannay, a Glaswegian, whose claim was verified by the Keeper of Minerals at the British Museum in 1880.

Kingdon knew that real success hadn't been achieved until 1953 when the Swedish company, ASEA, managed to produce diamonds of less than one millimeter. In 1955 General Electric of America also produced synthetic diamonds, and because of ASEA's secrecy, were granted a patent. But the diamonds were only suitable for industrial use.

De Beers also evolved a method of making synthetic grit, but it wasn't until 1970 that General Electric announced the production of gem diamonds – white with a few flaws.

The method was to *grow* diamonds from seed crystals with a catalyst in pressure chambers at intense heat. But there were several snags: the synthetic stones could be identified as such because, unlike most natural diamonds, they were electro conductive; they contained tiny blemishes and, most damning of all, they cost considerably more to manufacture than it cost to mine natural diamonds.

Kingdon didn't understand the Jager Formula but he had no doubt that it purported to have overcome these difficulties. He read the accompanying letter.

It will have come as no surprise to you to learn from our recorded message that a method of manufacturing flawless white diamonds, indistinguishable from natural crystals, has now been perfected. Nor will you be greatly surprised to know that the formula has been repressed by an international cartel determined to maintain the value of gem stones.

As you can now see from the enclosed copies we do have the formula. Furthermore we are in a position to go into immediate production; the subsequent glut of flawless diamonds will make existing stocks virtually worthless.

Ironically this formula will not enrich us because, of course, although we would be producing perfect diamonds, we would at the same time be killing our own market. We concluded, therefore, that the only way to profit from the possession of this formula is to sell it. We can assure you that it is the only pirate copy in existence.

If you arrange for five million dollars to be deposited in Account No. CR 5843/91812 of the United Bank of Switzerland, Zurich, by the close of banking hours the day after tomorrow, April 24th, you have our promise that the formula and our equipment will be destroyed and we shall not go into production.

We appreciate that you will want to verify the validity of this formula and we have no doubt that in your present circumstances at Bilderberg you will not find this difficult. Do not dispose of the envelope before examining it closely: it contains a small gift manufactured at our plant three days ago. One last condition: please make sure that you raise the money from your personal assets, i.e. not from your clients' investments.

Kingdon felt the bottom of the envelope with thumb and forefinger. The diamond had lodged in one corner; he turned the envelope upside down and the stone fell into the palm of his hand. It was about one carat and, as far as Kingdon could determine without a loupe, flawless. It looked as though it would rate high in the colour grading system, i.e. River or Blue Wesselton, second and third after Jager which was extremely rare. But doubtless the Jager Formula could reproduce a Jager.

Kingdon re-read the letter. *In the present circumstances*? He consulted the guest list. Among the visitors from Holland was van Wyk, chairman of one of the most famous diamond merchant companies in Amsterdam. Kingdon had met him when he was negotiating the purchase of the Kingdon Diamond. Kingdon thought about the diamond lying in its vault in the City of London. It had been described as priceless: if the formula in his hand was genuine it could soon be worthless. Flood any market and you drown it.

He picked up the telephone cradled in the black box, and asked the switchboard operator to put him through to van Wyk. Van Wyk agreed to receive him in his room in half an hour. Anticipating a sale, Kingdon thought sourly.

The diamond merchant was a big man, reputed to be homosexual, with a drum belly – Kingdon noticed a corset hanging in the wardrobe – and a jovial disposition that Kingdon suspected was spurious. He was wearing a gold silk dressing-gown.

'Coffee, Mr Kingdon?'

Kingdon shook his head.

'Something stronger? A little Bols gin perhaps?' gold teeth gleaming in his smile.

'Not at this time in the morning,' Kingdon said. Bols gin for breakfast, Christ! He handed van Wyk the diamond. 'Could you have a look at that for me?'

Van Wyk fetched a loupe from the dressing-table and inspected the diamond, chuckling as he did so. 'A little beauty if I may say so,' and, putting the loupe in the pocket of his dressing-gown: 'What have you in mind, Mr Kingdon?'

'Is it genuine?'

Van Wyk guffawed. 'As genuine as the Kingdon Diamond itself.'

'I'd like you to have a look at this.' Kingdon handed the diamond merchant the Jager Formula. 'Tell me if it's plausible.'

Van Wyk glanced at the sheets of paper. The joviality evaporated immediately. 'Where did you get this, Mr Kingdon?' His eyes had suddenly become as cold and hard as diamonds.

'It doesn't matter where I got it. I want to know if it's genuine.'

'This is a serious matter, Mr Kingdon, very serious indeed. If this were to fall into the wrong hands. . . .'

'As far as I know, it's the only copy. You can keep it if you want.' Van Wyk immediately opened his briefcase and slipped the sheets of paper inside. 'All I want to know is, would it work?'

'You must first tell me where you got it and what you propose to do with the information. Have you copied the formula?'

Kingdon shook his head. 'I can't tell you where I got it. It came into my possession, that's all I can tell you because that's all I know. And as for doing anything with it, the fact that I came to see you speaks for itself. I don't even understand the bloody thing.'

Van Wyk's dressing-gown slipped open and an expanse of taut belly came into view. He pulled the gold silk around himself and re-tied the belt. Then he said: 'You ask me if it will work. The answer is yes. As you probably know, gem diamonds were manufactured in 1970. All it needed was the application of sophisticated electronic equipment to perfect the process. This was achieved eighteen months ago –'

'But suppressed for the sake of the industry?'

'Of course. Why should the world's most precious possessions be devalued because of some mundane advancement in technology?'

'And diamond merchants' fortunes. . . .'

Van Wyk nodded. 'And collectors' fortunes. Which I pre-

sume,' he continued, 'is why you brought the formula to me.
You are presumably as anxious as the rest of us to make sure
that the formula should have a very limited circulation.'

'I merely wanted to find out if it's genuine.'

'Then I've answered your question. And now I shall have
to investigate this lapse on someone's part. Are you sure you
can't tell me how this came into your possession?'

'Quite sure,' Kingdon told him, and 'Thank you for your
time,' as he opened the door and went out into the corridor.
'You can keep the diamond,' he said over his shoulder. 'Who
the hell wants a hand-made diamond?'

In his room two doors away from Claire Jerome's, he sat
down on the bed and re-read the letter before taking it into
the bathroom and burning it in the washbasin.

Then he ran a hot bath. He lay in the water for ten
minutes thinking. The bastards! The prospect of parting
with five million dollars to extortionists filled him with self-
disgust. There was only one redeeming feature: the blackmailers would be receiving ransom which, if Pierre Brossard
was to be believed, would almost immediately be valueless.

Kingdon made his decision and reached for the bath-towel.

* * *

At 8 am Anderson made a routine sweep of the conference
hall.

When he reached the microphone, through which guests
made their speeches, a green light began to flash on the portable bug-detector.

Anderson examined the microphone and from the base
retrieved a primitive eavesdropping device. Frowning, he
slipped the bug into his jacket pocket. So now, he thought,
we have an amateur among us.

XXIII

Pete Anello had left the château at 5.30 am.

Since Claire Jerome had confirmed that she was selling to both Arab and Jew, he had been examining her morals. And his own.

In Nassau he had been a bum. But free with no bouts of introspection, nothing to fear except the nights when he smelled burning flesh and heard the screams. Now his emotions were complicated.

He opened a bottle of whisky in his room and, over a period of several hours, drank most of it. Then he went to bed and slept.

When he awoke he felt stifled by the atmosphere of the château, oppressed by the wealth slumbering beneath one roof.

He opened the window. It was still dark. Mist lay close to the ground, an owl hooted, the moonlit clouds were high and motionless.

He dressed in a fawn sweater and denim suit and picked up the keys of Claire's green Porsche, which he had driven to the château from Paris. He let himself out of the room and walked swiftly down the corridor to the elevator.

As he went past reception the night porter signalled to the dozing switchboard operator who made a house call.

Anello stood in the drive for a moment, breathing deeply to try and disperse the aftermath of the whisky; then he headed for the car park adjoining the stables at the rear of the château.

By the time he drove out a man wearing a soft brown hat and black knitted scarf had reached the blue Fiat 124 Sport parked in the drive. A gendarme at the gates checked out Anello, stepped back and saluted; thirty seconds later he repeated the performance for the driver of the Fiat.

Anello had no idea where he was driving to; he merely knew that he had to get away for a while.

He didn't drive fast – he had long since lost any sense of urgency – and the driver of the Fiat had no difficulty in following. Anello decided that if he came across a small hotel somewhere in the countryside he would spend the rest of the night there.

And then? Anello didn't know. But he had to reach a decision. He was being kept by a woman who dealt in arms. A woman, he had discovered, who saw nothing immoral in selling weapons to the Jews, her own people, and to their enemies.

Balance of power, shit! The Porsche accelerated out of a mist-filled hollow in the road, then slowed down again.

Ahead lay a main road. And on the corner a motel, its name picked out in stuttering pink neon: VOYAGEURS. Anello parked the car in the forecourt and went in.

He handed his passport to a resentful porter, registered and took the key to Room 303 which the porter flung on the counter. The room was shabby but it had style, flowered curtains, reproduction furniture, everlasting flowers in a vase; the French could invest a prison cell with charm.

He washed his face and hands, wished he had brought a toothbrush. The knock on the door startled him. 'Yeah, who is it?' finishing drying his face.

'We forgot to change the bed linen, m'sieur.'

Anello glanced at the bed. The sheets didn't look too dirty, but they didn't look too clean either. Someone else's infectious disease was all he needed.

He opened the door and stared at the man in the corridor. He was vaguely familiar but his face was partially concealed by a black scarf and the brim of his hat. The man was carrying an attaché-case.

'Who the hell are you?'

'May I come in? We have to talk.'

'Like fuck.'

Anello tried to slam the door but the man jammed it with his foot.

Anello took a step forward and threw a punch. Somehow

the punch missed and Anello's arm was behind his back; the man with the scarf pushed and Anello hit the wall on the other side of the room.

The man shut the door. As Anello began to get up, he pressed the rapid-release button on the handle of the attaché-case; the lid of the attaché-case flew open; with one hand he took out the Uzi sub machine-gun nestling inside, dropping the case at the same time.

He said: 'Neat, aren't they? The Special Branch carry them in Ireland. You're fully armed within three seconds.' He waved the gun towards a chair in the corner. 'I suggest you go and sit there.'

'What the hell is this?' Anello stood up rubbing his head where it had slammed into the wall.

'I'm sorry it has to be like this.'

'You're sorry!'

'I'm sure you'll understand when I explain,' the man said. 'You see I have a proposition to put to you.'

XXIV

The two top security risks arrived together by helicopter at midday. The President of France and the former American Secretary of State.

As the helicopter banked like a giant dragon-fly and began to descend, thirty or so delegates made their way to the helipad beside the car-park.

During the morning, the debate had been passionate. It had been scheduled to relate to the fuel emergency. But it had exploded into the whole Middle East crisis, the Soviet threat to the oil supplies there and the future of the Olympic Games. Hawks and doves angrily mounted the lectern; the possibility of the third world war had been discussed.

Most of the delegates were relieved when the roar of the helicopter – a twin-engined Bell 212, in which the ex-Secretary had been touring Western Europe – broke up the session.

The helicopter approached at an angle to avoid its own slipstream and settled on the helipad. The blades scythed the air a few times, stopped. The President emerged first, tall, angular, distinguished; the American, who had once travelled the world as other men commute from home to office, followed closely behind him, physically the antithesis of the Frenchman – dumpy, bespectacled, radiating energy.

The sun shone. The introductions were informal. An historic occasion. If there had been any cameramen there to record it.

Anderson watched from the wings, eyes scanning the backcloth to the scene for any movement, any incongruous detail. Security guards milled around in the background.

Beside Anderson stood Inspector Moitry, the local French plain-clothes police chief. He was stockily built with sleek greying hair and pouchy eyes. He carried with him an air of disillusion. A fall guy.

Anderson said to the Frenchman: 'A classic scene for an assassination.'

Moitry puffed nervously at his cigarette. 'Don't even say things like that.'

The introductions were concluded. The two statesmen went into the château followed by their personal bodyguards. Each had been allotted a suite of rooms on the top floor of the west wing; both suites had been double-checked that morning.

'At least they're safe inside,' Anderson said.

'I pray to God that you're right,' Moitry said lighting another cigarette. 'I'm afraid I have a premonition about this conference.'

But Moitry, Anderson thought, was the sort of man who shared his life with premonitions.

*   *   *

In the village at 3.15 that afternoon a series of events took place that would have fully justified Inspector Moitry's premonition.

Two years ago Jacques Bertier had taken up trout fishing. Today, instead of his rods, he packed the old German rifle into the long canvas container. He buttoned down the flap at the end and, as an extra precaution, bound it with twine. Into the pocket of the camouflaged jacket he wore on his fishing expeditions, he slipped six rounds of ammunition which his twin brother had stored in the old tin chest all those years ago.

He locked the door of the apartment behind him and descended the stairs humming to himself. He was pleased with his nonchalant manner because he felt far from nonchalant; his hands were greased with sweat and he could hear the thud of his heart.

He waved to the old woman in the *tabac*; the old woman waved back. Stick to the routine he had established: that was the secret. Which was why he dropped into the inn for a rum.

'To keep out the cold,' he told the black-haired woman behind the bar. It wasn't cold but it was his customary excuse.

'Are you going to be away long?' looking at him significantly because her husband was away and she had indicated that she would come up to the apartment later.

'About an hour.'

The thought of sex after the shooting excited him even more.

He was about to leave when the priest entered the bar. The priest ordered a glass of red wine and said: 'Can I get you one? Rum, I believe. . . .'

'No thank you, father. One's enough.'

'Going fishing?'

He smiled and thought: For big fish.

He walked into the daylight. The weather had changed and low clouds were scurrying across the sky. The village was at rest. Which was how he wanted it.

He set off at a brisk pace towards the river that lay half a mile from the village, waving to the uniformed *gendarme* posted outside the church.

The route he always took skirted the church. Today he paused in the shadow of a woody old yew tree. On the other side of the narrow road stood a hedge with a hole tunnelled through it by children taking a short cut through the graveyard to the shops.

He consulted his wrist-watch. Three-twenty-nine. Surely nothing could have gone wrong. . . .

One second later the small charge of explosive, attached to a crude timing device that he had fastened during the night to a gravestone on the far side of the cemetery, exploded.

Such planning. Such timing.

He heard the running footsteps of the *gendarme* on the other side of the church. He ducked through the gap in the hedge and, keeping low, made for the small door at the rear of the church leading to the vestry.

Six months earlier, while Mass was being celebrated, he had nipped into the vestry and stolen the spare key. He inserted it into the lock; it turned easily.

He moved swiftly through the vestry and the nave of the church. He took the stairs leading to the belfry two at a time. By now the priest would be on his way home for his afternoon nap. He was safe.

It was as he was sliding the rifle out of the canvas container that he heard the footsteps creaking on the stairs.

*   *   *

At the same time that Jacques Bertier was descending the stairs prior to drinking a rum in the village inn, two men met by arrangement in a room in the west wing of the Château Saint-Pierre.

The subject to be discussed: the extortion of $15 million from three guests – Claire Jerome, Pierre Brossard and Paul Kingdon.

One man was code-named King, the other Prince.

The man code-named Prince was wearing head-phones when his partner knocked on the door. He had been listening to a wire-tap installed in the telephonic control system in Pierre Brossard's room. The systems in each of the subjects' rooms had been sabotaged – phone-taps instead of tap-defeats.

Prince took off the head-phones, listened carefully to the series of knocks on the door – three short, two spaced out, two short – then opened it.

While he locked the surveillance equipment in a suitcase, the newcomer swept the room with an electronic bug alert equipped with visual and audio signals. Neither spoke as he meticulously carried out the search. Walls, ceiling, light fittings, every article of furniture.

The search was an unvariable preliminary to conversation.

Finally, the newcomer, King, grinned and said one word. 'Clean.'

'Our own control system?'

'I don't think anyone else would be bright enough to bug

an anti-bug gadget.' He shrugged. 'But I'll check.' Again he said: 'Clean.'

Prince glanced at his wrist-watch. It was 3.19. The third conspirator was four minutes late.

When he pointed this out, the man code-named King said: 'A minor unpredictable. There will be plenty of those around. Minor *and* major. Now let's get on with it. Time is what we don't have. How is Brossard reacting?'

'Like a dream. I heard him on the wire-tap making arrangements for the five million dollars to be transferred to Zurich. He sounded as though he was giving blood.'

'Likewise Kingdon. The beauty of it is that both Kingdon and Brossard reckon the money won't be worth the paper it's printed on. But for once in his life Midas is going to be wrong.'

'So what we're missing is the reaction of Subject No. 3, Mrs. Claire Jerome,' the man known as Prince said.

'She'll pay. She won't even miss five million dollars.'

'I'd like to know for sure.'

There was a knock on the door. Not *the* knock. They waited in silence. The door-handle turned but the door was locked.

A pause. Then footsteps retreating down the corridor.

'Probably the maid,' said Prince who occupied the room.

His companion said: 'I'm going to call the room.'

He held the receiver away from his ear. Together they listened to the phone ringing in another room in the west wing. No-one answered it. He recradled the receiver.

'I can't wait any longer,' Prince said.

'Give it another couple of minutes. We meet again in three hours, right?'

His companion nodded. 'I wonder if anything's gone wrong. . . .'

'Nothing can have gone wrong. We've plotted every detail. It's been a long, long time. . . .'

Footsteps in the corridor.

They stopped outside the door.

Three short raps, two spaced out, two short.

'You're late,' they both said as the third conspirator, code-named Vixen, entered the room.

'I know, I'm sorry,' as the door closed. 'I had to call Paris. But everything is going according to plan.'

The tension dissolved.

The three smiled at each other.

Owen Anderson.

George Prentice.

Helga Keller.

Part Four

XXV

As Owen Anderson had remarked, it *had* taken a long time.

Ever since the 1977 Bilderberg conference – the first that Helga Keller, alias Hildegard Metz, had attended as Pierre Brossard's secretary.

George Prentice had first seen her sitting alone in the Regency lounge of the Imperial Hotel in the sedate English resort of Torquay in Devon.

He hadn't taken any particular note of her. Nor had he realised that he was looking at a woman whose whole faith had recently been destroyed. . . .

Prentice had arrived in Torquay several days before the conference to complete his ground-work. So had Owen Anderson. (Six weeks earlier he had carried out a preliminary security check.) So had Helga Keller – to prepare the way for Brossard.

Prentice had been exploring the hotel 'patronised for more than a century by the Royal Households of Europe.' He found it to his liking. The ornate chambers, the air of dignified affluence that drew upon the past splendours of Paris, Vienna and Imperial Russia; the sense of the past brought up to date by the sauna, indoor and outdoor pools, conference room equipment with duplicators, spotlights, translation equipment and health and beauty parlour providing anything from ultrasonic diathermy to a seaweed bath.

As usual Bilderberg had chosen well.

Debating what to put in his first report to Ballard in London, Prentice made his way to the Regency lounge where, beneath a maroon ceiling, you could relax to the accompaniment of a small fountain splashing in one corner.

Prentice sat down and ordered a whisky and soda. It was 6.30 pm. There were about a dozen guests in the lounge. By the time the conference opened on April 22 they would all be gone except for a handful of permanent residents.

He stretched out his legs, sipped his drink. Tried to imagine the scene in the days when, so it was said, Edward VII had dallied there with Lillie Langtry.

After a while he became aware of the woman sitting two tables away from him. He should have noticed her earlier; part of the training was to assess men – or women – sitting by themselves: they were usually waiting for someone, and that someone was sometimes yourself. But, as he had acknowledged to himself more than once recently, he was becoming careless. Too old for the game.

He looked at her more closely. She wore a dark grey two-piece and a white blouse; her hair was severely styled and he decided that her eyes behind her spectacles would be blue-grey.

He was assailed by a vague sense of familiarity.

Who had arrived in advance of Bilderberg? Of course, Hildegard Metz, secretary to the Gallic pillar to miserliness, Pierre Brossard.

Why should I think I know Fraulein Metz?

When she took off her spectacles, Prentice noted that she didn't blink or squeeze the bridge of her nose as people who needed glasses did as they re-adjusted their vision. Plain glass?

Prentice frowned but was saved from further puzzlement by the woman who walked over to his table and said: 'Mr George Prentice?'

Prentice stood up, nodded. 'I don't think I –'

'I'm sure you do. I'm Hildegard Metz, Pierre Brossard's secretary.'

He pointed at a seat and said: 'Please sit down.'

'Thank you.' She sat down, pulled her skirt down over her knees and regarded him through blue-grey eyes that had never needed spectacles.

And now it was coming back: he was poised on the brink of revelation. Not Hildegard but. . . .

'You once knew me as Helga Keller,' she said.

He stared at her. Time was spinning and there framed in the sights of his rifle was Karl Danzer.

He began to speak: 'I didn't –' but stopped himself. He picked up his whisky and soda to gain time.

She said: 'Mr Prentice, how would you care to take a walk with me? It's not a particularly pleasant evening but I think the fresh air would do us both good.'

And walk into the sights of a rifle?

She understood and said quietly: 'There's nothing to worry about, I promise you. It was all a long time ago. . . .'

He stood up and said: 'Yes, of course,' and thought that, if he did get shot, it would be a fair and just penalty for becoming old and careless, affected by the tears in a woman's eyes.

It was dusk and a light rain was sweeping in from the sea, polishing the evening and stinging their cheeks. Across Torbay where Napoleon had sojourned on his way to exile in St. Helena, they could see the lights of Brixham, green and orange.

Seagulls flew low across the water crying about loneliness.

Prentice and Helga Keller wore raincoats and they walked with their hands thrust deep in their pockets. For a little while neither spoke.

Below them, as they descended the hill, small boats jostled each other in the inner harbour. Torquay is a resort for the retired; retirement, Prentice thought, must be infectious because the Strand was deserted, everyone at home settled in front of television.

He said: 'I didn't kill him you know.'

He had to listen hard to her reply as the wind grabbed her words. 'I know,' she said.

Silence, except for the sound of the water and the hiss of tyres on the wet surface of the road.

He asked her: 'Have you always known?'

She shook her head. 'For eight years I've done nothing but hate.'

He thought about his own hatred and what it had done to him. 'When did you find out?' he asked.

'Two months ago.'

'But you've always known about me?'

'Ever since Karl died, yes.'

They rounded the inner harbour and walked along the promenade beside the deserted Abbey Sands.

'We assumed you did,' Prentice said. 'But, of course, you disappeared.'

'I wanted to kill you. Ever since that day I wanted to kill you.'

'You understand that I intended to shoot Danzer?'

'You and Anderson.'

'Oh no,' Prentice said. 'Anderson didn't want to shoot him.' He was silent for a moment. Then he asked: 'Have *they* always known about Anderson and me?'

'Ever since Zurich,' she said. 'I told them. You command considerable respect. They've never known quite what to make of you. . . .'

'I'm flattered. But now,' as the rain drove at him and found its way inside the collar of his raincoat, 'you must tell me. You once wanted to kill me. Why not now?'

As they walked back towards the hotel she told him.

When she visited Litvak in Moscow it was obvious that he had little time left.

He was alone in his small poorly-furnished apartment near the United States Embassy. A pathetic place to die, she thought as she glanced at the crudely-made furniture, the newspaper stuck around the windows to keep out the knife-blade of cold, the shelf of dull doctrinaire books. . . .

He was sitting on a sofa, a blanket drawn up to his chin. Death had already touched him: his eyes were yellow and the skin was tight over his cheek bones.

He touched her hand and she felt his coldness reach her.

'I was glad you could come,' he said. 'Are you here on business?'

'I would have come anyway,' she told him.

She went into the minute kitchen and made tea, squeezing lemon into each cup. Litvak could barely lift his.

Outside flakes of snow touched the window. The street below, separating two apartment blocks, was covered with black ice.

She found it difficult to talk because they both knew he was dying.

After a while he said: 'There is something I must tell you.' A pause while he gathered his breath. 'You've always known how I felt about you?'

She leaned forward and held his icy hand. 'I guessed,' she said, remembering the day beside the river.

'Maybe I should have told you then. Except' – he began to cough and it was a few moments before he recovered – 'that you wouldn't have believed me.'

She frowned. 'Believed what?'

He pointed across the room at a dossier lying on the sideboard beside a bowl of plastic fruit. 'Could you please bring me that over here?'

Still frowning, she picked up the worn grey file. On the top were two words: KARL DANZER. She began to tremble because she knew that something indescribably terrible was about to occur.

'Yes,' he said again, 'I should have told you then. But I thought I would be destroying you. Now I know better. I am dying and I know better, and I know that everything behind me has been empty. You mustn't let that happen to you, my Helga.'

She moved her chair away from the sofa. 'Please . . . tell me. . . .'

The voice issuing from between his lips was like a voice on a scratched old gramophone record. Or a voice from the grave.

'Karl Danzer,' he said, 'was a traitor.'

'No!'

He waved his hand at the dossier. 'It's all in there. He was cheating the Soviet Union out of millions of dollars.'

Again she cried: 'No,' as the dying man continued to destroy the years behind her.

'The American and the British – this man Prentice –'

'He killed Karl –'

'No, *we* killed Karl Danzer.'

An alarm clock on the table beside the sofa ticked away Litvak's life as the snow flakes pressed against the window.

Litvak went on: 'The British and Americans found out about the money in a numbered account and they blackmailed him. He told them everything he knew about the KGB operation. Moscow decided to eliminate him. An agent from Department V – or 13 as it used to be called – was dispatched to Zurich. The obvious time to kill him was when he was on the way to his chalet. It so happened that the British thought along the same lines. It wasn't Prentice's bullet that killed Danzer – it was one of ours. . . .'

She felt faint and pressed her head down towards her knees. 'I don't believe it,' she said. 'I don't believe it.'

'I didn't think you would. That's why I obtained the dossier.'

She raised her head. 'Why did the British want to kill him?'

'Because he had sent many of their agents to their deaths.'

The ticking of the clock seemed to be louder.

She picked up the dossier but he said: 'Not now.' He reached out his hand once more and she took it, and he said: 'I'm sorry. . . .'

She said: 'How do I know whether this dossier is genuine?'

'I have no reason to fake anything. I have my contacts in Dzerzhinsky Square. They obtained it for me. Has it occurred to you why I wanted you to know?'

She shook her head.

'Because your life has been founded on hatred. I don't want to die knowing that it is going to continue that way.'

He sipped his cold tea, spilling some on the blanket. She took the cup from him.

'Go now,' he said, 'and come back when you've read it.' He managed a smile that momentarily lit his face. 'And one more thing. Always remember that afternoon beside the beach. We were close then, my Helga. . . .'

She took the dossier. She read it. Then she burned it and all the horror it contained.

When she returned to Litvak's apartment, the door was locked and a neighbour told her that he had died during the night.

'At first,' she told Prentice as they retraced their footsteps, 'I was numb. And then, little by little, I began to think about everything I had seen in Russia. I realised that Karl's beautiful dreams were nightmares – not, of course, that he ever believed them himself. I was just a pathetic little dupe. One of many, according to the dossier.'

Prentice took her arm; it was the only thing he could think of to do.

'I thought of Budapest and Prague. I thought of the millions enslaved and I realised that I must have been crazy. But, of course, they caught me young . . .' And Prentice knew that the tears had returned to her eyes and were mingling with the rain.

Still he didn't know what to say. After a while he said: 'So what are you going to do now?'

The rain was easing off. A tiny rent appeared in the clouds. A sliver of moonlight.

'I'm not sure. I knew that to stand any chance of survival I had to go on playing it their way. Then I saw you. It was, of course, inevitable that we would meet at Bilderberg. You were the symbol of my hatred and I knew that the hatred had been a wasting and I knew that I had to talk to you. . . .'

The rain had stopped; far out across the bay the moonlight silvered the water.

'Perhaps,' he said, 'you would have dinner with me. We have a lot to talk about.'

* * *

The plan was seeded that night without either Helga Keller or George Prentice realising it. It was clinched the following day by Owen Anderson.

XXVI

For Owen Anderson the day began well.

He breakfasted in his room gazing across the bay, which this morning was as blue as the sky. He opened the window and smelled rain-washed air and spring blossom. An English sort of day. Anderson enjoyed England – its unruffled ways, its touches of faded elegance, its sense of the ridiculous.

Perhaps, he reflected later, it was the English ambience that was partly responsible for the momentous decisions that were taken that day.

But, as he yawned and stretched in the very English room with its ornate ceiling and old-fashioned furniture, he would have regarded any suggestion that he would soon be involved in a plot to extort $15 million as extravagant lunacy.

He showered and shaved and dressed in a fawn suit with flared turn-ups, ordered more coffee from Room Service and, with Frank Sinatra singing to him through loudspeakers concealed in the walls, sat down at a desk and ran through the accommodation arrangements.

Kissinger in Suite 410 (personal guards next door) . . . Helmut Schmidt in Suite 210, guard dogs in tow . . . Lord Home, who was temporarily taking the chair after the Bernhard debacle, in the Chinese Room . . . David Rockefeller in one of the apartments adjoining the hotel. . . .

The coffee arrived. Anderson poured it black and strong, leaned back in his chair and picked up *The Times*.

And it was then that the sourness that for the past year or so had disturbed him returned. On the front page was a report of yet another investigation into the CIA. Allegations of surveillance on visiting statesmen; accusations of overspending. . . .

Anderson hurled the newspaper across the room. It read like an attack on the KGB rather than an attack on the

United States' own intelligence organisation. The syndrome of self-destruction.

But it wasn't until he received the coded cable from CIA headquarters in Langley, Virginia, that the day that had dawned so serenely broke up into shards of bitterness and anger.

It took a few seconds before the message sank home. *He, Owen Anderson, was under investigation.* After Bilderberg he was required to give an accounting of his expenditure over the past twelve months and details of an audio-visual tap he had planted on a team of East German industrialists visiting Los Angeles.

It didn't seem to matter that he had nailed them discussing industrial sabotage: all that mattered was that a dove-like senator with paranoic tendencies regarding the CIA, had exposed the surveillance. Once again the Agency was the enemy: the real enemy was a martyr.

The cable ended on a slightly apologetic note from Danby. It was, apparently, Anderson's life-style that had upset the self-appointed critics of what had once been the best intelligence network in the world.

His bachelor pad on the East Side! As though it were a baronial mansion, a seat of decadence and corruption.

Fuck them!

Anderson paced the room, thumbs stuck in the pockets of his waistcoat. He remembered his youth and his ideals and the unrelenting slog of achievement, and the anger surged inside him.

When the knock came on the door he shouted: 'Who is it?' And when George Prentice identified himself, he flung open the door and said: 'What do you want, for Christ's sake?'

Prentice said: 'I want to talk.'

'The last thing on this fucking earth I want to do,' Anderson said, bunching his fists, 'is talk to you.' He began to shut the door but Prentice pushed it aside, once again surprising Anderson with his strength.

Anderson swung at him with one fist; Prentice parried the blow, but its impetus sent him sprawling on the bed. He lay there gazing at Anderson in astonishment.

Anderson said: 'Now get out.'

'First hear what I've got to say.'

Anderson hesitated, lowered his fists. Prentice wasn't the enemy. Who was the enemy? He no longer knew. 'What the hell do you want?'

'Shut the door first.'

Anderson kicked the door shut.

'I presume this room is clean?'

'Does it matter?'

'It matters.'

Anderson went to the window and stared out across the bay. A few white sails had appeared on the sea which now looked like molten silver in the sunlight. 'It's clean,' he said.

Prentice said: 'Helga Keller's here.'

Despite himself, Anderson swung round. 'Helga Keller?'

'Where it all began,' Prentice said. 'Where it all began with us.'

'Where it all ended.'

'You're blown,' Prentice said quietly, swinging himself off the bed and sitting in a plush easy-chair.

Anderson stared at him. 'How do you know?'

'Because I had dinner last night with Helga Keller. Or Hildegard Metz as you have her on your guest list.'

'She doesn't look a bit like –'

'She's Helga Keller. I'll explain if you'll let me. Because, you see, I'm blown too. Shall we take a walk?'

'I've got a better idea,' Anderson said. 'Let's get drunk.'

But they didn't.

Instead they walked along the sea-front.

The day was warm; the flowers in the gardens had opened overnight and the sunshine had cleaned winter from the houses piled on the hills crowding the harbour. Dogs gambolled on the beach and nurses pushed invalid chairs along the promenade as their elderly charges emerged from hibernation.

Prentice told Anderson about the remoulding of Helga Keller. And he told him that the KGB had penetrated Bilderberg through Pierre Brossard.

'Brossard? Sweet Jesus!'

Prentice also repeated what Anderson had always refused to believe: that he hadn't shot Karl Danzer. And Helga Keller would confirm it.

'I wanted you to know,' Prentice said.

'Why? You *tried* to shoot the bastard. You even took a Soviet rifle with you to make it look like a Department V job.'

'But I didn't and I just wanted you to know.' Prentice stopped and gripped the rails overlooking the daintily-lapping waves. 'It's difficult to explain,' he said. 'You see I once loved a girl like Helga Keller. She worked for Danzer . . . after that everything was founded on hatred. . . .' His voice faltered, died.

They walked on in silence.

Finally Anderson said: 'Are you trying to tell me that there's something between you and this girl? After one night.'

Another silence extended in front of them. A pretty nurse pushing an old lady smiled at them, but got nothing in return.

Prentice broke the silence. 'What I'm trying to tell you is that, since yesterday, a lot has changed. Our values – my values – have all been wrong. . . .'

He stopped outside the Palm Court Hotel, recommended by local CID officers assigned to the conference at the Imperial.

'Come and have a drink,' Prentice said.

In the lounge he ordered two beers from the barman, Paul Jones, as famed for his prowess with cocktails as the barman who was to be present at another hotel in another time.

Holding the two beers, Prentice led the way to a table overlooking the sea. Sitting in one of the orange and mauve chairs was a young woman wearing spectacles and severely styled hair.

Prentice put the two beers on the table and said: 'I want you to meet Helga Keller.'

It took twenty minutes for the chemistry to begin fermenting.

Then Anderson began to laugh. Shared misfortune, a glimpse of an astonishing concept.

They smiled at him uncertainly.

He went to the bar and ordered two more beers and a glass of dry white wine for Helga. When he returned he was still grinning.

'All right,' Prentice said, 'I'll say it. What's so funny?'

'Us.'

'Us?'

'Sure, us. Three loyal servants and look at us. You,' nodding at Helga, 'have been betrayed ever since you were a kid and you,' nodding at Prentice before Helga could interrupt, 'have been living like a monk because of some infatuation that happened a hundred years ago.'

'That makes two of *us*,' Prentice said. 'What about you?'

Anderson told them about the cable.

It was Helga who said it and added an ingredient to the chemistry. 'Our people think more of you than yours,' she said to Anderson.

And as the chemistry began to bubble, Anderson said: 'Let's take a drive. I've read about Dartmoor. They tell me it's wild and free – the guidebook definition – and, as we're neither, let's go and sample it in my beautiful, rented, debugged automobile.'

They drove in the fawn Rover 3500 through Totnes and Ashburton onto the moors, where a breeze combed the grass and shook the dead flowers of the heather and the shadows of clouds chased each other across the distant hills.

Anderson had a map with him. He parked the car on a narrow road and pointed at the skyline studded with tors of rock. 'The future,' he said, and pointing in the opposite direction to a complex of grey-stone buildings, 'the past.'

Helga said: 'I don't understand.'

Prentice said: 'I do. That's Dartmoor jail. One of the worst in the country. Built to house prisoners captured in the Napoleonic wars.'

'I still don't understand,' Helga told him. 'We can't escape.'

'Why not?' Anderson opened the car door and climbed out

onto the springy turf; lapwings and golden plover rose from the bracken. 'Why not?' he repeated as they followed him. 'You know something? I've just had a vision. Although it's not quite clear . . .' as the chemistry approached exploding point.

They breathed the sweet air, turned their backs on the corpse-grey tombstone that was the prison.

'I figure,' Anderson said slowly, 'that we're all pretty much in the same boat. We've all served a cause; we've all served it well. But we've all been cheated. Which is not,' he corrected himself quickly, 'to say that we haven't enjoyed what we've been doing. Do you go along with that, George?'

'It was a substitute life,' Prentice said 'but, yes, I enjoyed it. I was never a kitchen-sink spy brooding over a gas-ring in St. Pancras. . . .'

'Wherever that may be,' Anderson said. 'But I take your point. The great days of espionage are drawing to a close. We're the rearguard of an epoch. Now it's the turn of the bureaucrats and computers. Do you agree?' addressing Helga Keller.

'I was never Mata Hari.'

Neither of the two men spoke but Prentice moved closer to her and wished she would un-pin her hair, take off her spectacles.

High above them a bird of prey hovered, plunged.

Helga turned to them. 'My life was certainly a substitute.' Karl Danzer briefly intruded, then vanished. Forever? Ever since the walk on the rain-spattered promenade with Prentice she had experienced a miraculous sense of uplift. 'Many people's lives are substitutes,' she said. 'Most of them never have the luck to realise it.'

'And I've got a feeling that we're going to have a slice of that luck,' Anderson said, a note of excitement in his voice.

His mood reached Prentice. 'We've certainly got the professional abilities to profit from any luck that comes our way.'

Profit! Thus did George Prentice make his contribution towards the chemistry.

Anderson said: 'Not much profit so far, George. I doubt

if any of us saved enough for retirement. In the style to which we are accustomed, that is.'

He looked at Helga and Prentice questioningly, and their silence said that no they hadn't.

'I don't have a dime,' Anderson said. 'But I've lived well.' He smiled reflectively. 'But what about our employers? They've lived well too. And I guess they'll go on doing so, indulging their weaknesses. . . .'

Weaknesses!

'Brossard certainly will,' Helga said, a little breathlessly.

'Kingdon has his diamonds,' Prentice said. 'Anyone who puts all his eggs into one basket is vulnerable.'

Vulnerable!

The chemistry exploded.

Synthesised into one word.

BLACKMAIL.

On the way back to Torquay, hesitantly at first, they explored the staggering possibilities of their shared inspiration. Like most inspirations it was simple: they merely had to draw on their joint funds of secret knowledge, and extract a fortune from a selected trio responsible for funding espionage of one sort or another.

Why not? They had spent their lives carrying out missions of dubious intent for their masters. By such standards there was nothing immoral in redirecting their skills for their own benefit. For the final pay-off.

Two subjects for extortion were obvious: Paul Kingdon and Pierre Brossard. They both deserved such a fate, it was agreed.

The third?

Inevitably their thoughts homed down on Bilderberg. And it was then that the third name occurred to Owen Anderson.

He swung the Rover into a turn and said: 'Claire Jerome. I've had to work for her a few times.'

Prentice, who was sitting in the back of the car with Helga Keller, said: 'A woman?'

'For Christ's sake cut out the English gentleman stuff, George. I've known you too long. She's in armaments, right? Can you see anything wrong in extracting our retirement pensions from the profits of a few arms deals?'

'I suppose,' Prentice said, glancing at Helga to gauge her reactions, 'she wouldn't miss a few quid.'

'The question,' said the new transformed Helga Keller, 'is how much?'

Prentice, who was delighted by her reaction, said: 'A lot.'

'Five million?'

'Dollars or pounds?' from Anderson.

'I was thinking in dollars. We don't want to get greedy. We've seen too many people end up in front of a firing squad because they were too greedy. Two and a half million quid.' He thought about it. 'I should be able to buy a jet-propelled wheel-chair with that sort of money.'

'A fair reward for services rendered,' Anderson remarked as they left Newton Abbot on the last stretch of road to Torquay.

It was as they were entering the outskirts of the resort that the ultimate beauty of the burgeoning plot occurred to George Prentice. He squeezed Helga's arm, tapped Anderson on the shoulder.

'We want this to be perfect, right?'

They both nodded.

'We want symmetry. We want poetic justice. We want a perfect irony.'

'Get it off your chest,' Anderson said. 'We don't want crossword puzzle clues.'

'We don't extort from our own subjects.'

Silence in the car as an ambulance overtook them, siren wailing, on its way to Torbay hospital.

'What I'm getting at is this. We use each others' strengths, rather like Judo. For instance you,' to Anderson, 'would take Paul Kingdon on information supplied by me. And you,' to Helga, 'would take Mrs Jerome on information supplied by Anderson.'

'And you,' Helga said to Prentice, 'would blackmail Brossard on information supplied by me.'

'Exactly. Three agents co-operating while their governments continue to do battle. Isn't that a beautiful concept?'

They both sighed. It was indeed beautiful.

It was left to Helga to sound the realistic note.

'After this,' she said, 'we mustn't be seen together. In fact,' she said, eyes searching Prentice's, 'we must go on hating each other. . . .'

'Hating?' Prentice frowned.

'We must continue as we were. If we don't we'll arouse suspicions. We have to go on acting out our hatred.'

She told Anderson to stop the car.

As he watched her walking away from them, Prentice wondered if he could be that good an actor.

They called the plan Operation Imperial, after the hotel. And they code-named themselves after two rocky tors on Dartmoor where inspiration had visited them – Vixen and Kings – and Prince from Princetown, the ugly little town where the jail was located. It was, after all, an escape that they envisaged.

The conference at the Imperial was par for the course; they endured it impatiently.

There was an unusually large gathering of journalists haunting the lobby, and delegates agreed that the expanded coverage might attract trouble at future conferences; but, on the whole, they were confident that their lives and their deliberations would be safeguarded.

Their confidence would have been severely eroded had they known that, quite by accident, Prentice had discovered a ridiculously easy means of listening to their debates. A means available to any curious member of the public, journalist or espionage agent.

XXVII

Of course the final act of the conspiracy had to be staged at a Bilderberg conference.

Separately each had come to the same conclusion.

Where else could the three of them work together? Where else could they synchronise Operation Imperial? What other venue could provide such an apt setting for its climax?

But the venue did involve certain disadvantages. The principal obstacle: time. In between each conference Anderson, Prentice, and Helga Keller dispersed across the world, and so opportunities to scheme were limited.

But they all agreed that everything had to be planned to the minutest detail. Method of extortion, timing, escape route, financing, final destination. . . .

Prentice had hoped to enjoy his retirement with Helga Keller – if, that is, things worked out in that respect (nothing had been said). Privately he wished that they could hurry things along. Did they have to be such perfectionists? *Of course they did,* Prentice the professional admitted to himself.

Another obstacle was the reluctance of the Establishment to invite Paul Kingdon to Bilderberg. Anderson was working on this when Pierre Brossard, promoted to the steering committee, stepped in and solved the problem.

It was also Brossard who inadvertently settled the date of the operation. Through Helga they learned that he was planning a final consummate coup that he hoped would smash the American dollar. If it was successful he would escape to Yugoslavia where he would be granted asylum.

If it was successful, then the $15 million ransom to be reaped from Operation Imperial would be worthless!

Until then the Brossard plan had appeared to be the simplest because Helga had copies of Gestapo documents indicting Brossard as a war criminal. Now the Frenchman had jeopardised the whole venture.

One late summer evening in 1979, Anderson, Prentice and Helga Keller contrived to meet to discuss the emergency. Owen suggested the Villa d'Este on Lake Como, Italy, where Bilderberg had once met before he got the security job. He had always regretted missing out on that one.

* * *

The Villa d'Este at Cernobbio, on the shores of Lake Como, might have been built with intrigue in mind. But intrigue on the grand, romantic scale – whispered conversations behind fluttering fans; assignations in the shaded parkland overlooked by green slopes, where once a beautiful widow had built imitation fortresses to please her handsome new husband, a Napoleonic general; cloaked figures lurking behind the great pillars in the hallway.

A cardinal had built the original villa in 1568. Its occupants had included the Sultan of Morocco, the ill-fated Caroline of Brunswick, Princess of Wales and wife of George IV, Empress Marie Feodorovna of Russia and, for a couple of days in 1965, Prince Bernhard and his very special guests.

Owen Anderson booked a suite of rooms. A noble suite of blue and gold with views of the lake which, with its two legs and arched back, has the shape of a flamenco dancer arrogantly poised on the borders of Switzerland.

Such were the airs and graces of the place that it seemed indecent to check the suite for microphones. But Anderson went ahead and did it.

When Prentice and Helga Keller arrived within ten minutes of each other, both by taxi from the silk-rich city of Como, he was ready for business. Chairs arranged around an inlaid table on which stood a carafe of iced water and glasses.

Already Helga had opened a joint numbered account with the United Bank of Switzerland in Zurich and arranged for individual accounts to be opened in other banks in Geneva, Basle and Berne.

Each of them had made arrangements to adopt a new identity after Bilderberg. (In their profession this presented few difficulties.) And arrangements were in hand to establish their ultimate destination in Rio de Janeiro.

'But,' said Anderson drawing up a chair, 'we have to speed things up due to the untimely intervention of Monsieur Brossard. It has to be the next Bilderberg.

Prentice and Helga nodded agreement.

'Okay, George,' Anderson said, 'you first.'

Prentice began to speak. He was professional, purposeful and his authority was noted by Helga.

He said: 'We have agreed that each operation should be conducted in three stages. The initial frightener followed by a lull, the reminder and then the hit. This way the subject becomes malleable; not only that, but he is less likely to respond hysterically.

'I'm lucky in that, in my case, the method of extortion is simple; I'm also lucky that, with a man such as Pierre Brossard, I don't have the slightest compunction in terrifying and robbing him. We have agreed that the first move should be the delivery of a significant date. Helga,' nodding at her, 'will find an opportunity to write or print the date on some of Brossard's Bilderberg correspondence.'

'A nice touch, George,' Anderson said. 'But won't he immediately suspect Helga?'

'Why should he? As far as he knows the date has no significance to her. At that stage he won't realise that the object of the exercise is extortion. And when the second message is delivered – in the form of cassettes as we've agreed – the voice will be a man's. Mine.'

Prentice paused and drank some water. 'Now, as we all know, thanks to Helga and her employers in Moscow, Monsier Brossard has chosen to complicate our plans. *He* also wants to retire,' permitting himself a fleeting smile. 'It is therefore vital that, having obtained the ransom, we negate the Soviet conspiracy to bring down the dollar.

'Vital not only for our own ends but for the future of our Society,' he added sombrely. 'I know that Helga has no idealistic objections to this. But perhaps she would like to elaborate. . . .'

For Anderson's benefit Helga told them how she felt about the beliefs she had held for so long.

'I was once a Communist,' she said. 'Passionately, totally dedicated.' She didn't elaborate on how this had come about: they both knew. 'When you're young and you live in a country where people *live* Swiss francs and you know about poverty and starvation elsewhere in the world, then you are disturbed by dreams of equality. But gradually – although I kept it from myself – I became aware of another kind of poverty. Poverty of the soul.'

She drank some iced water. 'Wherever I travelled in Eastern Europe, in Russia, I felt it. The greatest crime was originality. If you were found guilty of this heinous offence then you were exorcised. In jail, in a camp, in a mental home. It is very sad,' she said softly, 'that ideals should be disciplined and converted into doctrines.'

She paused. A vase of russet-coloured chrysanthemums stood on the table and she could smell their coppery scent. Autumn. Through the window she could see the cold blue waters of the lake and the green hills smudged with gold.

Then she smiled at them, at Prentice in particular, and said: 'No, I haven't got any idealistic objections. I think I've earned my retirement. . . .'

Anderson said: 'One thing worries me. Shouldn't we wreck Brossard's plan to bring down the dollar right now?'

Prentice shook his head, lit a cigarette. 'In the first place Helga hasn't got the full details yet. Although my guess is that the Russians will dump dollars and Brossard will try and frighten speculators into panic selling. If we act now it will be premature. Just another red-under-the-bed scare which the Russians will deny. The essence is timing – for them and us.'

Helga said: 'Don't forget Kingdon's part in it.'

Prentice explained to Anderson that, according to notes scrutinised by Helga, Brossard intended to collaborate with

Paul Kingdon. 'Why we're not sure. But an educated guess would be that he wants Kingdon's help – and will tip him off about the attempt to topple the dollar. If Kingdon believes that his money – and the money he hands over to us – is going to be worthless, then he is much more likely to co-operate with us.'

Helga said to Anderson: 'Don't worry about the dollar. George and I are working on it.'

George and I. She took off her spectacles and experienced an astonishing urge to shake her hair loose from its combs.

'So that brings us to Paul Kingdon,' Anderson said. He stood up. 'My own operation based on information supplied by George. And to an extent I'm going to have to enlist George's support as well as his information. In fact, we'll all have to mix it a little. You know, black dudes aren't that common in the City of London. Nor, from what George tells me, are they frequent visitors to Wentworth. So the first warning will have to be delivered by you, George. In Kingdon's telephone monitor – with a voice-cast provided by you, Helga, in case Kingdon recognises George's inimitable voice.'

He paused while Prentice and Helga nodded appreciatively.

'Kingdon's strength,' he went on, 'is his weakness. His ice, his diamonds. Make the Kingdon Diamond worthless and you've emasculated him.'

Anderson turned to Helga because Prentice knew most of the details. He explained that several companies were concentrating on trying to produce flawless gem diamonds. So far none had succeeded.

'But Kingdon isn't to know that,' Anderson told Helga. 'Although he *will* have heard of the Jager Formula. This is the one bandied around in the trade as being on the verge of success. And it so happens that George here, being the best industrial spy in the business, has managed to get hold of a copy.'

'I don't understand,' Helga said. 'If the formula isn't perfected yet –'

'Hear me out,' Anderson said. 'I'm afraid I've had to

invest some of our anticipated rewards.'

'How much?' Helga queried.

'A hundred thousand bucks.'

'Peanuts,' Prentice said.

Anderson went on: 'A Dutch diamond merchant named van Wyk is attending the next Bilderberg. He's not as wealthy as he appears. He's gay and, as he's also fat and ugly, he has to pay for his pleasures. He has agreed to accept a hundred thousand. In exchange he will verify the Jager Formula and express consternation that it has fallen into Kingdon's hands. We will also make a gift of a small diamond to Kingdon – a product of the Jager Formula. In fact, of course, it will be a genuine diamond.'

'I'd like to make a request,' Prentice said.

'Go ahead, George.'

'I want Kingdon to raise the five million himself. You know, save as much of the poor bloody investors' money as possible. There's just a chance that one day a few Honest Johns might take over Kingdon Investments and save some of their cash.'

'Can he raise it?'

'If he thinks it's going to be worthless and he's got his diamonds he'll raise it.'

'Okay,' Anderson said, 'we'll make the point.' He sat down. 'Helga, your turn.'

Helga began with an apology.

'I'm afraid the female of the species has come up with the most obvious plan. But, believe me, it will be effective. You see,' she said to Prentice, 'Owen has discovered that Mrs Claire Jerome is in love.'

She tasted the word. *Love*. She unbuttoned the jacket of her suit, cleared her throat and continued.

'She has fallen for a very unusual man named Anello. She's currently on vacation with him in the Bahamas. Judging by reports from the servants obtained by Owen's representative in Nassau, she would break up if he left her. So I'm afraid what I'm suggesting is an old-fashioned kidnap.'

Neither Anderson nor Prentice looked enthusiastic.

'However,' she went on, 'I do have some refinements in mind. A woman's intuition. I haven't had time to investigate the possibilities yet but I'll let you know.'

'A kidnap?' Prentice's voice was sceptical. 'I had hoped we would be able to dispense with marked notes, a secret rendezvous, car chases. . . . This has to be artistic perfection.'

If it had come from Anderson she wouldn't have minded so much.

'I'll bear that in mind,' she said coldly. 'First I have to deliver Mrs Jerome's note. Anello's date of birth – cut from an old copy of the *Washington Post*. Does that upset your aesthetic senses?'

And when Prentice shook his head she said: 'Then I think that just about concludes the business of this meeting,' sat down, buttoned up her jacket and replaced her spectacles.

*　　*　　*

She would soon be thirty years old and only one man had ever made love to her.

Ridiculous in this day and age. Pathetic.

In her room next to the suite Helga Keller stared in the mirror at Hildegard Metz.

No-one had ever made love to Hildegard Metz!

Would anyone want to?

For almost a decade I have been another woman. Behaved like her, thought like her. Is it too late to revert to Helga Keller?

On an impulse she went into the bathroom and took off her clothes. Removed her spectacles, shook loose her hair and stared into a mirror. And still saw Hildegard Metz.

Her breasts were firm and full enough, good legs. Good figure, in fact, apart from her waistline which was a little too thick. But she could diet and the plastic surgery on her face had only been minor. Then she would visit a hairdressers and a beauty parlour and throw away her spectacles. But not before Bilderberg.

But what about George Prentice? Just like Helga Keller

he had assumed an identity. Was it also too late for him to change?

She had admired him while he outlined his role in the operation. But she had been frightened, too. The calculating efficiency. The way he had snubbed her.

As steam from the bathwater began to blur the image in the mirror her thoughts became confused.

Helga Keller and the original George Prentice . . . Hildegard Metz and the original Prentice . . . Hildegard Metz and this man with an assumed identity. . . .

They were strangers twice over.

She touched her breasts, small pink nipples like those of a young girl, epitomising unfulfilment.

Since Torquay they had only met fleetingly. She wasn't sure about his feelings towards her; wasn't sure about her feelings towards him.

She imagined him making love to her. Incredibly her body responded to her imagination. After all those years of abstinence.

Then she considered the possibility that Prentice wouldn't even contemplate making love to her and the excitement stirring inside her receded.

She leaned forward and with one hand wiped some of the steam from the mirror.

For a fleeting moment it was Helga Keller who looked back at her.

* * *

George Prentice, too, was unsure of his feelings.

He was over forty and the character he had adopted had settled upon him. He was like an actor who has played a role for so long that he has subordinated his own personality to it.

Prentice didn't know if he could shed the role; it was as hard as a shell.

He *did* know that when he was in the presence of Helga Keller he was suffused with a warmth of feeling that he hadn't experienced since Annette du Pont had briefly intruded into his life and changed it.

It had been Lake Zurich in that long-ago period, that moment in his life. Now it was Lake Como, sometimes described as the most romantic lake in the world.

But once again they had no time. And all he had so far managed to do was establish hostility. *But, Christ, kidnapping!*

Prentice picked up the telephone in the lounge of the suite and called Helga's room.

Half an hour later as she poured him a whisky in her room, she said: 'Do you call your girl-friends at this hour?' It was 10.30 pm.

'I wanted to apologise for biting your head off,' he said as he took in the long hair falling around her shoulders, the swell of her breasts above the pink bath-robe; he wanted to reach out for her.

'I don't blame you. Kidnapping – it sounds crude. But you've got to believe me: it won't be.'

'I believe you,' Prentice said. Without spectacles she looked vulnerable; he wondered if she had looked very much different before the plastic surgery.

She sat down on the chesterfield and crossed her legs. Good legs.

'I wanted to talk about the future,' he said, lighting a cigarette. 'Our future.'

'The two of us or the three of us?'

'The two of us. Owen Anderson isn't the type to stay alone for long.'

'No,' she said, 'I suppose not.'

At least, without too many words, he had established a future. Togetherness. Sharing. . . . Suddenly Prentice wanted more than that. Cried out inside himself and heard his voice echo back through the empty years.

He went to her and, still standing, put his hand to her neck and slid it down her shoulder; her robe fell away exposing her breasts and she stared up at him with fear and hope.

He bent and kissed her lips. And then her breasts and what they had both thought would be so difficult proved to be the easiest thing in the world.

And, as he led her towards the bed, the voice in the past lost itself in its own echoes.

* * *

During the next seven months the three of them managed to meet five more times. On each occasion their mood was subtly different as the build-up for Operation Imperial accelerated. Tension was there, but so was an expanding sense of cameraderie. Three agents *jointly* defecting from their respective mentors, that was the beauty of it; three individuals combining to take on organised intelligence networks – and using the skills imparted by those networks to do it.

While plans to extort ransom from Brossard and Kingdon proceeded smoothly enough, Helga had to fall back on her reserves of ingenuity to refine the Claire Jerome operation. She had promised them sophistication: they should have it.

From intelligence gathered by Anderson, it had become increasingly apparent that Anello wasn't a work-shy gigolo: he was a casualty of war. Helga had in her possession his Army records and reports from various sources about his views on the arms race. The combination presented distinct possibilities; but first she had to gauge for herself the depth of his feeling.

One warm spring day while Claire Jerome was in New York Helga took the combs from her hair and, posing as an Austrian businesswoman, picked up Anello in a bar in London with an ease that delighted her. She was feminine, she was attractive – even if Anello was a little drunk.

During their brief association she discovered more about the man than his views on war and those who profited from it: she touched the nerve of his self-disgust.

'So we won't have to take him by force,' she told Anderson and Prentice at their final meeting – again at the Villa d'Este. 'Of course he may react violently at first. You, George, will have to take care of that business. We can't have the American Secret Service,' pointing at Anderson, 'leaving the Château Saint-Pierre.'

They were breakfasting in the same suite of rooms; beneath them the lake sparkled in the early morning sunshine.

Prentice sliced off the top of a boiled egg and said: 'It is without doubt sheer artistry. Cunning tempered by rough justice.'

'If it works,' remarked Anderson buttering a bread roll. 'If not, then it will have to be an old-fashioned, gun-point abduction.'

'I think it will work,' Helga told them. 'It will give Anello a purpose. And the method of operation will appeal to him. You see I know the man,' she said, finishing her grapefruit segments which, with a cup of black coffee, was all she now allowed herself for breakfast.

Posing as an anti-armaments group – terrorists in reverse – they hoped to persuade Anello to co-operate in a kidnap. Claire Jerome, he would be told, would be informed that he would be released if she issued a statement announcing that she was pulling out of armaments.

Anello wouldn't, of course, be told about the $5 million ransom.

The previous evening Anderson had revealed that they now had an unexpected ally: Israeli Intelligence who had persuaded Claire Jerome to do a deal with the Arabs for their own ends.

'It's the catalyst we needed,' Prentice said, reaching for a croissant. 'When Anello hears that she's double-dealing he'll jump in with both feet.'

'To be fair,' Anderson said, 'Mrs Jerome's motives can't be faulted.' He helped himself to another roll. 'But we have to make sure that Anello gets to know about the Arab deal. Which shouldn't be difficult as it's up to me to debug all the rooms in the château. In four rooms – Brossard's, Kingdon's, Mrs Jerome's and Anello's – I shall be guilty of dereliction of duty. . . .'

337

Prentice said: 'Tell me something, Helga, do you feel a little sorry for Mrs Jerome?'

Anderson cut in: 'Why should she? It's the sort of lesson she needs. Up to now she's always been in the driving seat. Omnipotent, impregnable. Not her fault, maybe, but her values are all screwed up. Maybe one day she'll be grateful to us.'

Helga said: 'He's right, of course. But,' looking steadily at Prentice, 'yes, I do feel a little sorry for her.'

'I'm glad,' Prentice said.

Part Five

XXVIII

The first of the unpredictable elements anticipated by Owen Anderson, was the discovery of the primitive bugging device planted in the microphone in the conference chamber of the Château Saint-Pierre.

The second was the attempt on Pierre Brossard's life.

It occurred at 3.43 on the afternoon of the first whole day of the conference.

As far as Brossard was concerned, the debates were now entirely superfluous. He had retired to his room to continue making arrangements for the transfer of the five million dollars to the bank in Switzerland and to make final revisions to his column. The financiers he had primed were poised to sell dollars on a vast scale, so was the Foreign Trade Bank of the Soviet Union and Brossard had recovered his poise since reading the ransom note. Five million worthless dollars. Not only that but two million of the ransom had been provided by Claire Jerome and would be transferred tomorrow from his account in Monaco to the numbered account in Zurich. It really was rather piquant.

He stood for a moment in front of the window, arms folded, gazing across the gardens. It was true that the cheaper rooms on the east wing weren't blessed with as much sunlight as those on the west wing. But why *pay* for sunlight? In any case the weather had changed and the sun shone only fleetingly through low clouds racing across the sky.

Brossard was in the middle of a yawn when the bullet shattered the window and spun him round. At first he had no idea what had happened. A stone? There was no pain. Merely an icy coldness in his shoulder, then warmth as blood began to course down his arm. He felt the hole in the cloth of his jacket with one hand, felt the wound, and understood. He sat down on the edge of the bed and stared at the splinters of broken glass.

He was reaching for the telephone when someone pounded on the door and a man's voice shouted: 'Are you all right, Brossard?' The door opened and the security guard came in.

'I've been shot,' Brossard said.

Anderson sat beside him, saw the blood oozing through the hole in the sleeve. 'Okay, I'm going to call the doctor.'

There were shouts in the garden and the sound of running footsteps along the corridor.

An FBI agent stuck his head round the door. 'What the hell's going on?'

'A shooting is what's going on,' Anderson said.

'Holy shit!'

'Now let's get the hell out of here before he takes another shot.' Anderson said to Brossard: 'Can you make it into the passage?'

'I think so.'

The FBI agent helped Brossard to crawl out of the room while, keeping away from the window, Anderson told the switchboard operator to send up the house doctor. Hugging the wall, he edged into the corridor.

He tried a door on the other side of the corridor. It opened and he helped Brossard to a bed.

He said to the FBI agent: 'Tell the French cops but tell them to keep a low profile.' He shook his head. 'I might have guessed it,' as the church bells began to chime.

'Guessed what?'

'It doesn't matter. You stay here with Brossard.'

As Anderson ran down the passage, other plain-clothes police were rounding the corner. Grabbing a British Special Branch officer he said: 'Seal off the corridor. Someone just took a shot at Brossard. If anyone asks what the noise was, tell them it was a jet crashing the sound barrier. Tell them anything you like but don't say anything about a shooting. Understand?'

'Perfectly,' the Special Branch man said.

In the lobby Anderson slowed down to walking pace in case there were any reporters there; he was lucky – the reporters had departed to file stories about the arrival of the former American Secretary of State and the French President.

Gaudin stopped him near the reception desk. 'What happened?'

Anderson told him. 'Stall everyone. But none of that "No comment" stuff. That's as good as confirming it.'

He ran to the car-park, gunned the black Chevrolet Caprice on loan from the American Embassy in Paris. At the gates he sounded his horn; a gendarme peered at him, opened the gates.

Anderson reached the village in three minutes, knowing it was too late. He parked the car in the street outside the church. A small crowd had gathered in the graveyard. The doors of the church were open, the recorded bells were still chiming.

He ran up the steps leading to the belfry. The uniformed gendarme who had been guarding the church was kneeling beside the priest. The priest was unconscious. His bleak face was ashen and there was an ugly purple swelling on the side of his head; a little blood seeped from it.

The gendarme said: 'I've sent for an ambulance.'

Anderson knelt beside the priest and felt his pulse. It was beating faintly and irregularly.

'What happened for Christ's sake?' he asked the gendarme.

'I don't know. There were two explosions in the graveyard. And in between them the sound of a rifle shot. I didn't know what was happening. I realised too late that the explosions were diversions. Whoever it was got in by the back door. And left the same way. . . .' His voice tailed away.

Anderson stood up, noticed an object gleaming in the dust below the small window that he and the priest had discussed. A cartridge case. He examined it and said: 'Well, I'll be damned.' It had contained a standard 7.92 German rifle bullet. Standard, that was, in World War II.

On the ledge of the window he found a handful of photostats. Copies of the Bilderberg guest list with crosses marked against certain names.

Through the window Anderson saw the ambulance arrive. Before running down to direct the stretcher-bearers, he switched off the record-player: the peeling of the bells was a joyous sound but there wasn't a lot to celebrate.

*   *   *

When he had heard the footsteps on the stairs, Jacques Bertier had flattened himself against the wall. As the priest entered the belfry, and stood hesitating between the door and the railing encircling the great bells hanging from the domed ceiling, he hit him from behind with the butt of the rifle.

Then he crossed to the window, opened it and gazed down the barrel of the rifle. His hands were shaking; he had to control them; he only had two minutes before the second charge exploded in the graveyard.

The trembling subsided as he fought it.

Peering through the gunsight he traversed the château. There were plenty of targets in the grounds and in some of the rooms. It didn't really matter who he shot but he was interested in one particular room occupied, according to his information, by the French millionaire Pierre Brossard.

Brossard had been at the conference at Mégève when Georges had been dispatched to a lingering death. What sweet, beautiful justice if Brossard materialised in the sights.

One minute had passed.

He thought he detected a movement in the room. Come on, you bastard. You filth. Another bout of trembling. In a few seconds he would have to line up the sights on another target.

Then Brossard walked into the sights, stood there yawning, and Jacques Bertier shot him.

He was exultant but calm as he stowed the rifle away in the canvas container. As he left the belfry, he stumbled over the body of the priest and fell against the record-player.

The bells began to chime.

Then the crack of the second explosion in the graveyard.

Bertier was out of the rear entrance, across the graveyard and through the hedge while the gendarme, and anyone else attracted by the first explosion, raced to the second detonation.

He rounded the church and walked down the main street in the direction of the *tabac*. He looked as theatrically nonchalant as any fisherman who has caught nothing.

When the inn-keeper's wife arrived at the apartment he thrust her into the bedroom and made love with savage abandon.

Just like rape, she thought in astonishment. But her only real complaint was that it was over too quickly.

* * *

Before the shooting Nicholas Foster had put on sports coat and blazer and headed into the village to keep his appointment with Suzy Okana.

His hopes were not centred on Suzy. He hadn't so far learned anything that would stop the presses, and the bug he had planted in the conference room had been tossed out by Anderson.

As he limped along the lane he admitted to himself that he would see Suzy irrespective of whether or not she had any information for him. It seemed to him that they had released in each other forces of which neither had been aware. Or perhaps that was how it seemed to every man she met. Suzy Okana had been around.

She was standing outside the inn smiling at him. She was wearing a dark green skirt – no slits today – and a pale green sweater and carrying a jacket over her arm.

At the Post Office he posted his notes. Then holding hands, they walked past the inn in the opposite direction to the château.

'Where are we going?' she asked.

'There,' pointing at a gap in the hedgerow.

On the other side of the hedge was an orchard. They sat down in the long grass and watched petals of appleblossom falling in the breeze.

'Well,' she said, 'how's it going?'

'Bloody awful. Did you find out anything?'

'Yes,' she said, 'and no.'

'Let's have the "yes" bit first.'

'I spoke to Kingdon.'

'And?'

'He's going to live in Switzerland.'

'Perhaps he's found a corner in cuckoo clocks.'

'And he said something about the financial structure of the world changing.'

Foster frowned. 'Was this connected with Bilderberg?'

'I think so. He was speaking as if everything was going to happen right now.'

Foster whistled. 'I wonder what the hell he was getting at. The dollar's pretty shaky at the moment. I wonder if he knows about some decision in Washington.' He sat back, hands around his knees. 'Did he say anything else? I mean did he mention dollars or marks? Or gold?'

'He said he was going to make a fortune,' Suzy said, plucking a blade of grass and nibbling it. 'And he said that the only other place he could go apart from Switzerland would be behind the Iron Curtain. But, of course, that wouldn't be for him, would it?'

'Then someone's plotting a run on currency,' Foster said thoughtfully. 'Kingdon makes a killing and quits. And why?' He snapped his fingers. 'Because he's got diamonds, the only stable currency if the financial structure of the world, as he puts it, changes. So it must be some sort of bear raid on a vast scale. Culminating at Bilderberg,' Nicholas said excitedly. 'Who has he been mixing with?'

'No-one in particular. But he did meet Pierre Brossard before the conference. I got the impression that they were plotting something. I had to leave the house.'

'Pierre Brossard . . . Midas. Brossard writes a financial column under the name Midas,' Foster explained. 'He's the most influential financial journalist in Europe. Anyone else?'

'He met a man named Gerard. He called him a pig.'

'The London end of the banking family,' Nicholas told her.

'He said it – whatever *it* is – would ruin Gerard.'

Foster was silent.

'And there was something else,' Suzy said, 'and this is why you're going to hate me and I'm sorry but,' with a shrug, 'there it is.' She plucked a fresh blade of grass. 'I promised him I wouldn't tell anyone. Not even you I'm afraid,' looking away from Foster.

Somewhere in the orchard a thrush began to sing.

Suzy said: 'You see, whatever you may think, I do have my own rules. . . .'

Nicholas tilted her chin and kissed her.

Then he lay back in the grass and pulled her close to him and, leaning on one elbow, looked down at her face as the breeze moved her black hair and the sun reached into the depths of her eyes.

'I want to tell you about why I am what I am,' she said.

'You don't have to.'

'I want to . . . I want you to know everything now. You know, so it doesn't all come out one day when we have a row. Not that there's anything dramatic about it. No mitigating circumstances. In fact,' said Suzy, looking at him and searching his face, 'it's all pretty squalid.'

'I said you didn't have to tell me.'

'There was a man once. There always is, isn't there? He had an MG and he used to take me around in it. I thought he was the greatest thing since Roger Moore, but when he dropped me outside the house in Cardiff he used to roar off like a bat out of hell. He used to like slumming, you see, but he didn't fancy one of the neighbours putting his boot through one of the headlights. What I didn't realise was he was going back to his mates and telling them about the slant-eyed little bitch he'd picked up in the gutter. Anyway the usual happened, you know – '

'I can guess.' Foster was vaguely aware of bells chiming.

'I told you it was pretty squalid. But let's get it over with.' She hurried on. 'I came up to London to get the usual job done. He paid for it to give him credit but after that there was no sign of the MG.'

'How old were you?' Foster asked.

347

'Eighteen. I had a few lousy jobs in London, then I answered an ad for this escort agency. Real money at last! You see the clients seemed to get a kick out of being seen with your actual Oriental. Trouble was,' smiling hesitantly at Nicholas, 'they always took me to Chinese restaurants. You know something? I never want to see a bowl of chop suey again for the rest of my life.'

Foster tried not to think about what her duties had entailed. Sanctimonious bastard, he thought; this is the age of liberation.

And because his thoughts were reflected in his face, she said: 'I warned you. But there isn't much more to tell. Anway you probably know most of it.'

'I read the papers,' Foster agreed.

'I left the agency because I didn't need them any more. I moved into High Society. Occasionally Royalty, would you believe. Some of the men I met were all right, some of them were sods. But none of them were very demanding; they were more interested in power and money and being seen in the right places with the right girl. A few even wanted to marry me. But somehow none of it meant anything to me. I remember thinking, when a photographer was taking a picture of my hat at Ascot, that I'd rather have been eating winkles at Southend.'

'Then why the hell didn't you get out?'

'No reason,' she said flatly. 'No bloody reason at all. I was sort of dead. Just waiting for something to happen. . . .' She turned her head away from him. 'It matters, doesn't it? It matters to you.'

'Of course it matters,' he said. 'It's you.' He turned her face towards him and saw that there were tears in her eyes.

'Does it matter . . . a lot?'

He was silent for a moment. Something was different. The bells had stopped ringing.

'You know I don't give a damn really,' she said. 'I can always go back to Paul. He's not so bad really. He's always been straight with me.' And then: 'For Christ's sake, say something!'

'You gave him your word that you wouldn't repeat what he told you, didn't you.'

She closed her eyes, nodded.

'That's what matters. You kept your word,' as he drew her to him again and held her close as the pink and white petals fell around them.

Five minutes later he glanced at his watch and said: 'And if I'm going to get this bloody great exclusive story I'd better get back.'

'In a way I hope you don't,' she said as she stood up beside him. 'But for your sake I hope you do.'

He kissed her. 'You stay here for a few minutes. We'd better not be seen together too much.'

As he walked back through the village he saw an ambulance pull away from outside the church. Then a black American limousine with Anderson at the wheel.

Journalistic instincts aroused, he walked swiftly – almost ran – back to the château.

* * *

Anderson went first to Gaudin's office. Gaudin was speaking on the house telephone. 'I'm very relieved to hear it,' he said, and to Anderson as he put the receiver down: 'That was the doctor. Brossard's all right. A small flesh wound. Apparently he's worried about the possibility of publicity.'

I'll bet he is, Anderson thought. 'How many people know about it?'

'Myself, you, the doctor, about four guards. . . . That's all I know of. But I shall, of course, have to tell the President and the other delegates. I can't suppress the fact that there's a gunman on the loose from guests.'

'I guess not. But tell them to keep quiet about it. That shouldn't be any sweat – they've kept their mouths shut for twenty-five years.'

'Have you an idea?' Gaudin asked. He discussed the attempted murder as though he were discussing a fault in the plumbing. And they talked about the Gallic temperament!

349

'Nothing much. The shot was fired from the church belfry.'

'Didn't you check that out?'

'Of course. I posted a gendarme outside. But the gunman was too clever for him. Clever and yet not clever. I don't think he gave a damn who he shot. . . . The situation I've always feared. Monsieur Gaudin, I think we've got a homicidal nut on our hands.'

'The irony,' Gaudin said, pressing the tips of his fingers together, 'is that if Brossard hadn't objected to the price of the room on the west wing he wouldn't have been shot.'

Ironic all right, Anderson reflected. He had gone to considerable trouble to arrange the accommodation so that Brossard, Kingdon and Claire Jerome had adjoining rooms.

In the lobby the reporter from *Paris-Match*, a big man with cropped hair, approached him. 'What's going on around here?' he asked.

'Nothing out of the ordinary. Why?'

'I saw you driving like a lunatic. Then I saw an ambulance.'

'I always drive like a lunatic,' Anderson said.

'And the ambulance?'

Anderson shrugged. 'How should I know? A road accident in the village maybe.'

'My photographer reckons he heard a gun-shot.'

'He's got better hearing than me. Although come to think of it,' Anderson said frowning, 'I did hear a jet crash the sound barrier about twenty minutes ago. Where were you twenty minutes ago?'

'Phoning Paris.'

'In a booth?'

'No, in a bar in Etampes.'

'There you are, a noisy bar. If you'd been outside you'd have known it was a jet.'

In the corridor in the east wing, Anderson spoke to the British Special Branch officer. 'Any trouble?'

'Nothing. We told Brossard not to speak to anyone about the shooting, but it wasn't necessary. He seems more anxious about keeping it quiet than us. But he did ask to see his secretary, a Fraulein Metz. Is that all right?'

'I can't see any harm in it,' Anderson said. 'I believe you're an authority on ballistics. Can you spare a minute?'

'Of course.' The Englishman, whose name was Crawford, followed Anderson silently on his crepe-soled suede shoes.

In his room Anderson threw the cartridge-case on the table and said: 'What do you make of that?'

'German,' Crawford said without looking at it. 'Last war.'

Anderson stared in surprise at the squarely-built policeman in tweeds who looked as though he had just been shooting grouse – except for the shoes. 'You can tell without even examining it?'

'Your colleague from the FBI found the bullet.' Crawford took it out of the pocket of his trousers and tossed it onto the table beside the case. 'Hardly damaged. It had spent itself. Brossard was well out of effective range.'

'Which is?'

'Well, my guess is that this was fired by a Karabiner 98. The Germans had them at the beginning of the war. Based on a rifle designed in 1898. Range? Anything between 2,200 and 3,000 yards maximum. Effective – not more than 600.'

'Could it have been fitted with telescopic sights?'

'No reason why not. In the early days of the war snipers used a commercial sight – the ZF 39 made by Hensoldt – on the Karabiner 98K. Later they used the ZF 42.'

'I was right, you do know your stuff. What sort of a killer would use a rifle like that?'

'A raving madman,' Crawford said. 'Certainly an amateur. A gun buff maybe?'

'Could be.'

'Do you think he'll have another go?'

Anderson shrugged. 'Like you said, the guy's a crank. What surprises me is that it's never happened at Bilderberg before.'

After Crawford had left the room, Anderson stared thoughtfully at the photostats of the guest list. What, he wondered, did the crosses beside certain names indicate? There was no obvious pattern to them; they were neither the most nor the least important guests. But there was a common denominator there somewhere.

Anderson knew from experience that homicidal maniacs frequently liked to give notice of intent. They wanted to prove how clever (not crazy) they were and they enjoyed observing the frantic evasive action taken by the intended victims and their guardians.

He had, therefore, to assume that the shooting was a notice of intent. And that in all probability it was a diversionary tactic to enable the gunman to sit back and enjoy the action.

A diversion from what? A bomb?

The powers behind the thrones of the Western world wiped out in one big bang. Brossard, Claire Jerome and Paul Kingdon eliminated – before they had finished transferring $15 million to the bank in Zurich. But that was academic: the three blackmailers would be dead too!

Anderson picked up the phone and called the hospital where the priest had been taken.

A woman said: 'He is as well as can be expected, m'sieur.'

'Is he conscious?'

'Who's calling?'

'Police,' trying to shed any trace of an American accent.

'No, m'sieur, he is not yet conscious.'

Gaudin was waiting outside the booth. 'Our own police would like a word with you,' he said. 'I have made my personal suite available.'

Before making his way to the suite Anderson called Brossard, now back in the room originally assigned to him in the west wing.

The suite had been assembled from the past. An amalgam of periods – Louis XIV, XV and XVI – packaged with grey and yellow moiré drapes and wallpaper. In front of the marble fireplace stood a 19th century table, fashioned from lime and sycamore with ormolu mounts.

Inspector Moitry was there, together with Sureté and SDECE agents from Paris and the representatives of other internal security organisations. They were sitting around a table which looked very fragile in their presence.

Anderson expected trouble. He wasn't disappointed.

Moitry took the stage, pouchy-eyed and hostile. Acting, Anderson suspected, on instructions from the Surete and the SDECE who would want him to exercise Gallic authority but remain the fall-guy in case anything worse followed the shooting.

When Anderson entered the room, Moitry stood up and said sarcastically: 'Good of you to spare the time, Monsieur Anderson.'

'My pleasure,' Anderson said, lowering himself gently into an antique chair at the table.

'I want to be as brief as possible. An attempt has been made to murder a French citizen on French soil. French authorities,' without identifying them, 'will therefore be in charge of the investigation.' He pointed one finger at Anderson. 'You seem to regard this château as a fortress, within which you exercise total power. As from this moment all that has changed.'

He was, Anderson concluded, undoubtedly saying what he had been told to say. Anderson felt a little sorry for Inspector Moitry; he was hopelessly out of his depth.

On either side of him the other Frenchmen listened expressionlessly. They had more on their minds than an attempt to kill a wealthy and influential businessman: the life of the President of France was in their hands. Anderson didn't doubt that he had already been urged to return to Paris; nor did he doubt that he had refused.

A German addressed Moitry in schoolboy French. 'What steps have you taken so far?'

'Purely routine measures. A full-scale search has been mounted. Road blocks have been set up. The movements of everyone in the village are being checked. We hope that if the priest regains consciousness he will be able to help, although it would seem that he was struck from behind.'

An FBI agent said in slightly better French: 'I hope you've impressed upon your men the need for absolute secrecy.'

'Of course. I am fully aware that the distinguished company beneath this roof has requested absolute privacy. Happily most of the Press were away telephoning stories at the time of the shooting. Although the *Paris-Match* team are proving to be a little difficult,' he added.

Anderson said: 'What about the people in the village?'

'They have been told that the two explosions in the graveyard were the work of schoolboys.'

'And the priest? That wasn't the work of schoolboys.'

'He was startled by the first explosion. He slipped and fell down the steps leading from the belfry. In fact,' Moitry said, gaining confidence as he listened to his own catalogue of efficiency, 'he shouldn't have been in the church at all. He normally has a sleep at that time in the afternoon. But apparently he had left a book in the church.'

'James Bond probably.'

'M'sieur?'

'It doesn't matter,' Anderson said. 'How do you know he left a book there?'

'He was taking a glass of wine in the village inn. He told some of the villagers.' Moitry lit a Gauloise from the butt smouldering between his fingers.

Crawford, the British Special Branch officer, said: 'Whoever shot Brossard knew the church pretty well. That indicates a local man.'

Moitry looked pointedly at Anderson. 'I believe you dealt with the villagers.'

'I didn't interrogate 800 people if that's what you mean. But I did check out all members of the hotel staff living there. And anyone with a police record.'

The SDECE agent spoke for the first time. He looked, Anderson thought, like a Marseilles gangster dressed by a Parisien tailor. He said in a flat, cold voice: 'It goes without saying that there has been a lapse in security. The church was insufficiently protected. It was the obvious vantage point.'

Anderson didn't like doing it to Moitry but he had no choice. 'I'm afraid that was the responsibility of the French police. Inspector Moitry did his best with the resources at his disposal.'

The FBI agent said: 'Even if the gunman did live in the village he sure as hell won't be there now.'

'We are, of course, checking to see if anyone is missing,' Moitry said with dignity.

Anderson said: 'Also check to see if anyone in the village owned an old *Wermacht* rifle.'

One of the German Chancellor's guards exclaimed: 'How do you know it was an old *German* rifle?' as though it surely couldn't possibly be the Germans who were going to be the villains once again.

Anderson tossed the cartridge case on the table. 'Ballistics. We've got the slug too.' He leaned down and picked up his briefcase; the other men watched him curiously. The catches snapped open and, with a pair of tweezers, Anderson lifted out the photostats. 'I'd like to know if you have any theories about these,' he said laying the sheets on the table. 'I found them beside the cartridge case.'

No-one had any notable theories. Only the obvious. The names *with* the crosses beside them were the intended victims . . . the names *without* the crosses were the intended victims . . . the would-be assassin was trying to tell them something – a familiar characteristic of a paranoic criminal. . . .

There were no crosses beside the French President or the ex-Secretary of State.

Nor, Andrson brooded, against the names of Pierre Brossard, Paul Kingdon or Claire Jerome. Which could be good news; or it could be catastrophic.

Anderson said to Moitry: 'I want these photostats fingerprinted.'

'It is not what *you* want,' Moitry said as the telephone on the desk by the window shrilled.

He picked up the telephone. His attitude changed. He almost stood to attention. Anderson felt even more sorry for him because he knew what was being said on the telephone. . . .

Before coming up to Gaudin's suite, he had told Brossard to call Paris. To use the influence that, according to Helga, he wielded with France's top policemen. Brossard certainly didn't want police checking him out, calling at his home, perhaps stumbling across some of his last-minute getaway arrangements.

Nor, for entirely different reasons, did Anderson want the police interfering with Brossard's private life. Questioning, for instance, the transfer of $5 million to an account in Zurich.

Moitry replaced the receiver. He didn't look surprised, merely resigned. He lit another Gauloise and in a quiet voice said that he had been told to co-operate with Anderson.

Anderson took over. He said to the men seated around the table: 'Now we have to take this place apart all over again, because the obvious danger is a bomb.'

He turned to Moitry. 'And I want you to telephone the hospital and authorise them to let me see the priest.'

'Whatever you say,' Moitry said dully.

* * *

The priest's face was serene but his breathing was stertorous. Judging by the wound, he had been hit from behind with the rifle butt. But it was just possible that he might have a theory about the identity of his attacker. Who, for instance, had access to the church?

The nurse said: 'One minute, no longer,' and added: 'You shouldn't be here anyway.'

The priest had just been wheeled back from the X-ray department. Anderson sat on a chair beside the bed. He spoke softly. 'Can you hear me, father?'

He thought he detected a movement of the eyes beneath the lids.

'It's me. Shaft. Remember?'

The priest's eyes opened.

'Who did it, father? Do you have any ideas?'

The beginnings of the wondrous smile. His lips moved. Anderson leaned over the bed to try and catch the words.

'A case for Maigret, my son.'

His eyes closed as he lapsed into unconsciousness again.

In the corridor outside, Anderson asked the nurse: 'Is he going to make it?'

'God willing,' the nurse said. 'He has a hair-line fracture of the skull and he's concussed. It's not very serious.'

Relief surged through Anderson. 'Call me at the Château Saint-Pierre when he regains consciousness.'

And such was his relief that he bent and kissed the startled nurse before striding out of the hospital to the Chevrolet.

*   *   *

Members of the steering committee of Bilderberg summoned Anderson to their presence at 5 pm.

They sat round an oval table in an ante-room overlooking the fountains. The walls were Regency-striped, the drapes heavy green brocade.

The New York banker, who was regarded as the doyen of Bilderberg, had been called to Paris that afternoon. In his place the chairman of a Texas-based oil company, Roland Decker, was doing most of the talking.

Decker wore rimless glasses and his eyes behind them were grey – like his suit and his hair. His accent was Bostonian, the tone rasping. He was also a member of the Council on Foreign Relations. He looked a mean bastard, Anderson thought, momentarily intimidated by the aura of power present. They looked dour. With good cause: they had been discussing the Common Market all morning. And now this.

Decker polished his spectacles with his handkerchief, replaced them and stared at Anderson. 'Well, Mr Anderson, how bad is it?'

Anderson reeled off the facts – or those he thought they ought to know.

'Well, gentlemen, what do you think?' Decker asked the other members of the committee.

Anderson surveyed them curiously. The omnipotent conferring with the omnipotent. How did they react to each other? Did some personalities still dominate? Did any one commodity – oil, steel, chemicals, money – predominate?

357

A steel magnate, also in grey, said: 'So you think he's out to get the lot of us?'

'It's a possibility.'

They regarded him without emotion, calculatingly, like first-night critics about to crucify an unrehearsed actor.

Decker said: 'Have you made any progress, Mr Anderson?'

'Not so far. It didn't happen all that long ago.'

'It shouldn't have happened at all. The church tower was an obvious vantage point for a sniper.'

'If it hadn't happened, then we wouldn't have had this warning.'

'Are you suggesting that your inefficiency had benefited us, Mr Anderson?'

Another Bilderberger spoke up. 'We wouldn't have had this warning about what?'

Anderson said: 'My guess is a bomb.'

'That shouldn't be too difficult to trace.'

'I guess not,' Anderson said.

'Are you sure you can handle it?'

'I can handle it. What you have to decide is whether you're going to pull out or stay put.'

Decker said: 'The question doesn't arise. Terrorism only flourishes through weakness. If we dispersed, the Press would get hold of the story. Capitalism routed by one freak. Next year we'd have a dozen freaks and maybe some pros as well. No, Mr Anderson, we don't quit although I don't doubt that you'd like us to.'

In a way you had to admire the old bastard. Anderson said: 'On the contrary, sir, I consider it a privilege to have your lives in my care.'

'Are you being sarcastic?'

'No sir.'

The second grey-suit said: 'It's a personal decision, of course. Everyone will have to be told about the shooting and Mr Anderson's fears for our safety. The French President has indicated that he intends to stay.'

'And we'll have to make damn sure everyone keeps their mouths shut,' Decker added. To Anderson he said: 'That will be all. Keep us informed of your progress.'

Outside the ante-room Anderson glanced at his wrist-watch. In one hour he had to meet more important people than members of the steering committee: he had to meet George Prentice and Helga Keller.

XXIX

Reporters have a habit of making friends with hotel telephonists. It helps if you are also a trainee manager.

After he had spotted the ambulance and the Chevrolet with Anderson at the wheel, Foster went straight to the switchboard. In the small cheerless room where it was housed he spoke to a pale girl with a wistful face.

'Are they keeping you busy?' He smiled at her.

'There have been a lot of calls today,' she said. 'London, New York, Tokyo, Zurich. . . .'

Why had Anderson been in such a hell of a hurry and why the ambulance? 'I thought the emergency might have overloaded the switchboard.'

'Emergency, m'sieur?' Her dark eyes looked at him questioningly. 'I did have a call for the doctor. . . .'

'Who wanted him?'

'Monsieur Brossard.'

Nicholas touched her shoulder. 'Well, if you have any problems you know where to find me.'

'Thank you, m'sieur,' as she reached forward and plugged a lead into the switchboard.

Foster helped himself to a pass-key from behind the reception desk and headed for Brossard's room in the east wing.

He knocked. No reply. He opened the door and felt the draught on his face through the broken window. On the carpet he saw broken glass – and spots of blood.

He thought: 'By Christ, I've got a story.'

But what sort of a story? An ambulance, an empty hotel room, blood and broken glass. . . .

He picked up the telephone. The voice of the girl with the wistful face answered him. He asked her which room Brossard had been moved to.

His original room in the west wing, she told him.

The excitement that every newspaperman knows at least once in his life gripped Foster. The window must have been broken by a bullet. He peered through it. A clear view of the church tower. . . .

Why had the church bells been chiming?

The awesome possibilities of the story began to unfold before him. But first some facts. The obvious person to confront was Brossard.

Foster closed the door behind him and made his way to the west wing.

*   *   *

Brossard had agreed to be transferred back to the west wing without protest. 'East wing prices,' Gaudin had told him comfortingly.

In Room 205 he had struggled into another suit and discarded the sling provided by the doctor – no need to be unnecessarily conspicuous. Then shock had set in. He began to tremble violently. When the telephone rang he started. It was Anderson.

'All right, I'll do it,' he said, and called police headquarters in Paris. Then he poured himself a large whisky and drank it neat.

The trembling subsided, the wound began to throb. He lay on the bed and tried to think who would want to kill him.

Not the blackmailers, certainly not until the money transfer had been completed. Kingdon? Again he was only useful to Kingdon alive. Not the Russians for the same reason.

During his life he had made many enemies. But none of them would choose to kill him at the one time that he was surrounded by police.

But he couldn't make a run for it; the last coup had to be carried out. If it wasn't, the Russians *would* kill him. The safest way to transmit the column was by Telex. No eavesdroppers. He called Hildegard Metz and asked her to come to the room to arrange his belongings brought from the east wing.

Then he went down to the lobby and asked a receptionist for the key to the Telex room. It was empty. He locked the door behind him. Instinctively he taped the column first: it was cheaper that way because you were charged according to the time you spent on the machine, and the tape, with its message punched out in tiny holes, raced through the machine.

It took him ten minutes to type the column on the keyboard. Then he called the office of his newspaper in Paris and asked for Mayard.

Back came the reply on the paper in front of him; they were fetching Mayard. Brossard waited impatiently until Mayard indicated that he was waiting to receive the copy.

Brossard pressed a red button and the punched-out tape began to speed through the Telex machine, rising from its own coils twitching on the floor.

In front of Brossard, the column appeared as it was being received in Paris. When it was finished he tore the typescript off the machine.

Finally he punched out two messages to banks in Monaco and Geneva, seeking confirmation that arrangements for the transfer of $5 million to Account No. CR 58432/91812 at the United Bank in Zurich were in hand.

Within five minutes he had the confirmation.

In the corridor outside his room he met a youngish man in a black jacket and striped trousers. He limped and his face was vaguely familiar, one of the under-managers.

Anderson had emphasised: 'Speak to no-one. No-one, do you understand, Monsieur Brossard?'

'Excuse me, m'sieur,' the young man said.

'Yes, what is it?'

'I wondered how you were feeling.'

Conscious of his injured arm stiff at his side, Brossard said: 'I'm perfectly well, thank you. Did Gaudin ask you to inquire?'

'We are all concerned.' Which wasn't any sort of reply.

A little clumsily, Brossard transferred the Telex copy and tape from one hand to the other. Then he opened the door to his room. 'I've no idea what you are concerned about,' he said and shut the door.

Inside the room he placed the tape and the copy into his briefcase.

*   *   *

Paul Kingdon was one of the last delegates to hear about the shooting.

During the last session of the conference a brief announcement was made by Roland Decker. Bilderbergers were told that it was up to them whether or not they quit; they were also warned that, if they did, Bilderberg would in future be a prime target for terrorists.

At the time Kingdon was making arrangements for $5 million to be transferred to Zurich, and it wasn't until a typewritten version of Decker's announcement was delivered to his room that he knew a gunman was on the loose.

Later he called on Brossard in the room next door. Brossard was sitting in an easy chair – well away from the window. He was drinking Scotch and seemed a little drunk.

Kingdon helped himself to some whisky and said: 'Who was it, Pierre? Has anyone got wind of your impending transactions?'

'Only the dealers who are selling. And you, of course.' Brossard stared at Kingdon.

'It wouldn't be in my interests to knock you off, would it? One of the speculators? Perhaps – if he's decided to pull a stroke. Maybe buy dollars instead of selling them. But I doubt it. The dollar's too shaky as it is.'

Brossard said: 'There wouldn't be any point.' He winced as he moved his wounded arm.

'Do the speculators know what's going into your column?'

'Some of it,' Brossard told him.

'Have you written the column?'

'Written it,' Brossard said, 'and sent it.' He drank some whisky; a little dribbled down his chin.

'Well keep away from that window,' Kingdon said. 'I

want you good and alive.'

Kingdon went down to the bar and ordered a beer. Gerard was standing there; Kingdon ignored him – you had to salvage some pride.

By now most of the staff knew that something had occurred in Brossard's room in the east wing; as usual Jules Fromont knew more than most.

Kingdon asked: 'What's new?'

'I understand they're looking for bombs.'

'Have they found any?'

'Not as far as I know, m'sieur.'

'Any idea why anyone should take a pot shot at Brossard?'

Jules shook his head. 'I gather the shot may have been fired from the church tower.'

'Makes sense. Lousy shot though. Although it wouldn't have made much difference if he'd shot him in the heart.'

'Why's that, m'sieur?'

'The bullet would have been deflected,' Kingdon said. 'Brossard's heart is made of stone.'

* * *

Claire Jerome walked in the gardens.

The air was chill but she didn't notice it. She hadn't eaten and her head ached.

She had paid off Tilmissan and Brossard; she was negotiating payment of the ransom money. A fortune disposed of in a few days.

But it wasn't money that she was thinking about. She wanted Pete Anello beside her. That was all she wanted, all she had ever wanted since she met him.

She ached for him.

She leaned on the wall of the water-gardens and stared down. Fat carp moved lazily in the mossy depths.

Supposing he was implicated in the plot. If he returned to her, she would never question him. So much for pride. There had been too much of that in her life: it could shrivel your soul.

She walked back to the château, past the maze and the fountains. In the lobby, detectives wearing earphones were searching for bombs with portable detectors that reacted to explosive vapours and the tick of timing devices. The Press had been banned from the building and the grounds.

She collected her key and went up to her room.

On the table was a vase of daffodils and narcissi arranged with maiden-hair fern. An envelope was propped against the vase.

She ripped it open. It was Pete Anello's hand-writing. She felt faint and sat down.

Dear Claire,

I am being held by a group called LAW – the League against Weapons. They say that they will release me on condition that you resign from all companies connected with the manufacture and sale of arms.

They insist that you make a public announcement in the media to this effect. The announcement must also urge:
(1) resumption of arms-control talks with the Soviet Union
(2) a total ban on the manufacture of sophisticated weapons of horror, such as the concussion bomb.

These people are not, I can assure you, freaks. They plan to pressurise arms dealers both outside and inside the Communist blocs.

Nor are they so naive that they expect your announcement to have any immediate effect. But, they say, it is a beginning.

As soon as your announcement is published I will be set free. The decision is yours.

Pete

P.S. I can't help wondering if the gun pointing at my head at the moment is one of yours.

A wave of joy swept through her. He was alive.

Beside her the telephone rang.

'Mrs Jerome?' The same woman's voice.

'Yes, who is it?'

'Did you receive the note with the flowers?'

'Yes, but – '

'Act on it, Mrs Jerome. For your own sake act on it.'

The line went dead.

Claire Jerome picked up the note. The *P.S.* was pure Anello. She smiled.

When the first wave of euphoria had passed, the problems began to present themselves.

She could hardly quit the armaments business and continue directing the other businesses. Marks International *was* armaments and it was the cornerstone of the whole empire.

Furthermore, what would happen to her father if she resigned?

But she had to obey the instructions in the note; of that there was no doubt. She picked up the telephone and called Stephen Harsch in New York.

Over there it was mid-morning. Harsch sounded surprised to hear from her. 'Hi,' he said, 'how's it going?'

Cutting through all such niceties, Claire said: 'I'm quitting, Stephen. Provided you agree with a few formalities you are, as from now, No. 2 at Marks International, which as you and the rest of the world knows means in effect No. 1.'

A long pause. Claire pictured Harsch staring at the telephone in his hand and wondering, because humour wasn't his strong point, whether she was joking, a frown on his tight, watchful features.

Finally he said: 'Are you kidding, Claire?'

'I want you to listen, Stephen. Tape what I'm saying.' As if he wasn't doing so already. 'I'm quitting on one condition – that you make provision for my father. He stays as President, right?'

'Sure, but – '

'I want you to sign an affidavit to that effect and I want you to promise me right now that you'll carry him whenever he gets a little lost. . . . It won't be for long, Stephen,' Claire said, 'we both know that.'

'Why, Claire?'

'Private reasons. I'm going to issue a Press release the usual way through Hartman and Wilson. Your appointment will have to go to the board, of course. But you won't have any trouble there; you're the right guy for the job. My father thinks so, even I think so.'

366

'I still don't understand,' Harsch said.

'You don't have to. One more thing, Stephen. . . . Has that deal with the Pakistanis gone through?'

'The one you made on the side? Sure it has. The stuff's on its way to the East Coast now.'

'Thank God.'

'Does it matter so much?'

'My last deal with Marks International. Of course it matters. And Stephen. . . . Don't try too hard.'

It took her half an hour to compose a Press release which she telephoned to an executive of the PR firm of Hartman and Wilson, who was so astonished that he asked permission to call her back and confirm it.

Two more formalities remained. To instruct the switchboard not to put any Press calls through to her – and to tell her father what she'd done.

It was a long time before Nathan Marks understood. When he did his thin old voice was incredulous. 'You're leaving me in charge? Are you out of your mind, Claire?'

'No, papa. I'll explain when I get back to New York.'

'But I can't carry it without you, Claire. You know that.'

She imagined his small, hunched body clad in the old dressing-gown sitting in the chair in front of the television. She knew that he was frightened; that this was one set-back that he couldn't turn to his advantage.

She tried to comfort him. Told him that he would have Harsch behind him and that she would always be close at hand.

Perhaps, she thought, she should persuade him to retire with her, but he answered her thoughts: 'Okay, okay, so maybe I can handle it. But why, Claire. Why?'

'Because it's time for me to get out, papa.'

'Tell me something, is it hot out there? Are you suffering from the heat, Claire?' She could hear his rapid, bird-like breaths. 'Are you out of your mind?'

'No, papa, I'm not out of my mind. Everything is going to be fine, I promise you. Now I have to go. Turn up the television again. Is it *Citizen Kane*?' And when he said it was: 'Take care, papa, take care. . . .'

So it had been as easy as that. A few phone calls and all that endeavour, that crusade begun when only men reigned in the kingdoms of industry, was terminated.

But she felt elated, and it was only later that evening that she found herself wondering whether Pete Anello had known about the demand for $5 million when he wrote the note.

* * *

Just before 6 pm that evening Pierre Brossard received a telephone call in his room. The President of France requested his presence in his suite on a matter of vital importance.

A request was a command. Brossard wished he hadn't drunk so much. He tried to get in touch with Hildegard Metz but she wasn't in her room.

He managed to slip the jacket of his suit over his shoulders, then, swaying slightly, made his way down the corridor towards the elevators.

When Brossard was safely inside the elevator, Nicholas Foster made his way to his room and opened the door with the pass-key. The Telex message: every journalistic instinct told him that was the key to the mystery.

Brossard's briefcase was beside the bed. And it was unlocked. He was rifling the compartments when he heard a key slide into the doorlock.

There was the tape, no time for the sheets of copy. In one movement he removed the tape, slipped it into his jacket pocket and closed the briefcase. As Hildegard Metz walked into the room.

'What are you doing in here?'

'I came to make sure that Monsieur Brossard had everything he needed. I thought I should check when there was no reply. . . .'

'Well, you've checked,' staring at him suspiciously.

Foster nodded and walked into the corridor as the door closed behind him.

At approximately the same time a Presidential aide was informing a puzzled Pierre Brossard that the President had most certainly not requested his presence.

'Lucky for him that he didn't,' the aide said to the guard posted outside the door, as they watched Brossard stumble away. 'The President abhors drunkards.'

The guard, who thought that a man who had just been shot had a reasonable excuse for getting drunk, didn't reply.

*　　*　　*

In a motel room eight miles from the château, Anello stood at the window watching the traffic speeding past on the highway. He wondered if Claire had received the note. Wondered if she would act on it.

The proposition which the man with the submachine-gun had put to him had made sense. He had told him to put away the gun, he wouldn't need it.

Anello suddenly found that he had a purpose. The effect on the international trade in arms would be negligible. But it was his own gesture. It *was* a beginning.

XXX

One disturbing aspect of the shooting nagged Owen Anderson, as he made his way to his room for the 6.15 pm meeting with George Prentice and Helga Keller. It looked as though the gunman had known that an empty room in the château had suddenly been occupied. Which means that, in all probability, he was inside the hotel.

All members of the staff living outside the hotel had been screened and cleared and there wasn't time to repeat the performance. All they could try and do was check their movements at the time of the shooting.

Where, for instance, had the trainee manager Nicholas Foster been? The previous day he had walked into the village; he may have done the same today. Anderson decided to check with the guards at the gate.

Anderson had a feeling about Foster: he was incongruous in this Gallic setting: he was also a comparative newcomer and his past history was vague. He didn't look like a killer, but Anderson had long ceased to equate looks with criminal intent.

Of one thing Anderson was sure: the shooting had been a diversion. The would-be killer had bigger things in mind.

Prince and Vixen were waiting for King in his room.

'Well,' he said, 'I promised you an unpredictable. I keep my promises.' He sat on the bed beside Helga. 'Kingdon is still making arrangements for the transfer of the money. How abour your two?'

Prentice said: 'Luckily we left the old bug in Brossard's original room. Brossard's as scared as hell. Who wouldn't be? But he's pushing the money through.'

Helga said: 'So is Mrs Jerome. She got the note from Anello. Thanks to George,' she added smiling at him.

Prentice lit a cigarette and leaned against the wall.

'Anello was as good as gold. A nice guy into the bargain. He seemed to think it's about time Mrs Jerome was taught a lesson.'

'Does he know we're demanding cash?'

Prentice shook his head.

Anderson turned to Helga. 'And our own financial arrangements?'

'Proceeding smoothly,' Helga said. 'I do. know about Swiss banking.'

Dollars deposited in Swiss accounts, to be converted into Swiss francs as a hedge against devaluation and inflation, were no longer welcome and the United Bank had readily agreed, at a price, to diversify the money. Some of it was being transferred to interest-earning accounts in Andorra, Luxembourg, Liechtenstein and the Bahamas. Some was being deposited in a fixed-time deposit account in the Zurich bank. Some was being deposited to earn interest abroad in the name of the United Bank to avoid Swiss taxation. Some was being gambled on currency speculation. Some was being invested in gold and silver. A comparatively small proportion was being channelled into Brazilian checking accounts for immediate use.

All the transactions were being conducted on behalf of fictitious persons whose identities, careers, nationalities and credibility had been fully documented from birth.

'So we have a situation,' Anderson remarked, 'where we still stand to lose if our assassin hits any of our subjects before they've completed the financial arrangements.'

'Fifteen million if he hits all three of them,' Prentice said. 'We've got another whole day tomorrow. And then till 4.30 pm the following day.'

'My guess,' Anderson said, 'is that the sonofabitch works in the hotel.'

'Which reminds me,' Helga said, 'the English trainee manager, Foster . . . I found him in Brossard's room. He claimed he was checking to see if Brossard had everything he wanted. He was lying.'

Anderson stood up. 'That,' he said, 'is very interesting. I shall have to pay a call on Mr Foster. By the way,' as he reached the door. 'That Yugoslav booze that was delivered to Brossard. A nice touch that, George. A touch of class.'

* * *

The Telex room was empty. Foster locked it from the inside and sat at one of the machines. The tape he had stolen from Brossard's briefcase was in three parts, one of them long, the other two short.

He switched on the machine, fed in the long tape and sat back to watch the message being hammered out at breakneck speed – as in the past he had watched his own stories being transmitted.

The byline, *Midas*, followed by the dateline and then the first paragraph. . . . After that Foster sat transfixed as one stunning revelation after another appeared in front of him.

The dollar about to crash . . . OPEC countries blocking all exports of oil to the United States . . . Russians dumping dollars . . . followed by the major speculators . . . whizz-kid Paul Kingdon involved. . . .

As the last serpentine coil of tape sped through the machine, Foster leaned back in the chair. 'Christ,' he exclaimed aloud.

He had infiltrated Bilderberg to put together an exclusive, but he had never envisaged anything on this scale: the facts in front of him spelled out the destruction of the Western economy.

But were they facts? He had no way of knowing; the story wasn't his. Certainly the author was one of the most reputable financial journalists in the world. But for Nicholas Foster, who had learned responsibility the hard way, that wasn't sufficient. It had to be his own story. He decided to call Lucas on the *Financial Times* and seek his advice.

Meanwhile what had he got? Sufficient, certainly, to file a story to the newspaper that had been primed to expect a call from him. It had now been established beyond all doubt that an attempt had been made on the life of Pierre Brossard.

372

It didn't require any stroke of genius to write the second paragraph to the story: —

Police and security guards responsible for the safety of some of the most powerful men and women in the Western world fear that the would-be killer may strike again.

Then the fact that the Bilderbergers, including the President of France and the former globe-trotting American Secretary of State, had decided to stay put. Followed by details of the search for bombs and the theory that the shot had been fired from the church tower.

All that was sensational enough. But Foster's instincts told him that there was more. Paul Kingdon had told Suzy Okana that the financial structure of the world was about to change: Kingdon was named in the story written by Brossard. . . .

He fed the two short tapes into the machine. Brossard seeking and obtaining confirmation that $5 million was being transferred to a numbered account in Zurich. Why had he waited until Bilderberg to make such a transfer?

Foster's thoughts raced ahead. It was significant that Brossard had been placed in a room next to Kingdon, even if he had asked to be moved. Significant, too, that Mrs Claire Jerome and her body guard Anello had been allotted rooms next to them, because he had just learned that Anello had apparently disappeared.

It was no coincidence that everything seemed to lead to that cluster of rooms at the end of a corridor in the west wing.

A conspiracy? Blackmail with Anello as the extortionist? Five million dollars from Brossard, maybe five from Kingdon and Mrs Jerome. He would have to find a way of checking whether they had made any similar transactions.

But first the story of the shooting.

He picked up the tapes, tore the messages off the Telex and slid them into the inside pocket of his jacket. Then he switched off the current and let himself out of the room.

It was 7 pm. Time to catch the first edition in London. The scoop of a lifetime.

Anderson met him at the entrance to the annexe. 'I'd like to have a little chat with you, Mr Foster.'

'Can't it wait?'

'No, Mr Foster,' Anderson said, 'it sure as hell can't. Shall we go to your room?'

Anderson locked the door behind them, drew the curtains, pointed to a chair and said: 'Sit down, Mr Foster, and tell me just what the hell your game is.'

Foster sat down while, fingers in the pockets of his waistcoat, Anderson regarded him from above. Nicholas could see the bulge of his pistol beneath the chocolate brown jacket of his suit.

'I asked you a question,' Anderson said.

The room seemed smaller than ever with Anderson standing in it. Not only that but there was something subtly different about it; Foster tried to determine what it was.

He said: 'I heard the question. What am I supposed to say? I'm a trainee manager. I know that, you know that.'

'We both know you're lying,' Anderson said.

'Correction. You think you know I'm lying. I know I'm not.'

'And I don't like smart-asses,' Anderson said.

Foster shrugged. 'Now if you'll excuse me I've got important things to do.'

Anderson dangled the door-key on one finger. 'Like what?'

Foster eyed the telephone. The time element was already finely balanced. He wasn't an accredited correspondent and they would have to check his story. But a newspaper's Paris correspondent was expected to have good police and political contacts. Foster also intended to give them the name of the doctor who had attended Brossard. They would put in a barrage of phone calls to the village and the hotel. From the denials and half-truths supplied by unwary members of the staff, the truth would begin to emerge; truth based on information supplied by Nicholas Foster who had established a reputation for reliability on Reuters.

But it was getting late for the first edition. . . .

'Like what?' Anderson repeated.

'Like the preparations for tomorrow's cocktail party.'

'They can wait.' Anderson reached into the inside pocket of his jacket. Foster expected to see a gun in his hand. Instead he brought out Foster's notes. 'Funny place to keep them. Under a floor-tile.'

Foster stood up: 'What right have you –'

'Every right in the goddam world.' Anderson pushed him back into the chair and stood over him menacingly. 'Just what the fuck are these notes?'

'What do they look like? Notes about the conference,' Foster said. So that was what was different about the room: it had been searched.

'Why would you want to make notes like that?'

'Because I have an inquisitive mind.'

Anderson scanned the notes. 'I see you recorded the numbers of every guest's room. Even Brossard's when he moved to the east wing.'

Suddenly Foster realised where the questions were leading. 'Christ,' he exclaimed, 'you don't think –'

'It wouldn't be the first time a journalist has created his own story. And you are a journalist, aren't you, Mr Foster?'

'You think I fired that shot?'

'I know you did.'

'This is bloody ridiculous. I've never fired a rifle in my life.'

'The man who fired the shot wasn't so hot. I'm going to hand you over to the French cops,' moving towards Foster.

'Just a minute.' Foster tried to marshal his thoughts. One thing was obvious: he wouldn't be able to file a story from a police cell. 'All right,' he said, 'I'm a journalist.'

'Okay,' Anderson said. 'Tell me all about it. We've got plenty of time – we've swept the whole goddam hotel and there isn't a trace of an explosive device. Did you intend to plant a bomb? Or was the story good enough as it stands?'

'Look,' Foster said, 'I'll be straight with you.'

He told Anderson how he had been sacked, how he had

got the job in the hotel. 'And I've got a hell of a story.' To prove it he handed Anderson the Telex messages. 'That's what Brossard filed to his paper.'

Anderson glanced at it, pursed his lips. 'Dynamite. If it's true, which I doubt.'

'Brossard is a highly respectable journalist.'

'So it's his story, not yours.'

A part of Foster's consciousness recorded the fact that Anderson didn't seem to react sufficiently to Brossard's sensational revelations. But he was now only concerned with proving genuine journalistic endeavour, establishing that he wanted to co-operate with the American Secret Serviceman.

He said: 'I'm also onto something else that will interest you.'

'You've been a busy bee.'

'A conspiracy involving Brossard, Kingdon and possibly Mrs Claire Jerome.'

Later Foster was to conclude that it was at this moment that Anderson's attitude changed. The toughness remained but it was compounded by a new wariness.

'What kind of a conspiracy?'

'I don't know. But I do know that Brossard and Kingdon are connected. You see, I found out that Kingdon knew what Brossard was going to write in his column. So my guess is that Brossard tipped him off so that he can make a killing before the bottom falls out of the market.'

'Interesting,' Anderson said. He sat down opposite Foster. 'I won't ask you how you know this. But carry on.'

'The rooms occupied by Brossard, Kingdon, Mrs Jerome and her bodyguard Peter Anello are all together, right?'

Anderson nodded, staring speculatively at Foster.

'Now all of a sudden Anello goes missing. I presume you must be working on the theory that he tried to shoot Brossard.'

Anderson measured his words. 'I can assure you that we have eliminated him from our inquiries. Is that all you have to tell me, Mr Foster?'

Foster shook his head. 'I have another theory. Supposing

Anello found out about the conspiracy between Brossard and Kingdon – through Mrs Jerome, perhaps – and decided to blackmail them.'

'Blackmail.' Anderson seemed to savour the word. 'Now just what the hell gave you that idea?'

'Because Brossard suddenly decided to transfer five million dollars to a numbered account in Zurich. Now why the hell would he decide to do that in the middle of the Bilderberg conference?'

Anderson's voice was taut as he asked: 'Did you get the number of that account, Mr. Foster?'

Foster fished in his jacket pocket and brought out the two short messages that the Telex tape had punched out. He handed them to Anderson who read them carefully.

'What's more I've memorised it,' Foster said and recited the number: CR 58432/91812.'

'Well I'll be a sonofabitch!' Anderson reached for the telephone and asked for Prentice's room, and when the connection was made said: 'George, get your ass down to Room 38 in the annexe. We've got trouble. And George – bring your medical bag.'

'What was that all about?' Foster asked.

'You got yourself a story,' Anderson said. 'Trouble is you've just blown it,' as he drew a .32 Cobra pistol from his shoulder holster and pointed it at Foster's head.

They told Foster to walk in front of them and head for the car-park. If he met anyone he knew, he was to acknowledge them politely and keep walking.

Anderson slipped the pistol into his jacket pocket. 'Try anything and you lose your head.'

Behind him Foster heard them talking in whispers. The rapport between the black security officer and the professor of economics baffled him.

Wasn't Prentice connected with Paul Kingdon in some way?

Intuitively Foster knew that he wasn't being taken to the French police. What he had told Anderson had changed everything. In particular the numbered account in Zurich.

Half way between the annexe and the car-park they met Suzy Okana.

She smiled at him. 'I was just coming to see you.' She ran towards him. 'I've just left Kingdon.'

'Good evening, Suzy,' he said.

'Nicholas, it's me!'

'I'm sorry, I haven't got time to talk at the moment.'

She stopped. She looked as though he had hit her across the face with the back of his hand.

'Nicholas. . . .'

'Some other time, Suzy.'

He walked on. He thought it was the worst moment of his life.

Prentice climbed into the driving seat of the Chevrolet.

Anderson opened the rear door, prodded the gun through the cloth of his jacket and said: 'Get in.' He sat in the back beside Foster.

The Chev took off without lights. At the gates Anderson lowered the rear window and spoke to the gendarmes. They opened the gates.

The Chev accelerated down the lane, its headlights suddenly carving light in the darkness.

Anderson said: 'Now lie on the floor face down.'

'But –'

'Move it.'

Foster calculated that they had been driving for about fifteen minutes when the car stopped. Prentice climbed out and opened the boot. He handed Anderson a rag through the window.

Anderson tied the rag round Foster's eyes. It smelled of oil and petrol.

'Okay,' Anderson said, 'now get out.' He prodded the barrel of the pistol in Foster's back.

Foster heard a key turn in a lock. Anderson pushed him forward. Foster smelled rotting vegetables.

Anderson said to Prentice: 'Put the blanket down there, George.'

Foster said: 'Do you mind telling me what the hell's going on?'

Prentice said: 'Don't worry, we're not going to hurt you.'

'The fact is,' Anderson said, 'you're too smart. We under-rated you.' He whispered to Prentice, then said: 'Okay, now take your jacket off and lie down.'

Foster felt the needle of the syringe slip almost painlessly into the vein on the inside of his arm. His last conscious thought was about Suzy. And how he had hurt her.

Then nothing.

*　　*　　*

Suzy Okana stood for a moment watching the retreating figure of Foster, followed by the black security officer and another man in a leather-elbowed sports jacket.

At first she couldn't comprehend what had happened. Nicholas, who a few hours earlier had been kissing her, understanding, had walked past her as though she were an overnight whore he wanted to forget.

But had he understood? Why should he? It was a dreary and sordid story. But I had to tell him. We had to begin with honesty. Perhaps even then he had only wanted to get away from her. To escape without fuss.

She began to walk towards the gates. Strips of light shining through slits in the curtains made zebra-skin patterns on the grass.

How could he behave so cruelly? It wasn't in his nature. But it happened, Suzy Okana.

Ahead of her, an American limousine with its lights doused sped down the gravel drive. It stopped at the gates; then the headlights came on as it accelerated in the direction of the village.

Suzy walked slowly along the lane between the hedgerows, so high in places that they formed a tunnel in the night. A few hours of hope, that was all she had been allowed. And somehow in the previous years she had always known that it might happen like this: that what she had been doing then

379

might erase her one chance.

But her way of life had been predestined. Just like her meeting with Nicholas. There was a pattern and you conformed and she would return to the regular symmetry of that pattern, and one day she would marry a rich man and never again would she come alive.

She went up the stairs to her room in the inn. In the morning she would pack and return to London, because she never again wanted to meet Nicholas Foster. First she would call Paul Kingdon; perhaps she would settle down with him; perhaps it was written.

She went to the window to close the curtains and noticed the American limousine parked down the street. She pulled the curtains, undressed and climbed into bed.

Once in the melting moments before sleep, she called out Nicholas's name. Then she slept unaware that, three doors away, he lay unconscious on a car blanket, his jacket draped over his chest to keep him warm.

*   *   *

Because of the presence of the French President, dinner that evening was more of a banquet.

The château specialised in recreating great meals from the past. Tonight it was the Dinner of the Three Emperors, served at the Café Anglais on June 7th, 1867, to guests including the Czar of Russia, Alexander II, the Czarevich who became Alexander III and the King of Prussia, later Emperor William I.

Among the courses: hot quail *pâté*, lobster *à la parisienne*, canapés of duckling, *aubergines à l'espagnole*, iced *bombe* and fruit. The wines were chosen to correspond as closely as possible to the originals – Château-Yquem 1847, Château-Latour, 1847, Château-Lafite, 1848. . . .

But there were no speeches. There had been enough of those for one day.

The President sat between the former Secretary of State and Bilderberg's Honorary Secretary General for Europe. Also at their table were the Austrian Finance Minister, the

German Chancellor, the Icelandic Prime Minister, the Foreign Ministers of Ireland and Portugal and a member of the British Labour Party's Shadow Cabinet.

The tubby American statesman ate frugally, the slender French President tucked in with enthusiasm.

Observing the Frenchman demolish his iced *bombe*, the American said: 'Mr President, you must let me into your secret. How do you contrive to eat with such obvious relish and at the same time retain your figure?'

The President considered the question. He was due to leave the château after the cocktail party the following evening. After the shooting he had been urged to leave earlier. He had refused because it was undignified to run away and, if he took notice of every threat on his life, he would spend the rest of his term of office taking evasive action. The shooting, however, had affected him more than he cared to admit. No-one seemed to have noticed it, but he and Pierre Brossard did look uncommonly alike.

He sipped his wine and took his time about answering the American. Then he smiled and said: 'As a matter of fact I normally eat very little. But I am a Frenchman and I do enjoy my food. And, you see, there is a possibility that this could be our last dinner. *Bon appetit*, my friend.' He finished his glass of wine and turned his attention to the fruit.

XXXI

April 23rd. The last full day of the conference.

Helga Keller's travelling alarm clock awoke her at 4.30 am. Thirty-six hours before they would know if they had pulled the coup off.

But a more immediate deadline was 7 am. That was the time she had to be in Paris.

She showered and examined her body in the mirror. She *was* slimmer, no doubt about it. She thought about Prentice and smiled; it was extraordinary how sensual their love-making had become. Her only criticism was its infrequency. But that would soon be remedied; they had a lot of catching-up to do.

She dressed quickly. Then checked in her handbag to make sure that the message she had dispatched to Mayard on the Telex the previous evening was there. The message would be on the machine in the newspaper office now waiting for him when he got to work.

She went downstairs, crossed the darkened gardens and climbed into her grey Renault 18.

Ten minutes later she was on the auto-route to Paris. Traffic was light and she drove at a steady 60 mph.

Thirty-six hours . . . but hazards were materialising. First the shooting which raised the possibility that the gunman was contemplating a mass killing.

Now the discovery that Nicholas Foster knew the number of the account in Zurich and suspected a conspiracy.

Anderson had acted with his usual authority. When he was checking out the village, he had come across the derelict building in the main street; in the rear was an outhouse that had been used to store vegetables; the owner was in the south of France.

Anticipation, Helga thought, was the key to success in

such operations. The hallmark of the professional.

Anderson, who knew all the tricks, had also taken the precaution of driving around the countryside for fifteen minutes to give Foster the impression that he was several miles away.

But Anderson didn't think Foster was the gunman. He was patently what he claimed to be, a journalist and a remarkably enterprising one.

Helga Keller had reached the outskirts of Paris. It was still dark but the city was waking. She imagined she could smell baking bread and coffee. She had enjoyed Paris in an introspective sort of way; but for her it had been a retreat. Difficult to believe now that she had dismissed the stories of tyrannical abuse of power in Communist countries as Western propaganda. Would she have treated the banishment of Andrei Sakharov to Gorky, the invasion of Afghanistan, similarly?

Not that she now believed totally in the political structures of the West. How could anyone accept a system that allowed such men as Pierre Brossard and Paul Kingdon to prosper? The point was that you had to equate one system against the other.

One day, perhaps, the equation would be solved. She had made her contribution towards its eventual solution; the time had come to take her just rewards and start being a woman.

She looked back at her ideals with affection but without sentiment.

She took the east fork of the *Autoroute de Sud* and drove onto the *periphique*, the great roaring highway that encircles Paris. Already, as the first greenish light of dawn began to glow on the skyline, the traffic was building up. She left the highway at the Porte de Vincennes and five minutes later pulled up outside a café optimistically called *Le Gourmet.*

A tattered awning hung outside and the grimy windows were covered with steam. Most of the customers sitting at the plastic-topped tables looked as though they had been there all night. One or two were asleep, heads resting on their folded arms.

The bearded shop assistant was sitting in one corner eating a croissant and drinking coffee. When she sat down opposite him it was exactly 7 am.

She ordered a black coffee from the unshaven proprietor. When he had placed it in front of her, coffee spilling into the saucer, she spoke quietly and urgently to the bearded man for several minutes.

Then she passed him a top copy and carbon of the Telex message she had sent to Mayard, concealed inside the pages of the previous day's *Le Monde*.

Less than two hours later she was back at the Château Saint-Pierre.

* * *

At eight o'clock that morning, while Helga Keller was on her way back from Paris, a telephonist at the château dealt with an incoming call that destroyed the illusions of any Bilderbergers who thought the shooting might have been an isolated incident.

She plugged into the call and said, 'Good morning, Château Saint-Pierre. Can I help you?'

A man's voice said: 'Do you have a pencil and paper?'

'*Oui, m'sieur.* Do you wish me to take a message?' The girl picked up the stub of a pencil and waited.

'Take this down.' The voice was gruff as though, she later realised, he was trying to disguise it. 'By tonight. . . . Have you got that?'

'*Oui, m'sieur.*'

'By tonight they will all be dead.'

'I'm not sure. . . .'

'Have you got it?'

'Yes, but. . . .'

The line went dead.

The girl stared at what she had written for a moment, then ran to reception. She was ushered into Gaudin's office.

Gaudin, who was enjoying his first coffee of the morning, stared at the message.

'When did you receive this?'

'Just now.'

Gaudin shook his head wearily. To think that he had regarded the decision of the steering committee of Bilderberg to stay at the château as the greatest accolade of his career.

He told the girl to sit down and called Inspector Moitry and Anderson.

Anderson studied the note, then handed it to Moitry who looked at it and said: 'We have to treat it seriously.'

Anderson said: 'I agree. But short of evacuating the place, there's not a hell of a lot we can do. What is this guy going to do? Drop an atom bomb?'

Moitry spoke to the girl.

'Was it a local call?'

'I think so but I can't be sure. It sounded very clear.'

'Was he a Frenchman?'

'I don't know. He said very little and his voice sounded . . . strange.'

Anderson thanked her. Moitry told her to get back to the switchboard. 'If you get another call like that try and keep him speaking and call Monsieur Gaudin. Tell the other girls.'

Gaudin said: 'Forgive me asking, gentlemen, but have you made any progress?'

Moitry said: 'I think you should address your question to my colleague here.' Anderson didn't blame him.

He told Gaudin: 'We have a few fingerprints on the photostats we found in the church. We checked them out in Paris and came up with something very odd. The prints belonged to a man with a criminal record. He was a political agitator but small-time.'

Gaudin looked at Anderson expectantly. 'So you think he's here?'

Anderson shook his head. 'He died in 1974. His name was Georges Bertier. So our assassin is not only crazy, he's a magician . . . as you probably know, no two people have the same finger-prints. Or so it was always believed.'

Gaudin turned to Moitry. 'What do you think, Inspector?'

Moitry, who was by now happy to have as little connection with a possible massacre as possible, said: 'I don't think anything. Monsieur Anderson is in charge of thinking.'

'What about this man Anello?' Gaudin asked. 'I understand he's disappeared.'

'He's in Paris.' Anderson lied with conviction. 'I checked him out there. He and Mrs Jerome quarrelled and he took off.'

'So what now?'

'God knows. One faint hope is that the priest may be able to help when he regains consciousness. He may be able to tell us who could have had access to the church. We're also double-checking on members of your staff who live in the village.'

'You did that weeks ago,' Gaudin reminded him.

'Sure, and they were all clean. But I don't believe the guy we're looking for has a criminal record. He's a freak, a weirdo.'

When they had gone Gaudin sipped the remains of his coffee. It was cold. Grimacing, he picked up the telephone and asked the telephonist to call Room Service and order some more. He also asked the girl to locate Nicholas Foster and send him to the office because he was late reporting for duty.

The girl said: 'I'm sorry, Monsieur Gaudin, we have been trying to locate Monsieur Foster but he is not answering his telephone.'

*   *   *

The subject scheduled for discussion that morning was the fuel crisis. But, inevitably, the resurgence of the Cold War following the Soviet intervention in Afghanistan intruded into the debate. And the American hostages in Iran.

Hawks sharpened their talons and raised contingency plans for military action to safeguard oil supplies in the Middle-East. And the cooing of doves was heard not at all.

Some of the delegates listened to the speeches through headphones supplying instant translation into French and English. Some scarcely listened at all, their minds on the threat hanging over the conference.

One or two founder members considered the possibility, tentatively discussed outside the chamber, that the gunman was a guest – and rejected the possibility as preposterous.

Gaudin had told Roland Decker about the telephone call that morning. But Decker had decided not to make an announcement. Members knew that a threat existed. They had all agreed to stay and there was no point in dramatising the situation. In their time most Bilderbergers had received threatening calls.

Brossard did not make an appearance. The conference was told that he was 'still shaky'. Helga Keller told the switchboard not to put any calls through to his room; any urgent messages were to be diverted to Hildegard Metz.

In the kitchens, preparations for the dinner that night after the cocktail party got under way. This time it was to be a Burgundy-style feast. Rich and spicy. Escargots, veal braised in varieties of Dijon mustard, wine from the Romanée-Conti vineyard. For those who would find such a menu unacceptable the head chef, who presided over twenty-five cooks, had on the advice of the Secretariat devised other meals, volubly expressing his disgust.

Lunch would again be a buffet, accompanied by a choice of wines from twenty-five vineyards.

As the day got underway, the switchboard dealt with an increasingly heavy load of international calls. The three Telex machines chattered unceasingly. Security officers again *swept* the hotel from cellar to attic.

During the morning the weather changed. Bruised clouds hung heavily from the sky. And, as the conference broke up for the mid-morning break, the first heavy spots of rain fell. Then the deluge.

The rain spattered mud as high as the ground-floor windows; it filled the gutters and devastated the clumps of daffodils; it drowned the splashing of the fountains and in the water-gardens the carp rose to the surface.

Claire Jerome attended the opening session of the conference. Members agreed that she looked exceptionally attractive – dressed in lime-green with gold hooped earrings

387

– but a little drawn. Which was understandable: the announcement of her resignation from the board of Marks International had been in most of the European newspapers that morning.

There was considerable speculation about the reasons for her resignation among the guests – as there was in the Press. Why had she chosen to synchronise the announcement with the convention? It only served to strengthen the hand of those who accused Bilderberg of intrigue and manipulation.

Perhaps it was connected with the disappearance of her bodyguard. A lovers' tiff. . . . How old was Claire Jerome anyway? 'God knows,' murmured one delegate to another. 'But if my wife looked like that at her age I wouldn't be spending tomorrow night in Paris.'

When they adjourned for coffee, Claire went to the porter's desk to pick up her key. In her pigeon hole was a bunch of messages, all requests for her to contact the media – the *New York Times*, NBC, CBS and ABC television networks, *Time* and *Newsweek* magazines. . . . She tore up all of them except one: *A Mr Tilmissan called. Please telephone him immediately in Beirut.*

She went up to her room and placed the call to the number he had given her at their last meeting.

While she waited for the call, she lay on the bed and watched the rain streaming down the window. It was typical of the middleman that he had reacted to swiftly to the announcement.

Before the men holding Pete Anello!

She closed her eyes. In the announcement she had fulfilled all their demands. Surely they should have released him by now? Unless he was one of the conspirators. . . .

In which case everything had been taken from her. The man she loved and the purpose in life which had sustained her before she met him.

The phone rang; she picked up the receiver attached to the control system.

Tilmissan said: 'Is it true?'

'It's true.'

'What about our deal?'

'Marks International doesn't renege on contracts. Your merchandise is on its way.'

'And future deals?'

'You'll have to consult Mr Stephen Harsch.'

'What surprises me,' Tilmissan said, 'is the abruptness of your decision. The timing. It's almost as if someone was standing behind you holding a gun.'

'One of mine, I hope.'

'Why, Mrs Jerome? Why?'

'I've been thinking about it for a long time.'

'You weren't thinking about it the last time we met.'

'As I recall it, we didn't discuss my personal life. You were dealing with Marks International then and you can continue to do so. You've got your million bucks, Mr Tilmissan. Just leave it at that.'

A million dollars, she reflected as she hung up the receiver, and an appointment with death in the shape of a ship-load of flawed weaponry.

The phone rang again. The telephonist said: 'A call for you from Washington, *Madame*. The gentleman on the other end of the line insists that he's not from the Press and says it's very urgent.'

'Put him on.'

In Washington it was barely dawn. Bein or Eyal?

The voice on the phone was flat and disciplined and dangerous. Bein. She imagined him not in Washington but in the desert wearing combat fatigues speaking into a field telephone, which was where he would probably prefer to be.

He said: 'I heard your announcement on the radio. I just wanted to know if this changes anything.'

'It changes nothing.'

'May I ask why, Mrs Jerome?'

'Personal reasons.'

'Then I respect them. Thank you for what you have done, Mrs Jerome. On behalf of my country.'

Then she was alone again in her room that was a cell, staring through the raindrops shivering on the window-panes before streaming down the glass.

* * *

There was a bus into Etampes at midday with a connection to Paris. Suzy Okana was packed and ready to leave by 10 am.

Dawn had been a bleak and hopeless experience. But now her despair was rasped with anger. No-one treated Suzy Okana as though she were dirt, as though she had been paid and dismissed for services rendered.

Watched suspiciously by the wife of the owner who had disturbed her packing, she walked to the public phone booth in the village.

The rain was just starting to fall. She called the château and spoke first to Paul Kingdon.

She said: 'I've been thinking about your proposition.'

'And?'

'Why not? I've got nothing to lose.'

'Your enthusiasm overwhelms me.'

'I haven't changed. It's just an extension of our relationship. Right?'

'I hope our relationship will change when this is all over.'

'Are they –'

'Not over the telephone,' Kingdon interrupted her. 'But nothing's changed. I have to pay the . . . the fee. Then we settle down in Switzerland.'

'I'm going to London first,' she said.

'Why the hell are you doing that?'

She said: 'It doesn't matter why.'

'As you wish. I'm going back tomorrow evening before flying to Geneva. I'll see you in London. Goodbye, Suzy.'

'Goodbye, Paul,' she said.

The anger was still there. She called the château again and said: 'Put me on to Mr Nicholas bloody Foster.'

'*Pardon, madame?*'

'Mr Foster. One of your managers.'

'I'm afraid Mr Foster isn't available.'

The smug bastard. 'Make him available. This is his sister. There's been a death in the family.'

'You don't understand. Mr Foster isn't in the hotel. We've been trying to contact him all morning.'

A whisper of apprehension. 'Have you tried his room?'

'*D'accord*. His bed has not been slept in.'

Fear pushed aside her anger.

The telephonist said: 'I'm putting you through to the manager. He asked – '

Suzy replaced the receiver.

The rain was thickening but Suzy was hardly aware of it. She went back to the inn and ordered a coffee. The woman served her in the bar and stuck out her hand for the money.

Suzy sipped the coffee and relived the terrible moments of the previous evening. 'Good evening, Suzy . . . I'm sorry I haven't got time to talk just now . . . Some other time, Suzy. . . .'

Nicholas would never have talked like that unless. . . . And she hadn't even questioned his attitude. Had instantly believed that he had snubbed her. So much for her trust.

She tried to think methodically. He had been walking purposefully as though. . . . Two men had been behind him. Anderson, the security guard, and another man.

She closed her eyes tight and concentrated on their images. The other man was vaguely familiar. Where had she seen him before? At Paul Kingdon's?

Anderson's image was unforgettable. Tall, black, commanding, immaculate. . . . But one of his hands had been in the pocket of his jacket. Awkward. . . .

It was then that Suzy realised that he had been holding a gun.

Somewhere Nicholas was a captive. If he was still alive. Shock broke up Suzy's reasoning and it was a few moments before she was able to concentrate once more on the sequence of events the previous evening.

Nicholas had been walking towards the car park with the two men behind him. She had waited for a few moments, then headed towards the gates.

Something had occurred on the way to the gates. Something only faintly printed on her consciousness.

Tyres crunching on gravel. A car. That was it. A car without lights on the drive. She saw its outline mistily. A big car, an American car. And it must have left the car park at roughly the same time that Nicholas reached it.

After it had passed through the gates, its headlights had been switched on. And then from the window of her room she had seen the same car. . . .

Suzy put down her coffee cup. The rain was sluicing down outside. She went upstairs and fetched her raincoat and tied a scarf over her hair.

The car had been six doors away. Which didn't necessarily mean Nicholas was behind that particular door. It was, in fact, the door to the bakehouse; a man with flour on his hands was standing in the doorway as she walked past.

He smiled at her and asked if she wanted to take shelter. She shook her head, crossed the street and surveyed the buildings. The rain was bouncing on the cobblestones; her scarf was saturated and water ran down her back.

Bakehouse, greengrocers, inn, *tabac*. . . . In the terrace, between bakehouse and greengrocers, stood a derelict house, its windows boarded, a wooden plank nailed across the door. Beside the house was a passage like a narrow tunnel.

Suzy recrossed the street and entered the passage. It was dry to start with, beneath the roofs of the adjoining houses, and Suzy paused. Should she inform the police? Then she thought: 'Anderson *is* police' and walked on into an overgrown garden. On one side was a dripping stone wall.

At the end of the garden, in which fresh green weeds were pushing through the dead tangle of winter, she saw an outhouse. She walked cautiously forward.

There was a padlock on the door. It was undone and hung loosely. She opened the door. The light inside was poor and on the floor were a few rotting vegetables.

She stepped inside. Nicholas was sitting to her left, his hands and feet bound by rope. His eyes seemed to be trying to warn her. . . .

Simultaneously she felt a gun barrel in her back and a very English voice saying: 'Please don't shout or move, Miss Okana.'

*　　*　　*

Paul Kingdon was puzzled by Suzy Okana's decision to

return to London but not perturbed. She had served her purpose, helping him to retain his image by bringing a girl 'of dubious reputation' into the château. The Establishment had trembled. (Nothing compared with the bloody great shudders when they read Brossard's column and realised the extent to which he had got out of dollars before them!)

So there was no further point in her staying in France. He would meet her in London and they would fly together to Switzerland, where he was already negotiating the purchase of gold from the traders on Zurich's Bahnhofstrasse and Paradeplatz. A compact, private fortune with a glittering core of diamonds.

The price: $5 million. Blackmail, but it wouldn't be the first time he had clinched deals through methods which weren't far removed from extortion. Five million *worthless* dollars, he reminded himself.

And if anything went wrong with Brossard's grandiose scheme, then he would go public and fight as he had fought before, because Paul Kingdon always hedged his bets, and when he'd won the fight he would get Prentice to recommence his investigations into the London branch of the Gerard banking family and uncover some deal that would put the flabby shit in the dock at the Old Bailey.

He invited Brossard to his room for lunch. They ate lobster and drank a bottle of fine dry Sancerre. Kingdon had considered checking the room for bugs but remembered that Anderson had swept all the rooms that morning; a thorough man Anderson.

Brossard picked at his lobster, took sparrow sips of white wine.

Kingdon said: 'All set, Pierre?'

Brossard nodded. His wounded arm lay on the table beside him. Like a cumbersome piece of cutlery, Kingdon thought. 'The column appears tomorrow. But some of it will be leaked tonight to catch the markets in different time zones.'

'And the Russians?'

'As I told you, they are poised to sell on a massive scale.'

'And the speculators?'

'You have nothing to fear,' Brossard said.

'What if the OPEC countries renege on their decision to cut off oil supplies to America? If that part of your story's true. . . .'

'It will be too late to save the dollar.'

Kingdon cracked a lobster claw and said: 'How did you get all this information about the Russians' intentions, Pierre?'

'You don't imagine I'll tell you?'

'Do a bit of work for the Russians on the side, do you?'

'I didn't accept your invitation to lunch to be interrogated.'

'Never answer a question, do you, Pierre?' Kingdon poured himself more wine.

'Not stupid ones.'

'Funny thing is, back in England you had me by the short and curlies. Now it's the other way round. You can't back out of a bleeding thing.' Kingdon drank some wine. 'You know what I think, Pierre?'

'I don't really care what you think.'

'I don't think anyone was trying to kill you yesterday. I think you work for the Kremlin. I think they were just giving you a little warning. Balls this one up, Comrade Brossard, and we won't miss next time.'

Brossard pushed his plate away as though he had lost what little appetite he had possessed.

* * *

Anderson pushed open the door of the outhouse, stared at Suzy Okana and said: 'How the hell did she get here?'

Suzy was sitting next to Foster; they were both bound hand and foot.

Prentice said: 'I left the door open because I didn't want anyone hammering on it and raising the whole village. And look what walked in,' he added smiling at Suzy.

'Double trouble,' Anderson said. 'What shall we do with you?' he asked Suzy.

'Let us both go,' Suzy said. The fear had left her now

that she was with Nicholas. 'We can't do you any harm. I don't even know why you're keeping us prisoners.'

'Unfortunately Mr Foster here does.'

'The bank account number I presume,' Foster said.

'What bank account number?' Suzy asked.

'Just a number,' he told her. 'It seems to mean a lot to these two gentlemen. And maybe to Hildegard Metz.'

'Jesus Christ!' Anderson exclaimed.

'Well I've been thinking,' Foster said. 'Maybe Anello isn't involved.'

'And what brings you to that conclusion?'

'Just a little theorising. You see, I remember you making damn sure that Mrs Jerome was given a room up at that end of the corridor. So let's assume that there's a connection between you and Mrs Jerome.'

'Go on,' Anderson said.

'I know that there's a connection between Kingdon and Prentice.'

'So?'

'It's only a hunch but to complete the pattern there should be a third connection. And the person most closely connected with Brossard is Fraulein Metz.'

'Bright as a button,' Prentice said.

Anderson knelt beside Prentice who was sitting on a pile of sacking. He carried a Pan-Am flight bag with him. He wore a dark blue raincoat and water dripped from it onto the floor.

He said: 'Really, I'm not kidding, you two could wreck everything.'

'What? Blackmail?'

'Do you have strong suicidal tendencies, Mr Foster?'

'I've got nothing to lose.'

Suzy said: 'I don't understand, Nicholas. . . .'

Anderson said to Prentice: 'Just in case there was any doubt, I compared the prints on the photostats with the prints on a drinking glass in Foster's room. They don't match up.'

'So we haven't got the gunman.'

'I never thought we had. But now Foster's been reported

missing, Moitry and company reckon Foster's the guy they're looking for. A weird situation – I want the guy with the gun found so that he doesn't louse things up for us but I don't want Foster found because he'll do likewise.'

'One thing's certain,' Prentice said, moving the sub-machine-gun as water began to drip through the roof, 'we'll have to shift both of them out of here because it's only a matter of time before someone else comes through that door. One of Moitry's men, for instance.'

'There's only one place we can logically shift them to,' Anderson said, 'because we don't have time to take them some place else. But this time it's completely sealed off and I have the keys.'

'The church?'

'The bell tower.'

Foster noted that the bantering note had disappeared from both their voices. They spoke briskly and coldly as though each had cast off a disguise. Suzy shivered and Foster pressed his body close to hers.

There would be no difficulty, Anderson explained, in spiriting them inside the church: he was in charge of security and the armed guards at either end of the church would carry out his orders. All he had to do was to instruct the guard on the far side to take a break while he took over for half an hour.

Anderson left first.

Prentice gave it five minutes before cutting the rope binding their ankles with a pocket-knife. He waved the muzzle of the machine-gun at them. 'Carry on down to the end of the lane where Anderson parked the Chev. Move!'

They walked swiftly through the wasteland on the other side of the outhouse. Prentice told Suzy to get in the back of the Chev. With the knife he slashed the rope round Foster's wrists and said: 'Get in, you're driving.' When Foster was behind the steering wheel, he climbed in the back aiming the gun at Suzy.

He said to Foster: 'Drive round to the back of the church and don't try and be clever because if you do Suzy will suffer.'

Raindrops spattered on the bonnet. Foster switched on the ignition and the wipers began to switch across the windscreen.

He drove along the muddy lane, emerging at the end of the main street.

'Now turn right,' Prentice told him.

'Stop here,' Prentice said. They were behind the Church beside a gap in the hedge. 'Through there,' Prentice said.

As they went through the hedge ahead of him, Prentice heard them whispering. He was crouching, pushing his way through the gap, when they made their move.

Suzy ran to the right, Foster to the left.

Prentice swore. They could only be a few yards away from him but they were hidden by gravestones.

He shouted: 'I know you can hear me. You can't both make it. If one makes a break then the other gets it. Got that?'

No reply.

Lightning barbed the sky to his left. A second later a crack of thunder. Rain streamed down the mossy gravestones and collected in puddles.

A movement to his left. He caught sight of Foster's sodden black jacket and squeezed the trigger of the sub-machine-gun, aiming wide, at the same time moving towards the gravestones hiding Suzy Okana.

The bullets thudded into a leaning gravestone, chipping away an already-eroded date so that only the deceased's birth-date remained.

Another flash of lightning and an almost simultaneous crack of thunder.

Prentice spotted a patch of blue in the dank grass at the foot of a gravestone. The dress Suzy Okana was wearing under her raincoat was blue. He made a crouching run for the gravestone – and picked up the blue wrapping from an ice-cream.

Another blurred movement to his left. Shit, he thought, they're getting away with it.

He straightened up and looked round as Foster reached

an elaborate marble tomb where three generations of one family had been interred.

Foster wormed his way round the tomb and rested beside a sad little inscription recording the death of Albert Jadot at the age of eight months. What about Suzy? The thing to do was to run towards the road, visible and therefore drawing Prentice's fire, but shielded by the tomb with its towering, black-marble cross.

He rounded a corner of the tomb and stared into the barrel of Anderson's .32 Cobra. 'Man, I really underestimated you,' Anderson said. 'Now stand up.'

Prentice saw them standing beside the marble tomb and shouted to Suzy: 'You can come out now. We've got Foster.'

She stood up, three gravestones away.

They continued on their way to the church, entering it through the rear entrance.

'You really are a couple of smart-asses, aren't you?' Anderson said, closing the door.

Foster shrugged and put his arm round Suzy who had begun to shiver again.

Anderson led the way down the aisle, past the empty pews, with Prentice bringing up the rear. They went up the staircase leading to the belfry.

It was dry and dusty up there, and there was a chalk mark on the floor where the spent cartridge had been. The great bells hung motionless on the other side of the railing.

Anderson unzipped the flight bag and took out six sets of handcuffs. 'Courtesy of the FBI,' he said.

'They're going to die of pneumonia,' Prentice said.

'Go and see if you can find anything, George.' Anderson waved the Cobra at Foster and Suzy.

Prentice returned with a couple of black robes and some thick old curtains that puffed dust when he threw them on the floor.

'Okay,' Anderson said to Foster and Suzy, 'strip off those wet clothes.'

Foster and Suzy stared at each other. Foster shrugged. They stripped to their underclothes. Anderson and Prentice looked appreciatively at Suzy but said nothing. She wrapped one of the robes around herself.

From the flight bag Anderson took a red Thermos flask and some white plastic containers. He poured coffee into the screw cup from the Thermos and handed it to Suzy. He opened the containers in which he had stuffed remnants of the cold lunch buffet.

Foster ate hungrily, washing down the food with hot coffee. Suzy said she wasn't hungry. When Foster had finished, Anderson locked the cuffs round their wrists and ankles.

Prentice spread one of the curtains on the floor. He went downstairs and returned with two worn hassocks. He placed them on the curtain as pillows and said: 'Now lie down.' He placed two more thick curtains over them. With the remaining two pairs of cuffs, Anderson locked their feet to the railings.

Anderson said: 'You can make as much noise as you like, no-one will hear you. And as for that scene when, back to back, one undoes the other's cuffs, forget it. I've got the keys,' as he dropped them into the pocket of his raincoat.

Prentice said to Anderson: 'Did you bring the other gear?'

Anderson nodded. From the flight bag he took a portable radio and a tape recorder.

He said to Foster: 'I presume it was you that put the bug in the mike in the conference room?'

Foster nodded.

'Not exactly a pro job. But full marks for initiative. And guts,' he added thinking about the graveyard. 'Do you want to take over, George?'

Prentice said: 'I gather you're a journalist and you've been preparing for this for a long time.'

'And, by Christ, I've got a story,' Foster said.

'If anyone will publish it. If anyone believes it.' Prentice switched on the radio to see if it was working, switched it off again. 'Well, we have decided that you deserve a story. You see at Torquay I discovered a way by which Bilderberg

399

can be penetrated. It's ridiculously easy and anyone can do it. All you need is a small radio with a VHF wave band.'

Foster watched him intently.

'You know, of course,' Prentice went on, 'that with VHF you can pick up all sorts of radio messages. In particular police messages.'

'But if you act on them you can be prosecuted,' Foster said. 'They sometimes broadcast phoney messages and when a reporter turns up to cover a fictitious robbery or something, they nick him. But I can't see how any of this applies to Bilderberg.'

'Think about it,' Prentice urged Foster.

'The interpreting apparatus!'

'Got it in one. You see ever since Bilderberg first employed the instantaneous translation system, any journalist could have picked up all the debates. You just fiddle with the tuner on the VHF waveband and, *Voila!*'

An English male voice issued from the portable radio. Precise and unemotional.

'A translation of the Swedish Prime Minister if I'm not mistaken,' Prentice said. 'Later on you'll hear me, "I rise in our defence" – that's my opening line.'

'Well I'll be damned,' Foster said. 'All that secrecy all those years. . . .'

Anderson said: 'Think what a spy could have found out.'

'And there's a lot of those around,' Prentice said.

'So what we do,' Prentice said, 'is switch it up nice and loud, and at the same time switch on the tape-recorder. And there, you have a complete transcript of what's left of the Bilderberg conference.'

Grinning, he turned and followed Anderson out of the door. Foster and Suzy heard a bolt slot into place and a key turn in the lock.

They lay back listening to the views of the Swedish Prime Minister on the fuel crisis.

XXXII

It was 9 am and within ten hours they would all be dead.

And he would be gone, identity assumed five years ago discarded. A nice touch that, to revert to your former self.

As he dressed in the apartment over the *tabac*, he ran over in his mind the final details.

All he had to do while panic reigned in the château was reach his new car hidden in a lock-up garage, change his clothes make a few alterations to his appearance – spectacles worked miracles – and drive away.

By the time road-blocks were set up he would be on the autoroute to Paris. And when the police stopped him, he would be Jacques Bertier with papers to prove it. No-one would be looking for Jacques Bertier. . . .

Once in Paris he would register at the small hotel where he had made an advance reservation and sit back and watch television as the first reports of the massacre filtered through.

The hierarchy of Capitalism removed from the face of the earth! By a man who had once been regarded as a nonentity . . . because he had possessed only half an identity.

Now at last Jacques and Georges Bertier were about to triumph in their pre-ordained crusade, which had faltered only because they had been born as two. . . .

An error rectified by death. He made the sign of the cross on his forehead.

When he had finished dressing he made some coffee, adding a little rum. The plan really had worked perfectly, so different from the crude methods of today's terrorists.

The old German rifle – returned during the night to the hiding place in the countryside – the photostats of the guest list. . . . What can they have made of the crosses against certain names? They would only find the solution later today, when it was too late.

When the filth had been exterminated!

Carefully he picked up the means of extermination and carried it down to his old grey van parked outside the *tabac*.

He placed it on the seat beside him where it could be plainly seen by any curious guards at the gates to the château.

Then he switched on the ignition, let out the clutch and drove in the direction of the Château Saint-Pierre.

XXXIII

Among those whose thoughts were concentrated that morning on Bilderberg was Nicolai Vlasov, chairman of the KGB.

And his thoughts were murderous.

Sitting at his enormous desk in his office in Moscow, he re-read the message that had just been brought to him.

If it was to be believed, then he had been betrayed and he would be plucked from his luxurious office with its Persian carpets and mahogany-panelled walls and tossed ignominiously into obscurity.

On the eve of his retirement.

Vlasov had been mounting his attack on the dollar for two years. It was to be his triumphant valediction. The monumental finale to a career always finely balanced between subversion and political conformity.

Along with the President of the Soviet Foreign Bank he had watched the carefully managed dollar reserves multiply. They had now reached such proportions that if they were dumped on the foreign markets they would, with sufficient support from other sources, launch a world-wide wave of panic-selling.

Opponents of the scheme urged that Russia needed the dollars to buy essential commodities. Not so, claimed Vlasov; if the United States was destitute they would sell their produce for chocolate bars.

The man who had first suggested the plan had been Pierre Brossard. Now, according to the message in his hand, Brossard had double-crossed them.

But had he?

Why should Brossard, like himself on the brink of retirement, destroy a future in which even his peculiar pleasures had been catered for?

No, the message stank.

It was allegedly a Telex communication transmitted by Brossard from the Château Saint-Pierre to his newspaper office in Paris, cancelling the vital newspaper column that would ignite the processes to bring down the dollar. It had been taken from Brossard's briefcase by Helga Keller and handed to an agent in Paris at dawn that morning.

If the Midas column failed to appear then the speculators, poised to sell, would draw back. And the Soviet Union would be left out on a limb selling dollars which might then rally. The Kremlin – not the White House – would be humiliated!

Banished to obscurity? Hardly a fitting punishment for such a catastrophe. No, he would be taken to Lubyanka Prison which lay somewhere beneath his own office. The head of the KGB suffering the same fate as the thousands he had personally consigned to the bleak white-tiled dungeons. Vlasov pondered on their fate and his soul was touched with ice.

He decided to visit the President of the Foreign Bank and seek his assessment of the crisis. He told his secretary to call his chauffeur.

The black limousine pulled away from the bleak building – part of it once owned by the All-Russian Insurance Company before the Revolution, the other portion built partly by Germans captured in World War II – and Vlasov settled back in the cushions.

He had three alternatives:

(1) Call the whole thing off. He would be disgraced and prematurely retired but at least he would be able to salvage some dignity.

(2) Proceed with the plan without consulting the Politburo, which would only acknowledge complicity in the event of success.

(3) Get to Brossard who was apparently *incommunicado* and force him to publish the column.

The whole operation, he ruminated, had started to go wrong with the attempt to kill Brossard. In all probability, according to a previous message from Helga Keller, the work of a madman.

The limousine stopped outside the headquarters of the bank and Vlasov was ushered into the presence of the President, Sergei Visotsky.

Visotsky, a bulky man with incongruously tiny hands, produced a bottle of Stolichnaya vodka and two glasses. He chain-smoked and his crumpled suit was scattered with ash. He always appeared to be weighted with worry, and when he sat down it was as though the weight had dragged him to the seat.

Vlasov handed him the decoded message, waited while he read it and said: 'Well, what do you think?'

'It's a disaster.'

Visotsky drank his vodka in one swallow and picked up the bottle again with his little hands.

Vlasov looked at him contemptuously. Fear should be contained in company: it was part of an unwritten code. He had seen men die under torture without displaying it.

'The point is,' Vlasov said, 'is it true?'

'How should I know? That's your job.'

'Agreed. But why should a man with everything to win and nothing to lose by publishing lies, suddenly back out? I'm asking,' Vlasov said, 'because you know the man as a financier. I only know him as a spy.'

'He would only do it if he thought the dollar was going to rally. Obviously he would buy then rather than sell.'

'Without informing us?' Vlasov put his fingers to his fragile-looking temples. 'No, Monsieur Brossard wouldn't do that. He knows the penalty for betrayal.'

'Are you suggesting he didn't cancel the column?'

'It's a possibility.'

'Then what are you going to do?' a little courage gained from the bottle.

Vlasov listed the three alternatives.

Visotsky said: 'In the circumstances we cannot possibly proceed without informing the Politburo.'

'That is for me to decide,' Vlasov snapped. 'All I want to

know from you is this: Can we succeed without Brossard's column?'

'It's possible – if other parties start selling on a large enough scale. And if we issue a statement through Tass which will be picked up by the Western media. But I wouldn't advise it.'

'I didn't think you would. Bankers are not by nature adventurous. But don't worry, comrade, it's my responsibility. You are under my orders and if anything goes wrong it is I who will suffer.'

They were silent for a moment, musing on the form the suffering would take.

'Anyway,' Vlasov said, 'we still have a little time. I have to make contact with Brossard.'

'Is that so difficult?'

'If he is reluctant, yes. As you know he is at Bilderberg – and he is surrounded by police. But I can make contact with his secretary. It so happens that she works for us.'

'And is she completely trustworthy?'

Vlasov, who trusted no-one, considered the question. Within his own personal assessment of human frailty, Helga Keller was as trustworthy as any agent. However. . . .

He told Visotsky: 'She has served us well,' and thought: 'It would be the simplest thing in the world for Helga Keller to have transmitted a false message to Paris.'

Vlasov stood up. 'Leave it to me, Comrade Visotsky. Stay close to your telephone.' He paused at the door. 'And please remember that this conversation has been confidential. You will not discuss it with anyone.'

'I understand,' Visotsky said, reaching once again for the bottle of fire-water.

Back in his office Vlasov composed a message to be coded and sent to the Soviet Embassy in Paris.

Then he picked up the dossier on Pierre Brossard. Really, the bastard didn't deserve to live. If he *had* betrayed them then, of course, he wouldn't. It would be a job for Department V.

*　　*　　*

Mayard read the Telex message, which had been waiting for him on the machine, when he got to the newspaper office.

He read it with relief.

The column had been altogether too sensational. Barely credible. Granted Brossard had access to exclusive information at Bilderberg. But surely a financial editor would have heard at least a whisper of such incredible developments.

The cancellation now presented one outstanding problem: a great blank space on the front page.

Mayard reached for a cigar from the box on his desk and re-read the message.

CANCEL COLUMN TRANSMITTED YESTERDAY STOP NONE OF THE INFORMATION CONTAINED IN THE COLUMN MUST BE PRINTED STOP REPEAT NONE SIGNED BROSSARD.

Did Brossard intend to write a substitute column?

In a way Mayard wished Brossard hadn't cancelled his story. If, as it appeared, the facts were wrong then Brossard would have become a laughing stock. Mayard would have enjoyed that.

Now he had to determine Brossard's intentions. He picked up the telephone, called the Château Saint-Pierre and asked for Brossard.

The telephonist told him that Brossard was not to be disturbed. All calls were being referred to Fraulein Metz. Mayard shrugged: it was virtually the same as talking to Brossard.

He waited for a couple of minutes while they contacted her.

'So,' Mayard said when she came on the phone, 'he has got cold feet. Quite rightly I should think. The point is, does he intend to write another column?'

'I doubt it,' Helga said. 'He's suffering from shock.' She told Mayard about the shooting.

Mayard listened incredulously and thought: 'Why did the stupid bastard miss?'

'Of course, none of this must be repeated,' Helga said. 'And naturally there must be no mention of it in the paper.'

'Naturally. So what shall I do? Write his column for him? You are his eyes and ears.'

'The decision is yours. After all, you are the editor.'

'Thank you for reminding me, Fraulein Metz.'

Mayard replaced the receiver and stared at the blank sheet of paper on which he had to make up the front page. Should he write the Midas column? No, he thought, to hell with it; another row within the EEC, blaming as usual the British, would suffice for the lead story.

But if only the gunman had taken better aim. . . .

* * *

In Washington Vlasov's opposite number on the CIA, William Danby, had also considered a report from the Château Saint-Pierre with alarm.

According to Owen Anderson, there was a possibility that their shared annual nightmare might come true: a homicidal maniac might have found a way to perpetrate mass murder.

Danby shook his head. No, that was crazy. And yet Anderson was a level-headed agent who had weathered the storm when he had been under investigation, apparently without rancour.

Danby had sympathised with Anderson; the self-righteous patriots were hell-bent on destroying their own country's defences. Nor had he been surprised when Anderson asked to be relieved of the Bilderberg assignment: Danby fully expected his resignation from the Agency to follow.

Who could blame him?

In fact Danby had also decided to quit. But he wanted an honourable discharge, not a resignation forced upon him by a debacle at Bilderberg.

He glanced at the clock on the wall of his office. It was 10.15 am, mid-afternoon in France. Another twenty-four hours until the conference broke up.

Danby asked his secretary to bring him another cup of coffee. Then he called the President of the United States because, irrespective of whether he was campaigning to remain in office, it was necessary to inform him about the threat to the government-outside-the-government.

* * *

In addition to Mayard, one other person tried to contact Brossard that day, a man named Yuri Shilkov, a second secretary at the Soviet Embassy in Paris.

Shilkov contemplated driving to the Château Saint-Pierre. But what chance did a Russian have of being admitted to Bilderberg? As much chance as an American being admitted to the Council of Ministers of the Soviet Union!

Instead he telephoned and Telexed Brossard. Both messages were intercepted by Helga Keller.

On the telephone she told Shilkov that Brossard had confirmed to her orally that he had cancelled his column. She also said that Brossard was in a deep, drug-induced sleep from which he could not be awoken.

Which was true because she had dissolved three barbiturate tablets in his after-lunch coffee.

XXXIV

At 3.30 pm George Prentice sat at a desk in his room putting the final touches to the speech he was shortly to deliver.

But his concentration was impaired by the knowledge that, provided a madman didn't find some way of liquidating the nucleus of the Establishment, he would soon be a millionaire.

He shuffled the papers in front of him. In a way the speech was his credo. The crystallisation of what he had learned from his professional life.

He was not against the Capitalist system. Far from it – as his address would avow. The delegates would doubtless listen with the soporific detachment reserved for speakers such as himself, invited for the sake of the Bilderberg image.

Until his closing remarks – the last paragraph on the last sheet of paper lying on the desk in front of him. George Prentice smiled to himself as he imagined the impact those last few sentences would have.

*   *   *

'I rise in our defence.'

'Listen,' said Foster as the spool of the tape-recorder whirred, 'that must be Prentice.'

'Is it?' Suzy pressed her almost naked body against his. He could feel the small breasts against his chest, the hardness of her nipples.

'I'm trying to concentrate,' Foster told her.

'Why?'

'Because it's important.'

'But it's being taped.'

Foster didn't reply. If they hadn't been bound hand and

foot by steel bands he would have left Prentice to the tape.

'Nicholas Foster, you're a hypocrite,' Suzy said.

'And a liar!'

She kissed him, and for a few moments he lost the trend of what Prentice was saying.

* * *

'Not merely in the defence of Bilderberg,' Prentice said, 'but in the defence of Capitalism.'

The delegates sitting at oak tables arrayed in front of the lectern, regarded him with ill-disguised boredom, their faces as expressionless as those of the ancestral portraits on the walls. The rain which had thinned to a drizzle, trickled down the windows overlooking the gardens.

'And in the defence of Communism.'

Those delegates who had heard him frowned. The grizzled features of the German industrialist who had just been appointed chairman contorted in dismay, and his hand reached for the button which lit the red light signifying that a speaker had consumed his allotment of time.

'You,' nodding towards the Bilderbergers, 'have all endured your share of criticism because you have committed the crime of acquiring riches either by inheritance or endeavour. Few of those who attack you have ever paused to consider the employment you have created or the enrichment which your products have given to the deprived.'

The chairman's hand withdrew from the button.

'Few who indict our system have ever paused to consider the alternatives. Blinded by the zealot's barb, they ignore the repression and the erosion of human dignity that has always accompanied the practical application of Marxist ideals.'

A few delegates nodded. Most of them looked puzzled: hardly a defence of Communism.

'I believe that the majority of those assembled here today go about their business honourably and for the benefit of our Society. There are, of course, exceptions such as those who, in the guise of philanthropists, persuade the relatively poor to invest in their enterprises; in these exceptions the only beneficiary is the benefactor.'

Paul Kingdon stared at him coldly and said: 'May I suggest that the speaker gets to the point.'

'I am about to. I am suggesting that we have reached a watershed in history. I am suggesting that the future of this small globe of ours is as bright as any star in the firmament.'

He raised his hand as though warding off objections to such an unfashionable philosophy.

'I said I would also defend Communism. By that I meant its origins and ideals. *The proletarians have nothing to lose but their chains. Working men of all countries, unite!* I don't have to tell you that I am quoting from the Communist Manifesto. And could any of you here today really say that there was anything reprehensible about such a rallying cry at the time it was made?'

No-one spoke. The chairman glanced at the clock on the wall.

'The point is that from the extremes of their conceptions both ideologies have been set on course to meet at the apex of a triangle, of which the base was – *was,* I remind you – inequality and injustice. That meeting is imminent. And that meeting, to quote your parlance gentlemen, will be a merger.'

Paul Kingdon stood up, bowed to the chairman and said: 'I'm afraid I cannot listen to any more of this drivel, Mr Chairman.' He walked out of the conference chamber.

Prentice went on: 'The evidence is all around us. In the West the trade union members – the true Socialists – are beginning to realise that militancy preached by some of their leaders leads only to self-deprivation. Instead, the enlightened are now choosing to accept the benefits of profit sharing.

'Within the Communist bloc a measure of free enterprise is now permitted. And we have witnessed the visit of a Pope to a Communist country. The Soviet Union has traded with the West and the control of arms has been discussed.'

Prentice held up one hand, anticipating objections. 'We all know that detente has apparently taken a battering over the past few months. It had to happen – two heavyweight pugilists do not fall into each other's arms – and it is surely all to the good. The United States has realised that it must be seen to be strong: the Soviet Union has realised that there is a limit to appeasement in the West.

'Detente, gentlemen, is far from dead but the merger needs a catalyst. It is just possible that we have such an instrument because we have an energy crisis. I said a watershed: a drought might have been more appropriate. Not so long ago, in terms of evolution, Man made a grave mistake: he struck oil and decided that it was his lifeblood. If he had raised his eyes to the heavens and looked at the sun, as his primitive ancestors once did, he might have perceived that salvation lay not beneath the soil but in the sun. I believe that the sun was always intended to be our source of energy and that within a hundred years it will have been harnessed.

'Meanwhile we shall profit by that mistake; that is the function of mistakes. Do not believe for one second, gentlemen, that the shortage of oil is confined to those countries that we represent here today – even though there are those who would have you believe it. As I have said, the separate ideologies are set to coalesce. The catalyst may well be the co-operative endeavour of the great powers to find the solution to the crisis which threatens to bring the world to a standstill.'

If he had made the address a couple of years ago Prentice would have stopped there. At least he had preached hope.

But now he had to add a clause – to prevent a crime of global proportions being perpetrated. And to safeguard his own future.

He said to the chairman: 'If you would spare me just one more minute of the conference's time. . . .'

The chairman nodded.

Prentice said: 'I should like to offer you a measure of proof of my optimism which is admittedly idealistic. At the moment the crisis is confined to oil. Can anything be more optimistic than the intelligence that has just reached me?'

He paused. Silence. He had his audience. They knew that George Prentice's sources were always good.

He waved a sheet of paper and said: 'I have just learned that the OPEC countries have agreed to lower – yes, lower – the price of oil and continue its uninterrupted flow to the United States of America.'

He sat down and watched as, one by one, those delegates who speculated in currency made their apologies to the chairman and headed for the telephones.

* * *

'. . . allow its uninterrupted flow to the United States of America.'

Suzy said: 'Three cheers.' And then: 'What do you think they're going to do to us?'

'God knows,' Foster said. 'They can't release us until they've escaped.'

'I wouldn't want to hand them over to the police anyway,' Suzy said.

'Nor me.'

'I don't think they would have killed us in the graveyard.'

'What I want to know is what the hell they're up to. It's got to be blackmail. And yet that doesn't seem like them. The victims would have to deserve being blackmailed.' He thought about it. 'Brossard, yes. Kingdon?'

'Why not?' Suzy said. 'He can afford it. He's robbed enough people in his time.'

'What about Mrs Jerome?'

'Arms,' Suzy said.

'So what form does the blackmail take? Brossard, for instance. I suppose we shall never know. If he hadn't been so bloody mean, he wouldn't have been shot in the first place. And if he had paid to teletype his column direct to Paris instead of cutting the cost by taping it, I might not have found it.' He sat up and switched off the tape recorder with his manacled hands. 'They're taking a break, we mustn't waste the tape.'

'What about Mrs Jerome?' Suzy said. 'How would they blackmail her?'

'Got to be something to do with arms dealing. Double-dealing probably. What about Kingdon?' staring down into her eyes.

'I promised.'

'My guess is diamonds. Something to do with all his lousy diamonds. Am I right?'

'You shouldn't ask me.'

'You're right, I shouldn't.'

'So let's assume they're each being blackmailed for five million dollars. Fifteen million to be split three ways because I'm sure Brossard's secretary's in on it. Fifteen million!' Nicholas whistled.

'You'll have quite a story to tell,' Suzy said.

'If anyone cares about Bilderberg after Brossard's published his column.' Nicholas lay back uncomfortably and stared at the bells. 'Wait a minute, if Brossard's right and the dollar crashes, then the fifteen million dollars ransom won't be worth the paper it's printed on.'

Suzy said: 'In that case they must be trying to kill his story.'

'Which will leave me with mine.'

'Just remember, don't get too successful.'

'It's got the lot,' Nicholas said. 'Shooting, blackmail, verbatim transcripts of secret meetings. . . .'

They heard footsteps on the stairs. It was Prentice. He brought more food and two bottles of wine, one red and one white.

He unlocked the cuffs around their ankles and took them to the rest room in the vestry separately, then he secured their ankles again.

He said: 'What did you think of my speech?'

'Great,' Nicholas said.

'I meant it, you know. It's got to happen one day. The game will shortly be up for those who feed off discord. Not necessarily through the energy crisis – I used that for immediacy. But we are merging.'

Nicholas and Suzy nodded.

Prentice poured them some wine. 'What did you think about the last part?'

'Getting in before Midas?' Foster asked.

'As I said, bright as a button.'

'If, that is, the Midas column ever appears. . . .'

'Too bright,' Prentice said and closed the door behind him.

XXXV

At 4.15 pm, a quarter of an hour before the Swiss banks closed for the day, Anderson telephoned Zurich. The United Bank had been alerted to expect large deposits in the numbered account but so far none had arrived.

He wandered into the bar where Jules Fromont was lining up his Bilderberg Specials on the bar for the cocktail party. He contemplated drinking one, opted instead for a beer.

He said to Jules: 'Anything more?'

'Nothing, m'sieur. Everyone seems convinced that the man who shot Brossard was Nicholas Foster. I did mention to you that he had been to the village with that Chinese girl. . . .'

Anderson said: 'Well, it isn't over yet. Keep your ears open.'

'*Oui, m'sieur.*'

Anderson stared through the French windows. The drizzle had thinned to a thick mist. The sky was grey and the gardens were a melancholy place.

The Tannoy crackled. 'Will Monsieur Anderson please pick up the nearest telephone.'

It was the hospital: the priest had regained consciousness.

He called Helga Keller, then drove to the hospital ten miles away.

The nurse he had kissed when he knew that the priest wasn't badly hurt, was standing beside the reception desk. 'Bad news, I'm afraid. He has relapsed into unconsciousness.'

'Does that mean he's worse?'

'We don't think so. He will drift back and forth for a little while now.'

'Okay,' Anderson said, 'I'll hang around for a while. Will you call me as soon as he comes round again?'

'Of course.' She looked at him warily but not, he decided,

without interest; then she walked briskly away.

But it wasn't until 6.15 that she returned. 'You can see him now,' she said. 'The doctor in charge says it's all right. But only for a few minutes.'

The priest was propped up against two pillows. His head was swathed in bandages. As before, the sight of him lying there wounded, angered Anderson more than anything else that had happened at Bilderberg.

The priest's smile spread between the bandages. 'Good evening, my son.'

'Good evening, father.' Anderson sat on the chair beside the bed and spoke urgently. 'Did you see who did it, father?'

The priest looked at him vaguely. 'You see,' he said, 'he knew I hadn't seen him. If I had he would have killed me.'

The priest was talking as though he knew the identity of his attacker. 'Who, father?' *Please God, WHO?* The priest closed his eyes but the smile remained.

Anderson sat back; sweat trickled down his chest inside his shirt.

The priest opened his eyes again. 'Monsieur Anderson, isn't it?'

'Yes, father, I'm Anderson. Can you . . . please . . . do you know who hit you?'

'You see,' said the priest, blinking his eyes, 'he must have heard my footsteps on the stairs. He was waiting behind the door. . . .'

'He? Who is he?'

'A wonderful scene for a thriller. I was always very fond of Dorothy L. Sayers. . . .'

Now Anderson was kneeling beside the bed. 'Did you know who it was?'

'Know? Of course I know. You see I could smell the rum on his breath.'

Anderson groaned aloud. He whispered into the priest's ear. 'Please father, please tell me who it was.' An inspiration. 'Tell Maigret. . . .'

The priest's eyelids were dropping. He whispered two words.

Anderson snapped up. He gripped the priest's hand. 'Thank you, father.'

Then he was in the corridor sprinting towards the admission desk. Holy Shit! They had double-checked every member of the staff that lived in the village. Nothing against any of them. What chance did you have of pinning anything on a madman who kept his madness to himself?

He dodged a stretcher being wheeled along the corridor by two male nurses. He slipped on the polished surface, picked himself up and raced on.

In the lobby visitors arriving to visit patients, parted as he broke through their midst.

At the desk he grabbed the telephone.

He glanced at his wristwatch.

6.25.

He had five minutes in which to stop Jules Fromont poisoning every Bilderberger in the château.

* * *

Engaged.

Shit!

Anderson dialled again.

The desk clerk was protesting. Anderson flung his ID cards at him.

A minute passed.

Engaged.

Once more.

'*Bon soir*. The Château Saint-Pierre.'

Anderson said: 'Get Gaudin. Tell him to stop the cocktail party.' He was shouting, gabbling.

'I'm afraid Monsieur Gaudin is attending the cocktail party.'

'Then call the bar.'

'I'm afraid. . . .'

'Call it!'

* * *

Jules Fromont picked up the telephone receiver on the bar. He spoke into it briefly, then replaced it. He placed cocktails on a silver tray and began to circulate among the few guests who hadn't yet been given a glass.

* * *

'I'm sorry, m'sieur, Monsieur Gaudin is not available.'

'Then Tannoy.' Anderson tried to control his voice. 'Tell them the drinks are poisoned.'

'I'm afraid that I cannot do that,' indicating with one forefinger to her head, to the girl sitting next to her, that she had a lunatic on the other end of the line.

'Then get me Monsieur Prentice.'

Two minutes before the toast to Bilderberg.

Prentice answered the phone in his room.

'George. Jules Fromont is the killer. It's my guess that he's about to poison every bastard in the place. Get the fuck down there.'

Anderson replaced the receiver. He sat down, head between his hands. There was nothing more he could do.

* * *

Prentice grabbed the attaché case containing the sub-machine-gun, burst out of his room and raced down the stairs.

It was 6.29 when he reached the lobby. He sprinted across the marble floor, charged through the swing doors.

Gaudin raised his glass. '. . . we hope that one day you will consider returning to the Château Saint-Pierre. I give you a toast, Bilderberg.'

Prentice shouted from the doors: 'Don't drink!'

Glasses wavered, stopped in front of lips. The French President and the former American Secretary of State stared at him in amazement.

Gaudin said: 'Monsieur Prentice, what –'

'They're poisoned. All those drinks are poisoned.'

Gaudin said: 'Are you out of your mind?'

No-one drank, everyone stared at him.

Prentice strode through their ranks.

He stood at the bar in front of Jules Fromont. He turned to the guests. 'I ask one thing. I ask that Jules Fromont, who mixed the Bilderberg Special, has the first drink.' He turned to the barman. 'Go on, Jules, pour yourself one.'

The barman's face was pale, sweat was beading his forehead. 'I never drink at work,' he said. 'And I think you, m'sieur, are drunk.'

Prentice took one of the two remaining glasses on the tray and handed it to Fromont. 'Drink!'

The barman hesitated for a moment. Stared at the pinkish-coloured drink.

Then he vaulted the bar and ran for the French windows. Behind him drinks crashed to the floor.

In one smooth action, Prentice released the submachine-gun from the attaché case and ran after him, feet crushing broken glass.

Fromont hit the French windows with his shoulder. They burst open and he was in the garden. In front of him in the misty half-light, the entrance to the maze.

When Prentice reached the French windows he had dis-appeared.

Holding the Uzi in two hands, Prentice entered the maze. He moved cautiously. For all he knew Fromont might be armed.

The hedges were well over six foot tall, jungle thick. Somewhere ahead of him he could hear Fromont running, cannoning against the clipped foliage.

Possibly Fromont knew the formula to get out of the maze. Most of them had one. But first he would have to reach the centre.

Silence. Except for the splashing of the fountains. The light was fading fast. The misty drizzle soaked Prentice's clothes and the machine-gun was slippery in his hands.

A movement through a gap in one of the hedges. Prentice squeezed the trigger of the machine-gun. It barked and shuddered in his hands.

No answering cry of pain.

He stalked on – and came to a dead end. He swore and retraced his footsteps. Another dead end. He went back and took another turn. And then he was in the centre. Two plane trees and a wooden bench. Fromont was slumped on the bench. Prentice approached, Uzi pointing at the crumpled figure. There was froth on Fromont's lips. Even in the fading light Prentice could see that already it was tinged with blood.

Fromont turned his head and stared at him. 'Filth,' he whispered. 'Filth!'

His face contorted.

Prentice bent down and smelled the bitter almond scent of potassium cyanide on his dying breath.

XXXVI

The morning of the day of departure.

A mass exodus. While Rolls-Royces, Cadillacs, Mercedes glided up to the entrance of the château and departed in a steady stream, Owen Anderson and Inspector Moitry stood in the apartment over the *tabac* in the village.

They had ransacked the rooms and found a wooden box. It had recently been painted brown. But through the paint they could see letters. When they scratched away the paint, they found that the letters had been indelibly stamped on the wood in black ink. SS PANZERDIVISION 'HITLERJUGEND'.

'One of the crack Panzer units in the German army during the last war,' Moitry said. 'The Germans had lost the war when these boxes were issued. Potassium cyanide capsules were supposed to be the honourable solution. But few SS men could see any honour in suicide. The *Hitlerjugend* must have abandoned this as they were being chased out of France.'

'And Fromont – or Jacques Bertier as he was once known – must have found it as a kid. Either him or his twin brother. A pity we didn't get the full details on Georges Bertier yesterday. Then we'd have known that he had a twin brother and we'd have known that the description fitted Fromont.'

'You,' – not *we*, Anderson noted – 'can't have been expected to realise that the reason the fingerprints checked out with a dead man's was because he had a twin. An interesting point of criminology that – identical twins' fingerprints matching.'

Anderson said: 'And your men on the gate' – not *mine!* – 'can't have been expected to know that all the bottles of liquor the barman brought into the château yesterday morning in his van, contained booze slugged with potassium cyanide.'

They closed up the apartment where Jacques Bertier had mixed his death cocktails and began to walk towards the château.

'Now, of course,' Anderson went on, 'I understand Fromont's obsession with Nicholas Foster. I implied I was interested and he tried to plant the blame. He didn't see Foster and the girl from the French windows on the day of the shooting: he saw them in the village.'

'One thing puzzles me,' Moitry said as they entered the lane. 'What was the significance of the crosses on the photostats of the guest list?'

Anderson grinned at him. 'Simple when you think about it. The crosses indicated the teetotallers.'

'But they were all going to be served with the same cocktail – the Bilderberg Special.'

'Not quite,' Anderson said. 'You see alcohol dissipates the bitter almond smell of cyanide, so Bertier had no problems there. But he did with the non-drinkers because they would have smelled the alcohol.'

'So he found something else to kill the smell of bitter almonds for the teetotallers?'

'Peppermint,' Anderson said. 'As simple as that. Here's to Bilderberg and down the hatch and the whole goddam lot of them would have been dead within three to five minutes.'

'Not necessarily,' Moitry said as they entered the grounds of the château and headed for the maze. 'It took Himmler twelve minutes to die.'

The body of Jacques Bertier was being carried away on a stretcher. Spring had re-assembled overnight and the daffodils were raising their rain-battered heads.

Staring at the stretcher, Anderson said: 'He was very sure of himself. Odd that he should have carried a spare capsule with him, as though he expected failure.'

'*He* didn't expect to fail,' Moitry said. 'It was *Georges* Bertier who expected to fail.'

'You know something? You're a dark horse, inspector,' Anderson said.

'I have my moments,' Moitry said smiling. 'But I wonder why Foster disappeared. . . .'

Anderson shrugged. 'God knows, maybe he stole some silver.' He put his hand on Moitry's shoulder. 'I'm going to put in a good word for you, inspector. Tell Paris that without your help we wouldn't have stopped Fromont.'

'And in return?' asked Moitry, who knew that there was always something in return.

'That reporter from *Paris-Match* is sniffing around outside. Lock him up for a week or so will you?'

'It would give me great pleasure,' said Inspector Moitry.

It was the least he could do for Nicholas Foster, Anderson reflected. Prevent him being scooped while he was locked up in a bell tower.

*   *   *

Prentice told Pete Anello about the attempted massacre. He said: 'Fromont could have knocked off the whole bunch of them with a poison made from the pips of apples or pears, or the stones of peaches or cherries. How about that?'

'How about that!' Anello sat down on the edge of the bed in the motel, picked up a morning newspaper and pointed at an item. MARKS INT. QUITS ARMS RACE. And underneath: SHOCK STATEMENT BY CLAIRE JEROME. 'Can I go now?' Anello asked.

'Not quite yet,' Prentice said apologetically.

'Why the hell not, she's done what we asked her to do?'

Prentice's eyes strayed towards the attaché case he had brought with him. 'There are one or two points – '

'Bullshit!' Anello lunged with one foot and kicked the attaché case across the room. 'You know something, old buddy, you look as much like an idealist to me as an Eskimo.'

As Prentice came towards him, he kneed him in the belly. 'And no Kung Fu stuff this time,' as Prentice grunted and collapsed on the floor. As he tried to get up, Anello hit him on the side of the neck. Prentice fell back paralysed.

Anello took the car keys from Prentice's pocket, went into

the corridor and locked the door. The Caprice was parked in the driveway; Anello drove in the direction of Paris.

He needed time to think. He had agreed to return to Claire when the announcement about her resignation was made. Now it had been. But what am I? A pathetic pawn, an object to be bartered?

What have you become, Pete Anello?

And why hadn't Prentice wanted him to go?

Ten minutes later he pulled into a lay-by. The spring sunshine beat through the windscreen. He curled up with his head on the passenger seat. He closed his eyes and soon he smelled burning flesh and cried out as the Viet Cong machine-gun opened up.

*   *   *

The first five million dollars to be received by the United Bank of Switzerland was the ransom transferred by Paul Kingdon.

Helga Keller called him from the booth in the village and said, 'Goodbye, Mr Kingdon. You have kept your side of the bargain, we shall keep ours.' She hung up.

Kingdon stared at the receiver for a moment, then replaced it in its cradle. He tried to contact Brossard, but the Frenchman wasn't taking any calls. Kingdon hammered on the door; no reply.

Could anything have gone wrong? Kingdon, who had left the conference chamber before Prentice announced the change in the attitude of the OPEC countries, shrugged.

He still had his diamonds.

He drove the Ferrari onto the auto-route and headed for Paris. Why the hell had that bastard Prentice suddenly turned on him in his speech?

Bilderberg. Never again. Kingdon shuddered as he thought of the glass of poison six inches from his lips.

He pressed his foot on the accelerator and the Ferrari surged forward at 100 mph.

*   *   *

The deposit of Pierre Brossard's ransom was confirmed by the bank in Zurich at midday.

Anderson telephoned Brossard from his room to dispatch him on his way and said to Helga Keller: 'You're sure he doesn't know anything about Prentice's bombshell at the conference?'

Helga shook her head. 'He's been sleeping the sleep of the dead. He's only just woken up.'

'And he hasn't contacted Mayard?'

'I've taken all the calls.'

'He may try to call Mayard now.'

'Then I'll have to attend to that.'

She opened the door as George Prentice staggered in.

'What the hell happened to you?' Anderson asked.

Prentice told them.

'It needn't affect anything,' Anderson said.

'Unless Mrs Jerome hears that Anello's got away. She could call off the deal.'

'She's late as it is,' Helga said.

'A woman's privilege,' Anderson said.

Helga went up to Brossard's room and knocked on the door. 'Who is it?'

'Me. Hildegard.'

Brossard opened the door. He looked terrible, Helga thought. His movements were slow and dreamy, his complexion grey.

He said: 'Call Mayard. Make sure the column's been published.' He hardly seemed able to control his voice.

'Very well, Monsieur Brossard.'

She called her own apartment in Paris and said: 'Monsieur Mayard, please,' and asked the phantom at the other end about Midas' column.

Brossard went into the bathroom. She replaced the receiver quickly and called out: 'Everything's fine, Monsieur Brossard. Mayard says the column is causing a sensation.'

Brossard came out of the bathroom. He seemed to have gathered a little strength. 'Help me pack my luggage,' he said. 'You will make your own way back to Paris?'

'As soon as you have departed.'

On the way to the Citroen, Helga told him about the mass murder attempt.

He leaned against the car as though he were about to faint.

'Good-bye, Monsieur Brossard,' she said as Brossard switched on the ignition. 'For ever,' she said as the Citroen moved away from her towards the gates of the château.

* * *

It was 4 am.

'What the hell's gone wrong?' Anderson asked.

They sat in his room. Their bags were packed. Helga's Renault stood in the driveway outside. Anderson had a chess problem in front of him, Prentice a crossword-puzzle; neither was making any progress.

'Maybe George was right,' Helga said. 'Maybe she's opted out. Maybe Anello called her.'

'Then why is she still in the hotel?' Prentice asked. He winced and put one hand to his neck.

Helga looked at him solicitously.

'Don't worry,' Prentice said. 'I deserved it. It's time I quit.'

Anderson called the bank again. Nothing. 'I wonder where the hell Anello is,' he said.

* * *

Claire Jerome finished typing her report for the President of the United States. During the conference she had learned about several big arms deals being negotiated by other czars of munitions. Behind every such deal was a notice of intent – the exchange of one super-power mentor for another, a shift from peaceable to aggressive policies. . . . The President and his advisers would be able to make much of her information and the intelligence supplied by other participants. Particularly with regard to the crisis in Afghanistan.

She finished the report with an air of finality: she had carried out all her commitments and she didn't give a damn about anything any more.

Her hair was disarrayed, her clothing crumpled. She wished she had drunk the poison.

The statement announcing her resignation had been published, but Anello hadn't come back. He was waiting for the five million along with the other blackmailers.

You poor pathetic bitch, she thought. How long ago had he planned it? How long had he been laughing at her? Had he been repulsed by her love-making?

Let him have his share of the five million. But what have I got? Nothing but the empty future. She refused to cry. She picked up her bag, opened the door and walked into the arms of Pete Anello.

And then she cried.

'Where have you been?' she asked a few minutes later.

'Thinking.'

'About what?'

'About us.'

For a moment she thought he was going to say that he was leaving. 'Did you reach any conclusions?'

'Sure I did. We're going into business.'

'I thought I just got out of business,' she said.

'Rehabilitation,' he said. 'Of Vietnamese veterans. The war's been over a long time, but a hell of a lot of us haven't been rehabilitated yet. There are various societies but they need money. . . .'

Then because she felt she might start to cry again she asked: 'When did you think all this out?'

'Maybe thirty minutes ago,' he told her. 'Sitting in the car. As though I'd been searching for the answer for a long time. How does it grab you?'

'It grabs me,' she said and: 'Pete, why did you come back?'

'Because I need you,' he said quietly. '*You* – not just your money.'

Soon, she thought as she went to him, she would tell him about the $5 million. But not now. There was plenty of time.

* * *

At 4.20 the phone rang in Anderson's room.

Anderson answered it, spoke briefly.

Then he turned to the other two and said: 'We are now richer by fifteen million bucks.'

He uncorked the bottle of champagne that had been waiting on ice. They touched glasses. 'Here's to an honourable retirement.'

'I'll drink to that,' Prentice said.

'And me,' said Helga, slipping one arm round Prentice's waist.

'And perhaps,' said Prentice, 'a toast to our benefactors. The United States of America, Great Britain and the Soviet Union.'

* * *

Anderson drove first to the village. While Prentice and Helga waited in the Renault parked behind the church, he told Foster and Suzy Okana about the poisoning attempt.

'There's just one thing,' Foster said after he had thanked Anderson.

'I know. How the hell can you send the story when you're trussed up like a Thanksgiving turkey. Don't worry, the French police will shortly hear about your plight.'

Foster said: 'Tell me one thing, why are you doing this for me?'

'I'm not. I'm doing it for Suzy. You'll need the bread you earn from the story to keep her in the style to which she's accustomed.' He grinned at them. 'Take care,' and was gone.

Anderson made one last stop before driving south to Auxerre where they would change the car and their identities, before continuing the journey to Madrid to catch a flight to Rio de Janeiro.

He pulled up outside the hospital where the priest was recovering and went inside carrying a bundle of books he had *borrowed* from the château library.

He met the nurse he had once kissed in the lobby, and asked her to give them to the priest.

She looked at the books in surprise. 'But they're all

thrillers. Are you sure he'll like them?'

'Tell him they're from Shaft, he'll understand.' He paused. 'Have you ever been to South America?'

'No, but –'

'I'll call you,' Anderson said.

*　　*　　*

After Anderson had gone, Foster and Suzy Okana continued the work they had begun during the night. Pushing and pulling with their legs, trying to dislodge the railings from their wooden foundations.

The hand-cuffs bit into their flesh and their ankles were raw and bleeding beneath the old curtains covering them. Once or twice Suzy had nearly screamed out, but now she had grown used to the pain.

The wood began to splinter . . . the railings to which their ankles were manacled moved. . . .

'We're nearly there,' Foster said.

'When the police arrive do we tell them about Anderson and Prentice?'

Foster shook his head. 'Of course not.'

Push, pull, push . . . the railings burst free from the woodwork and their feet shot through the space and hit one of the bells.

The bell swung against its neighbour and the chimes rang out across the countryside, summoning police instead of worshippers to the House of God.

*　　*　　*

Hearing the bells Anderson said: 'You know something? Right from the start I underestimated Foster.' He put his foot down on the accelerator. 'But if I'm any judge of human nature he won't blow us.' He glanced over his shoulder. 'What do you think?'

Helga said: 'I think he would have made a good spy.'

'Well,' Prentice said, putting his arm around her, 'there are a few vacancies around.'

431

Anderson drove onto the autoroute and together they headed south towards the future.

XXXVII

That day the dollar continued the rally that had started the previous evening, and there were those who blamed clandestine dealings at Bilderberg. But, as always, they were unable to prove it.

In his timbered home in Surrey Paul Kingdon digested two unpallatable facts:

(1) According to an expert in Hatton Garden, the Jager Formula was a fake and he had been conned out of five million dollars.

(2) He had been double crossed by Pierre Brossard whose Midas column had not appeared.

The first fierce anger had subsided. He poured himself a generous Scotch. The task at hand was to rally support for Kingdon Investments.

He raised his glass to the old, rust-coloured ten shilling note in the showcase on the wall. 'Here we go again,' he said. 'There's one born every minute,' and downed his whisky.

The front door bell rang, and Kingdon saw on the closed circuit television screen the figure of a policeman. He opened the door.

'Mr Paul Kingdon?'

'That's me.'

'I have a warrant for your arrest,' the policeman said. 'Failure to answer a summons for exceeding the speed limit. . . .'

Kingdon said: 'Don't stand out there in the cold, officer. Come in and have a drink. A Scotch maybe?'

'Well, I don't mind if I do.'

Kingdon smiled at him. There was still hope.

* * *

In Paris the wife of Pierre Brossard knelt in prayer in an apartment on Rue d'Alésia. Also kneeling were six of her new-found friends. But Madame Brossard's prayers were of a different calibre to those of the rest of the group. She was praying for deliverance – from her husband; praying that in some miraculous fashion the Almighty could intervene and prevent his return to Paris.

In Moscow Nikolai Vlasov, who had advised the Politburo to cancel the dollar operation, when the dollar began to rally the previous evening, issued one last command before penning his resignation.

The command was to Department V of the KGB.

Pierre Brossard was nearing the Yugoslav border when he noticed a flash of light on the mountains to his left.

A piece of glass, perhaps, or a discarded beer can.

For the second time in two days Brossard was framed in the telescopic sight of a rifle. The sight was trained on his head and this time the marksman didn't miss.

The Citroen wheeled off the road and smashed into a tree. The marksman, dressed as a peasant, ran down the mountainside to make sure that Brossard was dead. Not much doubt: bone and brain were spattered over the windows.

He collected three cans from his van parked down the road, doused the Citroen with gasolene and set fire to it.

Only a few charred remains of Marcel Rabier, architect, were later found by the Italian police.

Epilogue

Nicholas Foster was in despair.

It was ten days since Bilderberg and no-one would touch his story – the shooting, the attempt at mass assassination, the bid to bring down the dollar . . . everything given credibility by tapes of debates and the minutiae of his background material.

But Bilderberg was omnipotent.

Suzy watched him in her apartment in Chelsea as he pushed aside the telephone in disgust after a last abortive attempt.

'It's no good,' he said. 'They don't believe me. Or say they don't. For the first time in its history Bilderberg secrecy has been breached, but in the end they come out smelling of roses.'

'Don't worry, love,' she said. 'I don't really want to be married to a journalist anyway.'

He picked up a copy of *Paris-Match.* 'They made a stab at it – buried in a general piece about the conference – but, God, it's nothing like the truth. Just vague rumours. The sort that surround Bilderberg every year.'

'Do you want some plonk with your steak? You'd better wash it down with something, it's as tough as a legionnaire's boot.'

'And now there's a story in the papers that Pierre Brossard's missing. Backed-up, of course, by the statement that he left the conference in one piece. Bilderberg exonerated once again.'

Nicholas tried to cut his steak. She was right: tough was the understatement of the year.

'I know I can't cook,' Suzy said, sawing at her steak, 'but I am good on ideas.'

'Such as what?'

'While I was cooking – well, murdering – the meal, I was thinking.'

'And?'

Suzy put down her knife and fork, rested her chin in her hands and stared at Nicholas. 'I believe you've misplaced your talents. You should have been a novelist.' She stretched out her hand and touched Nicholas' cheek. 'Why don't you write a novel about Bilderberg? A novel based on fact.'

Nicholas persevered with his steak in silence. After a while he said: 'You're right, you are better on ideas than cooking.'

He stood up and went round the table and kissed her. Then he refilled his glass with wine, walked into the spare room, rolled a sheet of paper into his portable typewriter and, after a few moments' thought, he began to type.

Danzer didn't look like a spy.

THE RED DOVE

Derek Lambert

As the Soviet space-shuttle *Dove* orbits 150 miles above the earth on its maiden flight, Warsaw Pact troops crash into Poland. What is the deadly connection between the soaring bird and the shattering fist?

The seventy-two-year-old President of America wants to be re-elected, and for that he needs a spectacular. He needs to win the first stage of the war in space: he needs to capture the Soviet space shuttle. But as the President plans his coup a nuclear-armed shuttle speeds towards target America — and only defection in space can stop it!

ADVENTURE THRILLER   0 7221 5348 1   £1.95

Also by Derek Lambert:
I, SAID THE SPY
TRANCE
available in Sphere paperback.